DESTROYING MAGIC

BY DAVID MEYER

ACKNOWLEDGEMENTS

My deepest thanks and appreciation go out to Dr. Jose Lopez as well as everyone else at the Norman Parathyroid Center. I'm not sure this book would've ever been finished without your excellent surgical care. Also, thank you to Dr. Patrick Nguyen and Dr. Robert Silver for diagnosing my condition and encouraging me to deal with it.

Tremendous thanks as well to Julie, for your love as well as for editing this book. Thanks, Dad, for your promotional assistance. And finally, thank you, Ryden, for letting me see the world through your eyes.

WARNING!!!

Your life is in danger.

Don't laugh. This isn't a joke. Listen to me very carefully. I need you to look around. And if you see anyone watching you …

Run.

Run as fast as you can. Run as if your life depends on it. Because, quite frankly, it does.

You see, there's a war going on right now. A secret war, pitting me and my fellow dropouts against the greatest magicians in all of history. But don't worry about us. We're safe, at least for now. Worry about yourself. There are powerful people out there who will do anything—and I do mean anything—to erase our very existence from memory. So, please, for your own sake, read this book in private, away from prying eyes. And whatever you do, don't tell anyone what you're about to learn.

Last chance. Are you absolutely certain you want to do this?

You are?

Well then, welcome … welcome to the war.

Welcome to *DESTROYING MAGIC*.

CHAPTER 1

I, Randy Wolf, am a magic school dropout.

Yeah, you heard me right. Just fourteen years old and my future is already in serious peril. Now, you don't have to say anything. I already know what you're thinking. Namely, what the heck happened?

Well, I didn't drop out on some fool whim. And I certainly didn't do it because I'm a poor magician. Actually, I'm pretty good with a wand, not that that's a big deal. Most kids master the basic spells at a young age. That's why institutions like the Roderick J. Madkey School of Magical Administration—whew, what a mouthful, huh?—focus on other things. Theory, history, social commentary, interpretation, and the like.

No, I dropped out because—and this is embarrassing to admit—I racked up failing grades across the board in my first one and a half quarters. And the Roderick J. Madkey School of … let's just call it the Madkey School, okay? … doesn't tolerate failure. So, I was given a choice. I could either accept expulsion or drop out on my own accord. The latter, it was firmly suggested, would allow me to save face. Once I left Madkey, I could make up a reason for my early exit. Like maybe tuition proved too expensive. Or maybe I was allergic to sasquatches. Anything, really. Anything but the truth. Which was, simply put, that I couldn't hack it.

So, I dropped out. And yet, I didn't leave. I'm still at Madkey. Not as a student though. Rather, I'm a staffer, working an assembly-line job alongside other dropouts. Now, you're probably wondering why I'd suffer such an indignity. It's simple, really. Madkey isn't just any old school. It's *the* school. Heck, it's even bigger than that. Madkey is the birthplace of modern magic. It's the unequivocal center of the magic universe. I spent my entire life dreaming of its sacred halls. And I'm not ready to part with them just yet.

All told, I've got a roof over my head, a steady job, and best of all, I spend every minute at the greatest place on Earth. I should be counting my blessings. But instead, I'm walking around on eggshells. For if there's one thing I've learned from this whole experience, it's that there's no such thing as rock bottom.

Things can always get worse.

CHAPTER 2

Snap!

My wand, a brittle stick of aspen, splintered down the middle. The auburn glow faded away. My lip curled. Scowling under my breath, I slammed the broken tool onto my workstation.

Lifting my forearm, I wiped sweat from my brow. My workstation consisted of an old hickory table, rickety on four uneven legs. A ball of sticky, rock-hard dough rested on its pockmarked surface. My job was to knead the dough, then convey it to the next workstation. Simple enough, assuming one had a working wand.

A new wad of dough materialized on the table and I frowned in displeasure. Unless I called for a stoppage, which was unthinkable, the dough would just keep coming and coming. It would pile up, consuming every inch of my workstation. There was only one way out of this mess.

I needed a replacement wand.

Twisting my neck, I scanned the kitchen. Dozens of workstations, situated in four crooked lines, occupied the room. Staffers stood behind each workstation. Brows furrowed, they waved their wands, uttering the same spells over and over again.

If you're like most humdrums, you probably picture magic as this wondrous, spectacular gift. I mean, come on … who hasn't wanted to clean a room with the mere flick of a wand? Or even better, whip up some savory doughcream at a moment's notice? It sounds too good to be true, right? Well, here's the thing …

It is.

Take doughcream, for instance. It's baked ice cream, enchanted so as not to melt. It constantly changes flavors so you might get a taste of chocolate, pineapple, or pepperoni pizza at any time. Or you might get them all at once. It's the luck of the bite, so to speak.

If you want to make doughcream, you can't just say, "Go, doughcream, go!" and flick your wand. Oh, no. First, you've got to locate and reel in the ingredients and supplies (and don't even think about trying to conjure them up out of thin air). Next, you've got to enchant everything in very specific ways. Various levitation spells are required to get the right amounts of everything into a mixing bowl. And so on and so forth.

Now, you might wonder why this requires so many individual steps. Why, you might ask, can't they be combined? It's because magic is set in stone. This means we've got to work with the spells we've got. And as you've no doubt guessed, an easy doughcream spell simply doesn't exist. But more on that later. My point is this. Making doughcream by yourself takes *forever*. Assembly-line magic is much more efficient, especially when you're trying to feed a population as large as the one housed at Madkey.

My gaze fell on Jaxon "Jax" Vegrold, would-be senior and current Kitchen Manager. He'd dropped out of Madkey three years ago, during the middle of his freshman year. I didn't know the exact reason, but I suspected it had something to do with his temper.

"Busted wand," I called out.

He glared at me for a long moment. Then he pushed back a mop of blonde hair.

"What'd you do?" His tone was gruff and accusatory.

"Nothing." I held up the wand. "It just broke."

His cheeks grew rosy red. He was a bit on the short side and built like a wall.

"Dang it, Randy." His voice bubbled with righteous fury. "We don't have time for this."

"Hey, it's not my fault."

"Could've fooled me."

Jax was in an extra-foul mood and with good reason. He faced constant pressure to keep us on schedule. With the Victory Feast looming, that pressure was through the roof. Even so, I wasn't about to let him take out his anger on me.

"Talk to Galison," I replied icily. "Tell him we need better wands. That is, unless you're afraid of him."

Nobody dared stop working. But I noticed my fellow staffers stiffen up. A few gazes shot our way.

"You've got three minutes," he said, his look one of sheer contempt. "Then I'm writing you up."

"You're all heart."

I made a beeline for the door and hustled out into the adjoining hallway. This part of the school, consisting of dimly-lit corridors and dusty, unadorned rooms, was known internally as Shadow Madkey. It allowed us staffers to cross campus and perform our duties with minimal disturbance to the students and faculty.

Some staffers hardly ever left Shadow Madkey, choosing to avoid awkward interactions with those that we served. Others, like me, ventured out into the main facility whenever possible.

Just outside the kitchen, an enormous banner caught my eye. It hung from one side of the dingy, dank tunnel, boldly proclaiming, *Happy Victory Day!* in freshly-painted black lettering. The accompanying image was an impressive likeness of Lanctin Boltstar, Madkey's famous headmaster. A scrawled signature in the lower right-hand corner identified the artist as *Leandra*. That is, Leandra Chen, fellow staffer and one of my closest friends.

I hurried past the banner. The hallway was a tight squeeze, the available space reduced by decorations and magical gizmos. They were intended for that evening's feast, which marked the beginning of Madkey's Spring semester.

I squeezed past stacks of paper ribbons, emblazoned with Victory Day slogans and enchanted to unfurl, curl up, and unfurl all over again. I stepped past crates of bottomless goblets. And I passed by an enormous cake, covered with thick frosting and adorned with miniature cool-lights. A cool-light, by the way, is essentially bundled illumination at room temperature. Wrap your brain around that for a minute ... the *cool*-lights exist at *room temperature*. Yeah, I don't get it either.

In less than a minute, I reached a supply room. A dusty sign, stuck fast to the metal door, read, *Faculty and Students Are Your Priority. Serve Them Always and Without Question*. The mantra—a constant presence in Shadow Madkey—didn't bother me. But it irritated my fellow staffers to no end.

Twisting the knob, I opened the door. The room was spacious, quite tall, and filled with a musty scent. Metal shelving racks, piled high with mixing bowls, cauldrons, ladles and spoons, enchanted gloves, self-cleaning rags, and many other things, lined the walls. Chests of drawers, marked with scribbled notes, filled the middle of the room. Thanks to well-placed cool-lights, I was able to read some of the notes.

Baby "Nessie" Teeth: Acquired in blockbuster 1967 trade with Harley Fee (a.k.a. the Tooth Fairy)

Cursed Poster Boards (Warning: Do not, under any circumstances, show them scissors!)

Humdrum Magical Products (Contents include: tablets, light bulbs, power cords, cellphones, toy cars, etc.)

On any other day, I might've lingered in the room for a minute or two. But with dough piling up on my workstation, on a day where I'd already be working long into the night, I was in no mood to waste time. So, I crossed the floor, slipped between a couple of chests and headed to the far wall.

A rack, three times my height, awaited me. Thousands of wands, old and spindly, were piled upon its dusty shelves. A sign, black ink on white paper, read, *Wands: For Staffer Use Only*. As if anyone else would want them.

Staffer wands were notoriously poor quality, a fact that kind of amazed me. It wasn't like we needed the fancy wands given to incoming freshmen. But at least they could've given us ones capable of surviving more than a week.

Rooting around, I noticed a wand that was thicker than the others. Extracting it from the pile, I held it up to a cool-light. It was made of cypress and seemed relatively stout.

I gripped and regripped it. It was a far cry from the one I'd received at the Madkey Orientation. That wand, harvested from Boarst Sacred Grove, had molded to my hand. A dream to use, I'd hoped to keep it after dropping out of Madkey.

Unfortunately, it took flight almost immediately, presumably in search of a more deserving owner.

I maneuvered the wand a bit. It wasn't great, but it was serviceable. So, I stowed it in my pocket. As I turned to leave, a very soft noise—a shallow breath—accosted my ears.

Heart racing, I twisted around. My gaze fell on the far corner, which was shrouded in darkness. I didn't recall it being that dark on previous visits.

My curiosity was piqued, but I really needed to get back to work. I started for the exit. However, a faint snore stopped me cold.

My gaze twisted back to the dark corner. Someone was sleeping there? On Victory Day, no less, when it was all-hands-on-deck? Oh, boy. If Galison found out, he or she would be gone in an instant.

I ventured into the darkness. My heart palpitated and I found myself breathing faster and harder.

A mass took shape before my eyes. It looked like … yes, it was the curled-up form of a tall, lanky man. He lay in the corner, facing the wall. His dark gray pants and matching pea coat were smudged with reddish dirt. He wore heavy boots, which lay in a small puddle of water. His wand holster, attached to his leather belt, was empty.

Circling around, I glimpsed the man's olive-colored skin and gleaming white teeth. His dark hair was closely-cropped and he had a day or so of stubble on his chin. Surprise registered in my brain.

That's no staffer. My heart beat faster and faster. *That's MacPherson.*

Deej MacPherson was co-chair of the Magicology department. He was famous for his heroics on Victory Day. Alongside Headmaster Boltstar, he'd helped end the Chaotic tyranny once and for all, ushering in the Golden Era of

Structuralism. Since then, he'd carved out a career for himself as one of Madkey's most esteemed professors.

I frowned. Something was very, very wrong here. Outside of Galison, I'd never seen a single professor in the bowels of Shadow Madkey. The idea that he'd just wandered in here for a mid-day slumber struck me as absurd.

"Professor?" I whispered. "Are you …?"

I trailed off as more snores escaped his lips. Switching tactics, I gripped his shoulder and gave it a little shake.

"Professor?"

I gave him more shakes, each one harder than the last. Still, he refused to stir. Finally, I wrenched at his arm, causing him to roll onto his back. And yet, he remained fast asleep.

Saliva pooled in my mouth and I pulled my hands away from his body. Peering closer, I noticed his sickly pallor. He seemed to be biting his cheeks. His skin, normally a bit wrinkled, was stretched tight across his visage.

Beads of sweat ran down my arms as I gained my feet. This was dark, sinister. It had the whiff of magic to it. And yet, that was impossible. Sleeping curses, as everyone knew, existed only in the realm of fiction.

As I ran for help, I found myself inundated with questions. Who had done this to MacPherson? How?

And why?

CHAPTER 3

"Come, Mr. Wolf. We have questions for you."

The voice, rotund and perfectly enunciated, belonged to Professor Cherry Wadflow from the Numerology department. Skinny and severe, she wore a slim-fitting black dress and kitten heels. Her hair was pinned up on top of her head. Her hands were balanced on her hips and she stared at me like I was a pesky fly.

Nervously, I followed her into the supply room. MacPherson, still snoring up a storm, lay right where I'd left him. His Magicology co-chair, Professor Beatrice Norch, stood nearby. She was a refined, plump woman, wrapped up in a tasteful, flowery dress.

"Hello again, Mr. Wolf," she said, shooting me a sharp-eyed gaze. "Thank you for your patience."

Norch chirped her words as she spoke. Because of this, kids called her Bird Woman behind her back. But they didn't dare question her abilities. She was, after all, one of Madkey's most renowned witches.

"Sure," I mumbled. "No problem."

The door banged shut behind me. Glancing back, I saw Professor George Galison. He served as chair of the Conveyance Department and also held the position of Staff Advisor. In other words, he was my boss.

Galison was a tall, stocky man with pale cheeks. He'd stuffed himself into a too-tight dress shirt and a pair of too-skinny trousers. Suspenders, which were completely unnecessary, hung loosely from his thick shoulders.

"Tell us everything." His baritone voice reverberated with intense anger. "And I do mean *everything*."

I was still new to the staffer role. But I knew it paid to stay on his good side. And so, I proceeded to lay it all out. I told them about my broken wand and my trip to the supply room. I told them about the snores and how I'd found MacPherson fast asleep.

"Did you see anyone?" Norch asked when I was finished. "Anyone at all?"

I shook my head.

"Well, then did you notice anything out of the ordinary?"

I'd seen plenty of things, come to think of it. His empty wand holster, still attached to his belt. The red smudges on his clothing. Oh, and I couldn't forget that puddle of water under his boots.

"His wand's missing," I said. "And—"

"Did you see anything unusual?" Galison growled, interrupting me. "A flash of light? Perhaps a loose critter?"

I shook my head. "Nothing like that."

They asked a few more questions, but it was apparent I wasn't much help. Finally, the bell rang, indicating it was 11:25 a.m. and thus, the end of Fifth Period.

"That's all for now." Galison stared hard at me. "Does anybody else know about this?"

I shook my head.

"Keep it that way."

"If anybody asks why you missed work, tell them …" Norch scanned the room. Her gaze fell on a familiar chest of drawers. "Tell them the poster boards got loose and spotted a pair of scissors. That should keep people from asking too many questions."

"I will," I lied. Turning on my heels, I hiked to the door. I took my time about it, hoping to eavesdrop a bit.

"I don't get it." Wadflow shivered quietly. "What was Deej doing here?"

"I don't know," Norch replied. "He didn't say anything to me."

Crossing the room, I took hold of the knob. Gently, I cracked the door open.

"You're pretty quiet, George." Wadflow cleared her throat. "What do you make of this?"

"I don't know how he ended up here," Galison replied. "And frankly, I don't care. All I care about is this curse. It shouldn't exist."

"Who could've cast it?" Wadflow wondered. "I can't imagine—"

"Do you need something, Mr. Wolf?" Galison's tone was sharp and stern.

My cheeks flushed. "No, Sir. I was just leaving."

"See that you do."

And with that, I stepped into the hallway. Hands shaking, I closed the door behind me.

There was much left unsaid. But it seemed clear that the trio of professors knew what had happened to MacPherson. They'd called it a sleeping curse, which confused the heck out of me. Sleeping curses weren't real.

Right?

CHAPTER 4

My stomach churned uneasily as I stopped in front of the double doors. *Faculty and Students Are Your Priority*, the familiar sign read. *Serve Them Always and Without Question.*

With a deep breath, I pushed the doors open and strode out onto a wide bridge spanning the length of Lower-Torso. Lower-Torso, of course, was the lowest part of Torso, the tri-level, open-air structure that served as Madkey's beating heart.

The chest side of Torso consisted of thick glass plates, separated by iron bars. Rays of sunshine poured through the glass, filling the space with natural light. One could see for miles up here, making it a favorite of artist-types.

The side I stood on, the back side of Torso, held three levels of bridges. Lower-Torso bridge was the widest, jutting out well into the open-air section. Mid-Torso's bridge was the next widest while Upper Torso's bridge was the skinniest. Various doors led off of each bridge to places like Madkey Arena, Madkey Art Gallery, the Enchanted Game Lounge, and the Handy Candy Sweets Shoppe.

An open-air space rested between the bridges and the glass windows. It served as home to the famed Madkey Station Grille. Hundreds of enchanted tables floated within the Grille, along with nearly one thousand chairs. On any given day, students, faculty, and staffers sat on those chairs, oblivious to the heights at which they sat. Amazingly, nobody ever fell. Oh, people tried to fall, especially new freshmen. It was practically a rite of passage at Madkey. But the chairs were enchanted so as to keep everyone afloat at all times.

Now, that's not to say other things didn't fall from time to time. And that's when things got a little dicey. You see, the Grille was built upon the remnants of an ancient conveyance station. Once upon a time, that station provided access to the Floating Abyss, a sort of mystical ocean that connected Madkey to enchanted lands all across Earth. While no longer in service, its conveyance energy remained. So, anything that fell through one end of the old station had to come out the other end. Who could ever forget the time Calvin Hayes accidentally dropped his knife? It slipped through the thick black mist at the bottom of the Grille. One second later, it came screaming out of the mist at the top end, almost bludgeoning poor Dylan Kosward in the process.

The double doors closed over, separating me from Shadow Madkey. Massive statues, broken at the neck, stood on either side of me. They depicted Chaotic magicians, ones who'd fought the Structuralists on Victory Day. Sculpted from granite, they'd proven far too heavy to move in the aftermath. So, they'd been beheaded instead.

I paused for a moment, my gaze searching the Grille as well as the three bridges. Torso acted as Madkey's student commons and thus, was usually crowded. Today was no different. Throngs of students, their faces flushed with excitement, packed the bridges. More students were out in the Grille, chowing down on food and talking in loud tones.

A bunch of juniors bumped into me. Next thing I knew I was sucked into the frenzied crowd. At first, I tried to push back. But it was hopeless and I soon found myself propelled into a gold-plated, open-ended box. Known as a hoist, it worked a little like a humdrum elevator, only with magical propulsion. This particular one allowed people to travel between Torso's three bridges at breakneck speed.

Other people crowded into the hoist until we were packed in so tight I could barely breathe. A beep sounded and a gate slid upward, blocking would-be riders. Some people managed to hop over it in the nick of time. Others weren't so lucky and got knocked backward into the churning crowd.

The hoist shot upward like a rocket and my stomach surged into my throat. I didn't scream. Nobody ever screamed on a hoist. There simply wasn't enough time to do so.

The hoist slammed to a halt. The gate slid open. A harsh voice screeched, "Mid-Torso. Get lost and be quick about it."

Students and faculty filed off and others filed on. Seeing the sheer volume of people waiting for a ride, I chose to stay aboard. Again, the hoist flew upward and again, my stomach leapt to my throat.

The hoist came to another jarring stop. As the gate slid open, the same harsh voice screeched, "Upper-Torso. Get out already!"

Everybody left the hoist. I pushed my way through a thick horde of waiting students and looked around.

"Well, well, well ..." The unwelcome voice, soft and biting, caught me off-guard. "If it isn't everybody's favorite dropout."

Don't let him bait you, Randy, I thought, my fingers curling into fists. *He's not worth it.*

My gaze shifted to Porter Garrington. He was tall and sported a head full of curly, dark locks. A white dress shirt and power tie adorned his lanky, toned frame. His pin-striped slacks were neatly-pressed. A suit coat, also pin-striped, dangled from his fingertips.

Porter was handsome, popular, fabulously wealthy, and the leading candidate for class valedictorian. In short, he had pretty much everything a guy could want out of life. For some reason, he'd taken a dim view of my existence all the way back at the Madkey Convocation. That view had only gotten worse after I'd dropped out of school.

"Whatcha doing here, Wolf? Shouldn't you be slumming in Shadow Madkey with the rest of the help?"

"I'm on break," I replied through gritted teeth. I felt small in front of him, not least because of my attire. In line with Victory Day tradition, students were dressed in their finest clothing. Boys wore jackets and ties. Girls tended toward dresses, although some had gone with tasteful pantsuits or blouse and skirt combinations. Meanwhile, I wore the required staff uniform. Namely, a crimson collared shirt, black pants, and black shoes, all of which were well-smudged with grime and bits of dough.

"Madkey's paying you to stand here and look stupid?" He snorted through his nostrils. "What a racket."

I felt sorry for his future employees. The Garrington family owned and operated Garrington Magic Company. Garrington Magic, along with Alanskew and Casafortro, comprised the so-called Big Three of the magic world. Together, they held a vice grip on the enchanted product marketplace.

Before I could muster up a reply, Gordon Tancort sauntered across the bridge. Gordon was athletic and wiry, with bronze-tanned skin and a mouth that wouldn't quit. Sya Moren and Felicia Masters flanked him on either side. Sya was medium-height with long, blonde hair and a permanent sneer upon her lips. Felicia, meanwhile, had curly brown hair and a cherubic face. She was widely regarded as the prettiest girl in the ninth grade. But really, they were all good looking. That was the worst thing about Porter and his friends. They might've been miserable people. But they still had it all.

Dismissing me with a withering look, Gordon clapped his friend on the back. "Hey, man," he exclaimed. "You hungry?"

"Sure am," Porter replied.

With a smirk in my direction, Porter led the others to the nearest loading platform. Picking out chairs, they sat down. Immediately, the chairs zoomed off, taking them to the Mid-Torso section of Madkey Station Grille.

Slowly, I unclenched my fists. Walking to the loading platform, I scanned the Grille. Halfway between Mid- and Upper-Torso, I spotted Piper sitting alone at an isolated table.

I picked out a chair and sat down. With a rush of air, it lifted off the platform. Kicking my legs like I was swimming, I propelled it upward. Then I angled my body toward the Grille. Still kicking, I directed myself through the frenzied maze of students.

"Hey, Randy," Piper said as I pulled up to her table. "How are you feeling?"

Piper Shaw was short, a shrimp compared to other kids our age. Her dirty blonde hair was frizzy and hung down to her shoulders. Her mouth, while tiny, was capable of great volume. And yet, she had a quiet, bookish way about her. She was exceedingly smart and should've done just fine at Madkey. Unfortunately, she possessed an irredeemable flaw.

She was a poor test-taker.

Oh, she'd studied like crazy. She'd known the material of every class inside and out. But when it came time to be tested, she'd freeze up. Sometimes, she'd get hung up on the wording of questions. Other times, she'd check her work so much that she'd run out of time. Still other times, she just sat there, overwhelmed by it all. The faculty was sympathetic and had extended her multiple chances. But things didn't get better and she'd dropped out at the same time as me.

"I'm feeling fine." I directed my chair to the opposite side of the circular table. "Why?"

"Jax came by a few minutes ago, angry as a horned serpent. He said Galison pulled you from your shift even though you still had tons of dough to knead. Apparently, he and the others had to work overtime to get through it all."

"That's true. But—"

"Hey, guys." With quick, jerky movements, Leandra steered her chair to the table. "Say, what's this I hear about you skipping work, Randy?"

Leandra Chen was short and petite but carried herself as if she towered over everyone else. Her face was diamond-shaped with high cheekbones and a wide mouth. Her appearance was rather solemn, which stood in stark contrast to her jokester personality.

Like all of us staffers, she was a dropout. But it wasn't due to poor grades. In fact, she'd been a fairly solid student. Not the top of our class, but certainly not the bottom either. No, her problem was financial.

Tuition, room, and board at Madkey ran a steep 267,324 quadrods per year. To put that in perspective, the average annual wage in the magic community was less than 50,000 quadrods. So, when her folks ran into a bit of bad luck, unpaid bills began to stack up. Halfway through the second quarter, she was forced to drop out. She'd decided to stay on as a staffer, reasoning the room, board, and stipend would keep her from being a burden on her folks.

"I'm not sick and I didn't skip work." I lowered my voice to a whisper. "I stumbled on something. Something big."

"What?" Piper practically shouted.

A table full of sophomores looked at us with upturned eyebrows. I gave them an awkward smile. "We're, uh, just talking about proper assembly-line procedures. You know, ways to keep production really humming."

Rolling their eyes in unison, they turned away.

My gaze shifted to Piper. "Keep it down, will you?"

She blushed. "Sorry."

Leandra gave me a keen look. "What's this all about, Randy?"

I didn't feel like telling the story twice, so I looked around for the missing member of our foursome. "Where's Tad?" I asked. "He'll want to hear this, too."

"He's showing that new kid around," Leandra said. "Her name's Hannah, I think."

Most students matriculated at the beginning of the school year. But when someone dropped out, that opened up a new slot, which Madkey was always quick to fill. A staffer was then assigned to show the newcomer around school. Think about that for a moment. A *dropout* was assigned to help *the very student who'd taken his or her place*. Believe me, it's as humiliating as it sounds.

I scanned Torso one last time, then turned back to the table. "It all started when my wand broke mid-shift."

Leandra made a face. "I hate that."

"I ran to the supply room to get a new one. And that's when I heard the snores."

Piper frowned. "Snores?"

I nodded. "Someone was fast asleep in the corner. You'll never guess who it was."

Leandra arched an eyebrow. "This had better be good."

I paused for effect. "Professor MacPherson."

Her jaw dropped. "No way."

"Oh, it was him alright."

"What was he even doing there?" Piper wondered.

"I don't know. Nobody knows." I took a deep breath. "Because he won't wake up."

Piper's jaw dropped this time. Before she could say anything, the ghostly head of a man materialized before us. A straw hat partially covered his bald spot. His eyes were dark and swirling. His bulbous nose was bright red.

"Ahoy, mateys," he called out in a slurred, tired tone. "And welcome to—"

"Stuff it, Yordlo," Leandra said. "We don't need your fake pirate talk."

The head belonged to Yordlo Jellman, pirate and former captain of the infamous Warfire. Many years ago, far too many to count, Yordlo and his crew had preyed upon innocent airships as they sailed through the Floating Abyss.

"That's fine by me." He exhaled a long, slow breath. "You know, if I have to say that stupid line one more time, I swear I'll make one of you little urchins walk the plank."

"You talk pretty tough for a guy who can't leave his ship," Leandra retorted with a smirk.

Yordlo's reign of terror ended when he made the mistake of trying to pillage a small vessel on its way to New Orleans. One of the passengers happened to be an exceptional witch and she used her formidable skills to trap him and his crew into the planks of the Warfire. Sometime later, the ship was dismantled and Madkey purchased the hulk. Someone had the bright idea of turning the wood into finely-crafted tables and chairs.

Now, the crew's souls were trapped within the chairs. Yordlo, meanwhile, was trapped within the tables. With nothing else to do, he became a ghostly waiter. He could pop in and out of any table at a moment's notice, taking orders and checking in on customers. I'm sure he found it humiliating but hey, it was better than being firewood.

"I might be stuck here, lass," Yordlo seethed. "But I highly recommend you don't underestimate me."

"I highly recommend you take our order and be quick about it."

If looks could kill, she would've died right there on the spot. But since they can't, nothing happened. Well, nothing except that his face turned a fine tomato red.

A couple of juniors began banging silverware on their table. "Hustle up, Yordlo," Kell Masters, Felicia's older brother and Madkey's most promising ramball prospect, called out. "We don't have all day."

A scowl crossed the pirate's lips. "Duty calls, ye mateys," he said to us. "Now, what'll it be?"

I glanced down. The table glowed in front of me, listing a short menu of food and drink options.

"The Abyss Burger," I decided. "Medium-well. And I'll take a Sunrise Canfee, too."

Canfee was kind of this super-charged coffee that came in all sorts of flavors. I'm not talking licorice or donuts, either. No, canfee was charmed to taste like *an experience*. There was Beach Party, End of Exams, Stormy Seas, and that was just the beginning. My favorite was Magical Bliss. It had this warm, comforting taste that stretched through your body, exactly the way one felt while doing a spell.

Yordlo took Piper's order, then shot Leandra a look. "And what about ye, lass? Some boiled turnips, perhaps?"

"Gross." She studied her glowing menu. "Just bring me the same as Randy."

"How very original."

She frowned. "Hey, I was going to order it first but—"

He winked at me, then vanished.

She sputtered for a moment. "You know, I really hate that guy."

It wasn't true, of course. Sure, they needled each other. But that was how their friendship worked.

Piper grinned. "He can hear you, you know."

"I don't care."

"You'll care when you get your food." She turned toward me. "By the way, are you sure it's wise to talk about you-know-what here?"

Yordlo, it was generally believed, maintained a presence in all of the tables at all times. That meant he was probably capable of hearing every word that we uttered. I wasn't worried though. Yordlo was a lot of things. But he was no blabbermouth.

"It's fine," I said. "Now, have either of you ever heard of a spell that could induce a state of endless sleep?"

"Maybe it's one of the forbidden spells," Leandra suggested.

"I don't think so," I replied. "I mean, they definitely recognized it. But Galison also said something about how it's not supposed to exist."

"What's that supposed to mean?"

"I'm not sure." I frowned, mulling over possibilities. "They made it sound like it was a brand-new spell."

"You mean, like invented?"

I nodded.

"Well, that's impossible," Piper said. "So, it must be something else."

It's high-time I talked about how magic works in our world. You don't just mutter weird phrases and wave a wand in random fashion. Well, you actually do both of those things, but there's a bit more to it.

The process starts with the Capsudra. The Capsudra, named for its inventor, Xavier Capsudra, is essentially a giant spell book that can anticipate your needs. He created it centuries ago, but it only came into popular usage with the rise of Structuralism.

In order to cast a particular spell, one must enter a defined emotional state. Beginner spells require fairly simple emotions, like certain amounts of happiness or anger. More complex spells call for multiple emotions. In a way, it's like making a recipe. You know, a tablespoon of this, a cup of that. But instead of ingredients, magic requires deep and exacting feelings.

After ginning up the required emotions, a magician must perform a wand sequence and utter the correct phrase. But this isn't enough to complete the spell. The problem is that the Capsudra requires absolute perfection on the part of the magician. If something's even a little bit off, the spell will fail. That's where Instinctia comes in.

Instinctia is what allows different people with different wands and different inflections to do the exact same spells. It occurs when the Capsudra takes over your body. You heard that right. *It takes over your body.* Weird, right? Believe me, it is, at least at first. But it's kind of wonderful, too.

Here's how it works. You line up your emotions, wave your wand, and utter the correct phrase. That gets the Capsudra's attention. It reaches out and connects to you, putting you into a state of Instinctia. With full control over your body, it completes the spell on your behalf. Like I said, weird.

But still wonderful.

"I know it's impossible," I said. "But they still acted as if it were a new spell."

"Not to change the topic, but I've always wondered about something." Leandra furrowed her brow. "Where'd Xavier get his magic from?"

We stared at her.

"From himself," Piper said. "He was a Chaotic."

I blinked. "He was one of *them*?"

"Everyone was a Chaotic in those days. There was no other option, at least not until he invented the Capsudra. That's when the Structuralist movement really began." She paused. "Xavier infused the Capsudra with his own magic. Its spells are his spells. The emotions, wand movements, and words all come from him. That's why it can't be altered."

I considered that for a moment, then frowned.

"What?" Piper asked.

"You're right. I know you're right. It's just ..."

"What?"

"I hate thinking of magic as something that's, well, stagnant."

"Don't tell me you're going Chaotic on us," she said with a teasing, upturned eyebrow.

I didn't laugh. Not even a bit. You don't call someone a Chaotic. You just don't. That's a big no-no in our world.

"That's not funny, Piper," I said.

"You're right. Sorry. It's just that the Chaotics made a similar argument during the Philosophical War." She leaned back in her chair. "What would be the point of more magic anyway? We've got all the spells we need."

"Tell that to the humdrums," I replied. "Their magic—technology—keeps growing, keeps changing. And yet, we're stuck with centuries-old spells. And all from a single wizard, to boot."

"I'm with you on that," Leandra said, matter-of-factly. "The Capsudra could use a little witch influence."

"At least we're on a level playing field. Just imagine what it was like back in the Chaotic days. Some people could wave their wands and move mountains. Others, through no fault of their own, got stuck with toilet cleaning spells." A strange look crossed Piper's face. "You know, I just had a thought. Maybe the spell came from—"

I never heard the end of that sentence. For just then, something slammed into my chair. I caught a quick glimpse of Porter aiming his wand in my direction. And then he was gone and I was whirling like a top.

Right away, I knew it was Cordef Maklo. Don't ask me to explain the name. Like all Capsudra spells, the wording came from a different time and place. But that didn't make it any less effective. Cordef Maklo, properly deployed, caused an object to rotate in circles until the magic was all used up.

I pulled my wand out of its holster. But it danced out of my fingertips and bounced onto the Lower-Torso bridge. And so around and around I whirled. I whirled so fast and hard I thought I'd lose my lunch. And I hadn't even eaten yet.

I kicked my legs and waved my arms. But the chair gained speed with each revolution and I started to feel dizzy.

Blinking, I caught glimpses of blurry people. They were laughing and shouting at me. And it wasn't just kids. Professors Jillian Lellpoppy and Cory Stewart, situated at a Lower-Torso table, were chortling too, although they were more discrete about it.

Piper kicked her legs, directing herself around the table. She and Leandra tried to grab my shoulders, but I was moving way too fast.

I needed to get out of the chair. But how? It wouldn't stop spinning until the spell had run its course. And it wasn't like I could just leap off of it either, not when it was enchanted to catch me.

I spotted Porter as I continued to spin. He stood on his chair a few feet away, throwing mock bows at the teetering crowd. An idea entered my muddled brain.

I pushed my back against my chair. Still spinning, it tipped over until I was in a horizontal position. Gripping the seat, I kicked my legs hard, propelling my whirling body through the air.

Sya's face twisted in surprise. "Look out," she yelled.

But Porter was too busy soaking in adoration to take notice.

WHAM!

My chair caught his shoulder and shoved him out into open space. With a yelp, he plummeted toward the black mist that served as a kind-of-floor for the Grille.

His chair made a move to chase him. But I grabbed hold of the seat. Still dizzy, I managed to pull myself onto it. Immediately, I stopped spinning.

Both chairs paused for a moment, as if deciding on their next move. Then the whirling chair took off. At top speed, it raced between tables and seated students, all the way down to Lower-Torso. At the last second, it cut to the right and Porter landed on top of it. And then it was him who was whirling like a top.

"Help meeeee!" he yelled.

Felicia stared daggers at me. Meanwhile, Sya and Gordon kicked their legs and floated down to help him. Sya tried to grip his arm, only to get kicked in the stomach. Gordon grabbed hold of the spinning chair, clearly hoping to strong-arm it into submission. But it continued to rotate and his chair began to spin with it. With a soft grunt, he released his grip and spun away. His chair smacked into a table and he pitched forward. Pasta, bowls of steaming soup, muffins, and mugs of canfee went flying.

Nobody dared laugh at Porter's predicament. But memory mirrors appeared as kids raced to record their recollections. As for me, I felt pretty darn good. Dizzy of course, but still good. I hadn't had a lot of victories since coming to Madkey.

Leandra directed her chair to my side. "Time to go," she whispered.

As I caught my breath, she and Piper pushed me toward the Lower-Torso bridge. Glancing up, I saw Porter jump toward the bridge serving Mid-Torso. He fell short and the spinning chair caught him again. Desperately, he kicked his legs, only to have his rotating chair rocket toward the glass plates. A crash rang out and a faint smile crossed my lips. I'd gotten out of work early and now I'd managed to one-up Porter. This was turning out to be a good day. Nothing could ruin it.

Absolutely nothing.

CHAPTER 5

Leaving our chairs on the Lower-Torso bridge, we squeezed through a pack of gawking seniors. My stomach growled, but there was no way I was going to wait around for my food.

A sudden streak of almond-colored light caught my eye. Twisting around, I saw it careen into Porter's chair. The chair halted in Upper-Torso. Porter tried to sit up, only to splay out across the seat. Immediately, Felicia flew over to help him.

I tensed up. Spell colors were unique, like fingerprints. And I'd seen that color enough to recognize it as belonging to Galison.

Glancing up and down the Lower-Torso bridge, I caught sight of my wand. It lay just outside an arched doorway, framed by old stones. Letters carved out of the rock read, *Madkey Library: Est. 1676*. That's right. Madkey Library. Not *Roderick J. Madkey School of Magical Administration Library*. The carving came from the old days, when the school was simply known as the Madkey School.

Grabbing my wand, I threw the doors open. With my friends hot on my tail, I hustled into the cavernous space.

Madkey Library is, for lack of a better expression, a basilica dedicated to the glory of the written word. Holding over 500,000 unique volumes, it's widely regarded as the world's foremost collection of magical literature. Its tomes are spread out over eleven floors of towering bookshelves, carved columns, and decorative railings. Despite its size, it has a glorious intimacy to it that makes you feel like you can just grab a book and hole up somewhere in complete privacy.

I lifted my gaze. A massive memory mirror acted as the ceiling. Located over one hundred feet above the black marble floor, it was the library's pride and joy. Ancient memories, some of them thousands of years old, played on its glassy surface in a constant loop.

Memory mirrors, by the way, are like ordinary mirrors, only they aren't made of glass, can be folded up, and don't actually show one's reflection. Instead, they show memories, copied from one's brain in the blink of an eye. So, they aren't really much like mirrors at all, now that I think about it.

High above, the mirror shuffled scenes, revealing another memory. I saw a pair of witches—the fabled Crantee sisters—making their way through the primeval Stolen Souls Forest. Suddenly, roots surged out of the dirt. Whipping at the air, they attacked the sisters. The Crantees, caught off guard, were quickly thrown to the ground. But they were even quicker to rise. Back to back, they went for their wands.

The next part was kind of hard to see. I caught quick glimpses of the sisters. Their sweaty arms, their drawn cheeks, their churning legs. And I also saw the forest in attack mode. Its shrieking roots, its drooling, lunging branches, and its bristling, sharp leaves.

The battle was clearly epic. And yet, it was impossible to make much sense of it. Which was kind of the point.

The Crantee sisters had lived long ago, centuries before Structuralism. Their magic was what we today would call Chaotic magic. Of course, all right-thinking magicians know that Chaotic magic is bad news. That's why we celebrate Victory Day. For that was when the ancient and destructive reign of Chaotics finally came to an end, ushering in the modern era of safe, responsible magic.

But while Chaotics was now illegal, it also constituted much of our history. And that presented a significant problem. What do you do with embarrassing history? Do you try to forget it, to wipe it away? Is that even possible?

For the most part, we've settled on a whitewashing strategy. That is, we've stripped out the embarrassing parts of history—visuals of Chaotic spells, for instance—and acted as if they never existed. Hence, old memory mirrors that didn't measure up to modern standards were removed from public circulation.

You'd be surprised at how well it works. A tiny part of me realized the Crantees were using Chaotic magic. But for the most part, I was just wowed by the action. In fact, I was so wowed that I forgot to watch where I was going. Abruptly, I bumped into a table. It quivered and a stack of books, impossibly high, came raining down.

"Shh!" The librarian, Professor Johnathan Hope, gave me a nasty glare from behind his marble counter. He was tall and frail and had a love for history that few could match. He complained often of coldness and as a result, tended toward warm clothing. For today, he'd chosen long gray slacks and a purple sweater. A thick scarf, gray like his pants, was draped around his neck. "Madkey Library is a sanctuary, Mr. Wolf," he hissed. "You'd do well to remember that."

It wasn't difficult to imagine Hope wandering through the eleven tiers, bowing down to each and every stack as he praised their many books. The thought made me grin, a detail that wasn't lost on him.

"Think I'm funny, do you?" he said in a hushed, yet ferocious whisper. "Well, how's this for funny? Make one more outburst and I'll throw *the Book* at you. Got it?"

His hand drifted to the counter and came to rest on a large, leather-bound volume. The spine was cracked and the cover lacked ink. All in all, it looked hundreds of years old. And according to my buddy Tad, who practically lived in Madkey Library, that was about right.

I had no desire to test Hope's patience. I'd seen him throw the Book at people before and let's just say it wasn't a pretty picture.

"Sorry," I mouthed.

He stood there, glaring at me. I felt a sudden tug on my arm. Next thing I knew, Piper was leading me into the maze of stacks lining either side of the marble floor. She kept going and before long, I found myself staring at a tall chest of tiny drawers labeled, *Official Madkey Library Catalog*. There were dozens of such catalogs, all exactly alike, sprinkled throughout the many floors.

"Why are we stopping?" Leandra whispered. "We're almost to Shadow Madkey."

"I know." Piper gave the chest of drawers a thoughtful look. "But this could explain what happened to MacPherson."

Leandra tossed a nervous look over her shoulder. "What about Galison?"

"Maybe he'll let this go," I said. "After all, it's not like I did anything wrong."

"It'll only take a minute," Piper added.

Leandra sighed, then nodded her agreement.

As a student, I'd spent a fair amount of time in Madkey Library. And so, I knew better than to take it at face value. A lot of things could go wrong amongst the stacks, none of which was worse than a poorly-opened catalog drawer.

Steeling her muscles, Piper reached for a drawer marked, *Celery Stalks, Magical Applications of — Cistern Cleaning Enchantments.*

Slowly, she pulled it open as far as she dared, which was no more than a few inches. Holding her breath, she studied a row of cards nestled tightly within the drawer.

The problem with this drawer and the others had everything to do with volume and thoroughness. Each and every one of Madkey's 500,000 books had been placed into hundreds or even thousands of categories. A book like, *Instinctia: Separating Myth from Reality,* could be found under the Instinctia category. But it would also appear in categories like History, Magic History, Magic Know-How, Theories of Magic, and so on. Each drawer, enchanted to stretch to an incredible length, contained thousands and thousands of categories. Each category contained thousands and thousands of books.

In other words, each drawer was stuffed with cards. And that was just fine as long as you treated them with care. But if you happened to open a drawer too quickly or with too much force, they'd all fly out at once, nicking you with endless amounts of painful paper cuts.

"Chaotics," Piper said. "Comprehensive Spell List."

"Chaotics?" I frowned. "But I thought—"

"Shh." Leandra elbowed my side.

She was absolutely right. So, I shut my mouth, lest I confuse the catalog. Meanwhile, the cards began to riffle themselves. They shifted forward, then backward. Finally, a single card slipped out of the drawer and into Piper's waiting palm.

Almost immediately, it struggled to escape her grip. The thing about the catalog cards is that they're really homebodies at heart. Oh, they like to get out every now and then, mostly to stretch their edges. But they miss being in the drawers with their fellow cards. That longing intensifies if you shut the drawer before they can get back inside it.

Piper stared down at her palm. Leandra and I crept forward and peeked over her shoulder. The card was crisp and clean and perfectly white. Black ink, etched in an illegible handwritten scrawl, adorned its surface.

Abruptly, the text began to shift and change, transforming into a far more legible script. Clearly, it had been written in Living Ink. Living Ink adjusts itself for each individual reader. Scrawled handwriting turns into block lettering. Foreign languages are translated. The vernacular changes. Slang words are updated. The original meaning is even sanitized to reflect the whims of the current generation.

Some magicians, the same ones who argue we shouldn't whitewash history, find the process abhorrent. The past should be fixed in stone, they say. It should be preserved, not updated to match the ever-changing winds of time. But proponents of Living Ink disagree. What if a young woman stumbled across an old derogatory slang word used to insult witches? Should she be forced to subject herself to that kind of insult? It's better, the proponents say, if the word should simply cease to exist. Hence, Living Ink.

"A History of Chaotics," Piper whispered, reading the now fully-legible title. "Volume Eighteen. Spells, Curses, and Enchantments."

At the very bottom of the card, a line of text read, *Floor 8, Stack 46, Shelf 9.* We exchanged looks, then Piper released the card. Happily, it dove back into its drawer.

Taking our leave, we took a hoist to the eighth floor. The stacks were numbered on the sides so it didn't take long to find Stack 46. On the ninth shelf above the floor, we discovered a thick volume, covered in dust. The spine read, *A History of Chaotics: Volume 18.*

Piper pulled out the volume and hauled it to a table. Plunking it down on the wooden surface, she peeled it open.

"This book was published in 1936, six years after Victory Day," she said, leafing through the pages. "If the Chaotics had a sleeping spell, it should be in here."

Blinking, I stared at the tome. It appeared to be little more than a list of spells, along with their effects. There were no instructions on how to perform them.

In my weaker moments, I'd sometimes found myself wondering about Chaotic magic. How had it worked anyway? I mean, I knew it originated from inside a magician. But how did a guy like me actually call upon it? And if I ever did so, what kind of spells would I cast?

"You're wasting your time," Leandra said. "Chaotics died on Victory Day."

"Not completely," Piper replied. "A few practitioners escaped."

"But they were eventually rounded up."

"Maybe, maybe not."

She continued to page through the book, stopping occasionally to take a closer look at one of the entries.

"So, you think an honest-to-goodness Chaotic magician attacked MacPherson?" I arched an eyebrow in disbelief. The idea was so unthinkable, I almost laughed out loud. "Why now? Why not decades ago?"

"Maybe he or she wasn't alive decades ago," Piper remarked. "Technically, we've all got Chaotic magic. We've just advanced enough that we don't use it anymore."

"Oh, I see." I shifted uncomfortably on the balls of my feet. "So, you're saying it could be anybody?"

"Exactly."

"Then how does that book help us?" Leandra asked.

"Chaotic magic is hereditary," Piper explained. "Spells are passed down the line, so to speak."

"So, if we find the spell, then we can trace its lineage?"

"That's the idea."

I tended to trust Piper's instincts. Still, I found her theory hard to believe. It wasn't like Chaotics had ended recently. No, it had been dead for nearly a century.

Once upon a time, Chaotics was the dominant magical philosophy. Its adherents believed magicians should be free to practice magic without control or regulation. They turned their nose up at the Capsudra and instead, encouraged magicians to revel in their inner magic. Since such magic was unique to each individual, it proved impossible to control or even teach properly.

By the 1920s, a movement known as Structuralism had risen up to oppose Chaotics. Led by Lanctin Boltstar, the Structuralists promoted the Capsudra as a way to standardize magic. Rigorous early schooling would teach young magicians how to safely and effectively perform acceptable spells. Later schooling would provide magicians with the necessary tools to succeed in the workforce as well as in society as a whole.

The Chaotics, desperate to maintain power, fought the Structuralists at every turn. It all came to a head in 1930. On what we now call Victory Day, the Chaotics and Structuralists were scheduled to debate at the Madkey School. But the Chaotics launched a sneak attack instead. Fortunately, the great Boltstar was up to the challenge. Rallying his allies, he led a daring counterattack. When the smoke finally cleared, the Chaotics had been defeated. At long last, Structuralism reigned supreme.

Triumphantly, Piper stabbed her finger at a brittle page. "I found it."

Leandra and I edged close to the table. Peering down, I studied the block of text above Piper's outstretched finger. It was part of a section entitled, *Sleep Spells: Dreams, Nightmares, and Other Quandaries.*

"Hibernation Induction," Leandra whispered, reading aloud. "Also known as Hibernuction. Causes the recipient to slip into a state of blissful, unawakeable tranquility. Unique to the Hynor Family."

"The Hynor family?" I frowned. "Who's that?"

Piper gave me an exacerbated look. "Are you serious?"

"They were Chaotic bigwigs, right?" Leandra interjected.

"They were *the* Chaotic bigwigs," Piper clarified. "During the 1920s, Boris Hynor was the most well-known Chaotic on the planet. Also, he was behind the surprise attack in 1930, the one that led to Victory Day."

"What happened to him?" I asked.

"He was captured," Piper said. "But I don't know where they sent him. Probably Gutlore."

I shivered. Gutlore Penitentiary was the most feared prison in the magic world. Located somewhere in Death Valley, it housed the worst of the worst. Killers, magic-skinners, life-drainers, and the sort.

Soft ridges creased Leandra's brow. "Do you think it was him?"

"I don't see how," I said. "He'd be over a hundred years old by now."

"Boltstar's at least that old," Piper pointed out. "And he hasn't lost a step. But no, I doubt it was Boris. He'd never get past Madkey's border enchantments."

"Then who was it?" Leandra wondered.

Piper glanced down at the book. "It says here the spell is, 'unique to the Hynor Family.' So, it's a relative."

A throat cleared. "Mr. Wolf."

I froze, as did Piper and Leandra. It took me a full second to turn around. It took me another second to meet Galison's penetrating gaze.

"I heard about what you did to Mr. Garrington." His baritone voice barely concealed his fury. "Have you lost your mind?"

"Piper found something," I said hurriedly. "It's big. You need to—"

"What I need, Mr. Wolf, is an explanation."

"But—"

"Now."

I exhaled a long breath. "Porter fired the spell. Heck, I didn't even use my wand."

"Immaterial. Mr. Garrington will someday run the Garrington Magic Company. You are, and always will be, an assembly-line wizard. He's somebody. You're nobody. He's important. You're not. Do you get my point?"

Leandra's eyes narrowed to slits. "Just because he's destined to be some big muckety-muck doesn't mean he gets to push people around."

He gave her a fleeting glance. "What's the staffer motto, Ms. Chen?"

"But—"

"The motto."

"Faculty and Students are my priority," she said in a clipped tone. "I will serve them always and without question."

"How about you, Mr. Wolf?"

With a sigh, I repeated the words.

"Good." He pursed his lips. "It would behoove you to remember that. Otherwise, you'll be asked to leave."

"So, what should Randy do the next time Porter sics a spell on him?" Piper asked, her cheeks turning apple red. "Should he say, 'Thank you'?" Or better yet, should he save Porter the trouble and just sabotage his own chair?"

"Do you need to repeat the motto as well, Ms. Shaw?"

Leandra crossed her arms. "It's a fair question."

He emitted a tired, annoyed sigh. "If Mr. Garrington is causing you problems, find a professor and ask him or her to intervene."

"You can't be serious." Piper's eyes popped open in disbelief. "Lellpoppy and Stewart were there. They saw the whole thing and they did nothing."

"I'm sure they had their reasons," he said with a dismissive wave. "Now, I need to drop a little truth spell on you, Mr. Wolf. You won't work here forever. Eventually, you'll leave. And when you do, you just might find yourself in front of Mr. Garrington. He could be in a position to hire or fire you at a moment's notice. So, do yourself a favor and treat him with the respect he deserves."

He stared at me expectantly for a few seconds, as if he thought I'd thank him. Of course, I didn't. Snorting in disgust, he turned around and walked away.

After he'd passed out of earshot, Piper glanced at the book, still open on the table. "We didn't even get to tell him about Hibernuction."

"I bet he already knows," Leandra said. "I mean, he was at Victory Day, right? He probably knew Boris personally."

Piper nodded. "That's true."

Leandra turned her gaze to me. "By the way, Galison's a jerk. Don't let him get to you."

I didn't reply. What could I say?

Like it or not, the professor had a point.

CHAPTER 6

Jax's wand paused in mid-air, directly above a towering pile of sliced red apples. "I see you finally decided to come back to work," he said, rather crossly.

With long strides, I entered the kitchen. "That wasn't my fault. I—"

"Save it." Using his forearm, he mopped sweat from his forehead. "Galison said to excuse your absence so I am. Just don't let it happen again."

More apples materialized on his workstation. He resumed his wand work, quickly chopping the fruit into lots of little pieces. After speeding through a dozen of them, he conveyed them away with a swipe of his wand. Fresh apples quickly took their place.

I checked the clock. The time was 12:23 p.m. To my surprise, I was early. I still had a full thirty-seven minutes before my next shift. Part of me was tempted to return to the Grille, to grab the lunch I'd ordered. But another part of me was drawn to something else.

Quietly, I headed outside. Fighting off trepidation, I walked to the supply room. The door was closed and a handwritten sign had been attached to its surface.

"Cursed poster boards on the loose with scissors in the vicinity," I read softly. "Do not enter until further notice."

Checking both directions, I made sure I was alone. Then I cracked the door open and peered inside. The supply room looked much the way I'd found it. There were two big differences. First, the missing cool-light had been replaced. This shed light on the previously-dark corner, revealing the other key difference.

MacPherson was gone.

Galison, Norch, and Wadflow must've spirited him away to another location. That made sense. After all, they couldn't just leave him there for someone else to find.

A third difference, one that was also revealed by the cool-light, became apparent to me. Carefully, I knelt down. Scuff marks, nearly invisible, marred the floor. They led from the doorway to the corner, in an arcing path.

Thinking back, I was almost positive I'd seen them on my previous visit. That meant MacPherson's attacker had physically dragged him into the room. Which, in turn, indicated the Hibernuction spell had been cast in an entirely different location. That is, if a Hibernuction spell had been cast in the first place. Piper had made a pretty decent case for it. But the idea that someone would cast such a spell remained tough to swallow. I mean, come on ... a Chaotic spell? In this day and age?

Curiosity piqued, I walked back into the hallway. Studying the floor, I saw more scuff marks. They were even fainter than the ones in the room, which made sense given the amount of foot traffic that passed through the corridor.

A bit of sweat bubbled up under my lip. Wiping it away, I hiked through the hallway. More than once, I lost sight of the scuff marks only to find them again.

Walking around a tight bend, I halted in front of a hoist. Well, at least it looked like a hoist. In reality, it was a large dumbwaiter, powered by a steel cable and a pulley. It was used to lift supplies up from Right Foot. A real hoist would've been much faster and far less backbreaking. Unfortunately, there were no hoists in Shadow Madkey, a subtle but effective way of reminding us of our place.

Following the scuff marks, I walked into the dumbwaiter. A giant mass of loosely coiled cable lay on the floor. One end of it rose upward, disappearing into the ceiling. I grasped the cable, then disengaged the manual locks. Gravity took over, pulling the dumbwaiter down. I clutched the cable tightly and the line jerked to a halt, burning my palms in the process.

Grimacing, I let out the cable and the dumbwaiter continued its descent. I took it all the way down to Right Foot, then released the cable. I took a second to rub my aching hands, then stepped outside.

Immediately, I picked up the scuff mark trail. Exiting Shadow Madkey, I walked down a tube-like corridor. After a short distance, I came to the exit, which was really nothing more than a couple of large doors. Since they got a lot of use, my first instinct was to head toward them. But surprisingly, the scuff marks continued past the doors.

I kept following them and soon found myself surrounded by stacked, dusty furniture, dismantled and beheaded statues of forgotten Chaotic magicians, and cobwebs galore. This part of Madkey, the toes of Right Foot, was just a storage area. So, how had MacPherson ended up here?

Available cool-lights grew fewer and farther between. It became difficult to see. Pulling out my wand, I stared hard at the tip. Taking a deep breath, I rid myself of all emotions. Then I let down my guard and allowed in a touch of mischievous joy. I added a bit of depth to the joy, then layered in some awestruck surprise.

My wand glided through a sudden range of motions. The spell came to my lips, but I was no longer in control.

Warmth and drowsiness washed over me as I entered a state of Instinctia. It felt like I was taking a long, hot bath. My emotions shifted a bit as the Capsudra took control. My wand adjusted. My lips moved.

"Dayga Fluza," I whispered.

The tip of my wand began to glow with an auburn-colored light. Instinctia faded away, taking the warmth and pleasantness with it. Holding the glowing wand in front of me, I continued my trek. I walked through a section of old portraits, the faces of which had been torn to shreds. A little farther on, I saw something on the floor. Thin and roughly the length of my forearm, it lay in a small puddle of water.

I fell to my haunches. Hand trembling, I reached into the puddle. My fingers closed around a piece of wood. It was hard, yet flexible, and decorated with beautiful carvings. It was a wand. And not just any wand either.

It was MacPherson's wand.

CHAPTER 7

A breeze crested against me as I walked outside. I paused long enough to gulp down a few breaths of warm air.

Blinking hard, I looked up. The colossal Madkey School rose way over head, hundreds of feet into the air. I'd gawked at it the first time I'd laid eyes upon it. I still gawked at it. Partly for its size and partly for its shape.

Madkey, like all great magic schools, has a look uniquely its own. More specifically, it's housed within a statue. That's right. An honest-to-goodness *statue*, one of mammoth proportions. A colossus, really.

The statue stands atop the tallest mountain in New Hampshire. Even so, it's invisible to most people. You have to be admitted across the enchanted border to see it. And admission is limited to faculty, staffers, students, and alumni.

Which is too bad really, because the statue is something to behold. It depicts Roderick J. Madkey, the founder of our esteemed school. He's cloaked in flowing robes of bronze and steel. His right arm kicks out a bit at his side while his left one holds a wand aloft, as if he were about to cast a devastating spell.

Living within a statue is both amazing and horrible at the same time. On one hand, you've got eye-popping views of deep blue lakes, fertile valleys, and towering mountains. On the other hand, *you're living in a statue*. Just think about that for a moment. Not only do you sometimes have to travel from shoulder to foot—and in mere minutes to boot—but you also have to put up with the limitations of the structure itself. Hallways and corridors wind in weird directions, sloping up and down, left to right. Also, no two rooms are alike. Some classrooms are large and spacious, others are cramped with buckling floors and oddly-angled ceilings.

The worst I've seen is the one for Numerology 9, which is located at the tip of Right Knee. The room is tall and curved on the far end, but also extremely shallow. Because of this, there's only room for one row of desks. But since Numerology 9 is a required class, lots of students need to take it. So, desks are stacked on top of each other, supported by increasingly rickety platforms. And if that's not enough, the floor and platforms slope forward. So, you've got to constantly pull yourself and your desk backward. If you happen to fall asleep—like Royce Miller that one time—then you can expect to tumble off the platform, desk and all. And that means broken bones and worse, a trip to the clinic.

I shifted my gaze. The sky was a bit cloudy now, obscuring the afternoon sun. Enchanted cool-lights, mounted on poles, gave the school's exterior a haunted, majestic look. More cool-lights, embedded into the ground, lit up the grass at my feet.

Madkey straddled two separate peaks of Mount Ferocious, a hidden geological wonder. I'd exited out of Right Foot, which was situated on the subsidiary peak known as Mount Abner Ferocious. The area just outside of the exit was a designated picnic-zone. As such, it employed weather-controlling magic, designed to repel precipitation while maintaining a spring-like temperature. Past that zone, everything was natural all the way up to the enchanted border. In springtime, the entire outdoors would've been crawling with kids. But it was the dead of winter. And winter on a New Hampshire mountain meant near-freezing temperatures and snow.

Tons and tons of snow.

I felt MacPherson's wand, which I'd stowed in my pocket. All that snow was, of course, the reason for this visit. Water had been puddled under MacPherson's boots. I'd found more water surrounding his wand. And I'd noticed traces of dried water—dirt and minerals, mostly—in the scuff marks leading back and forth from the dumbwaiter. So, what if that water hadn't always been water? What if it had been snow?

It made sense to me. MacPherson was an outdoorsy guy who liked to take late-night hikes along our little slice of mountaintop. Nothing stopped him, not even a good snowstorm.

"Coming through." A tray floated past me. Seconds later, Gustav Firbottom, clad in shirt and tie, appeared. He gave the tray another push, then followed it to one of the tables.

I walked to the edge of the picnic-zone. Then I began to circle around the area, keeping a close eye on the white powder. Near a table full of quiet, studious freshmen, I found something interesting. A large boot had crunched the snow next to the grass. There were more footprints farther back, some of them partially obscured by fresh snow.

Steeling myself, I stepped forward. My shoes sank into foot-deep powder. The temperature fell to freezing.

"What's he doing?" Carlita Lopes whispered.

"Being stupid," Erin Dogger replied softly.

The table erupted into giggles.

Ignoring them, I hiked forward. Snowflakes whirled around me, covering my head in a light layer of chilly fluffiness. More snow slipped into my shoes and up my pants. I couldn't remember the last time I'd been so cold.

I followed the tracks until they veered off in a separate direction. Shivering, I studied the footprints. They indicated that the hiker—MacPherson, presumably—had been circling Madkey's exterior. He must've heard or seen something because his footsteps suddenly veered off-course and his stride lengthened. He ran back to the school and entered the corridor. Someone had attacked him, possibly with that Hibernuction spell. That same person then dragged him to the dumbwaiter, took him upstairs, and hid him in the supply room.

Retracing my footsteps, I walked back into the picnic-zone. The temperature warmed almost immediately. Ignoring the furtive glances of the freshmen, I brushed snow off of my head.

I turned my gaze skyward, taking one last look at Madkey's enormous head. A soft glow emanated from it, giving definition to the statue's weak jaw and high forehead.

Walking inside, I returned to where I'd found MacPherson's wand. A short distance away, I spotted five thin hallways, branching off from the main corridor. These were the toes of Right Foot.

My fingers trembled as I grabbed my wand. The odds of MacPherson's assailant returning to the scene of the crime were pretty low. But it sure didn't feel that way.

Checking the smaller toes, I found nothing but more junk. Heading into the big toe, I was surprised to find it empty. There was no furniture, no boxes of broken wands. I did find some grime on the walls, similar to the smudges I'd seen on MacPherson's clothing. There was a dusty, old plaque, too. But that was it.

Still, the grime seemed like an important clue. The professor must've confronted his attacker late at night inside the big toe. They'd fought and he'd been pushed up against the wall, smudging his clothing in the process. Then the attacker had thrust him out into the main corridor and somehow, sent him into a deep slumber, possibly with the Hibernuction Curse. The pieces all fit. And yet, it told me nothing. I still didn't know why MacPherson had been attacked.

And I was no closer to identifying the culprit.

CHAPTER 8

Madkey students are housed in dormitories by grade, which are located in contained sections of the school. They're assigned roommates and live in doubles, complete with comfy beds, sleek desks, a private bathroom, a walk-in closet, chairs and couches, and the best magical gear money can buy. Now, imagine the complete opposite of that.

That's what we get.

The staffer dorm was located at the end of Left Arm, specifically in the area encompassed by the wrist and hand. The view was pretty sweet, but the sloping floors, short ceilings, and cramped spaces were positively nauseating.

I strode into the dimly-lit dorm, which was really just a large room. Two community bathrooms, which also served as changing rooms, branched off of it. Curving rows of bunkbeds occupied either side of the dorm. They held ratty mattresses topped with musty bedsheets, all of which were student hand-me-downs. Tall dressers, one per staffer, separated the bunk beds.

As I returned my wand to its holster, I felt MacPherson's wand, which was still stowed in my pocket. I had planned on taking it straight to Galison. But at the last second, I'd veered off for the dorm, figuring I'd get ready for work first.

Ignoring the hunger in my belly, I made my way through the room. To my right, I spotted Leandra's dresser. A single memory mirror rested on top of it.

Memory mirrors go way back, thousands of years in some cases. Older mirrors were made by artisans and from a wealth of different materials. These days, they're made of remembra, a flexible, glassy substance. They can be used to record anything. Lectures, graduations, birthday parties, treaty signings, and so on. These memories can then be mass-produced into any medium that supports remembra, such as newspapers, books, posters, and lots of other things.

I studied Leandra's mirror for a moment. Its glassy surface began to swirl, as remembra always did when looked upon. An image of my buddy Tad Crucible appeared.

At a hair over six feet, Tad was tall for his age. He had dark brown skin and his black hair was closely cropped. Packed with lean muscle, he looked like the prototypical ramball player. And yet, he had zero interest in the sport.

Wearing a nicely-tailored suit and a beaming smile, he stood on the world-famous Lubbrick Stage, which was part of the Lubbrick Magic Historical Society. An adoring audience stared back at him, their hands poised for applause.

The memory mirror began to engage my other senses, emitting all of the information it had collected from this particular moment. I felt the heat of the stuffy room and heard light chatter in the audience. My body jiggled softly as Tad, waving at the now-applauding audience, began to walk across the stage.

Leandra, clad in a red dress and matching heels, stepped onto the right side of the stage. A sly look crossed her visage. Lifting her wand, she muttered a few words. Doughcream materialized in front of her. It smelled wonderful and my mouth began to water. Before I could stop to wonder why she was there or how she'd made doughcream appear out of nowhere, she waved her wand again. And just like that, the doughcream soared across the stage.

Gasps rang out and Tad swiveled around. A terror-stricken look crossed his face. One second later, the sticky dessert came crashing down on top of his head. It slipped down his sides and puddled around his feet. The audience exploded into laughter. Tad, his face twisted in horror, tried to run off-stage. But the doughcream stuck fast to his shoes and he ended up running in place instead.

I chuckled. The memory looked authentic, but I knew better. Tad was a dropout like the rest of us. While he would've loved to stand on Lubbrick Stage, it was little more than a pipedream. As for Leandra, she couldn't make doughcream appear on cue. However, she had a strong artistic side and was quite good at tricking memory mirrors into accepting false recollections.

I turned away and the memory vanished. Off to the side, I caught a glimpse of Jeff Candleshed, a would-be-sophomore-turned-staffer. He lay in his bed, reading a book, oblivious to what I'd just experienced. That was how memory mirrors worked. They only impacted those people who were actually looking at them.

I resumed walking through the curving rows of bunkbeds. The far side of the dorm had been turned into common space. It held threadbare couches and a coffee table. A couple of dog-eared paperbacks sat on the table, along with some old-fashioned board games. An enchanted clock was pinned to the wall. And that was it. Staffers didn't get the cool stuff allotted to students. No enchanted walls, cursed mystery games, or talking trashcans for us.

Stifling a yawn, I stopped at my dresser. It had been a long, weird day, interspersed with exhausting assembly-line shifts. And yet, I remained full of adrenaline. Less than two hours remained until the Victory Feast. Of course, I would've preferred to attend it. But working it was better than nothing.

Opening my top drawer, I retrieved a pressed pair of black pants and a well-starched, crimson dress shirt. I hesitated long enough to make sure no one was watching me. Then I pulled MacPherson's wand from my pocket. Quickly, I stuffed it into a folded shirt near the bottom of the drawer. Just as quickly, I shut the drawer again.

I felt immediate relief, followed by even more consternation. What was I doing? The wand wasn't mine.

Taking a deep breath, I promised myself I'd hand it over just as soon as the Victory Feast was finished. My consternation eased a bit.

I was about to get changed when I caught a glimpse of Tad, for real this time. He was curled up on one of the couches, his gaze directed at a memory mirror.

An orphan since childhood, Tad had grown up in a variety of living situations. As a result, he'd spent much of his life with no clue that he was a magician. That all changed when he experienced his breakout.

A breakout, by the way, refers to a magic breakout. Most kids learn how to perform spells at a young age. We learn how to hail the Capsudra and give ourselves over to Instinctia. Despite this, magic kind of builds up inside of a person. Eventually, it all comes out in one crazy burst of undirected energy. This usually happens between the ages of twelve and fourteen. Nobody knows why it happens. It just does.

The bigger the breakout, the more potential for greatness. At least, that's the general consensus. Then again, if breakout size was all that mattered, I would've been at the top of my class rather than working an assembly line. Regardless, magic schools are always scouting for new breakouts. Small breakouts draw regional attention. Bigger ones bring the elite institutions into the mix. The biggest ones of all are reserved for Madkey.

"What are you doing?" I asked.

"Watching memories," he replied.

"Aren't you showing someone around today?"

"You mean Hannah?" He didn't look up. "Nico offered to take my place. I think he likes her or something."

Kinico "Nico" Stotem was a staffer with two years on us. I didn't know him all that well, but he seemed like a decent guy.

I waited for Tad to look my way, but he kept his gaze locked on the mirror. He adored history and was always hitting up Madkey Library for memories. He could sit there for hours, perfectly happy, watching recollections of famous events. This single-minded devotion had helped him ace his first semester of Magic History 9. But he'd neglected his other courses in the process, a fact that eventually led him to drop out.

Tad, along with Piper and Leandra, was one of my best friends. He was nice and had a good sense of humor. And yet, I always felt kind of uncomfortable around him. It wasn't anything he'd done. Honestly, I couldn't even explain it. There was just something about him that irked me at a very deep level.

"Have you talked to Piper or Leandra?" I asked.

He shook his head. "Why?"

I told him about my morning, starting with the broken wand and running all the way through my discovery of Professor MacPherson. Finally, I told him about our trip to the library.

"Piper thinks she's traced the spell to a Chaotic family," I finished. "The Hynors."

"Impossible." Still staring at his mirror, he frowned. "Boris was imprisoned long ago."

"It doesn't have to be him. It could've been his kid or some other relative."

"Like I said, impossible. Here, let me show you something." His gaze swept across the mirror several times and I knew he was bringing a new memory to the forefront. Then he turned the mirror toward me.

One full-on glance caused the shiny remembra to swirl away. I saw a tall man standing in a snowy field. A black derby cap was pulled tight over his head. His mustache was thick and curly and he wore a worsted wool suit jacket with matching trousers.

"That's Boltstar." I recoiled in surprise at the sight of Madkey's famous headmaster. "He looks really young here. When was this captured?"

"1935. Five years after Victory Day."

A cold breeze caused me to break out in shivers. The scent of fresh snow floated into my nostrils. Shifting my gaze, I saw a second man standing across from Boltstar. He was short, with a heavy build. His clothes were rags and his face reflected sheer hatred.

"Who's that?" I asked.

"James Torwheat. The last of the Chaotics."

Ahh, a Chaotic. That made sense, seeing as how the very sight of him made me uneasy. "The last?" I asked.

"Victory Day ended Chaotics as a movement. But it took a few years for Boltstar to track down the stragglers." He nodded at the mirror. "James Torwheat was the last to fall."

"Yeah, but a kid—"

"Kids were imprisoned, too, Randy. Nobody escaped."

Frowning, I peered closer at Boltstar and Torwheat. "Who's providing the memory?"

"Galison."

I nodded to myself. Professor Galison might've been a jerk. But he was also a hero, having fought alongside Boltstar on Victory Day.

"It's just those two?" I asked. "They should've brought a havoc army with them."

"They did. But a storm stirred up and everyone got separated. Boltstar and Galison ran into Torwheat by accident. Most wizards would've waited for back-up." He shrugged. "Of course, Boltstar's no ordinary wizard."

Still watching the mirror, I saw Boltstar circle around Torwheat. "Lower the wand," he called out. "We can resolve this peacefully."

"Like the peaceful way you took down my friends?"

"They left us no choice."

Torwheat's wand moved swiftly, zigzagging through the air. His lips spoke a quiet incantation I didn't recognize. Three bolts of straw-colored light shot into the storm. I could feel their energy, their heat.

His lips moving fast, Boltstar waved his wand in response. Four cyan-colored lights shot forth. Three of them slammed into the straw-colored bolts, vaporizing them in an instant. The fourth light ripped into Torwheat's wand. The short staff crumbled into dust and blew away with the wind.

Torwheat stared at his empty hand in disbelief. Then he turned to run. But another cyan light caught him in the right leg and he fell to the snow.

"Don't move," Boltstar said. "Don't even breathe."

The remembra surface returned to normal. The chilly sensation and smell of snow and heat vanished.

"What happened to him?" I asked.

"Torwheat?" He shrugged. "He went to Gutlore. I hear he died a year later."

I gave Tad the once-over. His shirt was stained with sweat. Bits of reddish dirt colored his pants. "Are you working tonight?" I asked.

He looked at me like I was crazy. "Of course."

"And you're not ready yet?"

He checked the clock. Eyes wide, he jumped to his feet. The movement caused an object to slip out of his pocket. It fell to the floor and rolled up against my shoe.

At first glance, it looked like one of those little bouncy balls the humdrums buy for their kids. But this was no humdrum toy. Known as a fizzer, it was a product of Leandra's fertile imagination.

After practical jokes, her favorite hobby was tinkering with magic. She was always pulling apart items from the Big Three in order to see how they worked. Now, she was starting to bundle spells, making products of her own.

She'd spent two weeks creating the fizzer. It was so named because she'd enchanted it to fizz upon touching any kind of liquid. At her request, I'd tasted an earlier version of it. It felt like a firework show within my lips, one that only ended after I thoroughly washed my mouth out with soap.

Tad scooped up the fizzer and shoved it back into his pocket. "So, uh … you didn't see that, right?"

I grinned. "Planning a prank?"

"Yeah." He relaxed long enough to shoot me a smile. "On you-know-who. She deserves it after everything she's put me through."

We took our clothes into the bathroom and quickly changed. By the time we were finished, Jeff was no longer there. Neither was anyone else.

"What's your work schedule this week?" I asked as we hiked to the exit.

"Same as usual."

"Me too." A frown creased my visage. "It sure would be nice to get a day off once in a while."

"Yeah." His voice sounded sickly, almost listless.

"You feeling okay?" I asked.

"Sure. Well, no. Not really. Listen, I—"

A whizzing sound interrupted him. Right away, I knew it was a bubbler. Bubblers were used for long-distance communications. They could slip through door cracks and seep through windows. In short, they could go anywhere at any time, provided the sender had total access to the recipient. Most parents signed their kids up for bubblers at a young age in order to keep tabs on them. I was no different. Unfortunately, that meant I'd be at Mom and Dad's beck and call until I reached the age of eighteen.

"Nobody ever calls me," Tad said, looking around. "So, it must be your folks."

My parents liked to keep a close eye on me, which meant nightly bubbler chats. And unfortunately, those chats almost always devolved into lectures and shouting matches.

"Way ahead of you." I headed toward my bed. "Now, what were you saying? Make it quick."

He hesitated. "It can wait."

I leapt into bed and pulled the sheets and blankets over me. "Cover for me with Jax?"

He nodded. "Will do."

The door shut as Tad left the dorm. Meanwhile, the whizzing noise drew closer and closer. The temperature dropped a notch and vapor wetted my cheeks.

"Randy?" A familiar voice rang a discordant note in my ears. "It's Mom. We need to talk."

CHAPTER 9

Can't you see I'm sleeping? I thought. *Come back later.*

"Get up, Randy," Dad said in that tough, no-nonsense voice he uses when he's trying to, well, stop my nonsense. "We're not leaving until we've had a chance to talk."

Breathing softly, I remained still.

"We've got good news," Mom said. "Really good news, in fact."

I didn't move a muscle. A minute of silence passed by.

"Isn't the Victory Feast tonight?" Dad asked in a voice that indicated he already knew the answer.

"Why, yes, it is," Mom replied. "And seeing as how Randy's on staff, that means he'll be working it."

They had me and I knew it.

Unwilling to admit I'd been faking, I waited a little longer. Then I issued a big yawn and cracked my eyes open. "Whoa," I said, laying eyes upon my parents. "What are you doing here?"

A large watery bubble floated in front of me. It showed my parents sitting at the kitchen table back home. Ceramic plates, piled high with homemade spaghetti, sat in front of them. I licked my lips. The spaghetti smelled delicious and I was eager for a bite. A real bite, not just the taste of one. Unfortunately, that wasn't going to happen.

A bubbler is basically enchanted water, designed to carry sensory data from one location to another. It travels as water vapor, which enables it to slip through tight spaces. Upon reaching its intended recipient, the droplets form into a bubble of considerable size.

Bubblers are similar to memory mirrors in that they can communicate images, sounds, smells, tastes, and even touches. Which is good and bad. There's nothing like getting a hug from a distant loved one on a bad day. But it also means you might get a face full of Casafortro-branded Punishment Pudding instead.

"Quit it," Dad groused. "We know you weren't sleeping."

"Honey, that's not helpful." Mom patted his hand, then smiled at me. "How are you doing, Randy? Are they treating you okay?"

"I'm fine." I made a show of checking the clock, then jumped to my feet. "Wow, I'm really late."

"Don't worry. We'll make this fast." Dad dragged his fork through the spaghetti. "Your mom and I have talked it over. And we want you to come home."

"Yes," she said. "As soon as possible."

I frowned. "You mean for a visit?"

She shook her head. "For good."

I winced inwardly as I saw the barely-veiled shame in her eyes. When Madkey had first offered me a spot in its hallowed halls, she'd been so proud of me. She and Dad had told anyone and everyone about my matriculation. That pride quickly faded, however, as I began to rack up failing grades in nearly all subjects. They'd even begun to monitor me on a daily basis, sitting in on my classes via bubblers. But all that did was detract from my quickly-ebbing confidence.

And now they wanted me to do what? Quit my job? Go home with my tail tucked firmly between my legs? What would I even do at home? Get an entry-level position at Casafortro? Maybe painting labels with the other dropouts?

No, thanks. If I had to work an assembly line, at least I could do it from within Madkey's hallowed halls.

Mom traded glances with Dad. "Do you want to tell him, or should I?"

I frowned. "Tell me what?"

"I spoke to Ian last night," Dad said. "He's agreed to bring you aboard at YickYack for the fourth quarter."

YickYack, or the YickYack Academy for Magical Arts, was one of the regional magic schools operating out of New England. Its headmaster, Ian Clagheimer, was one of Dad's closest friends.

"YuckYuck?" I made a face. "No, thanks."

"Don't call it that," Mom replied sternly. "And there's nothing wrong with YickYack. It's a good school."

It wasn't, but that was irrelevant.

"I'm staying," I replied.

"No," Dad said. "You're not."

Like it or not, they were my guardians. If they wanted me home, I'd have no choice but to hop into one of Galison's conveyance portals.

"I need to get to the feast," I said, my voice icing over.

Mom shook her head. "You don't have to be a staffer, Randy. YickYack can—"

"I need to go."

"Fine." Dad sighed. "But this isn't over."

"Bye, Randy," Mom said.

"We love you," Dad added.

Mom stuck out a finger. Abruptly, the bubbler popped, spraying me with a soft mist, and they disappeared. The smell of spaghetti faded away.

And then I was alone.

CHAPTER 10

I was late.

Moving at a quick pace, I exited the staffer dorm and hurried through the forearm portion of Left Arm. The entire area was dedicated to staff and thus, was considered part of Shadow Madkey.

My feet struck ragged carpeting. A couple of armoires and old chairs were pushed up against the walls. The items were antiques, old and dull. Nobody cared for them because nobody really wanted them. At the same time, nobody wanted to make the effort to get rid of them either.

I broke into a trot. Reaching the elbow, I entered a crooked spiral stairwell. The walls were dented and the paint peeled in numerous places. The sickly green carpet was threadbare. Tapestries, tattered and fraying at the edges, hung from the walls. Overall, the area looked spic and span, thanks to regular cleanings from us staffers. But all of that elbow grease couldn't change the fact that Left Arm was long overdue for renovation.

Heading down the staircase, I hustled to a door. I caught a glimpse of the sign and its mantra—*Faculty and Students Are Your Priority. Serve Them Always and Without Question*—as I turned the knob.

Flinging the door open, I stepped out into the bicep portion of Left Arm. This section, which was occupied by the Conveyance department, sloped upward to the shoulder. Doors lined either side of the corridor, leading to various classrooms and offices. Gleaming sculptures of Structuralist heroes, exquisite paintings in polished frames, and cozy, plush furniture filled out the space.

As always, everything looked new and inviting. I sometimes lingered here on my way back and forth to the dorm. But since I was in a hurry, I sprinted instead.

I darted uphill to the shoulder, then walked out onto the Upper Torso bridge. Madkey Station Grille was in the process of a complete overhaul. A dozen staffers were busy covering tables with fine white cloth. Other staffers sat in floating chairs, now adorned with colorful bunting. Kicking their legs, they traveled amongst the tables, using their wands to convey silverware, plates, glasses, napkins, flowers, and other items into place. Still other staffers handled decorations. There were so many balloons, the place looked like a kid's birthday party.

I recognized some of the decorations from the Madkey Convocation. That event, which celebrated the beginning of the school year, had been one of the greatest experiences of my life. I still recalled the delicious food, the rousing speeches, and the astounding feats of magic. Most of all, I recalled the Critter Combine.

The Critter Combine was a ritualistic affair in which a magical creature was paired with the incoming class. For the next four years, the fates of both parties were completely intertwined.

The tenth through twelfth graders had previously been paired with the thunderbirds, the chupacabras, and the snipes, respectively. Meanwhile, the ninth graders—my class—had waited eagerly to see which critter would choose us. We'd gone bonkers when the sasquatches sent up a signal. Exhilarating at the time, it seemed like a distant memory now.

I looked around. An unfamiliar face caught my attention. It belonged to a raven-haired girl, accompanied by Nico.

A native of Guam, Nico stood a few inches over six feet. He had a relaxed way about him that hadn't played well in the hard-charging world of Madkey. He couldn't—or maybe wouldn't—keep up with his schoolwork. After three semesters, he'd dropped out. Displeased with the prospect of returning home, he'd become a staffer.

The girl at his side, I could only assume, was the new student. Hannah, according to Tad. Her face was perfectly symmetrical and featured a pair of green eyes that seemed to shine for miles. Dark hair, smooth yet wavy, bounced gently upon her shoulders. Her lightly-tanned body was toned with thin muscle.

"Wolf," Jax shouted. "You're late."

Cheeks burning, I froze in place. Jax knelt on a floating chair near the bridge. His arms were crossed. A scowl rested upon his lips. "You skipped the morning shift. Now, you're late to set-up. What's up with you, Wolf?"

"My parents sent me a bubbler. Didn't Tad tell you?"

"No."

I frowned.

"Speaking of Tad, where is he?"

"He's not here?"

He gave me a pointed look.

Quickly, I scanned Torso. Indeed, there was no sign of him. Genuinely puzzled, I thought back to our parting moments in the dorm. He'd sounded a little funny and I'd asked him if he felt okay. *Not really*, he'd said. But before he could offer an explanation, the bubbler had arrived.

"You and your friends better get it together, Wolf. Or else." With a fierce growl, Jax twisted his chair around and raced off to Lower-Torso.

I remained still for a moment, wondering if I should go look for my friend. But a shouted order from Jax put that idea to rest. Entering Shadow Madkey, I made my way down to the kitchen. I spent the next hour or so on the assembly line, busily putting together last-minute appetizers. I wrapped bacon around dates that had been stuffed with blue cheese. I spread enchanted caviar onto thin slices of cucumber. And I mixed up a smooth mixture of cranberries, honey, orange juice, and sea salt as prep work for cranberry crostini.

When I finally got a chance to breathe, the enchanted clock read half past seven. That meant the Victory Feast was already underway, a fact that kind of surprised me. I tried to picture it in my head. The performers, the speeches, the trays of delicious food emerging from the wall chutes. It must've been amazing.

"Psst," Jenny Lynch whispered.

I offered her a quick glance. "Need something?"

"Yeah. The truth." Her look turned conspiratorial. "What really happened in that supply room?"

Licking my lips, I recalled the cover story. "A bunch of cursed poster boards got loose. They spotted scissors and—"

"Stop lying." She made a face. "I mean, *come on*. Who's going to believe *that*?"

I hid a small smile. "It's true."

"I'm not an idiot, Randy. Now—"

"Oops." Leandra's wand squirted out of her hand. It slid across the floor and bumped into my shoe. She froze, her eyes focused on Jax.

He shot her a cold look in return. "What are you waiting for? An invitation?"

She scurried across the room. Stooping down, I grabbed her wand. Still in a crouch, I handed it to her.

She took hold of it. "Have you seen Tad?"

Checking Jenny, I saw she'd gone back to her work. So, I scanned the room. Extra workstations had been brought in for the evening, enough to accommodate staffers who normally worked in laundry, housekeeping, or one of the other assembly-line functions. As such, the room was practically bursting with staffers. But Tad wasn't one of them.

"No. Where is he?" I wondered.

"I was hoping you knew."

I glanced at Jax. He waved his wand all over the place, putting the finishing touches on bowls of bananas foster. "Has Jax said anything?"

She nodded. "I heard him grumbling about it a few minutes ago. He thinks Tad's playing hooky."

I frowned.

"When was the last time you saw him?"

"In the dorm, right before work. He had your—"

"My what?"

Back in the dorm, I'd thought Tad was planning a prank for Leandra. Now, I wasn't sure what to think. "He had your fizzer."

Thinking of Tad jogged my memory. I recalled how he'd looked a bit tired and beat-up. I recalled the reddish dirt on his clothes. I'd seen similar dirt on MacPherson's clothing.

"What a freak." Tossing her curly, red hair back, would-be junior Fyla Roice stormed into the kitchen. "I knew that kid was trouble."

"What are you doing here?" Jax frowned. "Get back to your post."

"I *was* at my post," she replied huffily. "Only that little creep snuck past me. He's out there, Jax. He's at the feast!"

Fyla was one of five watchers for the evening. Their job was to keep an eye on the feast and make sure everything went swimmingly. If a problem arose, they were empowered to pull out all stops to fix it.

"Slow down," Jax said. "Who went out there?"

"Tad Crucible."

He gave his temples a good, hard rub. "And you didn't go after him?"

"By the time I got onto the bridge, he was gone."

"Cripes, what is wrong with that guy?" Jax massaged his temples. "I'd better go … hey, Wolf … where do you think you're going? Get back here!"

But I was already out the door.

CHAPTER 11

I had to find Tad. And I had to do it before Galison or another faculty member caught sight of him. So, I hustled through Shadow Madkey at top speed, heading for the exit. Unfortunately, Jax was quicker.

"Wolf!" Grabbing my shoulder, he wrenched me away from the double doors. "What's Tad doing out there?"

"I … don't know."

His face reddened. "He's through. Finished. When the feast is done, I'm telling Galison everything."

I gave him a doubtful look. "You mean how you couldn't keep control over your staff?"

His gaze wavered.

"I can find him," I said. "I can bring him back."

He scowled at me. Still, I had him over a barrel and he knew it.

"Then do it." He released me. "But if you get caught, I'll make sure both of you get fired."

I hurried to the double doors and eased them open a few inches. My eyes shone with wonder. I'd heard stories about the Victory Feast ever since I'd come to Madkey. But this, well, it was beyond my wildest imagination.

Lovely moonlight, aided by well-placed cool-lights, cast an elegant gleam throughout the entirety of Torso. Lace cloth, along with polished silverware, pristine plates, and vases of aromatic daisies and lilies, covered the tables. Students and faculty members sat in various sections, situated on well-adorned chairs.

Students chosen by the Magictainment department floated amongst the crowd, performing to roaring applause. Chez Skalant, a senior, aimed spells at a dozen falling swords, continuously blasting them back into the air. Tara DuBois, also a senior, used her wand to sketch people in Living Ink. Moses Cole, Lola Neri, and Madhuri Data whipped spells at a series of metallic objects, causing them to reverberate gently. This created a variety of sounds that somehow melded together to form beautiful music. There were other artists and artisans, too. Dancers, singers, air tumblers, even woodcutters, which seemed to make the floating chairs more than a bit nervous.

Sneaking outside, I looked for Tad. He wasn't on the bridge and I didn't see him amongst the students and faculty. Thinking he might be on one of the other bridges, I took a hoist to Mid-Torso, exited, then ducked into the shadows.

A long table was situated on the Mid-Torso bridge. Its occupants included Galison, Wadflow, and Norch. There was an empty chair next to Norch, which was probably meant for MacPherson. And in the middle of the four regular chairs was an oversized seat. A throne, really, one fit for a king.

Out in the open, the Seniors and faculty occupied the tables closest to the long table. The Juniors sat behind them. The Sophomores and Freshmen were gathered in Lower- and Upper-Torso, respectively.

Curiously enough, the faculty section seemed a bit light on numbers. Looking around, I noticed a few professors situated around Torso's edges. Their eyes roved and they held their wands in tight grips. It occurred to me that they were on guard-duty.

Covered silver trays began to pop out of numerous wall chutes. They soared through the air, carefully skirted one another, and settled down onto the many tables.

Food was a big deal at Madkey and there was always plenty to eat. But the Victory Feast was special. A quick scan of the room revealed a variety of mouth-watering dishes. Jumbo shrimp wrapped in prosciutto ham and glazed with masala butter sauce. Cuts of orange-glazed beef fillet. Braised short ribs. Mashed potatoes. Potato cakes. Sweet plantains. Straw vegetables. And lots of other things, too. I knew the food well, having helped to prepare much of it over the last twenty-four hours.

Stomach growling, I searched for Tad. But all I saw was festive eating. The seated faculty members stuffed themselves silly amidst a great deal of laughter. The Seniors, Juniors, and Sophomores were just starting to dig in. Meanwhile, the Freshmen were in the process of placing their orders.

Another quick search revealed Porter's table. He sat with Gordon, Sya, Felicia, and a couple of other freshmen. They were situated just above me and I could hear every word emanating from their table.

"Ahoy, mateys." Yordlo, his ghostly face looking especially chipper, materialized before Porter. "Ye ... oh. It's ye."

"Yes, it's us." Porter frowned. "What took you so long?"

"Freshmen eat last, young Garrington. Ye should know that."

Sya rolled her eyes. "That's dumb."

"It's tradition, lass." He gave the table a cock-eyed look. "Well, what'll it be, mateys?"

"Pistachio crusted sea bass," Felicia said without hesitation. "Oh, and the lamb lollipops. And a soda, too."

The rest of the table quickly rattled off a bunch of dishes and drinks because, hey, why not? That was the whole point of the Victory Feast. To eat, drink, and celebrate like crazy.

Soon, a covered floating tray arrived at their table. Gordon removed the lid and passed around a bunch of bottomless goblets.

More trays arrived in short order. Years ago, trays could only float on a certain plane. They couldn't be lifted or lowered, which was apparently quite annoying. Mom and Dad, in fact, still complained about it. Usually in the middle of one of their *you don't know how good you have it* lectures. It was a rare bit of true innovation, courtesy of Alanskew.

I continued my search for Tad. Nobody, not even Porter and his friends, spotted me. They were too busy enjoying the festivities.

Meanwhile, Wadflow, Norch, and Galison finished up their salads, soups, and appetizers. Dirty plates and bowls were piled back up on the floating trays, which then whisked their way back to the wall chutes. Silver trays arrived soon after, adorned with covered dishes.

Galison removed the lid from a tray and sniffed the contents. I couldn't see it, but I sure could smell it. It was a bacon-wrapped cut of filet mignon along with salted, buttery potatoes. I salivated just thinking about it.

"Cook it," he told the tray. "Medium-rare."

The food, showered with enchantments, began to emit tiny, heatless sparks. Quite quickly, the filet mignon was cooked to perfection. Although we'd prepped the meat in advance, various spells were required to keep it fresh. Some magicians weren't fond of enchanted food. They considered it unnatural. But since it made my job easier, I loved it.

The assembled guests fell quiet. Confused, I watched Galison gain his feet. He stared out over the crowd, his visage full of grave certainty. "Welcome," he shouted. "To the Victory Feast!"

People went bonkers. The faculty remained seated, applauding loudly. Students, meanwhile, stood up in their chairs. They clapped and cheered and hooted at the top of their lungs.

With the crowd distracted, I hustled to the nearest loading platform. I climbed aboard a chair and it whisked me out into the Grille area. Sticking close to the windows, I circled the backside of Torso, my eyes peeled for Tad.

"First things first," Galison continued. "As many of you know, Professor MacPherson is an esteemed outdoorsman with a keen interest in sacred mountains. To further his research on the subject, he has decided to scale Arizona's Superstition Mountain. As such, he will be taking a temporary leave of absence. Professor Norch will assume his professorial duties for this semester."

MacPherson was well-liked by his students and I saw plenty of crestfallen faces amongst the crowd. The cheers faded away. The students sat down again.

"We here at the Roderick J. Madkey School of Magical Administration wish him all the best. Now, let us return to the matter at hand." Galison stroked his jaw. "This fine meal we share marks the official beginning of the second semester. But it also marks something else, something far more important. The first Victory Feast was held many years ago, way back in 1930. It was held to commemorate a victory. *The* victory."

The students remained quiet, listening to every word with rapt attention.

"I remember it like it was yesterday." He glanced around Torso, his eyes wistful. "This is where it happened. This is where the Philosophical War, for all intents and purposes, reached its conclusion."

The crowd was absolutely silent.

"Up until the 1920s, magic was almost entirely a Chaotic pursuit," he reminded the crowd. "But a few of us, led by Lanctin Boltstar, had begun to question the old ways. We saw the dangers inherent in boundless magic. And so, we proposed a new path, which became known as Structuralism.

"We fought an uphill battle for several years. But with time, we began to convince others of our righteousness. Soon, the Chaotics could no longer ignore us. And so, their leader, a rather cowardly man by the name of Boris Hynor, challenged our beloved headmaster to a debate. It was to be held here, in the glorious halls of the Roderick J. Madkey School of Magical Administration.

"We arrived on this very day, way back in 1930. We came seeking peace and understanding. But the Chaotics had other ideas. They saw us as a threat to their power, their very way of life. And so, without warning, they launched a vicious and deadly attack."

He paused for a moment. Deep lines etched their way across his face.

"The battle raged all throughout this great room," he said with a sweep of his hand. "Somehow we managed to repel the ambush. Under Lanctin's flawless leadership, we regrouped and launched a counter-attack. When the smoke had cleared, the Chaotics were pretty much finished."

Breaking their silence, the crowd hooted and hollered. And why not? The defeat of the Chaotics was, without a doubt, the single greatest moment in magic history.

"That night, badly injured and feeling low, we raided Madkey's kitchen," he said once the cheering had died down a bit. "We threw an impromptu meal, which helped us to momentarily forget the horrid events of that day. That meal became an annual tradition. And that tradition morphed into what we now know as the Victory Feast."

The crowd roared its approval.

"With Structuralism came a whole host of new things. Formal schooling, available to all, was introduced. Small businesses consolidated into the Big Three, allowing safer and more sensible products to reach the marketplace. Magical remnants of the old world—the Floating Abyss, for example—fell into disuse and were replaced by more efficient enchantments. And through it all, Lanctin Boltstar's popularity reached epic heights. People begged him to take power, to rule over us. But true to his nature, he wished to dedicate his remaining years to the youth. And so, he assumed the position of Madkey's headmaster."

The roar died down. Stifled, excited whispers took its place.

"Without further ado, please welcome the greatest magician of this or any other age. The scourge of the Chaotics, the hero of Structuralism." Galison's voice took on an admiring edge. "Lanctin Boltstar!"

Everyone, even the faculty, climbed on top of their chairs this time. People whistled, clapped, shouted, hollered, and cheered. The sound was almost deafening.

I knew I needed to keep looking for Tad. But the moment was just too big to ignore. So, I halted my chair near the windows, halfway between Mid- and Upper-Torso. My gaze turned to the Mid-Torso bridge.

The headmaster's door opened wide and Boltstar appeared in the frame. His short hair, a distinguished salt and pepper, was mostly covered by a black derby cap. His goatee and mustache, also salt-and-pepper, were neatly trimmed. For clothes, he wore a long-sleeve yellow collared shirt, topped off by a black bow tie and a brown herringbone wool vest. A pair of brown herringbone trousers covered his legs.

The noise grew even louder, so loud I could barely think. And when Boltstar leapt onto his chair, the place went nuts.

"The last thing any of you need is to listen to the prattling of an old man," he announced, a broad grin stretching across his face. "So, I'll keep this short and simple. Thank you for being here today."

The crowd roared again, the noise reached an all-new high. Boltstar played to them, encouraging even more excitement. And they responded with such applause that I was forced to cover my ears.

He waited for the noise to quiet down again. Then his grin turned into a smile.

"Now, enjoy the rest of the feast," he said.

The crowd voiced its approval. Meanwhile, new trays soared to the faculty section and settled into place. From my vantage point, I could just make out Professor Lellpoppy as she pulled the lid off of an oversized tray. Her eyes grew wide as she surveyed plates and bowls of doughcream, cakes, pies, ice cream, and other assorted treats.

A shadow caught my attention. Glancing up, I spotted movement near the Upper-Torso bridge, just inside Left Arm's entranceway. My gaze narrowed. Was that Tad?

"Kell! Kell! Kell! Kell!"

I shifted my gaze to the Junior section. Kell Masters stood on his chair, a bottomless goblet in his hand. It didn't weigh much, but his muscles were steeled anyway. With tremendous concentration, he started to turn the glassware upside down.

Bottomless goblets are a staple of Madkey dining. They're specifically enchanted so as to provide an endless supply of drink. Obviously, such a goblet could create quite a mess. That's why they're also enchanted to return to an upright position when not being held aloft.

Students and faculty alike twisted toward the scene. The chant grew louder.

"Kell! Kell! Kell! Kell!"

Lip curled, he turned the mug upside down. A small torrent of soda poured out of it, soaking the table cloth. Gritting his teeth, Kell struggled to keep the goblet aloft. But the force of the flowing soda was just too much. Suddenly, the goblet wrenched its way out of his grip. It reverted to an upright position in a split-second, landing neatly on the table.

The crowd laughed and applauded. Kell, his face red from exertion, took a few mock bows before plopping back into his chair.

I figured he'd held it aloft for maybe one or two seconds. That was par for the course. No magician could hold an upside-down, free-flowing bottomless goblet for long. The enchanted flow was way too powerful.

I was so busy watching his strong-man stunt that I nearly missed it. But as a pack of students crowded around Kell, a tawny hue caught my eye. Tawny was Tad's color. Clearly, he was casting a spell. But why?

Are you crazy? I thought. *Are you trying to get caught?*

The light, thin and barely visible, crested forth from the Upper-Torso bridge. Something was positioned at the front-end of the light, something small and round and contained by a soft glow. That caused my eyebrow to arch. It looked like he was moving something across Torso. But what? And where was he sending it to?

The object zoomed across open space with no one the wiser. Holding my breath, I watched it veer toward the Freshmen section. Then the light blinked out and the object splashed into Porter's bottomless goblet.

The faculty continued to enjoy their desserts. A large portion of the students were still focused on Kell. The rest had turned their attention back to their plates, eager to finish their food before the annual Philosophical War reenactment. Nobody else had seen Tad's spell. That was good. Maybe I could still salvage this.

A zapping sound, soft yet discordant, rang out. It was followed by a series of frenzied splashes.

Soda bubbled up inside of Porter's bottomless goblet and started to overflow the edges. My eyes widened as I realized what Tad had dropped into it.

The fizzer.

Liquid spurted into the air. It came faster and faster, like some super-powered geyser. In mere seconds, soda splashed onto dozens of people.

Porter and his friends, their jaws slack, kicked their chairs away from the table. Faculty and other students turned to see what was happening. For the most part, they seemed excited. And why not? They probably thought it was another performance. But I knew better.

The airborne soda gained volume and speed at a terrifying rate. It became a veritable tower, reaching all the way up to the ceiling.

What have you done, Tad? I wondered, my heart filled with awe and trepidation. *What have you done?*

CHAPTER 12

With a mighty ripping noise, the tower of soda broke apart. Brown liquid crashed over all of Torso. Ducking my head, I managed to weather the blow. Others weren't so lucky.

Royce Miller shrieked as a jet of soda knocked him off of his chair. The sound of brilliant music vanished as Moses, Lola, and Madhuri lost their balance as well. Students and faculty alike plummeted toward the black mist. Their ever-vigilant chairs raced off to save them.

The service doors flew open. Fyla and the other watchers hurried out onto the Lower-Torso bridge. But a giant wave of soda sent them tumbling across the stones.

Other staffers, including Leandra, emerged from Shadow Madkey. Pounding waves swept them out into the Grille area, where chairs caught their shaking, shivering bodies.

Even the sheer force of the fizzing soda couldn't upend the enchanted goblet. But it did cause it to spin in tight circles. Moments later, a particularly vicious rotation sent it shooting off the table. With soda spurting in all directions, the bottomless goblet fell past tables and chairs. It slipped through the black mist. Utilizing the mist's conveyance energy, it emerged from the mist along the ceiling, spurting soda the entire time. It dropped like a rock and fell through the floor mist before shooting out of the ceiling mist all over again.

I peered through the dense storm of fizzing soda. Floating tables had been knocked askew. Trays of fallen food were tumbling repeatedly through the mist. It was pure bedlam.

The students and faculty were in even worse shape. I saw a wave catch hold of Kell and send him careening into Calvin Hayes. Sya got blasted off her chair and slammed into an upended table. Professor Sadie Whitlock reached for her wand, only to get ripped clear off her seat by a vicious geyser. Nobody was spared. Even Boltstar, still situated on the Mid-Torso bridge, got sprayed from head to toe. But unlike the others, he didn't look worried.

Following his gaze, I realized he was watching Porter's goblet as it repeatedly dropped through the floor mist. Undoubtedly, he was trying to figure out a way to stop it.

A dark shadow fell over my chair. Peering up, I saw a tsunami of soda cresting high above me. Heart pounding, I kicked my legs and zipped through the open space, searching for refuge.

A jet of soda crashed into me. The chair twisted and turned, bucking me off my perch. Immediately, the chair turned to catch me.

My lungs emptied as my stomach smashed into the seat. I lay still for a few seconds, stunned, as more soda slammed into me. And that's when I caught my second glimpse of tawny-colored light.

Feeling exhausted and beat-up, I peered at the Upper-Torso bridge. Tad stood just behind the railing, his wand stretched outward, a tawny jet flowing toward the Grille. The streak started to weave, wrapping its way around the space. It continued to stretch and curl, enclosing everything, even the black mist at either end. I recalled how he'd always made me feel uncomfortable. Like I couldn't quite trust him. Apparently, my instincts had been on to something.

More soda smashed into me and I found it hard to think. What was he doing? And why?

I shook away the cobwebs and something occurred to me. Yes, his spell was encircling the Grille. But it was also encircling the ancient conveyance station. The station that had once allowed access to and from the Floating Abyss.

Was that his target? The station?

Prior to its abandonment, the Abyss was the sole means of transportation between magical realms. Adventurous witches and wizards used to travel through its inky, shadowy folds in search of new lands. But these days, travel is a cinch. All you need is humdrum transport and permission to cross the occasional enchanted border.

Waves crashed down on top of Tad, but he didn't move an inch. His wand remained steady and his spell continued to envelop the old station.

My brain screamed at me to get clear, to seek safety. Let Boltstar and the faculty deal with Tad. But at the same time, I felt something urging me on, driving me to confrontation.

I directed my chair forward and upward. A burst of soda knocked me back down. With liquid stinging my eyes, I noticed that I was close to the Mid-Torso bridge. Rising to my feet, I leapt for the railing. Immediately, I knew I was going to come up short. But a sudden burst of soda propelled me onward.

I crashed onto the bridge. A vicious jet of soda sent me skittering across the stonework. Blinking liquid out of my eyes, I scrambled to my feet.

Slipping and sliding, I entered a hoist. The gate closed over and it rocketed toward the ceiling. As my stomach surged into my throat, more soda crashed over me.

The hoist came to a jarring halt. The gate slid open and a nasty voice yelled, "Upper-Torso. Get out before I throw you out."

Dazed, I stepped outside. A fine mist of soda sprayed me in the face. Shielding my eyes, I looked at Tad. He stood at the railing, fifteen feet away. His posture was firm and tall, oblivious to the bedlam that surrounded him. His tawny light, meanwhile, had completely enveloped the ancient conveyance station.

I grabbed my wand out of its holster. The stick felt old and brittle, like it might break at any moment. I found myself wishing I'd brought MacPherson's wand with me.

A sideways geyser knocked the air right out of me. Somehow, I managed to struggle forward.

"Tad!" Jets of soda struck my shoulders as I drew within shouting distance. "What are you doing?"

He didn't even acknowledge me with a look. "You shouldn't be here, Randy."

I had no plan, not even an inkling of one. And I certainly wasn't a fighter. Heck, I didn't know so much as a single havoc magic spell. But that didn't stop me from jabbing my wand into his back. "Holster your wand," I growled. "Or else."

I caught a glimpse of the reddish dirt on his clothes, the same dirt I'd seen on MacPherson's clothing. Right away, I realized the foolishness of my actions. Tad had, in all likelihood, attacked MacPherson. He'd put the professor to sleep, somehow. How could I, a dropout, defeat someone with that kind of power?

His free hand snaked backward. It grabbed hold of my wand and he yanked it out of my sore, tired fingers. Without fanfare, he tossed it onto the bridge.

I stared blankly at it, then at him. "Why?"

"Just go. You don't want any part of what's coming."

"What are you talking about?" I shook my head. "What's coming?"

"I—" He paused as a mid-sized wave crashed over us. Through it all, he held his wand perfectly steady. "I'm not who you think I am."

The tawny light began to pulse and throb. Slowly at first, before picking up steam.

I froze, at once fascinated and horrified. From a certain perspective, this was a thrilling moment. The conveyance station had been sealed for decades. If Tad was opening it up, the Floating Abyss would be within reach. What was it like in there anyway?

The waves of soda began to ebb. Then they vanished altogether. Peering down, I saw Boltstar. He stood on a floating chair, wand in hand. Cyan-colored light connected it to Porter's goblet. Ever so slowly, the light crept over the drinking glass, capping it fully.

The waves vanished, leaving a receding sea of soda flowing within Torso. Galison, Wadflow, and Norch climbed onto floating chairs. Flying out into the open, they attacked the liquid with spells, causing it to evaporate into steam.

Everyone was so busy recovering that no one saw the newcomer. No one, that is, but me. He materialized within the Grille, looking dim and hazy at first before turning into a full-fledged person. He was a few years older than me. His skin was pale white. His hair was dense and black. He wore a tunic, belted with a steel blue sash. A wand, long and thin, filled his hand.

Instantly, I disliked him. I didn't know why. But it reminded me of the discomfort I'd always felt around Tad.

An empty chair flew up to catch him. Meanwhile, more people materialized within the Grille. They came in all skin colors and body types. I saw more men than women, but it was close. As for age, they ranged from teenagers to thirty-somethings.

With the goblet fully capped, Boltstar twisted around. He surveyed the newcomers with a hard eye. "You're trespassing," he announced. "Please leave at once."

The tunic-wearing kid kicked his feet from a standing position, driving the chair upward until he was level with Boltstar. "You must be Lanctin. We've heard a lot about you."

Jaw slightly agape, I glanced at Tad. "Who are these people?"

"My friends, my family. We're Chaotics, Randy. And we're here to reclaim what's ours." With his wand held firmly aloft, he gave me a quick look. "We're here for Madkey."

CHAPTER 13

Galison got off the first shot, sending a screaming almond streak at the tunic-wearer's head. The boy ducked the attack and lifted his wand. One second later, a magenta bolt raced forth. It hit Galison in the stomach and the professor doubled over in pain.

"They're Chaotics," Norch shouted. "They've infiltrated the school!"

Crisscrossing streams of light went airborne. A couple of Chaotics were felled quickly. Their chairs caught them, then hovered in mid-air, still and silent. But more Chaotics arrived to take their place. Lots of chairs flew up to catch them. So many, in fact, that I wondered if we'd run out of enchanted seats.

Taking stock of things, these new Chaotics went on the attack. A couple of faculty members, including Professor Lellpoppy, fell under the ensuing onslaught.

I watched all of this with a kind of detached awe, too horrified to even move. The Chaotics still existed? Admittedly, I'd briefly toyed with the idea after Piper had discovered the Hibernuction spell. But I hadn't really taken it seriously. Honestly, who could blame me? As a philosophy, Chaotics had died decades ago, long before my birth. Its adherents, to the best of my knowledge, had died as well. I'd grown up in a world dominated by Structuralism. To my generation, *Chaotic* was a serious and rude insult, used primarily by political types.

But now, I saw the error of my ways. The Chaotics, somehow, had survived Victory Day. Tad, my supposed friend, was one of them. Evidently, he'd used the Hibernuction spell on MacPherson after all. That meant he was related to Boris and part of the Hynor family. In other words, he was Chaotic royalty, if such a thing existed. Was that why I'd always felt uncomfortable around him? Had some part of me known the ugly truth?

"This is going to get nasty," he told me. "Get back to the dorm. Don't come out until it's over."

His wand was still aloft, still aimed at the ancient station. As the tawny light continued to pulse and throb, I started to put a few things together. Madkey, of course, was protected by enchanted borders. So, the Chaotics had planted Tad within the school. He'd opened the ancient conveyance station, allowing his people entrance via the Floating Abyss.

More newcomers materialized. Boltstar, Wadflow, Galison, Norch, and other faculty members rained spells upon them. The battle grew fierce and both sides lost wizards and witches. Meanwhile, Professor Whitlock took charge of the students and staffers, hustling them to safety inside of Madkey Library.

I turned an angry eye toward Tad. "Are you crazy?"

"Not at all."

"You're hurting people."

"It's the only way."

I stared at the developing action. Strange witches and wizards filled all of Torso, throwing weird spells at Madkey's professors. Josh Hunt, professor in the Magictainment department, took a bolt of light to the chest and went completely limp. And I do mean, limp. It was as if all the bones in his body had suddenly turned into jelly. Meanwhile, Professor Lidia Gaibie from the Conveyance department got hit by a spell and found her arms growing longer and longer.

They wrapped clear around her body, tying her into the oddest knot I'd ever seen.

I shook my head. "Why?"

"You wouldn't understand."

"Try me."

He didn't reply.

"Try me," I repeated.

He kept quiet, his attention focused on his spell. Frustrated, I grabbed his shoulder. His wand shifted and the tawny light broke off. Slowly, it began to unravel from the old conveyance station. A partially-materialized woman, attired in a loose-fitting dress and clutching a crooked wand, started to fade.

A violent push spilled me to the floor. Words, too quiet to hear, flowed from Tad's mouth. A new spell raced forth. It connected to the unraveling light, reforming the net around the ancient station. The woman fully materialized. A chair caught hold of her. Screaming like a banshee, she twisted this way and that, firing spells in multiple directions.

"We're the good guys," Tad said. "That's all you need to know."

"Could've fooled me." I retrieved my wand from the bridge, not really sure what I'd do with it. Havoc magic was a highly-specialized set of fighting spells, none of which I knew.

Tad's face twisted. "You don't understand."

"Then help me understand." I stepped between him and the old station. "Let's go somewhere, talk this out."

He gave me a long, steely look. "Move."

"No."

"I'll take you down. I don't want to, but I will."

I didn't back down. But that was only because I was too scared to move.

He broke off the spell. His wand zigged and zagged. "Blastfor."

I gasped as a heavy force struck my chest. In agony, I stumbled sideways and collided with the railing.

As I sank to the ground, Tad waved his wand again. Another spell raced forth, reconnecting to the original spell.

My breaths came in short, heaving gasps. My chest hurt so bad I wondered if I'd broken a rib. Feeling lightheaded, I glanced toward the Grille. What I saw caused my heart to palpitate. Madkey's faculty was world-famous. And yet, the Chaotics—despite fewer numbers—were winning the fight.

Professor after professor fell before their attacks. Only the presence of Boltstar, along with the faculty's larger numbers, kept it from becoming a complete slaughter.

My chest burned as I stood up. Yup, I'd definitely broken a rib. Maybe two ribs. I was in no shape to fight and I knew it. My best bet was to get clear.

Across the Grille, I spotted the woman in the loose-fitting dress. She was still whipping about, still wailing like a banshee. She was here now, but she'd almost missed her chance. When I'd grabbed Tad's shoulder, I'd interrupted his spell. She'd started to fade. Only by recasting the spell had he been able to ensure her arrival.

So, Tad hadn't just opened the conveyance station. No, he was *keeping it open*. If I could break his spell again, the station would close, shutting off the Chaotics pipeline. That might be enough to help Boltstar and the professors repel the invasion.

I zeroed in on Tad. No one seemed to notice him. Certainly, no one was going to stop him.

No one, that is, but me.

CHAPTER 14

I stuffed my wand into my pocket. My ribs ached as I marched forward. I felt winded and yet, I couldn't refill my lungs. But there was nothing I could do about that now.

This is going to hurt, I told myself. *Badly*.

I rammed my shoulder into Tad's back. Pain exploded in my head. It felt like my ribs were on fire.

His body careened into the railing and he dropped to the bridge. I collapsed on top of him and the pain turned agonizing. Tad tried to maneuver his wand, but I grabbed hold of his wrist. The spell broken, his tawny light began to unravel from around the station.

"You don't know what you're doing," he cried.

"Yeah, I do." My teeth clenched. "Stopping you."

He tried to squirm out from underneath me. But my weight kept him pinned down. Meanwhile, the fighting continued. Chaotics chased the faculty around Lower-Torso, spinning spells at every turn. But they were still outnumbered. And with Tad immobilized, the gate was now closed. That was all it took to turn the tide.

Standing tall, Boltstar roared through Torso, shouting orders in either direction. Riding their chairs, the faculty retreated to an area near Right Leg. Undeterred, the Chaotics attempted a full-on attack. They took out a few professors, but lost some of their own as well.

One kid in his late teens took an almond light to the neck. He fell to his knees, clutching his throat and gasping for air. Another boy, a few years younger, took one of Wadflow's spells to the leg. Bones crunched. Collapsing in his chair, he clutched his useless limb, shrieking at the top of his lungs.

Sensing an opportunity, the faculty surged forward. Dividing into groups, they raced to isolate and crush their opponents. The Chaotics, realizing at last that the ancient conveyance station had been closed, started to panic.

Tad jabbed me in the ribs with his free hand. My breath caught in my throat. Quickly, he slid out from underneath me. Standing up, he aimed his wand at the station. His lips started to move.

I struggled back to my feet. A few unsteady steps took me to the railing.

As his magic started to flow, Tad glanced in my direction. "Wait, Randy. Just wait. Let me—"

I felt a rush of air. Looking down, I caught a glimpse of Boltstar sailing through Torso, whipping off all kinds of spells. Some sailed harmlessly into the bridges or glass plates. But more often than not, he hit his mark.

He glanced over his shoulder, looking my way although not directly at me. His wand shifted and cyan light filled my field of vision. My eyes widened. I shied away even as I braced for the inevitable.

Air rushed out of my lungs as Tad crashed into me. I hit the ground and he landed on top of me. His wand squirted out of his hand. It rolled to the edge of the bridge, then dropped into open air.

He rolled away. His face twisted in agony and his hands clawed at his shoulder. Puffing his cheeks in and out, he shifted his arm, testing his range of motion. Then he looked for his wand, only to discover it was gone.

I blinked a few times and saw a hole in his shirt, surrounded by scorch marks. A small black dot marred his skin. It looked like someone had burnt him with a fireplace poker.

A sharp breath escaped me. I recognized that wound. I'd only seen it in books, but I recognized it all the same.

It was the Gratlan.

The Gratlan was a death spell, the only one of its kind. It was one of a dozen or so forbidden spells contained within the Capsudra. As such, its mechanics were unknown to the general public. But its effects were feared by all.

The Gratlan spread through a person with excruciating slowness, killing them bit by bit. The entire process could take up to forty-eight hours. Forty-eight agonizing, horrible hours.

"Your shoulder," I wheezed. "It's the Gratlan …"

He glanced at the wound again, then studied the battle. There was no anger or fear in his eyes. All I saw was sadness.

"Sorry, Randy." His voice was soft, strained. "I didn't want this. I didn't …"

Wincing, he checked his wound again. He touched the black dot, then yanked his hand away as if he'd burnt it.

With some effort, he rose to a crouch.

Then he hurried away.

CHAPTER 15

Running with busted ribs isn't easy. Or fun. Or even possible for very long. Still, I managed to keep up a decent pace as I hustled into Left Arm. Tad was heading toward the staffer dorm so it caught me by surprise when he cut his speed shy of Shadow Madkey. Throwing open one of the many doors, he vanished from sight.

I followed him in close pursuit. Reaching the door, I saw it was marked, *Warning, Foolish Traveler! Cursed Stars Lie Ahead!*

I'd passed the room plenty of times since joining the staff. So, I was familiar with the sign.

I just had no clue what it meant.

I pulled my wand out of its holster. Having lost his wand, Tad was no longer a threat. Not that I had any plan to engage him. No, I just needed to keep him in sight.

I opened the door. A winding stone tunnel, lined with small windows and bathed in moonlight, awaited me.

Exhaling, I felt a distinct ache in my ribs. Still it could've been worse. If not for Tad, I'd be suffering the Gratlan right now. Maybe he hadn't known it was a death spell at the time. And maybe he'd put me in danger in the first place. But still, he'd saved my life. From Boltstar, no less.

The headmaster's actions confused me. Why had he used the Gratlan? Casting such a spell was far from heroic. Then again, maybe I was being too hard on him. It wasn't like he'd just thrown the Gratlan out there for fun. He'd cast it while fighting Chaotics. He'd cast it in order to defeat an evil philosophy that had suddenly and violently returned from the grave.

I eased the door shut. Light clambering sounds caught my attention. Swiftly, I walked through the tunnel. It curved to the left and I soon found myself parallel to Left Arm's main hallway.

The stone floor began to slope upward. My brow furrowed as I rose higher and higher. I'd never been in this part of Madkey before and from the looks of it, neither had anyone else in a very long time. Where was Tad going anyway?

The path straightened out. A dull glow rose up from the floor. Chatter, too soft to discern, filled my ears. I walked a little farther and realized the glow came from a metal grating. Peering down, I found myself staring into Torso.

The battle was over. Numerous faculty members were strewn across the Upper-Torso bridge. They were all disabled in weird ways. Whitlock used levitation spells to direct the injured toward Right Arm. I assumed she was taking them to the clinic.

Tough luck for them.

Shifting my gaze, I saw Chaotics. Lots of them. They lay on the lower bridges, still and silent. Were they dead? Unconscious? Seeing them like that, vulnerable and defeated, sent tiny waves of sympathy through me. But my concerns were quickly crushed by righteous fury.

Plain and simple, they'd attacked us. They'd tried to conquer Madkey. Despite Tad's claim, they were the bad ones. They were the ones practicing a defunct, dangerous philosophy. As far as I was concerned, they deserved whatever happened to them.

Boltstar's voice floated up to me. "What's your name, Son?"

The headmaster and a group of professors stood on chairs floating in the middle of the Grille. They encircled a lone boy, dressed in a close-fitting tunic. It was the kid I'd seen earlier, the first one to come through the conveyance station. He appeared unharmed and a bit panicky. His wand, clutched in trembling fingers, was aimed at his throat.

"Ivan." The boy licked his lips. "Ivan Gully."

"It's nice to meet you, Mr. Gully. I'm Lanctin Boltstar."

"Spare me the pleasantries. I know who you are. I know *all* about you."

"Why don't you lower your wand? We'll go somewhere safe and talk." His face brightened. "Do you like canfee? We've got lots of canfee here."

"Spare me the nice guy act. I know the truth, even if none of your bootlickers do. I know what really happened on Victory Day." He spat the words, *Victory Day*, as if infuriated to even speak them.

"I'm afraid you have me at a loss, Mr. Gully. But if you just hand over your wand—"

"Why? So you can skin me? It won't work." Ivan leered. "I don't have an anchor. None of us do."

"That's quite alright, Mr. Gully. We—" Boltstar waved his free hand at the professors. "—just want to help you."

"Forget it." He jabbed the wand deeper into his neck, pinching the flesh. His lips began to move. He was quick.

But Boltstar was quicker.

"Drodiate," the headmaster called out with a sudden flourish of his wand.

A cyan spell barreled into Ivan's belly. It encompassed him, wrapped around him. His lips sealed shut and he stiffened up. He didn't move. He didn't even blink.

My heart slammed against my chest. Like the Gratlan, the Drodiation Curse was a forbidden spell. It was a rather cruel fate, even for a Chaotic. Essentially, Boltstar had turned the kid into a living, breathing statue. Ivan was fully awake and one-hundred percent conscious. He could see, hear, smell, and taste things. He just couldn't move.

More clambering noises caught my attention and I stared into the darkness. Tad was still out there. And while he'd lost his wand and been cursed with the Gratlan, I knew I couldn't take him for granted. He was a Chaotic, after all, and would do just about anything to avoid capture.

You've tracked him far enough, I told myself. *It's time to get Boltstar. He'll take care of this.*

It was a powerful argument and it almost swayed me. But after a brief internal struggle, I started forward again. Once Boltstar got involved, I'd never see Tad again. And I wanted one last chance to talk to him.

A short walk led me to a hallway. Men's and women's bathrooms lay on either side of it. I gave them a quick check before continuing on my way. At the end of the hallway, I found a ladder. Above, I glimpsed a hatch. It opened up into what looked like a large space, flooded with moonlight. Soft breaths, punctuated by the occasional gasp, reached my ears.

Ribs burning like fire, I scaled the rungs. I had to grit my teeth to keep going. Near the top, I slowed my ascent. My head swiveled in either direction. I didn't see Tad, so I kept climbing, albeit slowly and cautiously.

Peeking my head through the opening, I saw a large and well-appointed room. Odd bronze and silver contraptions rested on the floor, shrouded in thick layers of dust. Fine tables and chairs, clearly of a bygone era, were neatly positioned on a hand-sewn, decorative carpet. Busts and statues, beautifully carved, sat quietly on some of the tables as well as on the floor. Nearby, I saw a free-standing fireplace. It was free of dust, indicating it had been used recently. A circular chimney, made of smooth stones, lifted up to the ceiling. I saw no logs or kindling, indicating the fireplace was of the enchanted variety.

Most spectacular of all was the view. The walls and ceiling were made of glass and I could see for miles. The moon shone brightly and the stars twinkled in the sky. The natural light illuminated snow-capped mountains, crystal blue lakes, and the twin gondolas we used to go back and forth from Madkey.

I examined the stars for a brief moment. They reminded me of that sign I'd seen back in Left Arm. The one that had read, *Warning, Foolish Traveler! Cursed Stars Lie Ahead!*

A pained grunt caught my attention. Abruptly, Tad fell out of the chimney. With a sickening thud, he landed on the hearth. His soft moans filled my ears.

Chest heaving, he lay still for a few seconds. Then he rose to wobbly knees. Lifting his arms, he thrust them inside the chimney. His muscles quivered as he attempted to lift himself back into the stone cylinder.

Quieting my nerves, I climbed into the room. Holding my wand steady, I tiptoed to the chimney. And all the while, I continued to take in the space. It was well above Torso. And given its circular-like shape, I pegged it for the interior of the statue's head. It was kind of thrilling to see it. It had all the trappings of a fine apartment and I wondered if it had been built for Roderick J. Madkey himself.

The floor creaked under my shoe, just a few feet short of the fireplace. Tad froze.

"It's over," I said. "Come out."

He dropped back to his knees and crawled out from under the chimney. His back was hunched, his hair was dirty. His clothes were drenched in sweat and grease. Most disturbing of all, his brown skin had lightened a shade or two. Clearly, the Gratlan had already started its horrible work.

"Boltstar isn't who you think he is," Tad said.

I didn't know what to say or do. Truth be told, I hadn't thought this far ahead. All I knew is that I felt uneasy around Tad, now more than ever.

"And you are?" I retorted.

He stayed quiet.

"You lied to me."

"No. I just … I didn't tell you everything. And I'm sorry about that. But be honest, what would you have done if I'd told you I was a Chaotic?"

I would've reported him in an instant. My loyalties were to Madkey, to Boltstar. To Structuralism. "How can you be a Chaotic?" I asked, shaking my head.

"How can you be a Structuralist?"

"Easy, I—"

He grabbed my wrist and twisted. My wand fell to the carpet. He plowed into me and we fell over. Next thing I knew, he was climbing on top of me, pressing *my* wand to *my* throat.

My words ran dry. All I could do was look at him. Look into those dark, swirling eyes and wonder how he could've fooled me all of this time.

He held the wand close to my throat. I could feel it tickling the hairs on my neck. Gritting my teeth, I awaited the inevitable.

His muscles tensed. His lips quivered. He stared down at me, his eyes unreadable.

"I ... I can't." His body sagged and he dropped my wand. He climbed off of me, then backed away.

Scooping up the wand, I held it in trembling fingertips, wondering just how close I'd come to death. "Why not?" was all I could manage.

"Because we're friends."

"Not anymore." I inhaled softly and sharp pains shot through my ribs. "Not since you attacked us."

"I had a good reason."

"Did you have a good reason when you cast that sleeping curse on MacPherson?" I eyed him with disdain. "Don't deny it. I know it was you."

"He deserved it. He's just as guilty as the rest of them." Seeing my disgust, he hurried to explain. "But I didn't mean for it to happen. He caught me just as I was uncovering one of their darkest secrets. He attacked, I fought back."

"You put him to sleep."

"Not permanently. I always planned to undo it after ..." A pained expression crossed his face and I knew he was contemplating the failed invasion. "Well, just after."

He blinked away a few tears and I could see he was in pain. Shifting my gaze, I noticed the tiny Gratlan throbbing gently upon his shoulder. It looked a bit bigger, too, which was to be expected. The Gratlan wouldn't stop growing until it covered every inch of his body.

He still made me uneasy. At the same time, just talking to him felt, well, normal. Where did the Chaotic Tad end and the friend Tad begin?

Ultimately, it didn't really matter. I'd done what I'd come to do. Namely, track Tad to his hiding spot.

Even better, there was nowhere for him to go. The room had just one exit and the connecting tunnel had no other routes. In short, he was trapped. All I had to do was go out the way I'd come in and flag down some help.

And yet, I continued to linger. I didn't know why. Maybe I needed to understand his motives, to understand how someone could slip into darkness.

Turning in a half-circle, I took in the strange room. "What is this place?"

"A celestarium. There used to be lots of them, all over the world." He glanced at the glass ceiling. "This one used to house Madkey's Celestial Magic program."

"Celest ... what?"

"Celestial magic. It's the study of celestial objects— planets, stars, star clusters, galaxies—and how their motions influence spells."

I gave him a blank look.

"You saw the sign outside, right? The one that warned about cursed stars?"

I nodded.

"Well, people used to believe that back in the Chaotic period. They thought the motions of the planets and stars impacted one's ability to do magic."

A small grin creased my face. The ignorance of Chaotic magicians never ceased to amaze me.

"Yeah, it seems crazy these days." He shrugged. "After the Structuralists took over, fringe ideas like Celestial Magic were outlawed. Schools began to focus on concrete stuff, the things that could be proven."

"So, they just abandoned this place?" I looked around. "That's dumb. Why not use it for something else?"

"Probably because they didn't need the space. Madkey used to be an open campus. It was built to handle thousands of students. Now, we've got, what, maybe a thousand people between faculty, students, and staffers?"

I arched an eyebrow. "*We?*"

"You know what I mean." He sighed. "There's something you need to know. I didn't come here to make friends. Heck, this whole thing would've been easier *without* friends. But once I got to know you guys—you, Piper, and Leandra—I couldn't help myself. A lot of stuff about me was fake. But our friendship was always real."

"Forget it."

"Forget what?"

"I'm not letting you escape."

He sighed. "That's not what I—"

"Besides, the only way we can stop that Gratlan is to get you to the clinic. So, I'm going to get Boltstar and—"

"No, wait." He paused. "Just let me die."

I did a double-take. He spoke with ferocity, with absolute certainty. "I would never do that. Do you want to know why? Because I'm not one of you."

He exhaled. "If Boltstar finds me, he'll get my anchor. And I'd rather die than let that happen."

The word 'anchor' rang a bell for me. Ivan had mentioned something about it as well. "What anchor?" I asked. "What are you talking about?"

"What do you know about the Floating Abyss?"

I crossed my arms. "Other than the fact that your people used it to attack us?"

He exhaled again, deeper this time. "Think of it as an ocean full of constantly shifting continents. Nothing stays the same for very long. So, once you leave a place, it's nearly impossible to find it again."

"Go on."

"Now, there's no such thing as a Chaotic spell book. Chaotic spells differ from person to person."

Impatiently, I clucked my tongue. "I know that."

"Well, some people are able to cast a spell connecting themselves to a certain location. It's like an invisible thread that stays with you at all times. You can use it to send and receive messages, go back and forth, stuff like that. It's called an anchor and back in the old days, it was the only way to accurately navigate through the Floating Abyss."

"And you cast one of these spells?"

"Yes, right before I left home." Wincing, he glanced at his throbbing shoulder. "That spell you saw back in Torso was just me connecting to my anchor. In the process, it opened the station. And then—"

"—your people followed it here?"

He nodded.

"So, what took you so long?"

He frowned. "Huh?"

"You could've opened the station months ago. Why'd you choose Victory Day?" I arched an eyebrow. "Or did I just answer my own question?"

"Actually, MacPherson forced my hand."

"You mean because you cursed him."

He nodded. "It was only a matter of time before Boltstar started looking for me. I had no choice but to strike fast."

"So, that explains why you did it today." I gave him a thoughtful look. "But not why you waited so long."

His answer took a few moments to arrive. "Remember how I told you that MacPherson caught me uncovering one of their secrets? And that's why I had to curse him?"

I nodded.

"Well, that secret is at the center of everything. It's why I came here, it's why we staged the invasion."

"So, what is it?"

"You wouldn't believe me if I told you. Heck, you *couldn't* believe it."

The conviction of his words caught me by surprise. What else had Tad hoped to accomplish? And why was he so sure I wouldn't—or couldn't—believe it?

"Try me."

"It … doesn't matter." His face screwed up in pain as he massaged the deadly Gratlan. "All that matters right now is my anchor. I can't let Boltstar have it."

"And he can just take it from you?" I asked skeptically.

"If he skins me, he'll get my magic. All of it, including my anchor." He exhaled. "He'll use it to track down my people, Randy. My friends, my family. He'll kill them all."

I bristled with indignation. "Boltstar's no killer."

He turned his shoulder to me, showing off the Gratlan. "Are you sure about that?"

"That was an accident."

"An accident that almost hit you." He gave me a meaningful look. "If you turn me in, lots of people are going to die."

"Maybe they deserve it."

His eyes turned somber.

I frowned, unable to fully meet his gaze. "Can't you just throw off the anchor?"

"That's not how they work. They can only be removed from their point of origin." His gaze dropped to his shoulder. The Gratlan throbbed continuously under his watchful eye. "Or if their owner dies."

"So, if you die, the anchor's gone?"

He nodded. "Just pretend you didn't see me. Nobody will ever know you were here."

My ribs still ached and my breathing was turning raspy. A small part of me almost felt sorry for him. On the other hand, he'd attacked Madkey. He'd attacked Structuralism. And those things were everything to me.

"I'd know." I walked to the hatch, wondering if he'd try to attack me from behind. But he remained still, his gaze locked on the carpet. As I lowered myself to the waiting ladder, I gave him one last look. "I'll ask Boltstar to go easy on you. Okay?"

He didn't reply.

CHAPTER 16

Releasing the ladder, I dropped back into the stone tunnel. It was darker than I remembered. Shifting my emotions into place, I maneuvered my wand. Instinctia, warm and pleasant, took over for me, guiding the spell to completion.

"Dayga Fluza," my lips whispered.

A bit of auburn light appeared at the tip of my wand. Instinctia faded away and I started to feel cold and melancholy. Tad was a Chaotic. And Chaotics were horrible. But did I really want them to die?

I studied my glowing wand as I retraced my steps through the curving, sloping tunnel. The light was quite dim. I supposed it was always that way. It had never bothered me in the past, but now I found it annoying. What was the point of an illumination spell if it couldn't offer more light?

I slowed my steps. My chest felt raw and hot, like I'd taken a bath in molten lava. A short rest helped, however, and I continued forward.

I kept thinking about Tad. He'd betrayed us, attacked us. He was one of *them*. And yet, I couldn't help but feel guilty about turning him over to Boltstar. Why was that?

Because he saved your life, I realized.

He could've just let the Gratlan hit me. In fact, it would've gotten me out of his way. But instead, he'd jumped in front of me. And quite frankly, I didn't know a lot of people who'd do that.

I walked back to the grating. A pair of voices caught my ear. Curious, I paused for a quick listen.

"Have we identified the defector yet?" Boltstar asked, hopping off his chair and onto the Upper-Torso bridge. "The one who opened the station?"

"We believe so, Sir," Galison replied. "It was a staffer by the name of Tad Crucible. Several of his colleagues reported that he'd skipped out on his shift tonight. And three separate people identified his spell color."

"I don't believe I know him."

"He's a bit of a loner. But I've seen him hanging out with another staffer. A boy named Randy Wolf."

My name, uttered so casually, sent me into a seizure. Clutching my ribs, I took a few, gasping breaths.

"I'd like to talk to Mr. Wolf," Boltstar said. "As for Mr. Crucible, search every inch of the school. Every room, every hallway. If he's still here, I want him found."

"Of course." Galison bowed slightly at the waist. "Anything else?"

"Actually, yes. I want to create a new class, devoted to the art of havoc magic. Not in the daytime, of course. We don't want to interrupt the regular schedule. But we could do it at night, say, after dinner."

My eyes widened into saucers. Havoc magic was a highly specialized field of study, normally open only to qualified seniors.

"Are you sure about this, Headmaster?" Galison's tone turned doubtful. "Havoc magic is a difficult subject to learn, even for the most-disciplined of students."

"We'll stick to the basics. We'll teach just enough so that our kids can fight back in the event of another attack." He began to pace back and forth along the bridge. "I'll handle the instruction myself. We'll make it a requirement. No grades. Just pass/fail, based solely on my final evaluation. One more thing. Students won't be the only ones in attendance. I want staffers there, too."

Oh, great, I thought. *Another chance to embarrass myself.*

"The staffers, Headmaster?"

"Yes, George," Boltstar replied. "If the Chaotics launch another attack, we'll want as many skilled wands as possible on our side. And speaking of skilled wands, we will require some extra security for the foreseeable future. Recruit from the alumni. Give special preference to those who fought with us on Victory Day."

With respectful nods, they split up. Meanwhile, I resumed hiking through the tunnel.

A Havoc Magic class? Just thinking about it made my stomach queasy. Heck, it almost made me long for YuckYuck.

At least then I wouldn't have to worry about getting bombarded with spells from Porter and his friends.

With each step, I thought about all of the indignities I'd suffered during my time at Madkey. My poor grades and becoming a dropout. The never-ending insults. Being treated like a servant. And now, this new class.

I was sick of losing and just being a loser in general. My brain whirled and I thought about how it'd feel to take the Havoc Magic class by storm. To really dominate it and maybe put Porter in his place, too.

But how? It would probably be a bit more physical than other classes. But it'd still be a class. And I'd already proven to be a poor student. So, why should this be any different?

I had this sudden image of waving my wand at Porter and watching his arms stretch out to super-long lengths. Then his arms wrapped around his body, tying himself into a knot, just like that Chaotic spell had done to Professor Gaibie. The thought made me smile.

The aching spread beyond my ribs as I approached the exit. Carefully, I cracked the door open and peered outside. I heard footsteps and voices, but no one was in the immediate area.

Shutting the door behind me, I slipped out into the main hallway. I felt another sharp sting in my ribcage. After I alerted Boltstar to Tad's presence, I'd need to get some healing potion. Unfortunately, that would mean a trek to the clinic, which was located in Right Arm with the rest of the Cures & Curses department. Even worse, it would mean a face-to-face with Professor Tuckerson.

"Hey, Wolf?" Jax said. "Is that you?"

I whirled around. A couple of staffers, clearly harried, exited Shadow Madkey and strode into Left Arm.

"Yeah," I mumbled, suddenly feeling light-headed.

"That was crazy, huh?"

"I guess so."

"I heard Tad did it. He let them in."

"I saw the color." Jenny looked shell-shocked and beyond exhausted. Her clothes, meanwhile, were stained with soda. "It was his spell, no doubt about it."

My head felt woozy. My legs began to wobble and I had to steady myself against the wall. "Can you, uh—?"

"Hey, Randy." Piper darted out of Shadow Madkey. "We've been looking all over for you."

Leandra was close behind her. "Where's Tad?" she asked breathlessly. "Everyone's looking for him."

"There you are."

I felt dazed, like I was barely gripping to consciousness. Still, I managed to twist toward this new voice.

"First, a dropout. Now, best friends with a traitor." Porter, backed by his friends, strode toward us from the other direction. "You're just an all-out loser, aren't you Wolf?"

"There's no way that Tad kid acted alone," Sya added, her eyes icy cold. "You helped him, didn't you? You all did."

"Get lost," Piper said.

"No way." Gordon got in my face, jutting out his jaw so that it nearly touched mine. "Admit it, Randy. You helped Tad. You helped those … *those people*."

"Do you know how stupid you sound right now?" Leandra put her hands on her hips. "If you don't—"

But a growing crowd of students, obviously looking for Tad or at least someone to blame, drowned her out. They gathered around me, grabbing at my clothes and shouting insults and threats. Leandra and Piper tried to fight back. But they were outnumbered.

Darkness crept in at the corners of my vision. I realized I was drawing dangerously close to fainting.

"He's friends with the traitor!" a girl shouted.

"He *is* a traitor," someone else yelled.

"Get Boltstar," came a third voice.

"Did someone say my name?"

This last voice was pleasant, if a bit firm. But the crowd of angry onlookers stiffened up anyway, like they'd been hit with Drodiation Curses.

"Hello, everyone." Students and staffers, their jaws agape, slid to either side of the hallway. Then Boltstar appeared, wand in hand. "I'm looking for Mr. Wolf."

"He's right here," Porter snarled, jabbing his thumb at me.

Boltstar strode through the gap. I had to blink a few times to make sure it was really him. After all, it wasn't every day a dropout like me stood face-to-face with the greatest wizard of all time.

"Hello, Mr. Wolf. If you have a spare moment, I'd like to ask you about Mr. Crucible. You were friends, correct?"

I stood still, slack-jawed, shocked that he was even saying my name.

"Oh, they were friends, for sure." Felicia gave me a nasty look. "Best friends."

"Perhaps, Ms. Masters, perhaps. But let's not jump to rash conclusions. Mr. Crucible fooled us all."

Her cheeks reddened. "Yes, Headmaster."

"Well, Mr. Wolf?" Boltstar swiveled back to face me. "Come now, I don't have all night."

I could feel the eyes of the crowd. At the moment, they were angry, accusatory. But soon, they'd be back to mocking, condescending. At the same time, others stared at Boltstar with admiring, fawning faces. Why couldn't they look at me like that?

I shifted my jaw, ready to tell him about Tad. But then my mind fogged over from pain. And as I stood there, clutching my ribs, I found myself considering the unthinkable.

What if I didn't turn Tad in? What if, instead, I helped cure the Gratlan? In return, what if he taught me how to do Chaotic magic? With his help, I just might be able to turn in a respectable showing in Boltstar's new Havoc Magic class.

"I ... I ..." I doubled over in pain.

Then again, I loved Madkey. Maybe not everyone in it, but I definitely loved the school. Could I really help someone who'd attacked it? A Chaotic, no less?

Boltstar's look morphed into one of concern. "What's wrong, Mr. Wolf?" He gripped my shoulder. "Are you okay?"

"I took a spell to the ribs." My hand slipped off the wall. Cobwebs stretched across my brain.

I was no traitor. Then again, would helping Tad really constitute a betrayal? It's not like I'd be working with him, plotting another invasion. No, I'd just be providing him with shelter, like he was a prisoner of war. And hey, I could always turn him in at a later date, right?

"Yes, we are—were—friends. And yes, that was his spell, alright. I'd know his color anywhere." I fought the tide of creeping unconsciousness. "I ... I don't know where he is though."

And just like that, I made my choice. I felt a bit of regret and a whole lot of anxiety. If this backfired, well, there was a decent chance I'd get skinned and end up in Gutlore right next to Tad.

And with that uneasy thought in my head, my vision vanished. My body sagged. I heard Boltstar shouting for people to give me space.

And then I slipped off into unconsciousness.

CHAPTER 17

"He's waking up." Professor Donald Tuckerson's voice, brutally masculine and lacking even a trace of emotion, hit my ears like a lightning bolt. "Get the headmaster, Sally."

"Sure thing, Don." Clothing rustled. Chair legs squeaked across hard linoleum.

"Where are you going?"

"Getting the headmaster, of course," Assistant Professor Sally Kinder replied. "He's in his quarters, right?"

"In his quarters?" Tuckerson grunted. "Are you dense?"

"I—"

His voice grew louder, drowning her out. "I said, 'Are you dense?'"

Kinder sighed. "Yes, I'm dense, Don. Are you happy now?"

"Do you really have to ask that?"

"No, but—"

"The headmaster's in Room Twelve, checking on MacPherson. Now, go."

"Oh, that's right. I forgot he was here." A door opened. Heeled shoes click-clacked against linoleum.

My eyes fluttered open. I shifted my body, trying to get comfortable on a very thin mattress. Failing at that, I looked around. I was in a small room with eggshell-colored stone walls. A couple of cool-lights, fitted into the crevices, cast a fierce glow upon the space. My lip curled in fear as I recognized the location.

Madkey Clinic.

Pushing the back of my head into my pillow, I eased my brain into a state of relaxation. My mind wound through memories, starting with the Victory Feast and ending with me fainting in front of Boltstar, my friends, and those other kids. That last recollection caused my cheeks to burn in embarrassment.

Terrific, I thought. *I'm sure Porter's going to have a field day with this.*

Professor Tuckerson's pinched visage appeared above me. His eyes, like always, reflected sheer boredom. "Those ribs of yours better be hurting something fierce," he whispered. "Because you're taking up one of my beds."

Ahh, that was classic Tuckerson bedside manner. With some effort, I managed to sit up. I felt a bit sore. But that was it. Even my ribs, which had given me so much trouble, didn't seem all that bad. Instead of pain, I merely felt a slight itch.

I tried to speak, but my throat was parched. When was the last time I'd taken a drink anyway? "Water," I managed. "Need … water."

"Oh, you need water, do you?" he replied, mimicking my strained voice. "Well, tough break, kid. Because I—"

Assistant Professor Kinder poked her head through the doorway. "The headmaster is right behind me," she whispered hurriedly.

He gave her a terse nod, then walked to the door. "Hello, Lanctin," he said, adopting a formal disposition. "It's good to see you. I was just checking on our patient."

"Where is he?"

"Uh, right in here. In fact, I was just about to get him a drink. These kids can be such—"

"Later, Donald." Boltstar strode past Tuckerson and into the room. Pulling off his derby, he ran a hand through his short hair.

"Well, feel better, Mr. Wolf." Tuckerson checked to make sure Boltstar wasn't looking, then gave me a fierce glare. The message was obvious. Don't badmouth him.

Or I'd pay the price.

As Tuckerson shut the door, Boltstar pulled a chair over to the bed. "How are you feeling?"

I tried to speak. But just one word came tumbling out of my dry mouth. "Wa ... water," I croaked.

"Water, eh? I think we can do better than that." Rising to his feet, he walked to a tall cabinet. Swiftly, he rummaged through its contents. "There must be some canfee in here."

My mouth would've watered if it weren't bone-dry.

"Here we are." He removed a small carton and a glass from the cabinet. Filling the glass, he passed it to me.

My fingers trembled as I lifted the canfee to my lips. The taste of Afternoon Nap slipped down my throat. It was delicious and made me feel all warm and sleepy on the inside.

He retook his seat. "Is that better?"

I nodded between draughts. Within seconds, I'd finished the canfee. With my thirst slaked, I felt pretty good. Not great, though. My ribs continued to itch, a fact that was starting to annoy me.

"Good." He rested his hands on his knees, seemingly relaxed. But I could see hidden tension in his jaw. "Now, how are you feeling, Mr. Wolf?"

I scratched my chest. "Itchy."

"That's to be expected. Professor Tuckerson treated your chest with a Garrington Magic concoction." Seeing my horrified look, he rushed to soothe my nerves. "Don't worry. The itching is quite normal. It should go away in a few days."

"Yes, Sir," I said, half-heartedly.

Dedicated healers don't exist these days. Oh, the necessary spells are available to anyone. But putting them together is, like making doughcream from scratch, nearly impossible for a single magician.

Instead, healing is performed with magic potions, which are really just bundled spells prepared by assembly-line witches and wizards. They work just fine. The only problem is dealing with the intense pain that accompanies quick healing. That's a common thing with magic. You never get something for nothing. Anyway, Garrington Magic potions deal with pain by transforming it into itching. I'm no fan of pain. But you don't know how bad itching is until you've experienced a couple days of it.

"I know this isn't the best time, Mr. Wolf," Boltstar went on to say. "But I need to ask you about Mr. Crucible."

My heart felt like it would pound right out of my chest. "Okay."

"Did he ever give you any indication that he was planning an attack?"

I shook my head.

"Did he ever mention an affiliation or interest in the Chaotics?"

"No, Sir."

"Do you know where he came from? Where he lived?"

"He told me he was an orphan," I replied. "He said he grew up in a bunch of places."

"That was a lie," Boltstar told me. "We ran some checks on his background. He fabricated everything except for a short stint at Sunflower Farms Orphanage. That's where he experienced his breakout. Although now, of course, we're inclined to think he staged it in order to gain entrance to our school."

"Wow." I blinked, truly surprised. "I had no idea."

The conversation continued like that for several minutes. Boltstar would ask a question and I'd answer the best I could, making sure to conceal the truth at all times. I kept waiting for him to ask about my fight with Tad on the bridge. I had a story all ready about how he'd knocked me down, then escaped into the Floating Abyss. But the topic never came up and I soon realized the truth.

No one had seen me up there.

The more I thought about it, the more it made sense. The soda tsunami had thrown everyone into a state of disarray. Afterward, the faculty had fought the Chaotics. The students and staffers, meanwhile, were holed up in the library, unable to see much of anything.

After Boltstar asked his last question, he retrieved a handsome wooden rod, adorned with handcrafted edging, from his coat. "Do you recognize this wand?" he asked.

I nodded. "That's Tad's."

"It's not a staffer wand."

"No, Sir. He told us it was a present."

"From whom?"

"I don't remember."

Thoughtfully, he turned the wand over in his hands.

"How's Professor MacPherson?" I asked. "Did he wake up yet?"

He cocked an eyebrow. "You know about that?"

"I was the one who found him."

His gaze narrowed. "You've had a busy twenty-four hours, Mr. Wolf."

"Tell me about it."

Something about my tone eased his manner. "Professor MacPherson is still asleep."

"For how long?"

"It's difficult to say. But I expect the curse to run its course by the end of the school year. Of course, that timeframe will shorten dramatically if we capture the spellcaster."

"Tad?"

"We believe so, yes. Well, I think that's all I need right now. Thank you, Mr. Wolf." Donning his derby, Boltstar rose to his feet. "Oh, one last question, if you don't mind. What happened to your ribs? Professor Tuckerson tells me you cracked two of them during the attack."

"I snuck out of Shadow Madkey during the feast. Tad was missing and I'd hoped to find him before he got in trouble." I took a breath, preparing myself for the lie. "I got caught out in the open during the soda storm. When the Chaotics appeared, I tried to run. One of them zapped me with a spell. I don't remember a whole lot after that."

He rubbed his jaw, deep in thought. It made me wonder if he suspected something.

"Sir?" I hesitated. "What caused the soda storm?"

"Apparently, Mr. Crucible took some kind of gizmo from another staffer. A rather clever invention, really, created by a young lady named Ms. Chen. Perhaps you know her?"

I nodded. "She's good with that sort of thing."

"I questioned her about an hour ago. From all appearances, she's an innocent victim." He started for the door, then gave me one last look. "Do you need anything, Mr. Wolf?"

"I don't think so." I raked my fingers across my chest. "I just wish I wasn't so itchy."

"It'll get better. If you think of anything else, please come see me in my quarters."

I was suddenly very grateful to him. Very grateful and very ashamed. He'd shown me grace and courtesy. In return, I'd lied to him. But there was no going back now.

"Thank you, Headmaster," I replied.

He walked outside, shutting the door behind him. I heard some quiet chatter with Tuckerson, then silence.

A wave of warm, warbling energy passed through me, stretching all the way from my head to the tips of my toes. It felt deliciously sleepy and wonderful. I was tempted to stay in bed, to let the canfee do its work. But thoughts of Tad and the Gratlan propelled me into action.

Sliding out of bed, I crept to the cabinet. Rows and rows of small bottles rested on its sturdy wooden shelves. Hunting around, I found one labeled, *Garrington Magic, Stage Fourteen Healing Potion*. That would do the trick quite nicely.

I heard a deep exhalation, followed by faint rustling. Then Tuckerson's voice floated through the locked door.

"Go check on that waste-of-space staffer, will you?" he said. "See if that canfee put him to sleep."

"What should I do if he's awake?" Kinder asked.

"Hit him over the head with something."

I grabbed the potion along with a small carton of canfee. Then I raced to the bed.

The door cracked open just as I slipped under the sheets. Assistant Professor Kinder stuck her head into the room. "He's awake," she whispered over her shoulder. "Are you sure you want me to hit him?"

"Uh, no." A brief pause followed. "It was a joke, Sally."

"Oh."

"I'm feeling a lot better." I stretched my arms to the ceiling. "Can I go back to my dorm now?"

"The sooner, the better." Tuckerson appeared in the doorway. "But don't you dare faint. And if you do, you'd better not tell the headmaster that I let you out early."

"I won't," I promised. "Now, can I have a little privacy?"

Rolling his eyes, he closed the door.

I shed my gown and donned my clothing. Then I shoved the potion and canfee into my pockets and left the room. Walking to the exit, I found Tuckerson waiting for me.

"Shoo, shoo." He propelled me through the swinging double doors and out into Right Arm. "Oh, by the way, we send surveys out to all of our patients so make sure you give us good marks. Otherwise, I'll slip stomach bubble powder into your canfee when you least expect it."

I looked into his eyes, convinced he was joking. But nope, he was deadly serious.

Stomach bubble powder is a practical joke product, unique to Casafortro. If ingested, it causes your stomach to expand while making you ravenous for food. You can't help but stuff yourself silly, which is quite alright until your stomach begins to shrink again. I'd taken some powder on a dare once and believe me, it's the worst.

The double doors slammed shut and I turned toward Torso. My chest itched, but it wasn't too bad. As I walked through the hallway, I found myself thinking about Chaotic magic. All my life, it had been described as a fool's errand and dangerous to boot. Now, I was hoping to learn it for myself. Was I crazy?

I sure hoped not.

CHAPTER 18

Ignoring the urge to itch my ribs, I stared at the hatch. I'd left it open, but it was closed now. Had Tad closed it? Or was one of the search parties responsible for the deed?

I pushed the hatch open and crawled into the celestarium. Swiftly, I shut it and looked around. The room appeared empty. Everything was just as I'd left it.

"Tad?" I whispered. "You still here?"

There was no response. I was beginning to wonder if he'd fled the area when I caught sight of the fireplace. The hearth looked clean. But particles of dust, recently disturbed, wafted around it.

Walking over, I reached my arm into the chimney. My fingers closed around a piece of soft fabric and I gave it a yank.

With a quiet yelp, Tad came crashing down on the hearth. Rising to his knees, he coughed a few times. Then he rolled out onto the floor.

His eyes brightened as he caught sight of me. "I thought you were with a search party."

"Has one been through here already?"

He nodded. "Two hours ago." Then he gave me a curious look. "You didn't turn me in."

"No."

"Thank you. I really—"

"Yeah, yeah. Let me see your shoulder."

Brow furrowed, he unbuttoned the collar of his sweat-drenched, crimson dress shirt and squirmed his shoulder out. The throbbing Gratlan had tripled in size since I'd last seen it and now took up most of his shoulder.

Fishing in my pockets, I extracted the canfee. Gently, I tossed it to him. "Drink this."

He gave it a curious look. "Why?"

"Just do it."

With a couple of long draughts, he finished the carton.

I produced the bottled potion. Liberally, I applied its contents to the Gratlan.

"Okay," I said. "That should do it."

He stared at his shoulder. "Do what?"

"I just gave you some high-powered Garrington Magic healing potion. It should kill off the Gratlan within a few days."

At first, he looked pleased. But then his smile faded and I saw intense distrust. "Why are you helping me?"

I took a deep breath. "I need a favor."

"Anything."

"Can you teach me Chaotic magic?"

"Anything but that."

"Have it your way." I twisted around, ready to leave. "I guess I'll turn you in after all."

"Cripes." Slowly, he picked himself up off the floor. "Okay, you made your point. What's this all about anyway?"

Upon leaving the clinic, I'd seen dozens of signs about the new havoc magic class. It was to be held seven days a week for the rest of the quarter, from six to eight o'clock at night, in Madkey Arena.

"Boltstar wants the students and staffers to learn havoc magic. No credits, but it's a required class."

He gave me a strange look. "So?"

"So, I don't want to end up as Porter's punching bag."

He shrugged. "Study the lessons. Practice the spells."

"You're talking to a dropout, remember?"

"So are you." He stifled a huge yawn. "What kind of canfee was that anyway?"

"Sweet Dreams."

"You're putting me to sleep? Is this because of what I did to MacPherson?"

"No. But trust me, you'll appreciate it later."

Slowly, he sat down on the carpet. "Let me get this straight. You want to use Chaotic magic in your class?"

I nodded.

"What if you get caught?"

"Can you make it so that I won't?"

"Heck, I don't even know if I can teach it in the first place." His eyes fluttered and I could see he was having trouble keeping them open. "Do you even know what Chaotic magic is, Randy?"

I did. Well, at least I thought I did. Regardless, I didn't want to think about it. Like everyone else, I'd spent my whole life loathing the Chaotics. The fact that I now hoped to learn a little of their magic was already starting to weigh heavily on my conscience.

"It's a whole bunch of new spells." He started to protest, but I held up a hand to stop him. "Don't worry. I won't abuse it. I just need to learn a few havoc magic-like spells, only with ten times the force."

"That's not how it works." He sighed. "Not even close."

"What are you talking about?"

"Chaotic magic isn't a grab bag of spells, Randy. It's deeply personal."

"I don't understand. Are you saying I won't be able to do havoc magic-like spells?"

"I don't know. Nobody knows." He stifled another yawn. "Your Chaotic magic is decided at birth. It's a part of you, just like your arms or your legs. And it's not like the Capsudra where you've got a little bit of everything. Well, it could be like that. But you might also find that your Chaotic magic consists of plumbing spells and book-binding enchantments."

Disappointment began to set in. Right away, I banished it to the nether regions of my mind. "But I might have fighting spells."

"It's possible. There's really no way to know until …"

"Until what?"

He started scratching his shoulder in earnest. At the same time, yawns cascaded from his lips. "Until you start casting spells."

"Fine. So, will you teach me or not?"

"I'd need a wand."

I thought about MacPherson's wand, squirreled away within my dresser. "I can get you one."

"Are you sure you want this, Randy? I mean, are you absolutely certain?"

"Yes," I said with more conviction than I felt.

"Then I'll do my best. No promises, though. I've never tried teaching anyone before. I'm not even sure Chaotic magic can be taught. I've always just kind of ... done it." He continued to scratch his shoulder. His face contorted. I could tell it was taking every ounce of will power he possessed to keep from clawing the Gratlan right out of his skin.

At long last, his eyelids drooped, then closed. He sagged to the carpet. Soft snores escaped his lips.

I examined his shoulder. The Gratlan was still there, pulsing and throbbing. But it was a little smaller now. Its color had lightened as well.

I wondered if I should hide him. Ultimately, I decided it wasn't necessary. The search parties had already cleared the room. When they failed to find him anywhere else, they'd assume he'd escaped into the Floating Abyss.

Hunting about the room, I discovered a bundle of old cloth. Wadding it up, I shoved it under his head to use as a pillow. Then I draped a flannel blanket over him.

"Enjoy your nap," I said softly. "Because when you wake up, that itching is going to be a whole lot worse."

CHAPTER 19

My nerves went haywire as noisy chatter reached my ears. It was way late. For a variety of reasons, I'd hoped to return to a quiet dorm, one where everyone had been beset by sleep. Instead, it sounded like I'd be walking into the crowd of a hotly-contested ramball game.

Placing my ear against the door, I listened for a few seconds. Over a dozen voices reached my waiting ears. They came from all over the place. The lounge area, the bunks, even the little alcove close to the door.

I grabbed the knob and gave it a twist. Voices practically exploded in my ears as I opened the door. I had a story ready in case someone saw me. Something about how I'd been in the clinic this entire time. Hey, it was partly true, right? And as long as no one went sniffing around, my secret trip to see Tad would stay safe with me.

I slipped into the dorm and shut the door behind me. Chest heaving, I stuck to the shadows. Jenny, Nico, and Jeff were close by, regaling each other with what they'd seen and heard that night.

They were close enough to touch. Heck, I was practically breathing on Jenny's left arm. I kept waiting for one of them to see me, to say my name. But with every passing second, it became apparent that they hadn't noticed me.

Sucking in my chest, I slipped along the wall until I was past their little group. Then I stepped into the interior.

"Randy!" Piper darted over to give me a hug. "How are you feeling? Are you okay?"

A bunch of heads swiveled my way. I saw some suspicious looks. Some angry ones, too. But for the most part, it was just a lot of curiosity. Thankfully, it seemed that my fellow staffers were willing to give me the benefit of the doubt. Now, if I could just convince the students and faculty to do the same.

"I'm fine," I replied. "Itchy though."

"Itchy?" It suddenly dawned on her and she gave me a knowing look. "Garrington Magic healing potion?"

I nodded.

Leandra popped up on my left. "So, what's the prognosis?" she asked.

"Two cracked ribs," I replied.

"And you're up already?"

"It was either that or sleep in the clinic."

"Smart choice."

"Did you talk to Boltstar?" Piper wondered.

She spoke softly. And yet, chatter still died out all around me. I was acutely aware that every single staffer in the room was eavesdropping on our conversation.

"Yeah," I replied. "In the clinic. I don't think I was much help though."

They exchanged looks. "Us either," Piper said. "He questioned us for almost an hour. He asked about Tad's interests, his history, his favorite foods. Anything and everything."

"That includes my Fizzer, by the way." Leandra made a face. "He actually wanted to know why I'd invented it in the first place. As if I needed a reason."

The other staffers turned back to their conversations. Meanwhile, Piper steered us over to the bunks.

"Did either of you see any warning signs?" she whispered. "I mean, with Tad."

Leandra hesitated. "He always seemed a bit … off."

Piper nodded. "I know what you mean."

"But it was just a feeling," she was quick to add. "I never heard him talk about the Chaotics. Or say anything bad about Structuralism, for that matter."

"How about you?" Piper asked me. "You knew him better than us."

"Yeah," Leandra added. "Did you see this coming?"

I shook my head. "Honestly, no. It feels like a dream."

"Or a nightmare."

"I don't get it." Piper was silent for a few seconds. "I mean, yeah, Tad was kind of strange. But I never thought of him as a bad guy."

We stayed awake for another hour. One by one, the other staffers hit the sack. Soon, the lights flicked off and we were in near darkness.

At last, we said our goodnights. I was too tired to clean up so I climbed straight into bed. Pulling the covers to my neck, I lay there, still and sweaty.

Snores filled the air and it wasn't long before every single staffer was fast asleep.

Every staffer, that is, but me.

CHAPTER 20

I could take it no longer. Placing my wand on the workstation, I reached under my shirt and clawed away at my ribs. Scratching did me no favors, however, and I just found myself even itchier than before.

Frustrated, I picked up the wand. I knew I should be grateful. After all, things could've been much worse. Still, it was hard to feel appreciative when all I could think about was my next scratch.

It had been a strange, unsettling day, full of odd tension and vague unease. Students walked the hallways in small groups. Quiet and wary, they gripped their wands tightly, their eyes on a constant search for trouble. Staffers, with good reason, stuck largely to Shadow Madkey. There had already been six or seven ugly incidents in which students had cornered staffers in the corridors. They'd threatened them, roughed them up, and accused them of being part of a giant Chaotic conspiracy.

The faculty, for their part, seemed not to care about this feckless attempt at vigilantism. Instead, they patrolled the hallways between classes. They acted calm and in control. But their twitchy hands and sweaty brows gave them away.

Elsewhere, dozens of older witches and wizards— Madkey alumni, according to Piper—had taken up residence within the school. Wands at the ready, they roamed the three levels of Torso. They acted, well, normal. Like nothing was wrong. Which somehow made everyone way more uneasy.

A quick glance at the enchanted clock confirmed it was almost six. The new Havoc Magic class started soon. After four hours of restless sleep and a full day at the assembly line, I was drained of energy. Still, I felt a kind of nervous excitement deep inside my gut.

A whizzing sound interrupted my train of thought. "Bubbler at the door," Jax called out.

"It's probably my folks," Jeff said. "They must've finally gotten my message about the attack."

Other people chimed in that they too were waiting for bubblers. One by one, they looked at the door, then turned back to their workstation. Meanwhile, I stared straight ahead. I didn't look at the bubbler. I didn't have to.

I already knew it was for me.

Leandra fiddled with her hair. "Who wants to bet that Boltstar's got somebody spying on bubblers?"

"He can do that?" Nico asked.

"Why not?" She shrugged. "I mean, what can't he do?"

A discussion over Boltstar's magical limits started up between spells. Meanwhile, I spun toward the door. A watery bubble, two to three feet in diameter, floated at the threshold. Sure enough, my parents were in the middle of it. They sat at the kitchen table, same as the previous night. This time, though, there was no food.

"It's for me." I sighed. "I'll take it outside."

Jax shook his head. "Always finding a way to get out of work, eh, Randy?"

I blinked. "I—"

"Just go." He glanced at the clock. "Oh, and don't forget about Havoc Magic. If you're late, I'm not covering for you."

I hiked to the door. The whizzing noise burned my ears. A light mist sprayed over me.

"Randy," Dad exclaimed. "We—"

"Hang on." I squeezed past the bubbler and made my way into Shadow Madkey. I walked to the supply room and opened the door. It was empty, so I went inside and the bubbler followed after me.

"Listen, guys." I shut the door over. "I—"

"Let me look at you." Mom set down a steaming mug and I caught a whiff of fresh canfee. Specifically, Somber Silence flavored. She wiped her eyes with both hands. "Oh, thank goodness you're okay."

I couldn't remember the last time I'd seen her cry. I tried to think of something meaningful to say, but nothing came to mind.

"We got a mass bubbler from Lanctin a few hours ago," Dad explained. "He told us about the Chaotic attack."

"How come you didn't tell us first?" Mom wondered.

"I was in the clinic last night," I said. "And I've been at work all day."

"The clinic?" Her face tightened up. "What happened?"

It wasn't easy, but I managed to avoid itching my ribs. "Nothing important. I just needed to get checked out."

I caught a glimpse of the enchanted cuckoo clock hanging on the wall behind them. A quick check indicated I only had seven minutes to get to class. "Listen, I've got to go." I puffed my chest out. Of course, the class was mandatory. And it didn't really count for anything. Still, it was kind of nice to be able to tell my parents I was back at school again. "I've got class in a few minutes."

"We know. Lanctin mentioned it in his bubbler." Dad paused. "Just so you know, this doesn't change anything. We want you to come home, now more than ever."

I sighed. "I know."

"You've got a bright future ahead of you, Randy. But you've got to work for it."

And just like that, the conversation morphed into something more normal. Fighting the urge to itch my chest, I endured a full minute of veiled criticism. When I could take no more, I politely told them I was out of time and poked the mist, ending the bubbler.

As I headed for the door, resignation began to creep over me. My parents were being patient with me, but that wouldn't last forever. Sooner or later, they'd make me come home. I'd start school at YuckYuck. And then Madkey would be nothing more than a distant memory.

CHAPTER 21

My jaw slowly unhinged as I hopped over a short wall and landed in the heart of Madkey Arena. This certainly wasn't my first visit to the famous field. But it was my first time actually setting foot upon it.

Madkey Arena was an enormous circular structure, carved out of the statue's rear end. The field consisted of bright green grass, enchanted so as to grow without sunlight.

Stadium-seating, walled off at the bottom, revolved around the field at a very slow pace.

On any given day, a variety of goals, posts, walls, and other objects dotted the field, depending on the sport or game that was being played. As for the green grass, it could be covered at a moment's notice, replaced with a deep pool for PlankWalker or a ghostly graveyard for Hunters.

Between students, staffers, and faculty, close to one-thousand people called Madkey home. And yet, the arena could accommodate as much as ten times that amount, a fact that hinted at the school's much larger size during the Chaotic years.

At the moment, students and staffers were scattered about the field. Calvin led a bunch of sophomores in stretching. Nico sat in the bleachers, four or five staffers grouped around him. Hannah, the new girl, was in attendance, too, a couple of doting guys at her beck and call.

Piper approached me, a nervous smile upon her lips. "Well, this should be interesting."

"Oh, yeah." Leandra rolled her eyes. "I mean, who doesn't love school, right?"

"I'm surprised to see you here, Wolf," Porter taunted. "Haven't you failed enough already?"

He stood casually on the field, hands shoved into his pockets, wand tucked under his armpit. Sya stood next to him, arms crossed and leaning on one foot. Gordon and Felicia were there, too.

"He's not just a failure." Sya's face dripped with disdain. "He's a traitor, too."

"You're an idiot if you think that," Leandra said.

Ignoring her, Sya stared into my eyes. "Better be good, Wolf. Because I'm watching you."

I arched an eyebrow. "Don't look now, Porter, but I think your girlfriend's stalking me."

His face flushed. "You're pathetic, Wolf. And I'm going to prove it."

"Yeah? How?"

"By taking you out in the HMQ." He smirked. "And I'll do it in less than five minutes."

HMQ? What the heck was that? It suddenly occurred to me that I was in a bit over my head.

"Five?" I managed. "Can you even count that high?"

With a sneer upon his lips, Porter waved his wand at me. "Frube Paresnop," he said in a bold, clear voice.

I went for my wand. Suddenly, it erupted into fiery flames. The fire burnt my fingers and I dropped the stick of enchanted wood. The flames vanished and it landed safely on the grass.

With a chuckle, Porter lowered his wand. "That's an illusory spell," he informed us. "My dad taught it to me."

Porter already knew a havoc magic spell? Oh, boy. That didn't bode well for my chances in the HMQ ... whatever that was.

"Greetings and welcome to my class, Havoc Magic: An Introduction." Boltstar's voice cut through the crowd. Falling silent, we turned on our heels to face him.

He stood with his back to a descending ramp. The ramp led beneath the rotating wall and bleachers, all the way down to the sunken locker rooms.

"Please take a seat," he said, waving at a particular section of bleachers.

Along with everyone else, I hurried toward the stands. Vaulting the wall, I climbed a short staircase. A couple of staffers had carved out a small area behind the Sophomores. The Sophomores, wanting nothing to do with us, immediately relocated. Oh, well. More room for us.

Sliding into one of the rows, I took a seat next to Jenny. Meanwhile, the bleachers rotated in a clockwise direction, so slowly I could barely feel it.

Boltstar held his ground until our section of bleachers reached him. Then he hopped nimbly onto the wall. He was smartly dressed like always, his trademark derby hat cocked at a jaunty angle.

Reaching into his vest, he pulled out a thick tome and held it aloft. "This is the standard textbook for Havoc Magic 12, which some of you seniors are currently taking during normal hours. Written by one of our illustrious graduates, it's utilized by every major magic school in the world. You'll find copies under your seats. Please retrieve them and turn to Chapter One."

A textbook? Reading assignments? I'd expected it, but it still left me disgruntled. What did theory and interpretation have to do with havoc magic, anyway?

Reaching under my chair, I grabbed hold of an enormous book. Authored by Bella Cinda, it was entitled, *Havoc Magic: A Bare-Bones Treatise.*

Flipping pages, I turned to Chapter One. It was called, *The Art of Emotional Capture.* A quick perusal of the text nearly put me to sleep.

For the next hour, Havoc Magic was exactly like every other class I'd taken at Madkey. Boltstar lectured, occasionally citing the book for reference. Students and staffers alike took notes. Heck, even I took notes. Not because I thought they'd help me. I just didn't want to get called out as the only person not taking them.

I found it hard to pay attention. It wasn't Boltstar's fault. In fact, he was an exceptional lecturer. He used lots of movement and spoke in a variety of tones. He asked us questions and encouraged participation at multiple points.

No, the problem was with me. For whatever reason, my mind kept wandering and I couldn't stop daydreaming.

At precisely seven o'clock, Boltstar shut the textbook and placed it at his feet. "And that, ladies and gentlemen, is your first lecture," he announced. "But it's not the end of our time together. My goal is to teach you how to fight, not just how to think about fighting. As such, the first hour of each class will contain a lecture. We'll also go over reading assignments and I'll answer any questions you might have thus far. There will be occasional quizzes so that I can chart your progress. In short, it'll be quite similar to what you'd find in other Madkey classes."

I sighed.

"The second hour, however, will be very different," he continued. "During that time, we'll focus on practical, hard-nosed magic. You'll learn offensive and defensive spells. You'll be given ample opportunity to practice those spells in duels. And finally, you'll use those same spells in a series of games."

Locking his eyes on us, he began to pace back and forth along the wall.

"This class will continue until the end of the quarter. It's pass or fail, based solely on my evaluation. Specifically, you must convince me that you're able to handle yourself with skill and control in battle-type situations. Since this class isn't part of the core curriculum, I intend to grade all of you with a light hand. But that doesn't mean you can afford to slack off. Indeed, you must pass this class if you wish to continue on at Madkey, either as a student or as a staffer." His expression softened a bit. "After last night's attack, I think it's safe to say we live in dangerous times. The skills you'll learn here may one day save your life. So, please take your lessons seriously."

Visages turned somber within the crowd. A couple of students offered appreciative nods. A few others looked our way with tight jaws and accusatory eyes.

"Now, havoc magic is easy to learn, but difficult to put into practice. This is due to the emotional requirement. Ordinary spells, done under ordinary conditions, allow for complete concentration. As you'll soon discover, this is much harder to achieve while in the midst of battle." He paused in mid-stride. His gaze swept over the bleachers. "During the first half of class, we discussed two basic spells. Pobyl, which is used for defensive purposes, and Elertfa, which is utilized for attacks. We will now put that knowledge to practical use."

Next to me, Piper practically trembled with excitement. Thus far, she seemed thrilled to be back in school, even if the class didn't actually count toward a degree.

"Let's begin by viewing both spells in a real-life skirmish." Boltstar waved his wand and muttered a series of quiet incantations. A large memory mirror floated up from the sunken locker room area. "Specifically, the 1932 duel between myself and Mr. Colin Steadman."

Piper's eyes bulged. "Oh, wow," she whispered. "I've read about that one. It's supposed to be epic."

She was so amped up I thought she'd leap right out of her seat. As for me, I was puzzled. Who was Colin Steadman?

"Mr. Steadman was a Chaotic magician," Boltstar said, answering my question before I could ask it. "He eluded us on Victory Day. It took an additional two years to track him down. When we finally caught up to him, he refused to surrender, necessitating a duel."

The mirror flew across the field. Halting just shy of us, it proceeded to hover in mid-air.

Staring at the glassy surface, I watched it morph into a memory. The background was an old dirt road, framed by fields of dying grass. Two people faced each other, wands held aloft. Boltstar was decked out to the nines and utterly clean. Even his derby cap looked unsullied. Meanwhile, the other guy, who I took to be Steadman, was attired in rags. His eyes glimmered with fury.

Boltstar tried to get off a quick spell. But Steadman was faster. He waved his wand and muttered something too soft to hear. An orchid ray of light zoomed forth from his wand.

The young Boltstar, however, was not to be denied. Shifting course, he waved his wand and said, "Pobyl Caxtor." A flash, cyan in color, hit Steadman's ray and both spells evaporated into smoke.

Almost immediately, Boltstar waved his wand. "Elertfa Lokwhan," he said.

The resulting spell slammed into Steadman. The Chaotic wizard stumbled back a foot or so, then fell to a knee.

The memory vanished. The glassy surface returned. I blinked a few times, then turned my attention to Boltstar.

"Did everyone see that?" he asked.

Our heads bobbed.

"You call that epic?" Leandra whispered from the seat behind us. "They barely moved."

"Fighting was different back then," Piper informed her. "It was more refined. They didn't use fancy theatrics or enchanted weapons."

"Mr. Steadman fired the first spell, one of Chaotic origin," Boltstar said in a matter-of-fact tone. "I countered with Pobyl, then followed that up with Elertfa."

Felicia lifted a tentative hand.

Boltstar gave her a sideways glance. "Yes, Ms. Masters?"

"Why bother with basic spells? Why not just use the death spell?" She shrugged. "I mean, we're talking about Chaotics here."

"The Gratlan is well beyond the scope of this class," he replied. "But to answer your question, it's morally repugnant.

No decent magician would ever use it unless absolutely necessary."

I blinked in astonishment. Did he just say that no decent magician would ever use the Gratlan? What about the one that he'd fired our way? The one that had nearly killed Tad?

"From a practical standpoint," he continued, "a death spell is a bad idea. It's an escalation of force, one that could easily backfire on the spellcaster. Does that answer your question?"

Felicia, now slightly gray-faced, nodded.

"In any event, you don't need the Gratlan to be an effective havoc magician." He cast a glance over the crowd. "We're going to start with Pobyl and Elertfa. First, we'll nail down the particulars. Then we'll pair off and practice. Finally, we'll use them on the battlefield. Are there any other questions?" He scanned the crowd, then nodded. "Then let's get started."

CHAPTER 22

Sya Moren gave me a harsh, hateful look. Her lips moved. Her wand sliced menacingly through the air.

Twenty feet away, I itched my chest and fought to control my emotions. Part of me recalled pleasant memories. Nothing too pleasant, just run of-the mill stuff. Getting a hug from Piper. Laughing at Leandra's jokes. That night I crushed all comers in Sasquatch Summit Smash.

The other part of me ginned up recollections of painful, isolated surprises. I recalled the first 'F' I'd received at

Madkey. My legs getting tangled up and falling on my face as a kid. Tad breaking my ribs with a single spell.

Lifting my wand, I started to run it through the prescribed motions ... zig-zag to the left, then arching back to the right. As I opened my lips, Instinctia took over. My wand shifted. "Shumbla Dant," I said.

An auburn blaze left my wand. It careened into Sya and did ... nothing. Well, not nothing. Once again, I'd cast the wrong spell. Shumbla Dant was a speedwriting enchantment, which savvy students used to great effect in class. On the battlefield, however, it was pretty much useless.

I braced myself as Sya's spell raced toward me. One second later, it careened into my belly and ... nothing. I breathed a sigh of relief. Her spell was a dud, too.

"I can't concentrate." Disgusted, she lowered her wand. "It's your fault, you know. If I didn't have to do this with an actual Chaotic—"

"I'm not a Chaotic," I said, forcefully.

"Whatever." She stalked away. "I need a break."

Thus far, all of my attempts at havoc magic had come up short. Oh, I'd performed plenty of spells. Just not the right ones.

That's the frustrating thing about the Capsudra. When you attempt to cast a spell, it scans your emotions, wand, and lips to project your intentions. Then it takes over with Instinctia, completing the enchantment on your behalf. While that can be a big help, it's not a perfect system. If you aren't accurate enough to begin with, the Capsudra will misread your intentions and guide you to the wrong spell.

Making matters even more complicated, it constantly adjusts itself based upon those who use it. Imagine the Capsudra as a bundle of mystical energy. And imagine its spells as grooves upon that bundle. When a spell is performed, it temporarily deepens the groove. Over time, some spells develop deeper grooves than other ones. And the deeper the groove, the quicker the Capsudra senses your intentions and thrusts you into a state of Instinctia.

That's just fine if you're performing a popular spell. But if you're casting rare enchantments, like the ones used for havoc magic, it can be a real pain. The grooves are so shallow that you have to be extra-perfect with your initial emotions, wand sequences, and lip movements. Otherwise, you'll end up turning your opponent into a speedwriter by accident.

Wand in hand, I scanned the field. I saw no sign of Boltstar. After showing us the basics, he'd paired us off at random. Unfortunately, I'd ended up with Sya. While we began dueling—or at least, attempting to duel—he'd disappeared into the sunken locker room area.

A shriek rang out. And then Calvin Hayes floated gently into the air, like a balloon. Everyone turned to watch him, utterly dumbfounded. His partner, Gordon, stood beneath him, free hand covering his mouth. I couldn't tell whether he was shocked or trying not to laugh. Knowing Gordon, I suspected the latter.

Leandra was the only person who seemed to understand the gravity of the situation. Leaping up, she grabbed Calvin's ankles. But he kept gaining altitude and she was forced to drop back down to the grass.

For the moment, Calvin seemed safe. But one could never be sure when it came to magic. What would happen when he hit the ceiling? Would he gently bounce off of it? Or would the spell squash him against it until it—or he—broke?

Sya shook her head. "Calvin's such an idiot."

He was now twenty feet off the ground and still climbing. We all gawked at him, clueless as to how to remedy the situation.

Out of the corner of my eye, I spotted the ramp leading under the arena. I ran toward it, then darted down its soft grassy slope. The grass gave way to a concrete tunnel. A couple of enchanted fountains, situated in large basins, occupied the middle of the tunnel. Lined up one after the other, they featured stone figures playing a variety of sports, showered with streams of icy blue water.

"He's gone."

The voice belonged to Galison. Crouching down, I peered through the cascades of falling water. He and Boltstar stood between two of the fountains, well beyond the locker rooms.

"What happened?" Boltstar asked.

"Gully got his hands on a wand during an interrogation. He cast a few fancy spells, slipped the guards, and vanished."

Gully? As in Ivan Gully, the Chaotic magician that Boltstar had drodiated back in Torso?

"What kind of shape is he in?" Boltstar asked. "Will he hurt anyone?"

"I don't think so, Sir. We were starving him at the time, softening him up between interrogations. I imagine he's pretty hungry by now. Plus, the guards winged him during the escape and he lost his wand.

"I want Mr. Gully found," Boltstar said. "Immediately."

"Of course, Headmaster."

Boltstar stayed silent for a few seconds. "Did the interrogations yield any results?"

"Yes," Galison hurried to say. "According to Mr. Gully, Mr. Crucible was working alone when he opened the conveyance station."

"And you believed him?" Boltstar asked.

"I do."

"Anything else?"

"No, Sir."

"Very well. Find Mr. Gully."

"We will."

I took another look at Calvin. He was drawing close to the ceiling. As much as I hated to interrupt the conversation, I didn't see as how I had a choice.

I backed up a few steps, then made a show of running into the tunnel. My feet pounded against hard stone. My voice lifted to a shout.

"Headmaster," I called out. "We need you."

Galison and Boltstar fell quiet. I heard the sound of rustling clothes, followed by footsteps. Moments later, Boltstar appeared. I looked for Galison, but he was gone.

"Yes, Mr. Wolf?" he asked impatiently.

"Calvin Hayes is … well … he's floating."

Wasting no time, he ran out of the tunnel and up the grassy slope. Rather than follow at his heels, I lingered for a moment. Had they been holding Ivan prisoner here?

Letting my eyes roam, I stepped up to the first fountain. It depicted a couple of enchanted stone figures struggling for possession of a ramball. Water squirted up from the circular edging. The streams soared over the heads of the players, then turned into mist. Flashes of colorful light zigzagged amongst the water droplets. All in all, it looked like a hard-fought ramball game, drenched with stormy rain.

I leaned forward. A stream of water shifted course and squirted into my open mouth. As I drank, I peered through the streams of water. Farther back, I saw Galison. His shadowy figure moved to the end of the tunnel. He opened the last door on the right and strode through it.

Finishing my drink, I shifted back a few inches. The stream of water returned to its normal course. Heart pounding, I hurried after Galison. Sneaking up to the door, I placed my ear against it. I heard nothing, but I felt pretty sure this was where they'd kept Ivan.

Backing away, I sprinted after Boltstar. As I raced up the grassy ramp, I saw Calvin. He was now just ten feet from the ceiling, kicking his legs and waving his arms like he was operating a chair within the Grille. But it didn't help. He just kept right on gaining altitude.

Cutting my speed, I walked the final few steps to Boltstar's side. He was busy muttering an enchantment under his breath. A cyan beam emerged from the tip of his wand. It encircled Calvin's waist, arresting the boy's movement.

Muscles popping, Boltstar pulled the wand toward his shoulder. Calvin, still struggling, dropped a foot or so.

The headmaster snapped the wand forward, shortening the spell. Before Calvin could float away again, he yanked the wand back toward his shoulder.

Boltstar's brow formed into a hard, concentrated ridge. He continued to work the wand, reeling Calvin in like a fish. It took a few minutes but eventually, the boy's shoes were just a few inches off the ground.

Planting his feet, Boltstar steadied himself. "What happened here?"

Gordon was no longer laughing. "I learned some havoc magic at camp," he said. "I thought I'd give it a whirl."

"Let me guess. Catrew Corpa?"

Gordon nodded.

"I see." He raised his voice. "I'm well aware of the fact that some of you have experience in havoc magic. But from this point forward, I would ask you to refrain from using any spell we haven't covered in class. Is that agreeable?"

When someone of Boltstar's stature asks you if something's 'agreeable,' you'd better agree. And so, we did, nodding in silent unison.

"Uh, can someone get me down from here?" Calvin asked, trying but failing to hide his panic.

"Stay calm, Mr. Hayes." Boltstar caught sight of me. "I require your assistance, Mr. Wolf."

Boltstar was asking me ... *me!* ... to help him break a spell? Heck, yeah.

"What do I do?" I asked.

"His feet need to touch solid ground. Unfortunately, the enchantment grows stronger as he descends. It's a bit like gravity, only in reverse." Grunting, he strained his muscles. "Grab some friends and pull him down. Do whatever it takes."

Shouting for help, I grabbed Calvin's right leg. Pulling with all my might, I managed to lower him a few inches. Piper, Leandra, Nico, and Jax raced out of the crowd. Piper jumped onto the boy's left leg. Wrapping herself around it, she went dead weight. Leandra helped with the right leg. Nico and Jax threw themselves at Calvin's waist and violently yanked at it.

Inch by inch, he descended. Finally, his right shoe slid through the blades of grass and struck soil. The enchantment broke and we collapsed in a heap.

"Is everyone alright?" Piper asked.

Jax stifled a moan. "Just peachy."

"Thanks." Calvin flopped onto his back. Chest heaving, he stared at the faraway ceiling. "I owe you guys big-time."

"I think that's enough practice for today." Boltstar stretched his arms. "How are the new spells coming along?"

Silence greeted him.

"That good, huh?" He smiled. "Well, I think it's time for your first test."

A few people groaned. Piper bit her cheeks, looking as if someone had left a baby snallygaster on her front step. Regardless, we all started for the bleachers.

Boltstar looked puzzled. "Where are you going?"

"You said we were taking a test," Piper replied.

"Yes, a physical one." His smile widened. "It's time for your first HMQ game."

CHAPTER 23

"You know what I'd kill for right now. A bug repellant spell." Leandra waved her hand at a mosquito. "Seriously, where do these things come from?"

She swatted at the pesky insect and eventually, it moved on to annoy some juniors.

We watched with intense curiosity as a group of seniors, all students in Havoc Magic 12, marched out of the sunken locker room area. They moved slowly, their wands fixed on the objects levitating in front of them. Meanwhile, Boltstar produced an enchanted rope and proceeded to carve out a large rectangular-shaped section of the field. Unceremoniously, the kids dumped their objects into the roped-off section and went back to get more stuff. Before long, all sorts of items rested within the square. I saw an old table standing on end, a door jammed into the soil, empty ramball crates, and many other things.

My ribs itched, but the itching wasn't as intense as it had been the previous night. Still, I gave them a pretty good scratch before twisting toward Leandra and Piper. "What do you guys know about Chaotic magic?" I asked.

"It's bad news," Leandra replied, looking around. "And keep it down, will you? Most of these people already think we're Chaotics. The last thing we need is to give them more ammunition."

"Fine." I lowered my voice to a whisper. "Do you know how it works?"

"Of course not."

I switched my attention to Piper. "What about you?"

"I just know that it's magic at its most primal. It comes from a person's deepest emotions. Real emotions, not the ones we use for the Capsudra." She shrugged. "Of course, that's just what I've read. We'll never know if it's true or not."

"That's kind of sad," I said without thinking.

She gave me an odd look. "What makes you say that?"

"Uh, oh." Leandra glared at me. "You'd better not be a sympathizer."

My cheeks started to burn. "Hey, I don't like Chaotic magic any more than you guys. It just sucks that we can't use something that's a part of us."

"Would you expect an insane person to use their insanity?" Leandra arched an eyebrow. "And what about someone who's prone to violence? Should we just let them beat up people so they can be true to themselves?"

"Please direct your attention this way," Boltstar announced, his commanding voice carrying across the field. "Specifically, to the enclosed area. This is a Havoc Magic Quadrant, or HMQ, if you prefer."

He paused, giving us a chance to absorb this information.

"The HMQ is intended to simulate the conditions of a real-life battlefield. While certainly imperfect, it'll help you learn how to utilize objects for cover, as well as attack others from behind cover. We'll use the HMQ to play numerous structured games, which resemble different types of combat."

He glanced at our faces, then smiled. "Well?" he asked. "What are you waiting for?"

I exchanged uneasy looks with Piper and Leandra. At a quick pace, we trotted across the field. As I stepped over the enchanted rope, Porter caught my eye. With an oily smirk, he drew his finger across his throat.

I'd forgotten all about his promise to defeat me within five minutes. Now, I could think of nothing else.

"Your first HMQ game will be a Havoc Royal," Boltstar declared. "In other words, it's a free-for-all. Upon my whistle, you'll battle your fellow students. Anything goes. If a direct hit knocks you off your feet or renders you unconscious, you're eliminated. The last person standing wins the game."

Unconscious? My breaths turned raspy and I started to panic. This was insane. I couldn't perform a single havoc magic spell in a controlled duel. How in the world was I going to pull one off with spells flying all around me?

"Remember your spells. Keep your emotions in check. Watch your footwork and mind your surroundings. You have no idea how many times I've seen great witches and wizards lose to lesser ones because they tripped over something. Now, begin fighting on my mark." Boltstar walked partway up the bleachers. Sticking his fingers into his mouth, he emitted a low-pitched whistle.

Porter put on a burst of speed. "Elertfa Lokwhan," he called out, waving his wand in the prescribed fashion.

A chestnut blaze shot toward me. I leapt out of the way and his spell struck a refrigerator, jolting the giant appliance and singeing its surface.

Gasping for air, I slid behind an empty locker. I caught my breath, then peeked out at the HMQ.

Gleaming chestnut light barely missed my noggin. Instead, it knocked the locker back into me. The impact sent me sprawling to the ground.

"The Wolf's out," Porter crowed.

"Only a direct hit can cause an elimination," Boltstar reminded him. "So, Mr. Wolf is still very much alive."

Porter grunted. Another chestnut ray sent me scrambling for cover yet again, this time behind a stack of chairs.

"Let's go, Mr. Wolf," Boltstar called out. "Stop running and fight back!"

I frowned at his unyielding tone. What had I done to deserve his attention? And what kind of instruction was that anyway? I was supposed to, 'fight back'? How? By casting a spell I hadn't mastered yet?

But hey, his eyes were on me so I decided I had to do something. And since we'd only learned one offensive spell so far, it wasn't like I had much of a choice.

A glittering taupe spell careened into a chest of drawers. Piper yelped as they came crashing down on top of her.

My eyes widened. Everywhere I looked, students were zapping staffers, taking us out with ease. All thoughts of fighting went out of my brain. All I could think about was hiding just a little longer.

"Are you okay, Ms. Shaw?" Boltstar called out.

"Yes," Piper replied, painfully. "At least, I think so."

"The spell didn't hit you. So, keep fighting!"

Jeff ran past me, his untucked shirt flapping behind him. Gordon, Felicia, and Sya were in hot pursuit. Vicious bolts of light—ivory, fuchsia, and taupe—lit up the area around his feet. "Help," he shouted to no one in particular. "This is a madhouse!"

Gordon roared with insane laughter.

Dropping to all fours, I scurried into a fallen flowerpot. It was large enough to accommodate me and plenty dark inside. Curling my legs up, I tried to make myself invisible.

Nearby, Dorph Jenkins yelped. Leandra shrieked. Jenny grunted. They sounded like they were in agony.

Nico ran into view, dodging colorful spells.

"Psst," I hissed. "Over here."

But as he turned my way, a chestnut streak hit his right side. He went airborne, spinning like a top, before flopping onto his stomach. Groaning, he crawled toward the enchanted rope.

"I heard the Wolf," Sya yelled. "He's in that flowerpot."

Uh, oh.

Three blasts slammed into the flowerpot in quick succession. The first one sent it skidding backward. The next two caused it to roll like crazy, first to the left, then even more to the left. Gritting my teeth, I held on tight. Meanwhile, sweat oozed out of my pores and a pounding dizziness cropped up in my forehead.

The pot careened into another pot. The sudden jolt jarred me loose and I spilled outside.

Wand in hand, I rose to my feet. I tried to run, but I could only wobble. I had no sense of balance or stability. *This must be how it feels after drinking bizzlum*, I thought crazily.

Through dazed, blurry vision, I saw Porter. He was on the run, ducking and firing spells at Jax. He wasn't looking my way and I realized this was the best chance I'd get to take him down.

Waving my wand, I tried to pin down my emotion. The warm embrace of Instinctia wrapped around me. "Shumbla Dant," I said.

Auburn light careened into Porter. Of course, nothing happened. Just like in practice, I'd performed the stupid speedwriting spell.

Porter threw out another chestnut slash. With a pained shout, Jax bit the dust.

Looking over his shoulder, Porter caught sight of me. A devilish grin creased his lips.

Bam!

A brilliant chestnut glow, hard as steel, slammed into my gut. The back of my head hit the ground and I just lay there, too shaken up to move.

"You made it almost four minutes, Wolf," Porter crowed. "Maybe you'll get to five next time."

"You're out, Mr. Wolf." Boltstar called from his perch in the bleachers. "Please exit the HMQ."

Oh, I wanted to exit the HMQ. Anything to get out of there. Unfortunately, my muscles refused to respond.

"Did you hear me, Mr. Wolf?"

Somehow, I flipped onto my belly. Then I crawled toward the enchanted rope, Porter's vicious laughter ringing loudly in my ears.

CHAPTER 24

Beat-up and discouraged, I scaled the ladder. At the top, I lifted the hatch and peeked into the celestarium. Moonlight allowed me to see every inch of the space. And yet, I didn't see Tad.

I climbed into the circular room, taking care to close the hatch behind me. "You can come out," I said. "It's just me."

Scuffling noises arose from the chimney and a pair of feet dropped to the hearth. Ducking low, Tad made his way out of the fireplace.

"How was class?" he asked.

"Don't ask."

"That good, huh?"

My nose wrinkled. He smelled of sweat and grease. "I brought you some clothes." I peeled an old backpack off of my shoulders. "Some toiletries, too."

"Toiletries?"

I gave him a knowing look.

He sniffed his armpit, then made a face. "Whoa."

"Yup."

"There's a bathroom below us." He took the pack from me. "I'll get cleaned up."

"That's not all I brought."

He gave me a questioning look.

I nodded at the pack. "Look inside."

Setting the backpack on a table, he unzipped the zipper.

"I snuck some food out of Madkey Station Grille," I said. "It's not exactly fresh, but—"

Frantically, he dug into the main pocket. He came out with a banana and a bagged sandwich. Like always, the sandwich had emerged as a pile of enchanted, fresh ingredients. To make it easier to carry, I'd issued the preparation orders back in Madkey Grille.

Tad didn't seem to care though. He ripped the bag open and peeled the banana. Then he began eating with great gusto. In less than two minutes, he was done and licking his fingers.

"Wow, I needed that." He searched the rest of my bag. His face turned crestfallen. "That's all, huh?"

"I'll bring more tomorrow."

He nodded, disappointment evident in his features.

"How's your shoulder?"

He made a face. "Awful."

Truthfully, it didn't look that bad. The Gratlan had shrunk even more since I'd last seen it. It had also faded a good deal and was getting closer and closer to flesh-colored. "It looks pretty good to me."

"Oh, it's definitely better. But this itching is driving me nuts." He raked his fingernails across his shoulder. "Give me pain any day."

I scratched my itchy chest. "I know what you mean."

He left to freshen up. Meanwhile, I hiked to the glass wall and peered outside.

"I'm back," he said a few minutes later.

He'd shaved and his face looked freshly scrubbed. His hair was damp, but clean. Gone were the grease, the sweat, and most importantly, the stink. Decked out in a green shirt and jeans, he looked, well, almost normal.

"Thanks. For the food, clothes, everything."

"Yup." I hesitated for a split-second. "Do you know Ivan Gully?"

His head bobbed up and down. "Why? Is he okay?"

"I'm not sure." Quickly, I told him about the conversation I'd overheard between Boltstar and Galison.

"So, Ivan got loose, huh?" He stroked his jaw thoughtfully. "Good for him."

"Maybe not. He's injured. Starving, too."

"Really?" A pained look crossed his face. "If that's true, he won't last long on his own."

"You're probably right. But don't even think about helping him." I crossed my arms. "If Boltstar captures you, we're both screwed."

"If Boltstar captures me, he'll get my anchor. And then everyone I know will be screwed." He ran a hand through his hair. "Well, are you ready to get started?"

I hesitated.

"I get it," he said, grasping my shoulder. "The initial excitement's worn off, right? You're getting cold feet."

I brushed his hand away. He'd always made me uneasy and that moment was no different.

He took my rejection in stride. "What's the big deal?" he wondered. "Witches and wizards performed Chaotic magic for centuries, way before Structuralism came along."

"Yeah, I know." I exhaled. "It's just ... I'm worried."

"About what?"

I thought for a moment. "That I'm about to cross a bridge from which there's no return."

"Well, I don't know about that. But maybe this will make you feel better." He cocked his head. "Chaotic magic is nowhere near as dangerous as you've been led to believe."

"I'm sure it doesn't seem all that bad to you, but—"

"We don't have death spells."

"I ... what?"

"Okay, I'm sure some Chaotic magicians had deaths spells. But none of my people have ever cast one." He gave me a pointed look. "Which is more than I can say for you guys."

"That's different," I argued. "Boltstar was fighting an invasion."

"Yes. An invasion without death spells."

"He didn't know that." I bristled with indignation. "Anyway, that's not the point. Under your system, anybody could have a death spell. But under Structuralism, only Boltstar and a few others can access that kind of power."

"You mean they hoard that power for themselves."

I shook my head. "That's not it at all."

"Are you sure about that?" He continued to scratch away at the healing Gratlan without pause. "And what makes you think Boltstar deserves that power, anyway? He fired the Gratlan right at us, without even checking to see who he'd hit with it."

I suddenly felt very defensive. "That's because he knew it could be healed."

"Then why use it at all?" he challenged.

"I ... don't know."

"Let me make it simple for you," he said. "We're not savages. We've got laws, same as you. Laws that say you can't hurt other people. If you do, you get punished. It's as simple as that."

I tried to think of a snappy response, but nothing came to mind. So, I sighed instead. "It doesn't even matter. I won't be here much longer."

"Why's that?"

"My parents want me home."

"Because of the invasion?"

I shook my head. "They think I'm wasting my time here. They want to enroll me at another school."

"Gotcha." With tremendous effort, he managed to stop scratching. But in less than a second, he was clawing at his shoulder all over again. "Well, it's up to you."

I lingered for a second, torn by indecision. "Are you sure you can teach me? You didn't sound all that certain yesterday."

"No. But I'll try." He gave me a knowing look. "Of course, a wand would help."

I reached into my pocket and gently fingered MacPherson's wand. I'd anticipated Tad's request. Still, I wasn't exactly comfortable with fulfilling it.

With a sigh, I tossed him the wand. At the same time, my free hand went to my holster. Ahh, who was I kidding? Tad actually knew how to fight. All I seemed to be good at was helping people read faster.

But I needn't have worried. He took the wand in a careful grip, then held it up to the moonlight. "This isn't mine."

"Boltstar's got your wand." I nodded at the one in his hand. "That belongs to MacPherson."

He whipped it to the left, then to the right. He proceeded to run it through other movements, gradually getting used to the weight and feel of it. "It's nice."

I felt a pang of jealousy. Oh, how I'd wanted to keep it for myself. But it wouldn't be smart. If even one person spotted it, my growing web of secrets would unravel for all to see.

"I've given this a lot of thought," Tad remarked, alternatively playing with the wand and scratching his shoulder. "And it won't be easy. It'll be like teaching someone to walk on their own two feet after they've been riding hoists their entire life. But I still think we can do it."

"How?"

"First, I'll show you the steps. Then you'll mimic me. We'll practice over and over again until you get it right. Sound good?"

Actually, it sounded an awful lot like school, which didn't exactly encourage me. But since I didn't have any other ideas, I produced my wand. Thick and old, it paled in comparison to the one I'd given him. But hey, at least it hadn't broken yet. "Good enough," I replied.

"After you cast your first Chaotic spell, we'll test it a few times to see what it does. If it's useful, you can keep practicing it. If not, we'll move on. Okay?"

I nodded. "Okay."

He kept scratching. His face twisted, stricken between contemplation and frustration. "The problem, as I see it, is Instinctia. You enter it every time you try to cast a spell, right?"

"Of course." I shrugged. "But you knew that already."

"Do I?"

I gawked at him. "Are you saying you've never experienced Instinctia?"

He shrugged. "I never figured it out. I've been faking it all along, using my Chaotic magic to mimic your spells."

I blinked, still shocked. "That sounds hard."

"Oh, it was. Incredibly hard." He itched some more. "What's Instinctia like, anyway?"

"It's warm and comforting." I furrowed my brow, trying to figure out how to put it into words. "Like I've just come home for Christmas."

"So, it feels amazing?" he asked.

"You could say that."

"Ahh, that makes sense. Why else would you guys agree to it?"

"Agree to what?"

"Giving up control."

I blinked. I'd never thought of it that way. But wow, he had a pretty good point. The freakiest part about magic was losing control of oneself. Instinctia made that bearable, if not downright enjoyable.

"Chaotic magic is natural," he continued. "But Structuralism is anything but natural. It's someone else's emotions, someone else's spells. Even worse, it requires you to give up self-control, to let it take over. That's a tall order. Maybe the only reason you go for it is because Instinctia feels so utterly amazing. Maybe that Xavier guy made it that way on purpose."

I nodded. He was absolutely right. Chaotic magic probably felt pretty great. In order to compete, Structuralist magic—specifically, Instinctia—had to feel just as good, if not better.

"Have you ever rejected it?" he asked.

"Rejected it?"

"There's a moment where you cede control, right? Where you turn yourself over to the Capsudra's whims? Have you ever denied that?"

I shook my head. "I'm not sure that's even possible."

"Oh, it's possible. It has to be. You know why? Because *you've got free will*. We all do." He scratched his shoulder so hard I thought he'd draw blood. "You were trained to accept Instinctia. Now, you have to learn to deny it."

He made it sound easy. But I wasn't so sure.

Stooping down, he picked up a very old bust from the floor. It depicted a young man with scars on both cheeks.

Gently, he set the bust down on a table. "Let your mind go," he instructed. "And wave your wand."

I arched an eyebrow.

"Instinctia will kick in no matter what you do, right? So, just feel your emotions and wave that wand anyway you like. As soon as Instinctia starts to take over, deny it."

My eyebrow arched all the way to the top of my head.

He shrugged. "Who knows? Maybe it'll be easier than you think."

I wasn't used to feeling my own emotions, let alone waving my wand in haphazard fashion. Things just weren't done that way. So instead, I recalled what I'd learned about Elertfa Lokwhan. My emotions started to whirl. My wand sliced through the dust-clogged air. Instinctia reached out for me and I accepted it without question.

"Shumbla Dant," I said.

Auburn light raced out of my wand. It hit the bust and engulfed it, before blinking out.

Frowning, I lowered my wand. I hadn't even attempted to deny Instinctia. It just took over and next thing I knew, I was casting the spell. The wrong spell, as it turned out. Great, just great. Now, I was teaching statues how to speedread.

"Well?" he asked.

I shook my head.

"Try again."

And so, I tried again. Quickly, I entered Instinctia. And a few moments after that, I did the stupid speedreading spell all over again.

Tad cocked his head.

"It's not working," I complained.

"It will. Try again."

I shifted my emotions. My wand went to work. Instinctia took over and I fired off the wrong spell for a third time.

Tad saw the defeated look in my eyes. "Again."

I tried again. And again. And yet again. Eventually, he took over, casting Chaotic spells so I could see his process. I watched him carefully, then tried again.

And again. And yet again.

CHAPTER 25

The kid, awkwardly hanging around the Mid-Torso bridge, stuck out in almost every conceivable way.

For one thing, he wore a close-fitting tunic, belted with a steel blue sash. The garment, soiled and covered with sweat-stains, smelled faintly of body odor. Meanwhile, the other kids in the area, all students, wore typical Madkey casual attire. Slacks, polo shirts, and loafers for the boys. Colorful skirts, blouses, and closed-toe heels for the girls.

For another thing, the kid was ratty. Ratty and *old*. His skin was a ghostly white. His hair, thick, tangled, and black, looked like it hadn't been combed in weeks. A makeshift sling, made of torn fabric, supported his right arm. He was too old to be in a class, yet too young to teach one. Contrasted with dozens of well-scrubbed students, he looked totally out of place.

I halted partway across the bridge. My eyes traced his thin face and bony body. His image was burnt into my brain and I recognized him immediately.

It was Ivan Gully.

Seeing him there, just a few feet from Madkey Station Grille, shouldn't have surprised me. After all, that's where he'd first appeared. Plus, I'd overheard Galison say that they'd starved Ivan in order to soften him up. So, it made sense that he'd want some food.

But surprise me it did and for a couple of long moments, all I could do was gawk in his general direction. Thinking hard, I considered my next move. On one hand, I could report him. Heck, I could produce my wand and attempt to arrest him. On the other hand, I could just leave him alone. I could go about my day, pretending I hadn't seen anything.

Unable to make up my mind, I stood there, staring at him. Watching him as he licked his lips. Watching him as he stared longingly at the plates of food emerging from the wall chutes. He looked pretty harmless to me, especially with that sling on his arm. I didn't see a wand on him, either.

Students began to notice him. Slowly at first, but news of his presence quickly spread. Nervous students raced their chairs to the outer edges of Torso, trying to get as far away as possible. A few of the braver ones headed across the bridges, intending to alert the alumni. The bravest of all, Kell and some of his buddies, rode chairs out to greet the intruder.

"Chaotic scum." Kell spat at Ivan's feet. "Back for another round, eh?"

"Please." Ivan's voice cracked softly in the air. "I need … food … water …"

"Forget it." Growling, Kell raised his wand, moving it in the prescribed manner. "Elertfa Lokwhan."

To everyone's surprise, including my own, Ivan dodged the spell. With a soft grunt, he leapt out into the open. A chair rushed to grab him. But before it could arrive, Ivan slammed into Kell. The ramball star managed to stand his ground. But he was caught off guard nonetheless and Ivan was able to filch his wand.

Leaping onto the just-arriving chair, Ivan rode out into the middle of the ancient station. Alumni appeared from all corners of Torso, targeting Ivan, bombarding him with havoc magic spells. Ducking and weaving, he managed to steer clear long enough to embed himself amidst a group of terrified freshmen.

The alumni began racing about the bridges, checking the angles, trying to figure out how to sneak a spell through the group. Meanwhile, despite his ailments, Ivan began to fire attacks of his own. Kids screamed as he whirled amongst the frozen freshmen, his wand dancing in his fingertips. Strange curses and spells roared through the air. One spell hit Chez Skalant and he immediately sprouted long ears and a tail. Fur appeared as his body took on the shape of a donkey. Another one hit Kylie Davis and her limbs began to spaz in uncontrollable fashion.

I watched it all, frozen in place, consumed by awe and fear. A part of me wanted to reach for my wand, to cast a spell, to put an end to Ivan's reign of terror. Another part of me realized that I couldn't actually remember the havoc magic spells. Heck, I barely remembered my own name.

A cyan streak zoomed through Torso, threading a thin gap between two of the freshmen. Ivan managed to avoid it, but not by much.

"This is your last chance, Mr. Gully." Boltstar emerged from his quarters, wielding his wand in a firm, well-practiced manner. "Surrender. Now."

The Chaotic's confidence melted away, replaced by a most primal dread. He urged his chair toward the ceiling at a high rate of speed, leaving the freshmen cowering in his wake.

Boltstar fired another spell. It slammed into Ivan's back. The force knocked him clear off of his chair and he started to fall. The chair raced around and grabbed him up again. Then it hovered in mid-air, the unconscious Chaotic draped across its wooden seat.

Hard-faced alumni hopped onto chairs and rode them out into Madkey Station Grille. A few tended to the injured students. But most of the witches and wizards converged upon Ivan and soon, I couldn't even see him.

Quietly, students hurried to vacate the area. Rising to my tiptoes, I tried to catch another glimpse of Ivan. But the alumni were still packed tightly around him. Besides, it was difficult to see much of anything with so many students in the way.

They filed past me as if in a daze, alarm and shock etched deeply upon their visages. Once again, the Chaotic threat had reared its ugly head.

And once again, Madkey had seemed almost powerless to stop it.

CHAPTER 26

"I hope everything's okay." From our perch in the bleachers, Piper scanned the sunken locker room area. "It's not like Boltstar to be late."

"I bet he's still dealing with that Chaotic kid," Leandra remarked.

"You're probably right. But still …"

As she trailed off, I checked the enchanted clock hanging on the far wall. It was seven minutes after six o'clock. Indeed, the headmaster was late. Then again, he was the greatest magician of all time. As far as I was concerned, he'd earned the right to be tardy once in a while.

A yawn escaped my lips. For the last week, Tad and I had worked every night. I'd cast thousands of spells—maybe even tens of thousands of spells—over that period. And yet, I still hadn't come close to breaking Instinctia.

"I didn't see you last night," Piper said, changing the subject. "What time did you get to bed?"

"I don't know," I replied. "Midnight?"

"What were you doing?"

"Practicing."

"Really?"

"Really."

I didn't feel comfortable lying to her. Then again, it wasn't a lie. I'd been practicing alright, just not in the way she thought.

Gently, I scratched my chest. My ribs were nearly healed. All that remained was a bit of light itching. But even that was enough to drive me batty.

"How about you guys?" I asked.

"I stayed up until eleven," Piper said. "I would've liked more sleep, but I had to finish the reading assignment."

Leandra looked up just long enough to chuckle. "Finish it? You told me you read it twice."

"Well, how else am I supposed to remember it?" she replied, defensively.

"It's just busy work."

"Tell that to the kids who got cursed today."

"If you think reading a book will help you do havoc magic, then you've truly lost it."

"It's not just that." Piper frowned. "This is our big chance, Leandra. Randy sees that. Why can't you?"

"Hang on a second," I said. "What do you mean this is our big chance?"

"This class is our path back into Madkey," she replied. "You know that. That's why you're practicing so much."

"That's not why I'm practicing."

She frowned. "It's not?"

"I'm practicing because I'm sick of losing," I told her. "Just once, I'd like to put Porter and the others on their backs."

"Now, that's a cause I can get behind," Leandra said.

Piper stared deep into my eyes. "What's up with you?"

"What do you mean?"

"You've been acting really weird lately."

I had good reason to be acting weird, but I wasn't ready to tell her about it. So, I sought around for an alternative explanation. "My parents want me out of here," I replied at last. "They're threatening to enroll me at YuckYuck."

Piper's face turned sorrowful. "You can't leave. It won't be the same without you."

Despite my revelation, Leandra remained quiet, her attention focused on her lap. A quick glimpse revealed a sizable mirror resting upon her legs. It looked a little like a memory mirror. However, the remembra was rather warped compared to that of a normal memory mirror.

"What's that?" I asked, eager to change the subject to something else.

"A simulator mirror," she replied.

I stifled another yawn. I'd only gotten a few hours of sleep before I had to wake up for my shift. So, I was pretty exhausted. "A what?" I asked.

"A simulator mirror. It's like a memory mirror, but, you know, different."

I arched an eyebrow. "Okay …"

She sighed, then looked up. "A normal memory mirror takes possession of a memory, capturing all relevant sensory information. Then it replays the memory upon eye contact. The effect is to make the watcher feel as if she's seeing the memory in real-time."

"I know how they work," I said impatiently.

"Awhile back, I had an idea. What if the watcher didn't just observe the memory? What if she was able to participate in it?"

Piper arched an eyebrow. "Come again?"

"You know how memory mirrors can be tricked into accepting false memories?"

I recalled her memory mirror back in the dorm. The one that showed Tad getting a doughcream surprise.

"Of course," I replied.

"I'm trying to create something that not only lets you see a false memory, but actively participate in it as well."

"That's possible?"

"I think so."

Piper ran a hand through her hair, in a hopeless attempt to smooth out the frizz. "How?"

"It's kind of hard to explain. But the idea is to let the watcher do things. To let her change parts of the simulation as well as be impacted by what she experiences."

"What if someone does something completely unexpected?" I asked. "Something the mirror couldn't possibly see coming?"

"Then the simulation ends." She shrugged. "But it's easier than you might think to keep a person engaged."

"That's amazing," Piper said. "How come you never told us about it?"

"Because it's not done yet."

"You must've been working on it for a long time," I said.

"A couple of years," she replied like it was no big deal. "I did most of the work before I came here."

"Is that why you dropped out? Because you wanted to finish it?"

"Nope. But it's given me more time to work on it."

"What are you going to do with it once it's done?"

"Sell it. Hopefully, for enough money to get my folks back on their feet." She smiled. "There's loads of potential. Take this class, for instance. With simulator mirrors, we wouldn't need to fight in a lousy HMQ. We could train on any terrain and under any conditions. And rather than silly games, we could practice real missions. Like rescuing friends or fighting great magicians."

A hush came over the crowd. A couple of kids jumped to their feet. Looking around, I saw everyone swivel toward the locker rooms. Naturally, I followed suit.

Nearly the entire faculty stood at the edge of the field. They were dressed in their finest attire and carried themselves with solemn purpose. Boltstar, derby in place, stood before them. His back was ramrod straight and he clutched his wand in an outstretched hand.

Silently, he waved the wand and white sparks soared into the air. The faculty members stepped to either side, forming an aisle that led back to the locker rooms. A couple of figures appeared within the aisle. Squinting, I saw Galison and Wadflow. Sandwiched between them was Ivan Gully.

"That's him, right?" Leandra's eyes widened. "The Chaotic from this morning?"

I nodded.

"What's he doing here?" Piper wondered.

A couple of faculty members stepped away from the others. They swept their wands in quick, flourishing movements. The sounds of instruments—trumpets, drums, and horns—filled the air.

Tucking his wand under his armpit, Boltstar strode toward us. Galison and Wadflow prodded Ivan along after him. The Chaotic looked considerably more polished than he'd appeared that morning. He wore fine silk slacks and neatly polished shoes. A dress shirt, sans tie, covered his washed, gaunt frame. Staring hard, I saw his eyes were clear and focused. His jaw looked strong and defiant. Despite the fact that his right arm was in a sling, he appeared ready to fight at a moment's notice.

The faculty fell in line. Silently, the procession marched to the middle of the HMQ. Boltstar waved his wand again, emitting yet another brilliant shower of blazing white sparks. The music stopped. Faculty members streamed into the bleachers and took seats in the upper levels.

Galison and Wadflow spread out on either side of Ivan. Boltstar, meanwhile, gave us a sweeping, contemplative look.

"Good evening, everyone," he said. "Before I begin, I'd like to ask all of you to please excuse my tardiness, the reason for which will become apparent shortly."

Piper cocked a quizzical look at me. *What the heck is going on?* she mouthed.

I wasn't sure. But it had to be big. It wasn't every day the faculty got together in one place, let alone with such pomp and solemnity.

Boltstar's shirt was smooth and unrumpled. His cheeks looked healthy and his eyes were filled with light. Turning sideways, he cast a long look at Ivan. Then he turned back to the crowd. "This is Mr. Ivan Gully. Mr. Gully is a confessed Chaotic magician. One week ago, he attacked this fine institution of ours without cause or provocation. He escaped custody shortly afterward, only to attack us again this very morning."

Angry faces appeared all around me.

"As all of you know," he continued, "the Roderick J. Madkey School of Magical Administration is a self-governing entity. And our laws strictly forbid sedition or other actions designed to overthrow the existing administration. As headmaster, it's my responsibility to make sure these laws are followed. If someone chooses to break them, it's my duty to mete out an appropriate punishment. After much thought, I've reached several decisions on Mr. Gully's future."

All around me, students inched forward in their seats. Their jaws were set. Their eyes burned with anger. They didn't want justice. They wanted revenge. Revenge for the two attacks, of course. But also, revenge for their fear, for their lost innocence.

Boltstar turned toward Ivan. "After careful consideration, I find you, Mr. Ivan Gully, guilty of sedition, the usage of non-sanctioned magic, and injurious actions to Madkey magicians as well as school property."

I held my breath. What kind of punishment would he receive? An extended stint at Gutlore? Maybe hard labor?

"Since you and your fellow conspirators refrained from killing anyone, I've decided against the death penalty. However, your actions still merit a stern response. Thus, I've decided to skin you of your magic."

The faculty remained stone-faced. But judging from the reactions, pretty much everyone else was caught by surprise.

Eyes wrenched open. Jaws dropped and dangled in mid-air. There were a few cruel smiles, too.

I shuddered under my breath. Magic-skinning was a particularly heinous punishment. Not only did victims lose their ability to do magic, they also lost a part of their souls. Specifically, the part that was emotional and artistic. They became little more than joyless shells, permanently detached from the rest of the magic community.

"Upon completion of the skinning ceremony, you will be transferred to Gutlore Penitentiary," Boltstar continued. "You will spend the rest of your life there, isolated and despised by all right-thinking magicians."

Someone, I think it was Felicia, started to applaud. Others joined in and the noise turned thunderous. Tara

DuBois whistled. Tom Foundry hooted. Even Piper and Leandra got in on the excitement with some light clapping.

Cheers ended. A chant rang out, loud and clear. It started in the field, amongst the faculty members. Quickly, it spread to the bleachers.

"Struc-tur-al-ize," Madkey chanted as one. "Struc-tur-al-ize. Struc-tur-al-ize. Struc-tur-al-ize."

The occasion felt, well, oddly joyous. But I didn't feel a whole lot of joy. Oh, I screwed my face into a smile and pretended to clap with enthusiasm. But deep down, I felt conflicted.

Yes, he'd invaded our school. And yes, he'd used illegal magic, hurting people in the process. But if he could be skinned, then the same thing could happen to Tad. And that didn't seem quite right to me.

Boltstar adopted the gravest of visages. "As is my discretion, I've decided to carry out the first part of your punishment here, in front of the very institution you attempted to destroy. May your name be forgotten from this day forward and all through the annals of time so that those you love and that love you in turn may be spared your everlasting shame."

I had to give Ivan credit. He didn't try to run or call for mercy. Instead, he stood tall, a steely, unreadable expression plastered across his face.

Boltstar's wand raced through a series of complicated, dazzling, spark-inducing movements. His lips mashed together as he repeated unmentionable incantations.

A sharp jet of cyan light slammed into Ivan's chest. His lip trembled. For a split-second, he fought to control his emotions. Then he reared back and screamed.

Magenta light began to pour out of his mouth, his ears, his nostrils. It came slowly at first, but soon sped up. The boy's voice rose in pitch until he was almost shrieking.

With a soft pop, the magenta light broke free of Ivan's body. He collapsed into a heap, weakened but still conscious.

Breathless, I watched this odd-shaped bubble of skinned magic float in mid-air. It frothed and lurched from side to side, as if searching for a place to call its own. It reminded me of a lost child, frightened and trying to find its parent.

Still whispering words, Boltstar waved his wand. A cyan glow flooded out of his wand. He spoke faster and faster, working himself into a small frenzy.

The glow quickly surrounded the bubble. Then it reversed course. Slowly, it vanished back into Boltstar's wand, reeling the magenta bubble along after it. The bubble grew, well, panicky from the looks of it. It fought hard to escape and I couldn't help but feel a little sorry for it.

But Boltstar was relentless. With some wrangling, he managed to bring the skinned magic close. Then he whipped his arm and the magenta bubble vanished into his wand.

I released a long breath. I'd never seen someone skinned of magic before. It was just as horrible as I'd imagined. Actually, it was even worse than that. The skinned magic had looked so frightened, so unwilling to go with Boltstar. At the same time, one look at Ivan's dead eyes and pale, sweaty skin was enough to fuel a lifetime of nightmares.

"What does this mean?" Leandra whispered, her voice uncharacteristically shaky. "Does Boltstar have, like, his memories and thoughts?"

Piper shook her head. "No, just his magic. Technically, he's capable of doing any spell Ivan could do."

"But he'd never do Chaotic magic."

"Of course not. But he could if he wanted to." She paused. "As for Ivan, well, he's lost his magic."

"It's not just that," I said, my voice cracking at the seams. "He's lost his soul, too."

"That's just an old-wives' tale," Piper claimed.

"Yeah? Look into his eyes and tell me what you see."

We looked at Ivan. Even from this distance, we could see that his eyes were dull and listless. It was almost as if a light had gone out inside of him.

"Magic isn't just a part of us," I said. "It's who we are. You can't rip it away and expect that everything's going to be hunky-dory."

"It's finished." Boltstar looked refreshed, which was no surprise given that he'd just received a magic transfusion. "Please take Mr. Gully back to his cell and prepare him for transfer to Gutlore."

Gutlore's exact location was a secret and thus, nobody knew much about it. What kind of people worked there anyway? Were they even people? Or were they something else?

Galison and Wadflow hauled Ivan to his feet. The faculty stood up. Seeing this, the students and staffers followed suit. I was the last to stand, but not because I was trying to make some kind of statement. Rather, I was too stunned to do much of anything at the moment.

"That concludes the skinning ceremony, ladies and gentlemen," Boltstar said. "The faculty is hereby excused."

Galison and Wadflow took Ivan back to the locker room area. Meanwhile, the faculty exited the arena.

"Before we begin class, I have two announcements." Boltstar turned to face us. "First, all outside activities, games, and sports are cancelled for the remainder of the school year. This, of course, includes ramball."

Jaws dropped throughout the arena.

"While unfortunate, this is a necessary measure until we get a better handle on the Chaotic problem. Rest assured I will do whatever it takes to keep this school safe." His eyes were hooded and dark. His voice carried the tiniest bit of menace to it, a detail that cut to my core. "If that means skinning more magicians—invaders and traitors alike—then so be it."

CHAPTER 27

Grass green light, nearly impossible to see on the HMQ field, zoomed over my shoulder. Picking up speed, I rounded a corner. I was moving fast and with good agility. Unfortunately, the same couldn't be said for my wand work.

After the magic-skinning ceremony, Boltstar had led us through a long—and rather boring—lecture. We'd covered the previous night's reading assignment and had even been forced to take a pop quiz. He'd told us it was meaningless, something to help chart our progress thus far. I hoped that was true, seeing as how I'd almost certainly failed it.

We'd spent some time in practice duels. Then, under Boltstar's direction, we'd fought a couple of Havoc Royal matches. Kell, enraged by the ramball news, won most of them. But Porter took one, too. Regardless, I'd gotten knocked out early in every single game. Now, it was almost quitting time and I was in danger of yet another early elimination.

Sprinting around some metal barrels, I caught sight of Ophelia Wepper. Her back was to me. She was on her haunches, her gaze directed at a group of sophomores.

It was almost too easy and right away, I suspected a trap. But when I whirled around, there was nobody there.

Ducking down, I fought to get my emotions under control. Then I lifted my wand and took a deep breath.

I swept the instrument through its required motions. My lips began to speak the necessary incantation. And then the comforting embrace of Instinctia took over. It grabbed hold of my emotions, my hand, my lips. It felt utterly amazing.

At that exact moment, I sensed a small voice deep within me. It called out, telling me to forget the spell, to let my magic free. But the voice was quickly drowned out by the all-powerful force of Instinctia.

"Elertfa Lokwhan," I said.

An auburn flash zoomed out of my wand. It hit a small box next to Ophelia's head, blasting it right off of a stack of barrels. She gave me a surprised look, then fired off a spell of her own. I leapt out of the way, barely dodging it. When I looked again, she was gone.

"Come on, Mr. Wolf!" Boltstar called out. "You look terrible out there."

In previous classes, Boltstar had displayed the persona of a tough, but fair instructor. However, a different side of him had emerged that night, presumably due to the Ivan incident. The moment we stepped onto the HMQ, he became harsh and ruthless, with little to no patience for imperfection.

He was hard on the students. But he treated us staffers with almost utter disdain. Piper thought it was a case of headmaster bias. That is, he preferred people who stayed in school over those of us who'd been unable to handle it. But Leandra and I believed it was because he cared only about results. And so far, the students had outclassed us at every turn.

A bright, multi-colored glare caught my eye. Panicking, I slid behind a large sign, which was embedded deep into the ground. Loud blasts sounded out as the spells struck metal. I stayed low, eyes wide, as the sign bent and crinkled under the onslaught.

The sign dented one more time, then all went still. Breathing hard, I got my first good look at it. A painting of the elusive jackalope, peeling heavily, adorned the surface. In big block letters, somebody had written, *Jackalopes Rule. Others Drool.* Ahh, how clever.

I peeked over the top of the sign. Almost immediately, a blaze of chestnut—Porter's color—shot my way. I was so startled, I didn't even move.

The spell soared past my ear, missing it by mere inches. More chestnut beams followed in quick succession. This time, I ducked and the spells flew overhead.

"Quit hiding and fight, Mr. Wolf," Boltstar growled.

I wasn't sure what was worse. The prospect of getting knocked out by Porter again or Boltstar's constant complaints about my subpar performance.

I crawled through the short grass like a snake. Felicia cut about twenty feet in front of me and ducked down behind some empty cases of … was that bizzlum? I looked closer. Yup, that was Casafortro's bizzlum label, alright.

I ginned up new emotions and locked them into place. But as I waved my wand, I spotted a glint of chestnut.

My feelings shifted into a different combination. My wand glided through a sudden range of motions and I achieved Instinctia.

"Pobyl Caxtor," my lips called out.

An auburn spell exploded out of my wand. It zoomed across the HMQ and crashed into Porter's spell. The two lights blinked out in a puff of smoke.

My confidence soared like a rocket. That was my second havoc magic spell in the same number of minutes. Even better, it was completely unplanned. Maybe I was starting to get the hang of these new spells.

"Excellent attack, Mr. Garrington," Boltstar called out. "Mr. Wolf had luck on his side. You'll get him next time."

Instantly, my ego deflated. Just then, a powerful flare, chestnut of course, hit my side. I spun around in a half-circle, then pitched to the ground. My jaw slammed into the field and I got a mouthful of soil and grass.

"You're out, Mr. Wolf," Boltstar shouted. "Again. Please exit the HMQ."

I dragged myself to the magic rope and rolled under it. Over a hundred kids had been sent to the bleachers ahead of me, so I wasn't entirely discouraged. On the other hand, hundreds of kids were still on the HMQ, still running, still fighting.

I checked the clock. It was almost eight. Scanning the bleachers, I saw Leandra sitting in her usual seat. Her gaze was focused on her lap and I assumed she was working on her simulator mirror. Piper, textbook in hand, sat in front of her. She was reading intently, as if the book could help her get a step up on the competition.

I ascended the stairs. They didn't even look up as I grabbed my backpack. Quickly, I headed for the exit. Right before leaving, I heard a soft crash.

"Excellent shot, Mr. Garrington," Boltstar called out. "You, too, Mr. Masters. Both of you are turning into fine havoc magicians. In fact—"

I didn't hear the rest.

I was already out the door.

CHAPTER 28

"He did *what*?"

I knew Tad was looking at me, but I couldn't bring myself to return the gaze. "He skinned Ivan."

He dropped the chicken salad sandwich I'd picked up for him. Lifting the small jug of canfee—Death-Defying Escape—he poured himself a drink.

"Wow," he said at last. "I just ... wow."

Quickly, I filled him in on everything that had happened that day, from Ivan's appearance in Torso all the way up to the skinning ceremony. "Boltstar said he was guilty of sedition and illegal magic," I finished. "Plus, injurious actions to others."

"What a load of garbage." He itched his shoulder. He was still scratching, but not nearly as much as the previous week. "Ivan's a good guy. He deserved better."

I forced myself to look at Tad. He still bothered me in a way I found difficult to define. At the same time, I felt an odd kinship to him.

He finished his food and we moved to the middle of the room. For the next hour, I performed spell after spell. But try as I might, I couldn't deny Instinctia.

"That's enough." Disgusted, I stuffed my wand into my holster. Then I began to massage my sore, cramped fingers. I was tired from the drills. Plus, I was exhausted and beat-up from the HMQ games. Maybe it was time to call it a night.

"Can I ask you something?" Tad asked.

"Sure."

"How often do you feel your emotions?"

I looked at him.

"Just humor me."

I shrugged. "It's not like I keep track."

"Do you use them a lot? Or a little?"

"Well, when I'm casting spells—"

"I don't mean *those* emotions. I mean *your* emotions. Your true feelings."

I frowned. "What are you getting at?"

"Chaotic magic is fueled by personal emotions. But you've spent your life living emotional lies." He paused just long enough for the revelation to sink in. "Think about it. When you cast spells, you're not feeling your own emotions. You're feeling Xavier Capsudra's emotions."

His point resonated with me on a very deep level. In order to cast a Structuralist spell, one had to memorize and duplicate Xavier's original emotions. And my job as an assembly-line magician required me to cast *a lot of spells*. Heck, I probably spent more time with Xavier's feelings than my own.

"So, what am I supposed to do?" I asked. "Get in touch with my emotions?"

"That's the idea."

"How?"

"Easy. Just do it."

"That's real helpful."

His face screwed up in thought. "What's your approach? Are you letting your emotions—your real ones—lead you? Or are you casting Xavier's spells, using his emotions?"

"The latter," I admitted. "I cast a spell I already know, then try to deny Instinctia when it occurs."

"So, try the former."

"It's not that simple."

"Sure, it is."

"Structuralist magic is just so … so …" I sought around for the right word. "… natural."

He gave me a withering look.

"No, I mean it. It comes easily to me. It's what I know."

"That will change with time." He gave me a meaningful look. "But first, you've got to let go, Randy. You've got to feel your own feelings if you want this to work."

I wasn't sure I could do that. But even if I figured it out, there was still another problem. "Let's say you're right. Let's say I let go and start to cast a Chaotic spell. I'll still have to deal with Instinctia. It'll guide me toward the closest Capsudra spell."

"Perhaps. But at least you'll be on the right track. And who knows? Maybe emotional honesty will make it easier for you to deny Instinctia."

Exhaling, I produced my wand. My eyes closed over and I cleared my head of all thoughts. I began to sense deep-rooted emotions, ones I'd been ignoring for a long time. Fear of getting caught. Admiration for Boltstar, compounded by guilt that I hadn't turned Tad over to him. Frustration over my lack of progress in Havoc Magic class. Gratefulness to Leandra and Piper for their friendship. Distrust toward Tad, tempered by the fact that I genuinely liked him.

I focused in on the bust. It was so old, so dirty. For whatever reason, this piqued my frustration.

My wand began to move. My lips pursed, ready to speak. And then Instinctia roared through me. It grabbed hold of my emotions, my wand, and my lips.

"Grundel Saiurf," I said.

A spell flew out of my wand and wrapped itself around the bust. The old object began to emit smoke.

Instinctia faded quickly, leaving me with a cold, empty feeling. Frowning, I snapped my wand back. The spell broke and the smoke dissipated in the air.

Tad glanced at me, his eyebrow arched high on his forehead. "So, what happened?"

"Grundel Saiurf is from the Capsudra," I replied. "It's a heating spell."

"But did you feel your emotions? Your real ones?"

I nodded. "But Instinctia still hijacked me."

"Let's try again."

"Can I just fabricate the emotional component for now?" I exhaled. "This is hard enough without having to worry about my feelings."

He frowned.

"They might be fake, but at least they won't come from Xavier Capsudra," I argued. "They'll be my emotions."

"Fine." He sighed. "But I'm not letting this go. Sooner or later, you'll have to depend on real emotions."

I cast spells long into the night without ever once breaking Instinctia. When the enchanted clock finally struck one in the morning, I knew it was time to call it quits.

"Okay," I said. "That's enough for tonight."

"You're doing good. Real good, Randy."

"Yeah, yeah." Holstering my wand, I started for the hatch. "See you tomorrow."

"Say, can you do me a favor?"

I felt a rising sense of irritation, which I quickly smothered. "Sure."

"Could you bring a couple of books next time? Or better yet, a memory mirror? It gets lonely during the daytime."

"I'll try."

He cocked his head. "What's wrong?"

"Nothing."

"Emotional honesty, remember?"

I exhaled, then met his gaze. "You want the truth? Well, here it is. I feel like a traitor."

"To the school? Or to Boltstar?"

"Both, I guess."

He nodded. "Anything else?"

"Yeah." I looked away. "I don't trust you."

He was quiet for a moment. "I see."

"If I'm being honest, I've never trusted you. Not really."

I expected him to look shocked or at the very least, hurt. But instead, he peered at me with no malice, no disappointment. Rather, his face was lit up like a jack o'lantern.

"I get it now," he said, his voice brimming with excitement. "I know what the problem is."

"What problem? What are you talking about?"

"I know what's keeping you from denying Instinctia, from doing Chaotic magic."

I blinked. "You do?"

"Last week, you asked me why I'd waited so long to open the conveyance station. I mentioned a secret. A secret that was at the center of everything."

"I remember. You said it was something that I wouldn't—or couldn't—believe."

He nodded. "That secret is Womigia."

I shrugged, unimpressed. "Never heard of it."

"I'd be surprised if you had. Few people know it exists, let alone that it's stored here."

"What is it? And how's it keeping me from doing Chaotic magic?"

"To answer those questions, you'll have to see it for yourself."

"But I don't even know what it is."

"You will. Now, Womigia is stored in Madkey Archive. To get there, go to the end of Right Foot. In the big toe, you'll find a plaque. A conveyance portal lies behind it." He gave me a firm look. "When you find Womigia, you'll need to remember a date ... February 1, 1930."

I frowned. "But that's Victory Day."

"Yes."

I shook my head. "Why can't you just tell me what this is all about?"

"Because seeing is believing. But fair warning ... once you see Womigia, you won't be able to unsee it."

I didn't care much for all of the secrecy. Still, I was mildly intrigued. "I'll check it out tomorrow. Right now, I need sleep."

Reaching down, I grabbed hold of the handle. With a yank, I opened the hatch wide, revealing the ladder and stone tunnel beneath me.

"One more thing," he said.

I exhaled. "What?"

"Madkey Archive is protected by a rotating trap."

"A what?"

"A rotating trap. It was installed centuries ago, long before any of us were born. It changes whenever someone tries to enter it, adjusting itself to the current period."

"Well, how do I get past it?"

"Since the trap is always different, it's impossible to say with any certainty. Regardless, it won't be easy. Heck, I was lucky to get through in one piece." He scratched his shoulder. "In other words, you're going to need help."

CHAPTER 29

"Hey, stranger." Piper took the seat next to mine. Ten minutes remained until the start of class and the bleachers were just beginning to fill up. "You weren't at lunch."

"I wanted to get in a little extra practice." That, of course, was a lie. In-between shifts, I'd hustled down to Right Foot and got the lay of the land. Since it allowed access to the outside picnic area, it saw some decent lunch traffic. But that was it. Not a single soul had ventured all the way down to the toes.

"Did you do the reading assignment?"

"I, uh, well ..." I stammered.

"Relax." With a little grin, she nodded at the copy of *Havoc Magic: A Bare-Bones Treatise*, which rested in my lap. The spine was perfect, utterly uncracked. "I'm just giving you a hard time."

I chuckled.

"You look famished. Did you eat?"

My stomach growled and I shook my head. Oh, I'd grabbed breakfast, alright. Some fruit and pastries, to be specific. But I'd skipped lunch altogether.

She frowned. "You really shouldn't skip meals, Randy."

"I'll make up for it at dinner."

Reaching into her bag, she brought out a sandwich, wrapped in wax paper. Her smile turned dazzling. "Why wait?"

My eyes opened wide. I took the package from her and unwrapped a corner. It was a bagel sandwich, dripping with mayonnaise and mustard and piled high with turkey, bacon, cheddar cheese, lettuce, and fresh tomatoes. It smelled so good I thought I'd faint right there on the spot.

"Thanks," I mumbled, shoving the food into my mouth.

"No problem. And sorry it's not fresh. I didn't feel like bringing a tray with me."

"Hey, guys." Leandra took the seat directly behind Piper. Digging into her bag, she took out her simulator mirror. "What's new?"

"I've been reading. Randy's been sneaking away to practice." Piper shrugged. "So, it's the same old, same old."

"Yeah? Are you two going to crush the HMQ today?"

I took a giant bite of sandwich and paused, enjoying the food. "I'll be happy if I get a couple of spells off."

Leandra gave the locker room area a furtive look. "So, what's on the agenda for today? Another skinning?"

Piper made a face. "I don't think I can stomach another one."

"I could watch them all day." Hiking up the steps, Nico joined our little group. "There's nothing better than seeing a Chaotic squirm."

I'd been gearing up to ask Leandra and Piper for their help with entering the archive. But Nico's presence now made that impossible.

"Have any of you guys seen Hannah?" he asked. "I was supposed to walk her to class, only she never showed."

Piper shrugged. "Not me."

"Me either," I said.

He sighed. "Okay. Thanks anyway."

"You were going to walk her to class?" Leandra frowned. "Why? You don't like her, do you?"

"No. Well, maybe." He sighed again. "I'd like to get to know her, I guess. She's a real nice person."

"And a real looker, too, right?"

He blushed.

"Trust me, you're better off without her." Leandra went back to her simulator mirror. "Hannah's the worst."

"She's not that bad," Piper protested.

"No, it's okay. It's actually kind of true. She treated me like a servant from the moment I met her. Now, she barely talks to me." He shrugged. "Life of a staffer, right?"

We nodded in unison. We'd been there so we knew what he was talking about. Students and staffers just didn't mix. Oh, I'd tried to keep up my friendships after dropping out of school. But my old friends just blew me off. It was like they didn't want to be tainted by my failure.

Piper nodded at the field. "Speaking of Hannah …"

She appeared, gliding across the grass with undeniable grace. Kell, dressed in an old chupacabra shirt, was right beside her, a sly smile on his visage. Yup, Kell Masters, ramball star, seemed to have the hots for Hannah. And she flirted right back with him.

"Kell?" Nico made a cross face. "What's he got that I don't have?"

"Awful breath for one thing," Leandra remarked, her nose buried in her simulator mirror. "He tried to talk to me once and all I wanted was for him to shut his mouth."

That cheered Nico right up. "I'm going to say 'Hi,'" he said. "I'll be back in a minute."

Rising to his feet, he proceeded to gallop down the stairs. He ran out to greet Hannah. She didn't seem to mind the attention. In fact, she openly flirted with him, which drew a sour look from Kell.

"He's fooling himself," Leandra said without looking up. "She'll never date a staffer."

I devoured the rest of the sandwich, then stuffed the wax paper into my pocket. A few minutes later, Headmaster Boltstar walked out of the locker room area.

With perfect posture and the kind of confidence money can't buy, he hiked across the field. Climbing onto the wall, he waited for everyone to take their seats.

Half-heartedly, I listened to his lecture, doodling all the while so that it looked like I was paying attention. Afterward, we discussed the reading assignment and split off into pairs for practice duels.

We still only knew the two spells we'd learned on the first day of class. A couple of students had begged Boltstar for more magic. However, he preferred we master the old spells first.

The dueling progressed without incident for about twenty minutes. Finally, Boltstar cleared his throat. "It's time to put your skills to the test. Everyone, please head to the HMQ."

Leandra, who'd been dueling nearby, joined up with me. Adopting a slow pace, we hiked across the field.

"Come on, guys." Piper clapped us on the back. "What do you say we go show everyone how we do havoc magic?"

"You mean poorly?" I asked.

"Ouch." Leandra winced at Piper's touch. "Felicia nailed my back two days ago and it still stings."

Piper frowned. "Come on, guys. Get excited."

"For what?" I wondered. "Another thrashing?"

"This could be our day, you know."

"Yeah," Leandra quipped. "Our day to get crushed."

"Again," I added.

Laughing, we entered the HMQ. It felt good to laugh, even if only for a short while. It reminded me of how much they meant to me. I knew there was no one else I'd want by my side when I faced the archive's rotating trap.

"Today, we're going to start with a basic Havoc Royal match," Boltstar announced once everyone had entered the HMQ. "The rules are the same as always. Attack anyone and everyone and make sure to defend yourself at all times. The last person standing wins the game."

Wordlessly, the staffers gathered on one end of the HMQ. Meanwhile, the students split up by grade and went to other parts of the quadrant.

Thus far, our HMQ training had consisted entirely of Havoc Royals. And those Havoc Royals had begun to develop a pattern. Us staffers huddled together while the students separated off by grade. Once the game started, the students turned our way. They rained spells down upon us, picking us off with brute force. When our numbers began to dwindle, they'd turn on each other. Then it was all-out war.

I saw the value in HMQ training. It was intense. And even though I wasn't much of a havoc magician, I knew I was getting faster and stronger.

"Ready?" Boltstar called out. "Go!"

Right away, Jenny took a gunmetal gray spell to the face. With a soft groan, she melted to the ground. Meanwhile, the rest of us hunkered down behind a string of enchanted barriers.

"Cripes," Jax shouted. "That was way too fast."

"Yeah," Nico said sullenly. "It's almost as if they don't like us or something."

"Off the field, Ms. Lynch," Boltstar called out. "And staffers, please get your heads into the game. You look like a bunch of fools out there."

"I hate that man," Leandra said. "So much."

"You and me both." Steeling his jaw, Nico slid to the end of a barrier. He started lobbing Elertfa spells out into the open, forcing the Sophomores to take cover. The rest of us spread out and followed his lead. This was our normal strategy. We couldn't defeat all four grades by ourselves. So, we sought to repel the attackers long enough for them to turn on each other. It was a decent strategy considering the rules of the game. But I had my doubts about its real-life practicality.

Elertfa spells kept coming. We stayed low and didn't bother with deflections. Pobyl Caxtor was a good spell, but it wasn't much use against a barrage. So, instead we stuck to our game plan, throwing off just enough Elertfa spells of our own to keep the students from overrunning us.

Swishing clothes and pounding footsteps caught my attention. Peeking over the barrier, I saw Sya fall to the ground, then slide across the grass on her back. Her attacker, Calvin Hayes, raced behind a stack of lashed-down floating trays before the other freshmen could respond.

"A strong effort, Ms. Moren," Boltstar called out. "But unfortunately, you're out."

"Sorry, Ms. Moren," Leandra muttered, mimicking Boltstar. "It's sooo terrible that you're out. I just adore you and the other students."

Leandra, Piper, and I snickered. I still admired the heck out of Boltstar. But it wasn't like the students needed his encouragement. They were already outperforming us in every conceivable way.

"That was Hayes," Porter snapped. "Focus your spells on the Sophomores until he's gone."

Radiant streaks filled the air as the two grades duked it out. Gordon took a mauve spell to the gut, but managed to stay on his feet. Stumbling away, he shot a spell over his shoulder. It struck Liza Raico's belly, scorching her t-shirt and causing her to drop to all fours.

Spells started to fly between the Juniors and the Seniors. Alliances quickly broke down and the four grades, along with us staffers, began fighting in all directions at once.

I'd made it this far. But to make it much farther would require a miracle. Keeping low, I manipulated my emotions into place. Pursing my lips, I began to move my wand. I felt Instinctia take control and my body threw out a pair of spells. Twin auburn jets raced across the field. One streak sent Charlie Ridges to his knees. The other one narrowly missed his classmate, Posey Unydo.

I blinked, shocked by my success. It normally took me at least a dozen tries to correctly fire an Elertfa spell. Even better, Charlie was my very first elimination.

"Tough break, Mr. Ridges," Boltstar shouted from the bleachers. "Don't take it too hard ... it was a lucky shot. Oh, and excellent footwork, Ms. Unydo. You're doing great out there."

Sheesh. I couldn't even eliminate someone without a dose of veiled criticism.

Piper, red-faced, rose up from behind our barrier. Angrily, she unleashed a couple of spells. Right away, I knew she wasn't thinking straight.

She was kind of a mixed-bag when it came to HMQ sessions. On one hand, she was a good strategist and knew how to take advantage of the terrain. On the other hand, she lacked aggression. More than once, I'd seen her shy away from making a big hit, only to get knocked out in return. Mercy might've had its advantages, but not in the HMQ.

I grabbed for her leg, intending to pull her out of harm's way. But a spell caught her in the shoulder first. The impact sent her airborne and she did a half-twist in mid-air. It actually looked kind of graceful.

Until she landed on her face.

"That was awful, Ms. Shaw," Boltstar bellowed. "Please leave the field before you embarrass yourself any further. And Mr. Wolf, where were you on that one? Why didn't you back her up?"

Leandra got off two quick spells, then ducked down next to me. "Where were you, Mr. Wolf?" she quipped, mimicking the headmaster's voice. "Why are you so terrible at everything, Mr. Wolf?"

I grinned. "Why can't you save everyone and stop everyone, too, Mr. Wolf?"

She howled with laughter.

"Get it together, Ms. Chen," Boltstar hollered. "The only thing worth laughing at around here is your performance."

More people fell victim to Elertfa spells. With few easy targets left, the grades began to turn on their own.

Checking on Piper, I saw she'd made it to the sidelines. Then I shared a look with Leandra. We rarely made it this far and thus, had no real plan to keep going. She flashed me a hand signal, then hopped the barrier. Swiftly, she headed toward a partially-overturned table. I went in the opposite direction, taking cover behind a pair of lockers.

I snuck a glimpse at the field. I saw plenty of kids locked in individual duels. No one seemed to be looking my way so I slid out from behind the lockers. A bolt of iris caught my attention. My emotions shifted all at once. My wand twirled. My mouth opened wide.

A tingling sensation coursed through my veins as I entered Instinctia. My emotions lined up perfectly. My hand became foreign to me, a slave of the Capsudra. My lips moved as if I was a puppet on strings.

"Pobyl Caxtor," I said.

An auburn glint left my wand and smacked into the iris bolt. They vanished in a bit of smoke.

"Nice try, Ms. Tuck." Boltstar cupped his hands around his mouth. "Your Elertfa spell is definitely improving. You'll get him next time."

I caught sight of Daisy Tuck. Already, she was maneuvering for another attack.

Prepping my emotions, I whipped my wand in a well-practiced sequence. With the spell on the tip of my tongue, I opened my mouth.

The familiar tingling sensation shot through my veins as I entered Instinctia. My emotions slid out of my control, lining themselves up with the Capsudra's demands. My hand moved fast. My lips even faster. At least that's what I think happened. It's hard to know for sure because at that very moment a substantial force hit my belly.

I groaned and my stomach muscles tightened on reflex. And then I was on the grass and in agony. I ached all over. Even my teeth hurt.

"Excellent spell, Ms. Tuck. I told you that you'd get him next time." Boltstar's head shifted toward me. "That's it, Mr. Wolf. Please exit the HMQ immediately."

Painfully, I rose to my knees. As I crawled off the field, I felt a sense of deep dissatisfaction well up inside of me. My best performance yet and I was still just a punching bag for the students.

"You're out, Ms. Chen." Boltstar exhaled. "That wasn't bad … for you. Now, please exit the field."

I waited for Leandra just outside the magic rope. Piper had found a spot of grass to sit upon so we made our way toward her.

Leandra flopped onto the ground. "How long is this class going to last anyway?" she groused.

Piper touched her shoulder and winced. "The rest of the quarter, at least. If we survive that long."

As they lapsed into silence, I screwed up my courage. I knew that taking them to the archive would be dangerous. But like it or not, I needed them.

"I need your help," I said softly, my gaze flicking back and forth between them.

I expected Leandra to crack a joke. But instead, she studied my face, then furrowed her brow. "With what?"

"I can't tell you."

They exchanged curious looks.

"You should know it could get you into trouble. Maybe even kicked out of Madkey for good."

They sat in silence for a few seconds. Then Piper cleared her throat. "Is it important?"

"Very."

"Then we're in."

CHAPTER 30

"I've never been here before," Piper whispered as we slipped down the big toe hallway of Right Foot. "What's it used for?"

"Nothing," I replied. "At least on the surface."

We continued to creep down the tube-like hallway, all the way to where Tad and MacPherson had fought. At the very end of the toe, I laid eyes on a small plaque. During my previous visit, I'd paid it little attention. But now, I studied it in earnest.

"There's nothing here," Leandra said, looking around. "Just that plaque."

Piper leaned closer to the metallic slab. "This institution is dedicated to the great Roderick J. Madkey, esteemed wizard and friend to one and all," she read aloud. Then she rubbed her chin, deep in thought. "It's dated March 1747. It's amazing to think this place is still standing on its original foundations. These days, you're lucky if an enchanted building lasts a decade."

"That's great," Leandra said, clearly disinterested. "So, is this it, Randy? You dragged us all the way down here just to look at some old plaque?"

"Yes." I grabbed one end of the metal slab and gave it a tug. Noisily, it slid across the stone, revealing a swirling bundle of brightly-lit magic. "And no."

"A conveyance portal?" Piper's eyes sparkled with curiosity. "How'd you find it?"

Tad had told me what to expect. Still, I couldn't help but feel a bit surprised. It wasn't every day one uncovered a secret conveyance portal.

"Someone told me about it," I said.

"Who?" Leandra asked.

"I can't tell you."

She frowned. "Well, then where does it go?"

Conveyance portals required fairly complex spells and always came in pairs. If you went in one portal, you'd come out the other one and vice versa.

"Madkey Archive," I said.

Piper blinked. "Madkey has an archive?"

I stared at the swirling, churning portal, too entranced to answer her question. "I'm going in," I announced. "Are you guys coming or not?"

They looked a little less certain now. Nevertheless, they approached the portal. We shared looks, then each of us extended a hand toward the bundled magic. It buzzed softly and suddenly, we were zipping through complete darkness.

Riding through a conveyance portal is generally a rollicking good time. The closest thing I can think of to describe it is sailing down a long, twisty water tube, only in complete darkness. Sometimes, you're flying straight as an arrow. Other times, you're tumbling around a steep curve backward and with your legs above your head. That's why we'd entered at the same time. There's nothing worse than sliding through a portal just ahead of someone else. That's a good way to get your head kicked in.

Now, you might think the amount of time one spends in a conveyance portal has everything to do with the actual distance between the two points. But you'd be wrong. As far as I've been able to determine, the length of the ride, as well as the twists and turns along the way, are random.

Abruptly, all three of us slid onto a smooth platform. With a jarring smack, we careened against each other and then bumped into a gate.

Piper was the first to get up. Groaning, she lifted her back off the ground and started to feel around in the darkness. "I think … yes, we're in a hoist."

The hoist shuddered as Leandra and I gained our feet. Then it began to descend at a slow pace. Cool-lights flicked on and I saw we were entering a large room.

"That's not an archive," Leandra said.

"No," Piper breathed. "It's a garden."

The room held a magnificent garden of such beauty and lushness that I knew magic had to be at work. The grass was green and just a bit on the long side. Trees towered overhead, their leaves letting in a cozy amount of illumination from overhanging cool-lights. A gazebo, freshly painted, sat in the middle of the garden.

Shifting my gaze to the far corner, I saw a stone platform. A fountain, spouting crystal blue water, occupied part of the platform. I also saw a small table, covered in a red-and-white checkerboard cloth. Mouth-watering goodies—fresh sandwiches, bananas, and doughcream—rested on its surface, offering up an incredible scent that couldn't be challenged. In the very back corner of the platform, I noticed a fire pit with roaring flames. Beneath it, I caught a glimpse of bright, swirling colors.

"There's another conveyance portal over there," I said with a nod.

"Will it take us to the archive?" Piper asked.

"I think so."

"Why the extra step?" Leandra wondered. "Why didn't that first portal just take us straight there?"

I was pretty sure I knew the answer to that question. And I was even more sure they wouldn't like it.

"I think this room is a trap," I said.

Leandra gave me a wide-eyed look. "A what?"

"A trap." I swallowed. "Actually, a rotating trap. It changes every time someone comes in here."

Piper frowned. "By trap, do you mean *death trap*?"

I said nothing.

"Why are we only hearing about this now?" Leandra wondered, her eyes ablaze.

Again, I had no answer.

"Terrific." Her hands met her hips. "Just terrific."

A wave of guilt swept over me. "You don't have to go any farther." I nodded at the hoist's conveyance portal. It was still there, swirling endlessly. "That should take you back to Right Foot."

"We're not leaving," Piper said. "Right, Leandra?"

She sighed. "Right."

The hoist came to a stop and the gate slid open. I took another look at the garden. If it contained a trap, it was well-concealed.

Hesitantly, I stepped off the hoist. Suddenly, the ground buckled under my weight and I began to sink into the soil. I tried to climb out, but the more I struggled, the deeper I dropped.

"Randy," Piper shouted.

I was sinking fast with no end in sight. Twisting around, I lunged for her outstretched hand. She caught hold of my fingers. Leandra grabbed my other hand. Swiftly, they wrestled me back into the hoist.

I lay there for a second, gasping for air. "Thanks," I managed. "How big was that hole anyway?"

Leandra glanced at the garden. "It's kind of hard to tell."

Catching my breath, I sat up. The grass was back in place, pristine as ever. There was no sign that I'd even set foot upon it.

Piper aimed her wand at the far platform. Her wrist shifted. Her lips moved. She stiffened up and her eyes took on a glassy appearance as Instinctia took hold. One second later, a raspberry streak burst out of her wand. It hit the platform, then blinked out of existence.

"What spell was that?" Leandra asked.

"Calfrock," she replied, referring to Calfrock Zopra, a painting spell. "Only it didn't work."

"Let me try." Leandra waved her wand and started to speak. Entering Instinctia, she threw out a spell of her own. An aureolin bolt shot forward with great promise. Then it vanished without a trace.

I frowned. "This room is magic-proof?"

"Apparently." Piper exhaled. "So, how are we supposed to get to the portal?"

A tree stood near the hoist. Its branches, wide and sturdy, extended over the garden. It would take a pretty exceptional jump to reach the gazebo. But if we could manage it, we'd be within reach of other trees. From there, we just might be able to access the platform.

"How do you feel about a little climbing?" I asked.

"Great," Leandra said. "Assuming it doesn't involve a little falling as well."

Stowing my wand in its holster, I tested the tree's roots. They felt pretty firm. Taking a deep breath, I stepped forward, putting my full weight upon them. To my relief, they didn't collapse or sink.

Feeling emboldened, I grabbed a branch. Kicking my shoes against the bark, I propelled myself up the trunk.

"How sturdy is that branch?" Piper called out.

"Pretty sturdy," I replied as I climbed atop it.

"What happens if it breaks?"

I looked around, searching for a back-up plan. But I saw nothing. If the branch broke, I'd fall to the grass. That crazy soil would take care of the rest.

"Then I guess we get free burials," I replied.

Rising to a crouch, I stepped into a crevice. Using knots and branches, I proceeded to scale the trunk until I was twenty feet off the ground. Then I crawled onto a long branch that led directly over the middle of the garden.

Meanwhile, Piper stepped to the roots. Once she was on solid footing, Leandra followed suit. As they scaled the trunk, I began to edge my way across the branch. At the halfway point, it started to sink. Rising to my feet, I took a few careful steps. But the branch was dropping way too quickly. I'd never reach the gazebo from this height.

I backtracked and the branch returned to its former height. Heart racing, I took a deep breath.

You can do this, I told myself. *Don't think. Just do it.*

Putting on a burst of speed, I darted forward. The branch started to sag so I poured on even more speed. At the last second, I leapt into the air. Arms and legs flailing, I soared toward the gazebo. My legs came up short but my upper torso smashed into its side. I felt a jolt of searing pain and air whooshed out of my lungs. Frantically, I scrabbled at the tiled roof and pulled myself on top of the structure.

"Very graceful." Leandra smirked. "A sasquatch couldn't have done it any better."

Piper giggled. I suppose I would've joined in if my chest hadn't hurt so badly.

Piper walked onto the overhanging branch. Bouncing up and down, she tested its strength. Then she sprinted forward and made the leap.

Her feet landed on the gazebo's edge. She tried to put on the brakes, but her momentum carried her forward. I braced myself. She ran into me and we collapsed in a heap.

"Whew," she said. "That was close."

Leandra was the last to make the jump. She came up a bit short, but Piper and I grabbed her clothes and yanked her onto the roof with us.

As she caught her breath, I twisted toward the platform. Colorful lawn chairs were strewn about the area along with a ramball and other summer essentials. Meanwhile, flames raged within the fire pit, partially obscuring the portal.

I approached another branch. Breaking off a few twigs, I tossed them onto the dirt. Instantly, the ground roiled and yawned open. Just like that, the twigs were gone.

I fought back an urge to panic. Gently, I tossed some twigs onto the stone platform. They bounced a few times before coming to a rest. And that was it. The stones didn't try to swallow them or spit rocks or do anything else nasty.

Feeling a little better, I hiked out onto the branch. It started to dip under my weight.

"Hey, Randy." Piper cleared her throat. "I just had a thought."

"Can it wait?"

"What if the platform employs some kind of pressure mechanism? What if the twigs were too light to set it off?"

The branch dipped and I plummeted toward the ground. My feet touched the platform and I bent low, absorbing the impact. I braced myself for something, anything.

But I was safe.

Seeing this, my companions followed me down to the platform. Almost immediately, Leandra took a whiff of the air. "That smells awesome."

Piper positively salivated. "Sure does."

From across the room, the picnic spread had looked and smelled amazing. But up close, it was absolutely stupendous. Dueling aromas of doughcream, pulled pork, and barbecue ribs filled my nostrils. It took everything I had not to march over and start eating.

We hiked to the fire pit and watched the flames crackle for a minute or so. Then I put my hands up close before quickly withdrawing them. The fire was definitely real and definitely hot.

"I guess we need to put out the flames." Leandra gave the picnic spread a fleeting look. "Any ideas?"

Grabbing an empty pitcher off of the table, Piper walked to the gurgling fountain. Carefully, she dipped it into the water.

I tensed up, waiting for something bad to happen. But everything went according to plan and a few moments later, she returned with a full pitcher. She studied the flames, then poured the liquid into the fire. The flames sizzled.

Then they exploded.

Giant, greasy bits of flame leapt out of the pit. One barely missed my shirt. Another passed between Leandra's legs and struck a lawn chair, igniting it. More bits of fire collided with the doughcream and other decadent dishes. Within seconds, the entire platform was in flames.

"Well, that's a nice how-do-you-do," Piper sputtered as we backed up against the wall. "When did water become flammable anyway?"

Just then, flames hit the fountain and it erupted into an enormous blaze. Leandra grabbed the now-empty pitcher and stuck her nose into it. She sniffed, then recoiled in disgust. "That's not water. It's bizzlum. The food must've masked the scent."

"We can't stay here," I warned.

Piper glanced at the trees. The sagging branches we'd used to cross the garden had reverted to their original positions. "Well, we can't backtrack either."

Leandra clenched her jaw. "Can't stay, can't go … that doesn't leave a whole lot of options."

"Just one, the way I see it." I took a deep breath. "We do exactly what this garden wants us to do."

She looked at me like I was crazy. "Which is?"

"We touch it."

"And get buried alive?" She shook her head. "No, thanks."

"I'm not talking about making a run for it. I'm talking about gathering dirt and using it to put out the flames."

She eyed the inferno. "That's going to take a lot of dirt."

"We don't need to put out those flames. Just the ones blocking the portal." I held up the pitcher. "I'll use this to get the dirt. I need you two to keep me from falling in again."

"I'm lighter," Piper said. "Let me handle the pitcher."

I considered that, then tossed it to her. She slid to the edge of the platform. Leandra and I grabbed her shoulders and braced ourselves.

Taking a deep breath, she plunged the pitcher into the rich, soft soil. Instantly, it gave way to a deep, crumbling pit. Caught off guard, she lurched forward. Only our steady grip kept her from falling.

She scooped up some loose dirt and we pulled her back. Hustling to the pit, she dumped the soil onto the fire.

The flames winked out. Air rushed all around us, clearing away the smoke. For a moment, we stared at the swirling bundle of magic.

"Are you sure this is a good idea?" Leandra asked.

"Would you rather stay here?" Piper wondered.

The platform fire lurched toward us. In unison, we stepped forward.

The portal buzzed softly.

And then we were gone.

CHAPTER 31

I shot down a long, formless tube, tumbling end over end, trying to keep my wits about me. Abruptly, space unfolded upon itself. An enormous crack rang out. And then I came hurtling out of the void.

I smacked into something hard and unforgiving and lost my wand. Scrambling along a curved stone floor, I grabbed hold of it. Then I looked around. I didn't see anyone. But what I did see was weirdly awesome, causing my jaw to unhinge and flap gently in the light breeze.

Piper peered up from where she lay on the floor. Her eyes grew large with wonder. "Wow."

'Wow' was right. Thanks to a decent array of cool-lights, I could see an enormous room, perfectly spherical in shape. Tall shelving racks lined the wall, following its curves from side to side as well as from floor to ceiling. Objects of all types littered the shelves. I saw crystal balls, dusty wands, the stuffed head of what I took to be a hodag, and an entire section of talismans.

Focusing in on one shelf, I saw two tall poles. An iron ball swung back and forth between them without pause. It looked like a perpetual motion device.

"It's like a museum," Leandra said, her voice full of wonder.

"It *is* a museum," Piper said. "Most of this stuff comes from way before we were born."

Not only did the objects come from before our time but I was pretty sure they pre-dated Structuralism, too. Eyes wide, I studied the strange and wonderful things dotting the room's many shelves. Many of them were a complete mystery to me. Actually, my entire generation would find them mysterious. For nearly a century, they'd laid in this room, untouched, unseen, and unstudied by modern magicians.

Now, this wasn't my first brush with Chaotics-era magic. No, that had happened months ago, back when I'd first laid eyes on the enormous, statue-shaped school. Even so, the room astounded me. What long-lost secrets did it hold? What kind of strange, unknown spells did the objects possess?

It didn't take us long to realize the floor was curved like the rest of the sphere. With a soft yelp, Leandra lost her balance and pitched backward. Fighting to stay on her feet, she surged forward. But she over-corrected and stumbled toward a towering rack of shelves. She tried to put on the brakes, but her legs got tangled up and she collided with the metal structure.

A dull thud rang out. Old ramballs, looking like they pre-dated even Madkey itself, rolled off an upper shelf. In typical ramball fashion, they fell at varying speeds.

Leandra picked herself up off the ground. Annoyed, she gave her head a good shake. Just then, one of the ramballs bounced off of her noggin.

Clunk!

Her mouth dipped open and her eyes unfocused just a little. Still standing, she stumbled to the right, then to the left, leaving her wide open for the other ramballs.

Clunk! Clunk! Clunk!

She thrashed about, waving her arms over her head. But the ramballs just kept coming, zigzagging past her outstretched hands and bumping her body. Finally, her legs gave out and she collapsed to the floor. "What ... was that?" she asked, her tone slurred with befuddlement.

It took all of my willpower not to whoop with laughter. "I think you just made some new friends."

Piper covered her mouth with her hand, biting back a wave of giggles.

Leandra's gaze steadied. Peering at the ground, she gave the ramballs a dirty look. Suddenly, she reached down and grabbed hold of one.

"Wait ..." I said, the warning dying on my lips.

"Take a deep breath," Piper advised her. "They were just having a little fun."

Ignoring us, Leandra put her face up against the ramball's chalky, pockmarked surface. "Think you're real tough, don't you?"

It squeaked in protest.

Ramball is easily the most popular sport in the magic world. It's played with ramballs, living, breathing creatures that love the game even more than we do. Setting aside the rules, one's success at the game depends on two factors. First, tremendous athletic ability. And second, a winning, extroverted personality. The sport isn't suited for introverts because it requires one to bond with the ramballs while they're attacking you. Believe me, that's not easy.

"Relax," I said slowly, keeping an eye on the other ramballs. "Just relax."

"It attacked me! And it's not going to get away with it either." Taking aim at some faraway shelves, she threw the ramball with all of her might. In fact, she threw it so hard, she spun in a complete circle, lost her balance, and fell back to the floor. "Where'd it go?" she asked weakly. "Did it hit the shelves?"

I hid a small smile. "Not exactly."

Her eyes popped as she spotted the ramball just a few feet away. Waving me off, she struggled back to her feet. "They should turn the whole lot of you into enchanted glue," she grumbled.

They quivered, which was their way of chortling. Apparently, they'd taken a liking to her. That was a good thing. The last thing we needed was a room full of pissed-off ramballs.

"Well, this place is pretty amazing." Piper spun on her heels, taking in the massive sphere. "So, why are we here?"

"We're looking for Womigia."

A strange look crossed her face. "I've heard of that."

"You have?"

"I think … yes, it was in one of my books. I just can't remember …" Her brow formed a tight ridge as she tried to recall what she'd read. Finally, she shook her head. "It was a long time ago. So, what's Womigia?"

"I don't, uh, know."

She cocked a curious eyebrow at me.

Peering up, I stared at the vastness of Madkey Archive. About three-quarters of the way to the ceiling, I spotted a massive sign. Bolted to a shelving unit, it read, *Enter Here for Womigia*.

I pointed at it. "Up there."

Her eyes followed my finger. "How do we get to it?"

I looked around, searching for a hoist or even a staircase. But all I saw were the shelving units, following the curves of the spherical room.

"We could climb," I suggested.

"Are you crazy?"

"Do you see another way?"

"No," she admitted. "But ..."

I saw the apprehension in her eyes. She and Leandra had already done way too much for me. "Take it easy," I said. "I'll be back soon."

"Not a chance." Leandra hiked toward us, booting ramballs out of her way. In response, they quivered with delight. "We didn't come this far just to get put on the bench. Right, Piper?"

She nodded. "Right."

I exhaled. "Then let's get to it."

I crossed the archive to the appropriate shelving unit. With trepidation, I traced my eyes over it. My body hurt just thinking of what lay ahead of us. Man, what I wouldn't have done for a hoist at that moment.

This far down in the sphere, the rack was nearly horizontal to the ground. Farther up, the shelves began to rise at a gentle slope, like a staircase. The rack became increasingly vertical, until the shelves resembled steps in a ladder. The really scary part was the midway point. That's when the rack began to slope backward. At the very top, the shelves faced the floor. I could see objects stowed within those shelves, lashed down by chains. How crazy was that?

I hiked the first few shelves with ease. Leandra and Piper clambered up after me. Each step caused the rack to rattle and sway. At first, it wasn't too bad. But as we gained altitude, it got worse. It felt like a single misstep could send the entire rack crashing to the floor.

Eventually, we ran out of easy steps and the rack took on a more vertical alignment. Kicking aside a mass of enchanted netting, I leapt up and grabbed hold of the next shelf. Then I kicked my left foot onto the metal and strained my muscles. Hauling my body upward, I rolled onto the platform.

I caught my breath, then helped Leandra up. We both assisted Piper. Then we moved onto the next shelf, with Leandra leading the way.

We climbed like that, one going first then helping the others, for what felt like hours. Finally, we reached the archive's midpoint.

After a brief break, I strode to the edge, took a breath, and jumped into the air. My fingers latched onto the upper shelf. With a soft grunt, I pulled myself onto it, then peered down.

"Who's next?" I asked.

"I guess I am." Piper trembled as she approached the edge. She inhaled a few times, then leapt up. Her fingers touched metal, clasping onto it. She tried to pull herself up, but the arduous climb had left her fatigued.

"A little help?" she gasped as she thrashed about, trying to pull off a miracle.

Leandra grabbed her legs, steadying her. Meanwhile, I grasped her hands and pulled, dragging her to safety. She collapsed on the shelf, jittery and red-faced. While she recovered, I helped Leandra up.

After a short breather, we went back to climbing, with Leandra and I doing most of the heavy lifting. The rack began to curve backward. The shelves started to tilt toward the floor. Ropes and chains were everywhere, helping to secure the archive's magical items from the force of gravity.

"This Womigia thing better be worth it," Piper groused as we pulled her onto yet another shelf. She tried to stand up, but the slope was too steep. So, she grabbed hold of a metal strut instead.

"Look on the bright side." Leandra tilted her head upward. "Just a few more shelves to go."

Releasing a strut, Leandra twisted around. My breath caught in my throat as she leapt upward and outward.

A soft, metallic thump filled my ears. She hung from the upper shelf for a moment. Then her legs kicked and she pulled herself out of sight.

I exhaled a big breath. For a moment there, I'd thought she was a goner.

My gaze strayed and I caught a glimpse of the floor. My head began to spin.

"Are you okay?" Piper asked.

"Yeah." I began to sway. Clutching a strut, I forced myself to remain still. "I'm fine."

"Who's next?" Leandra called out.

I looked at Piper. "Go for it."

She took a few halting footsteps toward the edge. At the last second, she twisted around. Following Leandra's lead, she jumped upward and outward. Flesh banged against metal. Her legs kicked frantically as she got pulled up.

"We're ready for you, Randy," Leandra called.

I wasn't sure I was ready. But I released my strut anyway. I took a few stumbling steps toward the jumping point. Twisting around, I surged outward and upward. My hands clanged against hard metal. My fingers burned as I clutched hold of the shelf. Leandra and Piper grabbed hold of me almost immediately, yanking me upward.

Leandra directed me toward the nearest strut and I wrapped my arms around it. I felt exhausted. How in the world were we going to make the return trip? But my negativity drained away as I caught sight of the enormous sign bolted above my head. *Enter Here for Womigia*, it read.

Adrenaline pumping, I turned around. A door was built into the back wall. A sign, etched out of well-tarnished silver, read, *Danger: Restricted Area. Authorized Wizards Only.*

Right away, I knew the sign was very old. These days, such a notice would've read, *Authorized Magicians* rather than *Authorized Wizards*. The *Enter Here for Womigia* sign looked quite old as well. It occurred to me that Womigia—whatever it was—had been kept at Madkey for a very long time.

The shelf lay at an extremely steep angle. Fortunately, there were plenty of handholds. Releasing the strut, I grabbed a chain, one of over a dozen that secured a pile of tightly-bound brooms. Hand-over-hand, I hiked to the door. Testing the knob, I discovered it was unlocked. That surprised me at first. But the more I thought about it, the more it made sense. If a magician made it this far—through the rotating trap and up the curved shelving rack—then he or she had to be authorized to enter the room.

Blinding light greeted me as I opened the door. It came from the center of the room and I was forced to shield my gaze. Even so, I caught glimpses of the enormous space. It featured vertical walls, lined with life-size statues of witches and wizards. Soft carpeting covered the horizontal floor. I stepped onto the flat surface and instantly, my calf muscles relaxed. My legs sagged and I uttered a soft, contented sigh.

Piper appeared at the threshold. Immediately, her face lit up. "Whoa," she said.

My eyes adjusted and I followed the bright light to its source. A strange pocket of energy, roughly the size of a cottage house, resided within the room. Sparks of colorful magic zoomed through it. Sometimes, the sparks ignited other sparks, which ignited still other sparks. Sometimes, sparks dimmed or died out. Other times, they gained energy and intensity.

Intrigued, I took a few steps forward. I began to notice little bits of imagery amongst the sparks. First, a spectacular ramball play, pulled off by Adelaide Ulit from the New Orleans Nightmares. It was from last year's Ramball World Championship game and I remembered it well. Next, I noticed Guy Ford, Chief Magician of the United States, speaking before a vast audience. It was his inauguration speech and I recalled watching it at home.

"These are memories," I realized.

"Memories of big moments," Leandra added. "Important moments."

Piper seemed almost in a state of shock. "I just remembered what I read about Womigia," she managed. "I know what it is."

"What?" we asked in unison.

"It's the collective memory. *Our* collective memory." Her eyes took on a faraway look. "We shape it and it shapes us."

I knew she was right. I didn't know how I knew it.

I just did.

CHAPTER 32

"Hold on." Leandra looked lost. "What's this about a collective memory?"

"It's all the memories shared by a group of people. It's all the stuff we *know* to be true." Piper looked excited enough to burst. "For instance, we *know* that the Farwads enslaved the witches and that the witches fought the Freedom War to throw off their shackles. None of us were actually there, but we still know about it through books and plays, memory mirrors and oral history. We visit the memorials and celebrate the holiday. Little girls dress up like Rose Derfon and play-act her famous duels. We still say the Witches Creed when faced with extreme sexism and oppression."

Leandra waved a hand at Womigia. "So, those little sparks flying all over the place ...?"

"Memories. Powerful ones. Powerful enough to make it into the collective memory." She rubbed her jaw, deep in thought. "These are the memories we share, the ones that bind us together. They give us an identity, a sense of community. Without them, the magic world as we know it would cease to exist."

"So, this is what we came to see?" Leandra glanced at me. "Don't get me wrong. It's definitely interesting. But what's it got to do with us?"

A glimpse of odd light caught my eye and I tore my gaze from the interior. An object—a long, thin mirror—was embedded into Womigia's surface. The frame was made of gold and adorned with ornate decorations. The glass was wavy, like a churning sea.

The mirror's base was inscribed with ornate lettering. Rising to my tiptoes, I gave it a quick look.

Boris Hynor, the inscription read. *April 17, 1928 speech entitled, The Right to Perform Chaotic Magic. Given at the Magical Structuralism Society. Removed from Womigia on February 1, 1930.*

Tad was related to the Hynor family. But beyond that, the mirror was a mystery. Why had this speech been removed from the collective memory? And how was that even possible?

Cautiously, I peered into the mirror. The glassy surface twisted, turned, and churned before my eyes. Then I saw a rather tall man with dark brown skin, dressed in a silk jacket and matching breeches. A knee-length coat and buckled shoes topped off the ensemble. He stood before a seated audience of men and women. The image was normal enough. And yet it had a strange color scheme to it that made it look rather old.

"Good evening, lords and ladies," Boris said. At least I thought it was Boris and I was pretty sure that's what he said. Unfortunately, he wasn't wearing a name tag. As for his words, the guy's voice was scratchy and difficult to hear. "My name, as you well know, is Boris Hynor. Today, I wish to discuss the most basic building block of all. The fundamental right that gives rise to this wondrous society of ours. That is, of course, the right to perform Chaotic magic."

The mirror began to impact my other senses. I tasted sawdust on my tongue. The air smelled of perspiration and barely-contained body odor. Wrenching humidity caused sweat to dribble down my cheeks.

"Since the dawn of civilization, magicians far and wide have sought to push the boundaries of magic. And they—"

"Liar!" a woman cried out. "Deceiver!"

"Struc-tur-al-ize," another voice chanted. "Struc-tur-al-ize. Struc-tur-al-ize. Struc-tur-al-ize."

Others joined in and the chant gained volume.

A man jumped to his feet. "Leave, villain," he shouted, jabbing a finger at Boris. "Your magic has no place here."

Lines formed on Boris' forehead as he leaned over the podium. "Please sit down, Sir."

The man went for his wand. People seated nearby cleared away. Others exchanged frightened glances. Even so, the *Struc-tur-al-ize* chant grew louder and louder.

Boris produced a wand from inside his coat. "You may attack me all you like, friend," he said. "But do it with your words, not your wand."

The man paid him no heed. "So, you like Chaotic magic, do you? Then you should enjoy this!"

The chant faded away. Everyone was on their feet now, backing away as quickly as their stuffy outfits would allow.

The man waved his wand. "Ventham," he shouted.

A thin, wavering spell went airborne. Boris leapt out of the way. The amethyst streak collided with the podium and a cloud of smoke appeared. It quickly wafted away and I could see the podium again.

Or rather, what used to be the podium.

The Ventham spell had turned it into a weird mess of wood and nails. It took me a moment to realize that it had split apart at the seams and the various pieces had joined together in new ways, forming an entirely different object. Holy smokes, I didn't even want to imagine what that spell would do to a living, breathing person.

Boris rolled to a crouch. Wand drawn, he took aim at his attacker. "Arresta," he said.

Another streak, thick and saffron-colored, appeared. The man dove to the floor in the nick of time and the spell hit his seat. Sturdy chains materialized, wrapping snugly around the chair.

I tore my eyes away from the mirror and my senses returned to the present. The air tasted of dust and grit. A cool breeze chilled me to the bone.

Leandra gave me a funny look. "Are you okay?"

"Huh?"

"You stopped answering me. It was almost like you'd been hypnotized."

I nodded at the mirror. "I was watching that."

"What'd you see?"

"Well, it was supposed to be a speech, given by Boris Hynor. Only the speech never happened."

Piper cocked her head to one side. "Why not?"

"Boris started to talk about Chaotic magic, but the crowd shouted him down. Then a guy attacked him and Boris fought back." I shrugged. "That's when I stopped watching."

Leandra studied the frame. "It says here that this memory was removed from Womigia."

"Let me see that." Piper gave the mirror a close look.

I frowned. "How is that even possible?"

"I'm not sure," Piper said slowly. "But if I had to guess, I'd say the mirror took possession of the memory and somehow extracted it from Womigia."

"What does that mean?" Leandra asked. "That it's impossible to remember?"

"Not necessarily." She stopped to think. "I imagine anyone who was actually there would still remember it. But *the way* they remember it might have changed."

Now, Leandra looked really confused. "Huh?"

Piper glanced at me. "Tell me exactly what you saw."

I gave them a quick rundown of Boris' speech. "Of course, I don't know the context," I said. "But the crowd shouted Boris down before he even had a chance to speak. Then an audience member attacked him."

"How do you feel after watching it? Are you more or less sympathetic to Boris?"

"The audience was rude and the attacker made the first move. On the other hand, Boris was polite and defended himself. So, I guess I should feel a little better about him." I shrugged. "But I don't."

"I thought so." She nodded sagely. "Here's how I think it works. If we'd been in that audience, we would've remembered everything that happened. But it wouldn't have changed the way *we felt* about the Philosophical War. In other words, it would've had no impact on our feelings toward the Structuralists or the Chaotics."

"I get it." Leandra looked troubled. "But what's the point? Who cares if Boris comes out looking good once or twice? He was still a lousy Chaotic."

"I don't know," Piper admitted.

I recalled Tad's instructions to me. "Do me a favor. See if you can find a memory dated February 1, 1930."

"This one is dated February 1, 1930." Leandra began studying the many embedded mirrors. "This one, too. That's the original Victory Day, by the way."

That was true and a curious observation. Apparently, a bunch of memories, maybe even all of them, had been extracted on the very day that the Structuralists had won the Philosophical War. "I don't mean when the memory was removed," I replied. "I mean when it actually took place."

Splitting up, we scoured Womigia. Hundreds of mirrors stuck out of its surface. They looked like crude, unnecessary additions to a gorgeous masterpiece.

Leandra cleared her throat. "This one is pretty close. It says, 'Boris Hynor denounces protestor violence and vows to carry his message forward. April 18, 1929. Collected at the Tuckhouse School of Magic. Removed from Womigia on February 1, 1930.'"

"That's interesting," Piper commented.

"What's interesting?"

"I've always thought of the Philosophical War in a certain way. That is, the Structuralists were the scrappy underdogs, trying to achieve victory through peaceful means. Meanwhile, the Chaotics brutalized them at every turn. But these mirrors show a different side of the conflict. One where the Structuralists weren't always so innocent."

"If memories of Structuralist violence were removed," I said, slowly, "but memories of Chaotics wrongdoing were left intact ..."

"… then that's all we'd know about today," Piper said, finishing my thought.

I continued walking, checking mirrors at every step. They came in all shapes and sizes. Many sat in luxurious, fancy frames. I saw numerous types of glass, ranging from thick to thin and from cloudy to clear. The only thing they had in common was that none of them were broken.

The inscriptions, for the most part, pre-dated Victory Day. They dealt almost exclusively with events pertaining to the Philosophical War. I saw plenty of names, but few that I recognized.

As I worked my way around a corner, I noticed a mirror off by itself. It was long and thin, with bubbly glass. Its inscription read, *February 1, 1930 Battle at the Roderick J. Madkey School of Magical Administration. Removed from Womigia February 1, 1930.*

My heart seized in my chest and I found myself barely able to breathe. "Over here," I announced.

Piper and Leandra beat a path to my side. We exchanged uncertain looks, then turned our attention to the mirror.

The glassy surface began to swirl before our eyes. A large crowd of witches and wizards appeared. They were crammed onto a hoist. Their cheeks were severe, their jaws were hard as rock. I recognized some of them. Lanctin Boltstar. George Galison. Angela Tyca. Deej MacPherson. Beatrice Norch.

The hoist jolted to a halt, the gate opened, and the witches and wizards stepped outside. They gave quick looks at Boltstar.

He gave them a nod and they returned it. Then they headed off in various directions.

Leaving the hoist, Boltstar entered the Upper-Torso section of Madkey. The floors, walls, windows, and elevated bridges were all the same. The doors and hoists were the same as well. And yet, this version of Torso still looked quite different compared to modern times.

The open-air section was empty, completely free of tables and chairs. A single walkway, originating at the Lower-Torso bridge, extended out into the middle of the space. It was abutted by waist-high railings, mounted on steel poles. Swirling, black mist hung over the entire area, shrouding it in beautiful, regal mystery.

It wasn't just the looks that differed, either. Torso *felt* different, too. I'd always felt a weird vibe within it, part wild and carefree and part stressed to the edge of insanity. But this older version was neither of those things. It didn't seem like the type of place where students would go to blow off steam or study for a big exam. Instead, it had a mystical, almost reverential feel to it.

It took me a moment to put it together. Madkey Station Grille didn't exist at this point in time. Instead, I was looking at Madkey Station itself, the infamous conveyance portal that led to the Floating Abyss.

Lots of people were gathered upon the bridges. They were, I realized, Chaotic witches and wizards. They looked nervous and on edge. More than a few of them kept their hands near their wands. When people spoke, which was rare, they did so in quiet, reserved tones.

I watched as Boltstar joined a small group of people, whom I took to be Chaotics. They greeted him politely, if not amicably, and everyone chatted for a few minutes. Even in those days, he was eminently likeable and everyone seemed to warm to him rather quickly.

He moved from one group to the next, engaging people at every turn. After a bit, the palpable tension began to fade. Bizzlum and other drinks began to flow. I heard a few chortles and guffaws. Before long, laughter and chatter rang out, loud and clear.

David Meyer

I spotted a petite woman circling the edges of a small group. She carried a tray of champagne flutes in her right hand. With a sweet smile, she offered them to all in attendance. Some waved her off. Others took flutes with gracious gratitude. Afterward, she moved on to another group. But my gaze was still directed at the witches and wizards she'd just served. For although they hadn't noticed it yet, they'd been robbed.

Of their wands.

Shifting my gaze, I watched the woman offer more drinks to more unsuspecting people, all the while pilfering their wands. And she wasn't the only one doing this.

All across the bridge, waiters and waitresses were slipping from group to group, relieving magicians of their wands. What was going on? And was this happening on the other bridges as well?

Turning back to Boltstar, I saw he already had a flute in his hand. I couldn't see his wand. And that was when it hit me.

This was it. This was how it all went down. For it was on this day that the Chaotics launched their sneaky ambush. Boltstar and his allies took the initial lumps before managing to turn the tables. They had won the day—Victory Day, as it was now known—and at long last Structuralism became the dominant magical philosophy.

I didn't recognize any of the affected magicians. But it was pretty easy to figure out what was happening. Madkey's staff consisted of Chaotics. They were meticulously disarming the Structuralists in preparation for the battle.

My heart began to thump against my chest. It was so weird, watching this monumental event, and being unable to do anything about it. I wanted to warn Boltstar, to tell him everything. But all I could do was watch. Watch as history unfolded before my very eyes.

Smiling broadly, Boltstar rapped a silver spoon against his flute. Conversation died out and all eyes turned his way.

"Good evening," he began. "For those of you who don't already know, my name is Lanctin Boltstar. I wanted to take this opportunity to thank you—our hosts—for your gracious hospitality."

There were a few smiles here and there. I heard some polite applause, too.

"This conflict of ours, the so-called Philosophical War, has taken a terrible toll on all of us," he continued. "Whether you're a Chaotic or a Structuralist, I think we can agree that it needs to end."

The applause grew a little louder. But I also saw plenty of frowns amongst the gathered Chaotics. And why not? They were about to launch the most important battle in all of magic history.

"We need a clear and lasting resolution." Tipping the glass to his lips, Boltstar downed the champagne. "And we need it *now*."

Soft rustling rang out as magicians stepped away from their respective groups. They—Galison, Tyca, MacPherson, Norch, and others—went for their wands and took aim at surprised witches and wizards. Those people, in turn, went for their wands only to find empty holsters.

"Say, what is this, Lanctin?" a man shouted.

"This, my dear Corbin, is how the war ends." Boltstar's wand shifted. "Drodiate."

A blaze of cyan careened into Corbin and the man froze up stiff. I blinked, astonished and confused. This wasn't right. The Chaotics had attacked Boltstar and the Structuralists, not the other way around.

Panic ruled the day as the Chaotics tried to flee. But the Structuralists were ready. Colorful light filled the room. The effect was disorienting and I had trouble keeping track of everything.

All my life I'd heard about the epic brawl that had taken place on Victory Day. How Boltstar and his allies had hunkered down, regrouped, and put on a dazzling display of magic, the likes of which had never been seen before. But the fight I was watching was short on heroics. In fact, it was just plain short, lasting a mere three minutes.

As the spells died off, I got a good look at the bridge. What I saw made my skin crawl. Some Chaotic magicians, infected with the Gratlan, writhed from side to side. Others had been drodiated and remained utterly still, their bodies frozen in contorted positions.

When the last spell had flown, Boltstar hiked across the bridge. The waiters and waitresses, armed with wands, greeted him at the halfway point. The petite woman stepped out in front.

"We owe you a hearty thank you, Cherry." He took hold of her hands. "Because of your bravery, as well as the bravery of your peers, the violence has finally come to an end."

The woman looked a bit shaken. Turning her head in either direction, she stared at the fallen magicians.

"You look troubled," he said. "Is something wrong?"

"It's just …" She exhaled. "They were good people, you know. Good, decent people. My people."

"I understand." He gave her a soft smile. "Give it time. I think you'll remember them very differently in a day or two."

She offered a slight bow, then stepped away. I got a good look at her. She was younger then. More petite than skinny and severe. But I recognized her all the same. It was Cherry Wadflow, esteemed Numerology professor. If I understood this correctly—and that was a big 'if'—she'd originally been a Chaotic. Then, at Boltstar's urging, she'd betrayed her people.

Boltstar walked over to Galison, Norch, and MacPherson. They held wands to an unarmed man. He was a few years older, but I still recognized him as Boris Hynor.

"Hello, Lanctin," he said in a cool, crisp voice.

"Hello, Boris."

Hynor's gaze drifted to his defeated allies. "Using violence to stifle debate, I see."

"You left me no choice."

"There's always a choice, Lanctin."

"You speak to me of choice?" Boltstar shook his head. "How convenient, considering your entire philosophy eschews choice."

"Chaotics allows magicians to reach their fullest potential."

"But not their deepest desire. Under Structuralism, anyone can be anything."

"One doesn't preclude the other. As I've said many times before, the two philosophies can coexist."

"If only that were true."

"It *is* true." Hynor arched an eyebrow. "And that's why this little power play of yours will fail. Once people learn what you did—"

"They won't. For you see, we've crafted an alternative narrative about what happened here today, one in which your side launched the initial attack."

Horror dawned on Hynor's features. "You wouldn't."

"I must. This 'power play,' as you put it, must be pure and pristine if it's to last the test of time. There can be no doubt as to who was right and who was wrong."

"No one will believe you," Hynor said, his face growing pale. "I've devoted my life, my very being, to peace."

"You forget that we're now in control of this entire institution, Boris. That includes Madkey Archive and more importantly, Womigia."

His eyes bulged.

"Starting today, we can shape the collective memory any way we like. We can remove memories of Structuralist wrongdoing. And we can remove memories that shine a positive light on your people. By the time we're done, society will have a very different viewpoint of the Philosophical War."

"This is madness."

"This, my friend, is progress." Boltstar's wand shifted. "Drodiate."

The resulting spell smacked Hynor square in the chest. Shock registered on his face as he stiffened up.

I could take no more. With a yank of the head, I tore my eyes from the mirror. Instantly, Torso vanished and I was back in the archive, standing in front of Womigia.

I thought about Tad, about what he'd told me of Womigia. He'd said it was at the center of everything. It was why he'd come to Madkey in the first place, why he and his people had staged the invasion. Now, I was beginning to understand what he'd meant.

The Chaotics had been wronged not once, but twice. First, the leaders had been disarmed, then killed or drodiated. Second, the followers had been uniformly and unfairly portrayed as monsters. Many had likely converted in the aftermath. The holdouts had been hunted down and taken out of commission.

Piper, jaw agape, turned to look at me. "Was that ... real?"

"Yes," I replied. "Yes, it was."

CHAPTER 33

"I can't believe it." Leandra stepped back from Womigia as if it might burn her. "Boltstar's a jerk. But he wouldn't hurt people for no reason."

"He had a reason," Piper pointed out. "He was trying to end the Philosophical War."

"With violence? And murder?"

"It probably seemed essential at the time. Remember, Chaotic magic is dangerous, lethal even. He must've figured an ambush was the lesser of two evils."

"Not just an ambush. A cover-up, too." With a sigh, I glanced at the floor. "All our lives, we've been told that the Chaotics attacked the Structuralists that day, not the other way around. And it was all just a lie."

"How'd they get us to believe it?" Leandra studied the mirror, especially the end sticking into Womigia. "Do you think they planted a fake memory in there?"

"They wouldn't need to," Piper pointed out. "Boltstar killed or drodiated anyone who might disagree with him. After that, he was free to spread his story far and wide."

"So, it entered Womigia on its own accord?" I asked.

She nodded. "Exactly."

Leandra exhaled. "Well, what now?"

"We tell people," I said. "Today. Right now."

They stared at me.

"It's the right thing to do," I argued.

"Yeah," Leandra said. "If we want to end up like the Chaotics."

"She's got a point," Piper said. "What about Boltstar?"

"What about him?" I snapped.

"I'm on your side, Randy. You know that. But you saw the mirror. You saw what he did to those people. What do you think he'll do to us if we cross him?"

"What if we just break all of these mirrors?" Leandra wondered. "The collective memory would go back to normal, right? I assume the effect would be instantaneous, with everyone suddenly realizing we've been wrong about everything."

Looking thoughtful, Piper gave the frame a good yank. But it didn't budge.

I studied the mirror. It was sturdy, but I'd yet to see a glassy substance that could survive a good beating. It made me wonder why Tad hadn't tried to break it. Had he been unable to do it? Or unwilling?

"If we broke it, Boltstar would just fix it again," I realized. "People would have a sudden awakening, only to have it snuffed out again."

"Maybe we could—" The sudden sound of grinding gears caused Piper's spine to stiffen. "What was that?"

I hustled to the door. Peeking up, I saw the ceiling start to move. Then I glimpsed swirling colors, indicating the presence of a conveyance portal. The edges of a hoist appeared. Slowly, it descended into the archive. Boltstar was its sole occupant. He held a wand in one hand. Despite the late hour, his attire was immaculate.

"That's not the way we came in," Piper said.

Leandra inhaled a sharp breath. "He must have his own entrance."

Sweat oozed out of my pores. What if he saw us? Would he skin us? Send us off to Gutlore, maybe?

I snuck another glimpse at the hoist. To my surprise, it was no longer going down. It was moving sideways.

"He's coming this way." Leandra grabbed my arm. "We need to hide."

Softly, I closed the door. Turning my gaze inward, I studied the statues lining the walls. Then I looked at Womigia. Unfortunately, hiding spaces were few and far between.

"Back here." Piper dragged us behind Womigia. "Hurry!"

One of the taller statues threw off a decent-sized shadow. We hunkered down within it and turned our attention to the doorway. Leandra took her wand out of her holster. Piper and I grabbed ours as well.

The sound of shifting metal faded away. Footsteps shifted across the shelf. Then the door popped open. Boltstar, wand drawn, stepped into the room. He took a moment to shut the door, then hiked forward.

"There's no use hiding," he announced. "The archive floor is enchanted. The moment you stepped out of the portal, a bell rang in my quarters."

His revelation filled me with dread. But it also gave me the slightest bit of hope. He didn't actually *know* someone was in the room. He was merely aware that someone had entered the archive. And for all he knew, the intruder had already vacated the area.

"Only five people, including me, know how to find this place," he continued. "I'm guessing you're not one of them."

He checked the left wall, then the right one. Then he hiked toward Womigia.

Heart-pounding, I shrank into the statue's shadow. An elbow jabbed me in the ribs. At first, I ignored it. But a second jab caused me to twist around.

"What?" I mouthed.

Piper didn't say a word. Instead, she pointed up at the statue. I gave it a good look, recognizing it as a rather good likeness of Boris Hynor.

"So, what?" I mouthed.

"It's him," she whispered. "It's *actually him*."

Frowning, I glanced again at the statue. This time, I recoiled in horror. It wasn't a statue at all.

It *was* Boris.

Boltstar must've moved the man's drodiated body to this particular room. A quick check confirmed the other statues were also Chaotic witches and wizards from that fateful night. They'd stood here for decades, unable to move or talk or do anything. All they could do was observe. Observe and think and despair. Truly, it was a horrible fate.

But I didn't have time to ponder it. In a matter of seconds, Boltstar had walked around Womigia. The shadow, while dark, wasn't nearly dark enough. A few more steps and he'd see us for sure.

"Last chance," he said. "Come out now or else."

I had to do something. Lifting my wand, I tried to think. But fear consumed me and no spells came to mind.

Footsteps pressed against the carpet. They drew closer and closer. I decided right then and there to cast the Elertfa spell. If I could catch him by surprise, it might give us a chance to escape.

I focused my emotions and directed my wand through a series of movements. My lips pursed and I felt that sweet state of Instinctia. I felt its pull, its wondrous power. It was so addictive, so intoxicating, so *easy*. And that's when I sensed it.

A slight urge. A spontaneous tug. It was an appeal to something different, something deep inside of me. Something primal that I'd never actually touched.

New emotions—my emotions—swirled within me. I felt fear for my friends and for myself. Plus, loads of anger toward Boltstar along with epic frustration that he was about to catch us.

My lips continued to move and my wand shifted course, encompassing the three of us. This was my doing. I didn't fully understand why I was doing it. But for the first time ever, the Capsudra had no control over my magic.

The warmth of Instinctia faded away. A new feeling arose to take its place. It wasn't as safe or as comforting, at least not on the surface. But it was oddly satisfying on a very deep level. If Instinctia was like waking up to a huge pile of presents on Christmas morning, this was like revisiting a beloved childhood home I hadn't seen in years.

"Vanista," I whispered. I wasn't sure why I said that. It just felt, well, right.

Auburn light—unusually radiant—left my wand. It swiftly engulfed the three of us, then disappeared just as swiftly. And then ...

Nothing.

We were still there, still hunkered down in the shadow. Confused, I looked to either side. I'd denied Instinctia. And in the process, I'd cast a different spell. *A Chaotic spell.* But what had it accomplished?

Boltstar's shoe pressed against the floor. His chin tipped down and he stared right at us. Try as I might, I couldn't meet his gaze. Instead, I stared at the floor, my heart hammering at my chest. This was my fault. And now, we were all going to pay the price for my foolhardiness.

His chin jutted forward and I cowered back a few inches. I figured he wanted us to say something, to explain ourselves. With that in mind, I began to clear my throat. But just then, the craziest thing happened.

He walked away.

Gawking, I watched him stride all the way around Womigia. He halted for a moment. His eyes traced the walls, the ceiling, the carpet. He wore a puzzled look upon his face and I experienced a sudden realization.

He didn't see us, I thought. *He can't see us.*

Piper's lip quivered even as the rest of her remained stiff with fear. Leandra, her face pensive, knelt in the shadow. Sweat dripped down her face and collected above her upper lip, but she didn't dare wipe it away.

He reached the door, then paused in the doorframe. Twisting around, he studied the room yet again. His brow knitted in confusion. Then he walked outside.

As the door swung shut, I touched their arms. They jolted slightly, as if emerging from a daze. "Come on," I mouthed. "We're getting out of here."

Leandra's lips moved. "Are you crazy?"

"It's okay. We're invisible."

She considered that for a moment. "Are you sure?"

"Pretty sure."

She didn't look convinced. "Why now?" She nodded at the headmaster. "Why not wait until he leaves?"

"Because of the alarm," Piper mouthed.

I nodded. "Remember, he said the archive floor was enchanted. If someone crosses it, a bell rings in his quarters. Well, we need to cross it again to reach the portal."

"And since he's not in his quarters, he won't hear the bell." She exhaled, then nodded. "Okay, follow me."

She led us to the door. We cracked it open and peered outside. Boltstar and the hoist were nowhere to be seen. Moving swiftly, we slipped out to the waiting shelf.

A quick glance confirmed that Boltstar was busy riding his hoist down to ground level. Steeling our muscles, we began our descent. It was easier going down then coming up and we made good time.

We reached the halfway point just as he touched down on the archive floor. Exiting the hoist, he hiked to the pile of fallen ramballs. They just sat there, looking about as sheepish as a bunch of ramballs can get. He gave them a few stern words and the ramballs, their sides pink with embarrassment, scurried back to their former shelf.

We continued our silent descent, gaining speed as the shelves began to slope inward. Meanwhile, Boltstar scoped out the archive floor for a few minutes. Finally, he returned to the hoist.

Just as it lifted into the air, we stepped onto the archive floor. We raced to the portal and leapt into it. The last thing I saw before leaving the room was a glimpse of swirling color as Boltstar's hoist settled back into the ceiling.

I tossed and tumbled my way through the portal before it finally spat me back out into the rotating trap room. This time, however, the room was bare. Nothing but big blocks of stone and the hoist in the opposite corner.

"No trap," Leandra said, clearly pleased but also more than a bit suspicious.

"No sense in wasting one on the return trip," Piper reasoned.

While they discussed it, I reflected on the last couple of minutes. I'd done it. I'd actually done it. I'd denied Instinctia. I'd performed a Chaotic spell. In so doing, I'd fooled the greatest magician of all time. It was truly an eye-opening experience, one that made me question everything I thought I knew about magic.

Leandra touched my shoulder. "How'd you do that?"

"Yeah," Piper added. "I didn't even know the Capsudra had a vanishing spell."

"It doesn't." There was no point in deceiving them any longer. "That was Chaotic magic."

Piper's eyes narrowed to slits. She looked at me as if she barely knew me. "But ... how?"

"I had help." I took a deep breath. "Come on. There's someone you need to see."

CHAPTER 34

"What is this place?" Piper wondered as she followed me up the ladder.

"A celestarium." Climbing through the hatch, I gained my feet. "People used to study the stars and planets up here."

"You mean celestial magic? That's a bunch of hooey."

I shrugged. "You're probably right."

She climbed out of the shaft. Her hair hung from her head in damp curls. Her jeans and dark red t-shirt were stained and sweaty. If not for her eyes, which looked like they were on fire, I would've pegged her as exhausted.

Leandra was next to arrive. Her eyes were hooded and deep lines creased her face. She, too, showed signs of severe fatigue. Yet, a single look at the celestarium changed that completely. Her eyes widened and the lines vanished. Face full of wonder, she turned in a slow circle.

"How'd you find this?" she wondered.

"Someone, uh, led me here." Clearing my throat, I glanced toward the fireplace. "You can come out now."

The fireplace remained still.

"We can trust them," I added.

Rustling noises filled the area around the chimney. Then Tad dropped to the hearth. Ducking under the lip, he climbed outside. His hair was tousled. He'd showered recently, but a few dirt smudges remained behind his left ear.

Piper produced her wand.

"Hang on," I said.

"He betrayed us," she said angrily.

"He was fighting for his people."

"Uh, guys?" Tad blinked. "Where are you exactly?"

I looked at him and saw the blank look upon his face. *It's the Vanista spell*, I thought. *He can't see us.*

"We're still invisible," I said, turning to Piper and Leandra.

"Well, reverse it," Leandra replied.

"I don't know how."

"I might be able to help." Tad furrowed his brow and waved his wand. Tawny light flooded into us. "Ahh, much better."

"You can see us?" I asked.

"Sure can." He glanced at Leandra, then Piper. "Hey guys. I know I'm probably the last person you want—"

"Don't talk," Piper nearly shouted. "Don't you dare."

"Piper," Leandra said softly.

"Don't Piper me." She rose to her full height. "He attacked Madkey. He attacked us."

I saw her anger, her fury. But I also saw pain and question marks in her eyes.

"He and his people attacked Boltstar," I said gently. "And after what we've just seen, can you really blame them?"

Tad exhaled. "I take it you found Womigia?"

I nodded. "And we almost got nabbed in the process."

He gave me a startled look.

Quickly, I told him about Boltstar's appearance, the enchanted archive floor, and the alarm bell in the headmaster's quarters.

"I had no idea," he said when I was finished. "I must've gone in there while he was out and about."

I shrugged. "Regardless, we know the truth now. We know what really happened on Victory Day."

"That's good." He looked relieved, as if an enormous burden had been lifted from his chest. "That's something, at least."

"You shouldn't have attacked us," Piper said, her anger beginning to fade. "You should've found another way."

He chuckled darkly. "Like what?"

She frowned.

"No offense, but you're not one of us. You don't know what it's like."

"So, tell us." Leandra arched an eyebrow. "What's it like being a Chaotic magician in this day and age?"

"Pretty awful, actually." Holstering his wand, he shoved his hands into his pockets. "Womigia touches everyone, including us. It influences the way we think about things. When Boltstar changed it, he turned everyone against us."

I caught a weird hint of anguish in his tone. "Everyone?"

"Yeah, *everyone*."

Piper's eyes widened. Leandra emitted a light gasp.

"We hate ourselves," he continued. "We know the truth. We know what Boltstar did to our people. But we still hate ourselves. We can't help it." He started to choke up and quickly turned away. "I grew up despising myself. Despising myself and my people for something we never did, all because of the stupid collective memory. Do you know what that's like? Do you know what it's like to wake up every morning, *knowing* you're the worst of the worst?"

Piper cringed. "It sounds awful."

He sighed. "If Boltstar had just destroyed our ancestors, maybe we could've lived with it. Don't get me wrong. What he did was lousy. He stole our property, our livelihoods, our good names. Still, we could've moved on. But having to live each day with the lie that we're evil villains? That was something else altogether."

Looking at Tad, I still felt a bit of revulsion toward him. Suspicion, as well. That, I now realized, was because of Womigia. Or rather, because of the changes Boltstar had made to it. I could scarcely imagine how that felt from Tad's perspective. To labor under the false notion that one was a monster, beyond any hope of redemption. It sounded horrible.

The last trace of Piper's anger disappeared. Racing forward, she embraced Tad in a big hug. Tears bubbled up and she began to cry.

Taking turns, Tad and I got her and Leandra up to speed. They didn't ask any questions. In fact, they didn't say anything at all during the entire story. Instead, their jaws just kept dropping lower and lower to the floor. By the time we were finished, they could barely speak.

"I hate to admit this." Leandra stared at Tad as if seeing him for the first time. "But I never trusted you. I mean, I tried to. But something about you just …"

"No need to explain," he replied. "I feel the same way every single day."

Leandra, Piper, and I filled Tad in on our trip to the archive. We told him about the trap and the ramballs. We told him about my Chaotic spell and our escape. By the time we were done, it was his turn to be nearly speechless.

"So, you did it?" he asked excitedly. "You cast a Chaotic spell?"

I nodded.

"Then it worked."

"What worked?"

"My plan. You see, you grew up under Structuralism. You believed in it, depended upon it. Even worse, you were taught to despise Chaotic magic. To hate it, to fear it. That's why I sent you to find Womigia. I needed to open your eyes. I needed to challenge your faith."

"And that's why I was able to cast a Chaotic spell?" I frowned as something occurred to me. "But here's the weird thing. I don't feel different. I mean, I know the truth. I know what Boltstar did to your people. But it's like my brain doesn't care. The thought of Chaotic magic still puts a bad taste in my mouth."

He nodded sagely. "Believe me, I understand."

"So, how do we fix that?" Leandra asked.

"Are you sure you want to help?" He paused. "If it doesn't work—and there's a good chance it won't—you could end up in a whole heap of trouble."

"Then we'd better make sure it works."

"Easier said than done. As long as Boltstar is in charge, he'll be able to counter any changes we make to Womigia."

"Then we have to take him out of play." Piper began to pace back and forth. "And he's not the only one."

"Oh?"

"While he was searching for us, Boltstar said five people, including him, knew about the archive. I assume he was referring to Galison, MacPherson, Wadflow, and Norch. We have to assume they know how to fix Womigia as well."

He exhaled. "Terrific. I guess we'll have to put them out of commission as well."

"Can you contact your people? Can you bring them back here?"

"I'm still anchored to home. So, I can definitely contact them." He shrugged. "But they'd need an access point. And I'd be willing to bet Boltstar's keeping a close eye on the old Madkey Station portal these days."

"He brought in loads of alumni to watch over it," I confirmed. "We might have a chance at odd hours, though."

"There's another way we could grow our numbers." Leandra began to pace opposite of Piper. "Remember those

Chaotic magicians in the archive? The ones that got drodiated all those years ago? If we could free them somehow ..."

"I tried," he replied. "It didn't work."

We talked a little longer, brainstorming all sorts of ideas. Soon, my eyes began to droop. A yawn escaped my lips.

"Let's sleep on it," I suggested.

The others murmured their agreement. Leandra, Piper, and I snuck back to the staffer dorm. Splitting off, I climbed into bed. As I pulled the covers over me, I found myself afflicted with a sense of worry. Helping Tad seemed like the right thing to do. But at what cost? How far would I go to do the right thing? Would I risk capture and imprisonment? Would I throw my life away? Truthfully, I wasn't sure.

And that scared the heck out of me.

CHAPTER 35

"Okay, Randy." Tad nodded in my direction. "Give it your best shot."

It was late in the evening, five days after our little escapade in the archive. After class, Leandra, Piper, and I had snuck up to the celestarium. For several hours, we'd worked independently. Piper browsed through armfuls of books she'd borrowed from the library. Leandra spent much of her time working with her simulator mirror.

As for me, I practiced my magic. With Tad's guidance, I'd gotten pretty good at denying Instinctia. This opened things up, allowing me to cast a variety of Chaotic spells.

They were, unfortunately, not all that promising. My most interesting spell so far created little bursts of light, like a string of firecrackers. But they'd died out far too quickly to be of much use. The weirdest spell was undoubtedly the one that had bounced off the statue and careened into Tad's stomach. Afterward, he'd experienced an urgent need to visit the bathroom. On the bright—and really gross—side, I now knew how to spoil a person's bowels.

With each new spell, bright auburn light would careen into the bust. We'd check the results, then Tad would record everything in a notebook, along with the associated emotions, wand movements, and words. That was his idea and it seemed like a pretty good one. That way, I could remember how to do each and every spell. And if I happened to come across a really good one—say, a spell capable of turning Porter into a squonk—I could practice it to my heart's content.

All my life, I'd been lectured about the dangers of Chaotic magic. Now that I was actually doing it, it felt a bit unsettling. But it was also liberating and I found myself awaiting each spell with bated breath. The only strange part was that my emotions were more controlled than ever. That's because I had to keep manipulating them into new combinations in order to see what happened. But I figured that was a small price to pay for the ability to do Chaotic magic.

Letting my mind go, I relaxed every muscle in my body. Then I whirled my emotions into an untried combination. My wand began to move, in tune with my emotional state. I entered a state of Instinctia and felt the warm embrace of the Capsudra. I longed for it, but had little trouble denying it.

"Immaculatize," I uttered. My emotions may have been contrived. But the wand sequences and words that followed were derived from instinct. Like Structuralism, emotions were the driving force behind Chaotic magic.

An auburn bolt shot out of my wand. Half-curious, half-wincing, I waited to see what it would do to the bust. Deep down, I hoped it would pulverize the thing.

Striking the statue, the auburn light blobbed across its entire surface. Then it vanished. The whole thing took less than a second and left no residue behind. In fact, the marble-like material was now a beautiful white.

"You cleaned it." Tad whooped with laughter. "Way to go, Randy."

I shook my head, trying to imagine the entry he'd write in his notebook. Something like: *Spell 45: Immaculatize— Blobbed across statue at high-speed, leaving it in pristine shape. Look out maids and butlers … a new housekeeper is on the scene!*

"Hey," Piper groused. "Watch it!"

She sat at the table, just beyond the now-clean statue. A pile of books was scattered before her.

"Watch what?" I asked.

"You almost hit me!"

"I did?"

She gave me a withering look. "Do me a favor and keep your spells to yourself."

It was all rather odd. I thought the spell had disappeared upon cleaning the statue. But apparently, it had continued onward. Deep in thought, I walked to her table. Glancing through the books, I noticed one in particular. It was old and dusty. Its leather cover was ripped and showed signs of fading. Green stuff—mold, I figured—had taken up residence on the spine.

In other words, it was perfect.

"Hey!" she protested as I picked it up.

"This will only take a second." Cracking the book open, I stood it on end. Then I lined it up behind the bust.

Grumbling softly, Piper went back to her reading. Meanwhile, I walked back to my original spot. My mind became a blank slate. My muscles fell limp. Carefully, I stirred my emotions into the proper blend. Instinct sent my wand into action. The temptation of Instinctia came and went.

"Immaculatize," I said.

An auburn glow zoomed across the room. It blobbed over the bust so fast I didn't even have time to blink. The spell vanished for a split-second and I wondered if it was gone for good. But no, there it was, just beyond the statue. Instead of disappearing, it had broken free and continued along its way. Moving just as fast, but with considerably less volume, it blobbed over Piper's book. By the time it broke free, it was almost gone. It had just enough juice left to engulf a surprised Piper. Then it blinked out.

I darted to the table and checked my work. As I'd expected, the book had undergone a radical transformation. It was still old and its cover was still ripped. But the dust was gone and its leather had been polished. Even better, there was no sign of that disgusting mold.

"Looks like you cleaned two objects for the price of one." Tad grinned. "Not bad."

I glanced at Piper. Her hair was greasy and she had some smudges on her face from the evening's HMQ games. "Piper's still dirty," I said before I could stop myself. "But, uh, check out her—"

"*I'm dirty?*" She glared at me. "Real nice, Randy."

Tad followed my gaze. "Wow, I see what you mean."

Seeing our stares, she looked down. Grabbing the bottom of her t-shirt, she stretched it outward. Before, it had been a sweaty, grimy mess. Now, however, it looked brand new. "How in the world ...?"

Tad, sporting a big grin, began scribbling in his notebook. Leaning over, I checked the entry.

Spell 45: Immaculatize—Engulfs everyday objects at top-speed, cleaning them in the process. Proceeds onward, but at smaller size. Doesn't clean people though ... Piper is still dirty!!!

With a soft chuckle, I returned to my mark. Working up some new emotions, I cast another spell. Then another one. And then another one. Unfortunately, none of my spells resembled havoc magic. But I wasn't discouraged. I just needed to keep going, keep experimenting.

It was only a matter of time.

CHAPTER 36

"Out already, eh, Wolf?" Porter, perched on the edge of the HMQ, looked away from me just long enough to utter a spell. Chestnut light spewed out of his wand. Gustav Firbottom moved to block it, but the spell caught him in the stomach. He bent over, cringing and gasping for breath. "Too bad. I was hoping to do the deed myself."

"Don't worry." Gordon grinned. "You'll get another chance soon enough."

"Good thing, too." Twisting slightly, Porter finished off Gustav with yet another spell. "The HMQ isn't the same without my favorite Chaotic sympathizer."

My face burned with humiliation. I'd learned plenty of Chaotic spells over the last few days. But unless I wanted to start cleaning everything in sight, none of them were going to be particularly helpful. Well, except for Vanista. But I was too afraid to use that one, lest someone notice my sudden disappearance.

That left the spells we'd learned in class. Unfortunately, I found it increasingly difficult to do Capsudra-based magic. Even the spells I used on the assembly line were becoming a challenge.

"Check this out, Wolf." Gordon aimed an ivory bolt at Nico. The staffer hit the ground, rolling and shrieking for help. "What do you think? Does he really look like he's on fire to you?"

By now, most of the class had gained basic competency with Elertfa and Pobyl. So, Boltstar had decided to expand our spell book. During class time, he'd instructed us on the nuances of the infamous Genphor Nokrem. Genphor was a real doozy. From what I understood, it made one's body feel like it was on fire. And from the look on Nico's face, I'd say that was a pretty accurate description.

"Okay, huddle up." Jax lowered his head and a bunch of us eliminated staffers gathered around him. "I know we haven't had much luck lately. But we're getting better. We just need to keep holding them off and—"

"And what?" Nico, holding his side and grimacing in pain, limped over to us. "We'll get crushed again?"

"Face it, Jax," Jeff said. "We're never going to win. We're going to wind up on the ground like always, getting called Chaotic wannabes or some such nonsense."

Jax shook his head. "You can't think like that."

"Why not? It's true. We're dropouts and they're real students. End of story."

"Jeff's right," Jenny added. "I haven't been able to cast Genphor yet. Meanwhile, the students are throwing it around like it's kid stuff."

"So, forget Genphor." Jax grunted. "Use the stuff you know. It works just as well, right?"

They nodded reluctantly.

"Good. Now, once the next game starts, we have to stick together. Forget personal glory, forget showing off. Watch each other's backs. If we turn this into a defensive struggle, one of us might have a chance. Okay?"

Nobody looked convinced. But we all nodded anyway.

Boltstar blew a long whistle. "Mr. Garrington wins the game. Excellent job out there."

The students, many of whom were nursing wounds, gave a half-hearted cheer. Us staffers remained silent.

"We've got time for one last game," the headmaster announced with a pleased glint in his eye. "Everyone, please return to the HMQ."

We made our way onto the field. Like always, I took up position behind the string of old enchanted barriers along with the other staffers.

"Maybe they'll go easy on us," Nico said, hopefully. "Show us a little mercy for once."

Boltstar whistled again. Immediately, spells slammed into the barriers, causing them to rock on the soil.

Hunkering down, Leandra eyed Nico. "So much for mercy."

"Aim for the barriers and smoke them out of there," Porter yelled above the fray. "The rest of you watch for counterattacks. If they lift their heads, light them up."

More bolts of magic careened into the barriers.

"Excellent work, Mr. Garrington," Boltstar shouted. "Good job taking a leadership role and developing a viable strategy."

"Great strategy, Mr. Garrington," Leandra muttered in her best Boltstar voice. "Excellent job getting everyone to gang up on the weaker kids."

"Jeff, Nico, Randy ... stabilize the barriers," Jax called out. "Everyone else, go on the attack."

Piper and Leandra crawled to opposite edges of our barrier. The other staffers took up similar positions at the other barriers. Meanwhile, the spells kept coming and the barriers began to rock back and forth. Jeff, Nico, and I managed to keep them from toppling over onto all of us. But we couldn't stop them from falling the other way. If that happened, we'd be easy prey.

The barriers slammed into us yet again. We pushed back with all of our might.

"Where's our support?" Nico shouted.

Piper threw off a quick spell. She had no time to aim so I wasn't surprised when no one screamed in response.

"Whoa." With a yelp, she threw herself to the grass. Two dozen streaks soared overhead, missing her by inches.

"Ooo, that was close, Piper," Sya called out in a singsong voice. "I almost had you."

Five staffers rose up. They started to cast spells, but were greeted with a smothering wave of magic. Four of them broke off mid-spell and dropped back to the ground. But Jenny wasn't so lucky.

"Ouch!" Ecru-colored light struck the side of her head. Dropping her wand, she grabbed hold of her ear. "It burns," she shrieked.

A ruby-colored blaze crashed into her side. A pearl spell collided with her left elbow. And then she was on the ground, wailing and crying for help.

"You're out, Ms. Lynch," Boltstar said. "Again. Please exit the field."

Jenny rolled back and forth, trying in vain to put out the imaginary fires. Desperately, I tried to recall the counter-spell we'd learned in class.

"I got this." Nico pulled away from the barrier. His face twisted up and he waved his wand. "Antra Corderal."

A new spell, the color of sand, rushed out of his wand. It crested into Jenny's writhing form. She kept screaming, so he cast it two more times, neutralizing the other Genphor spells that had hit her. At last, she fell still, gulping at the air, her face contorted with pain and embarrassment. Then she crawled toward the sideline.

More spells hit the barriers, rocking them into us. Again, we pushed back and they swung the other way. Only this time, they swung too far.

"They're tipping," Jax screamed.

I lunged forward, but the edge slipped out of my fingers. Seconds later, the string of barriers fell face down in the grass. Cringing, I stared across the HMQ. Sadistic faces stared back at me. Then streaks of light hurled in our direction and we scrambled for cover.

I darted behind a stack of wide, sturdy wheels. Leandra popped up next to me, her hair mussed. Several other staffers, used to hiding by now, also made it to safety.

"Form up," Calvin yelled to the Sophomores. "Move in and finish—"

A chestnut spell slammed into his cheek. Shrieking in agony, he dropped to a knee. Immediately, the Sophomores turned their attention to the Freshmen. And then everyone was firing at everyone.

"Excellent work once again, Mr. Garrington," Boltstar shouted. "Fantastic job catching your alliance by surprise."

"I love you, Mr. Garrington." Leandra rolled her eyes. "Great job betraying your friends, Mr. Garrington. That'll come in handy when you're managing your family's company, Mr. Garrington."

I chuckled. But that chuckle died quickly as I surveyed my fellow staffers. Jeff, clutching an injured arm, crawled toward the sideline. Fyla was on her back, twitching and moaning.

An Elertfa spell knocked Dorph off his feet. He flopped onto his side, then slapped the ground in frustration. But as he headed for the magic rope, a second spell hit his rear. Screaming, he collapsed on the ground. Meanwhile, Gordon, who'd delivered the extra blow, howled with laugher.

Leandra watched Boltstar, evidently waiting for some kind of admonishment. When it didn't come, she tilted her head out into the open. "Hey, that was a dirty hit," she shouted. "Dorph was already—"

A fuchsia jet hit her cheek. Leandra's anger turned into agony and she fell down, clutching her face. Nightmarish screams escaped her lips.

"Excellent work drawing the enemy out of cover, Mr. Tancort," Boltstar said. "And that was a well-placed shot, Ms. Masters. Now, please leave the field, Mr. Jenkins and Ms. Chen."

But Dorph and Leandra were in no condition to leave. In fact, they were in no condition to do much of anything.

Again, I tried to recall the counter-spell. And again, I came up short. Was I supposed to swing the wand left then down and to the right? Or right, then down and to the left? And what were the emotions again?

Finally, Boltstar produced his wand. He issued two quick spells, one after the other. Dorph and Leandra fell still, their chests heaving up and down, their faces contorted with pain.

"Please exit the field," he said.

His casual manner made me mad. And yet, I still couldn't help but admire him. I knew that was due in part to Womigia. And that, of course, just made me even madder.

Daisy went down hard, the victim of a Kell Masters spell. I saw her pain, her agony. She looked close to passing out. One of her fellow sophomores issued a quick counter-spell.

Her face relaxed a bit and she emitted a deep sigh. Quickly, she headed for the sideline.

I closed my eyes and took a deep breath. For a single second, I found myself thinking of all the indignities spooled out by Boltstar and the Madkey School in general. I thought about how I'd dropped out of school. And I thought about Tad, about how he hated himself. My anger started to boil, but I managed to cut it off. Like it or not, the situation called for control.

A serene calmness spread through me. Something deep inside reached out and something out there reached back. We met in the middle and my eyes opened wide. Crazy amounts of energy began to surge through my veins.

Raising my wand, I stepped out from behind the piled wheels. Gordon saw me first. With a leer on his lips, he sent a spell screaming in my direction.

I ducked it, feeling relaxed and at peace. And yet my emotions and wand were going crazy. "Elertfa Lokwhan," I whispered as I entered a state of Instinctia.

The resulting spell popped him in the mouth. He collapsed next to Sya. Seeing this, she dove to the side. But I threw off another spell and it knocked her to the turf.

An unwelcome presence appeared behind me. I whirled around and saw Felicia. Her wand was extended and a smirk rested upon her lips. Her trademark fuchsia magic streaked toward me.

"Pobyl Caxtor," I said, still caught in the bliss of Instinctia. "Elertfa Lokwhan."

My wand blasted twice. The first blaze of light took out her spell. The second one caught her in the gut and she fell to the grass.

Others, sensing something strange and new was afoot, turned in my direction. I dodged or deflected their spells while lighting them up with my own. With each elimination, whispers began to filter in from the sidelines.

"Wow," Calvin said. "I can't believe it."

"How's he doing that?" Sya groused.

Felicia grunted, obviously in pain. "He's cheating. He must be."

Suddenly, a voice, loud and clear, rang out.

"There's just four of you left, Randy." Piper shouted. "You've got this!"

My bliss-like state vanished and I found myself standing in the middle of the field, far away from cover. Turning my head, I saw most of the class, as well as Boltstar, staring at me. For once, the headmaster was speechless.

Shifting in a semicircle, I saw over a dozen students crawling toward the sidelines. I was barely even aware of the fact that I'd defeated them. Or rather, that Instinctia had beaten them. But hey, I was happy to take the credit.

Across the field, I saw my remaining opponents. Given her newbie status, I was a little surprised to see Hannah still out there. But I was less surprised when I saw Kell at her side, throwing off vicious spells. Porter, meanwhile, was hunkered down behind a locker. He looked like he was in trouble, not that I was about to help him.

Adrenaline pumping, I worked my way across the field. All along, I'd hoped to use Chaotic magic to outshine my peers. But now, I wondered if I really needed it. I'd gotten this far with Structuralist spells, hadn't I?

A healthy buzz ran through the crowd. The staffers cheered themselves hoarse. Meanwhile, the students lifted their voices, cheering for the other three competitors.

Kell whispered something to Hannah. Then he circled to his right, keeping up a tight string of Genphor spells. Hannah, meanwhile, circled around to the left, keeping behind cover and throwing out Elertfa spells. I was impressed. She might've been new to Madkey. But clearly, she was no slouch with a wand.

However, Porter was no slouch either. He was a regular in the final four and had won about a quarter of the HMQ games to date. So, when he realized they intended to surround him, he made his move.

Rolling out from behind the locker, he took aim at Hannah. She ducked behind an empty metal crate. Undeterred, he adjusted his aim.

With a loud crash, the crate jolted backward, bumping into Hannah. With a shriek, she flopped on the ground. Dropping her wand, she reached for her nose.

Kell stood up straight. "Hey, you can't—"

Porter rolled again and fired off a quick Elertfa spell. It caught Kell's side and the older boy grunted. The force drove him back a foot, but he remained on his feet.

Wasting no time, Porter threw out a Genphor spell and Kell went down hard. Squirming in pain, he managed to perform his own counter-spell. Red with anger, he dragged himself to the sidelines.

Porter whirled back to face Hannah. She looked so vulnerable laying there that I wondered if he might show her mercy. He answered my question by zapping her with an Elertfa spell.

The roar from the crowd turned ferocious. Students began to chant his name.

"Por-ter! Por-ter! Por-ter! Por-ter!"

Porter was a popular guy. Even so, I knew they weren't cheering for him so much as they were cheering against me. Well, forget them. I'd made it this far, hadn't I?

Spinning around, he laid eyes upon me. I stared back at him, my lip curled with malice. His shirt was soiled and drenched in sweat. I could see he was panting heavily from all of the exertion.

I raised my wand. My emotions slid into place and I entered Instinctia.

"Elertfa Lokwhan," my lips whispered.

An auburn bolt shot out of my wand. At top speed, it hurtled across the HMQ, leaving a sizzling trail in its wake.

Unpanicked, he worked his wand. "Pobyl Caxtor."

A chestnut streak crashed into my auburn bolt. They erupted into a colorful ball of smoke, then dissipated.

He broke into a sprint. Arms pumping, he raced behind some piled furniture and I lost sight of him.

Overturning a table, I dove behind it. In the process, I caught sight of Boltstar's stony expression. Was he surprised by my performance? Pleased, even?

A blast of magic dislodged the table and sent it careening into me. The sudden jolt knocked me backward and I landed on the soft grass. With the scent of smoke wafting in my nostrils, I scrambled back to a crouching position.

"Por-ter! Por-ter! Por-ter! Por-ter!"

The chant gained volume. If anybody was cheering for me, I sure couldn't hear them.

I peeked out from one side of the table. My gaze swept the HMQ and I saw Porter holed up behind a mid-sized flying boat. Named *Revenger*, it was one of twelve crafts utilized for Madkey's annual Air Pirate Games. But at that moment, it was a cover position, a place for him to hide while he drew closer to me.

This wasn't good. Any spells I fired at the boat would merely ding its siding. Meanwhile, Porter could keep his head down and continue to pound away at the table I was using for cover.

A frustrated grunt left my lips. Porter might've been a jerk, but he was fast and highly-skilled. How in the world could I hope to beat him? I lacked his knowledge, his discipline. He was a star pupil, capable of learning and casting spells in no time. Meanwhile, I was a dropout, unable to handle even a full semester of formal schooling.

Yeah, it was a harsh assessment. But it was also true. Despite my little run earlier in the game, I was still outmatched. Porter was better at school, better at Structuralist magic. That was obvious to everyone, including me.

So, maybe it was time to try something else. Why not set aside Structuralist magic for a spell or two? Why not give Chaotic magic a try?

I racked my brain for a decent spell, something that no one would recognize as Chaotic magic. Unfortunately, none of the ones I'd practiced with Tad would be useful in a fight. What good would, say, Immaculatize do for me? It just cleaned stuff, moving from object to object and …

My brow furrowed. My gaze moved to the boat. It was a relatively new addition to the HMQ, brought in to replace some demolished rolly-carts. Because of this, it was quite clean. Would anyone notice if it got a tad bit cleaner?

I relaxed, allowing my frustration and nervousness to melt away. Carefully, I massaged my emotions into place. My wand began to sweep back and forth. My mind zeroed in on the cleaning spell and my lips moved to speak it.

Before I could get the words out, Instinctia appeared within me. I felt a moment of blissful peace as I connected to the Capsudra. My wand, my emotions, even the words on my tongue, began to shift toward a separate spell.

Fight it, I told myself. *Deny Instinctia!*

I clawed back control of my emotions. My wand returned to its original sequence. My lips quivered as I prepared to cast the Chaotic spell.

"Immaculatize," I whispered.

An auburn blaze, barely visible, streaked forward and hit the boat. A normal spell would've died right there. But the cleaning spell engulfed the boat in the blink of an eye, leaving a gleaming craft in its wake.

Clearing the boat, the spell continued onward. As I'd hoped, Porter caught a glimpse of the approaching light. Frantically, he dove out into the open.

My eyes locked onto him. Swiftly, I lined up my emotions. My arm shifted as I maneuvered my wand. The lure of Instinctia appeared and this time, I let it take control.

"Elertfa Lokwhan."

My spell smacked into Porter's chest. He reeled backward, then fell. His rear struck the ground, driving a small cloud of dirt into the air.

The crowd fell silent. I stood still, panting softly. Goosebumps covered my arms. Sweat dripped down my wrist and laced through my fingers, causing my grip on the wand to turn slippery.

"Mr. Wolf ..." Boltstar blinked. "... is the victor."

A collective groan rang out from the students. Meanwhile, the staffers raced into the HMQ. Reaching me first, Piper slapped my back. Leandra slugged my arm. Then I felt myself hoisted upward, onto the shoulders of Jax and Nico. They paraded me around in a circle to raucous staffer cheers. The students, meanwhile, stared at us in stony silence.

Boltstar watched this all unfold with a serene, emotionless expression. "Class dismissed. Remember to read the first section of Chapter Twelve for tomorrow." Leaving the bleachers, he made his way onto the field. "A word, Mr. Wolf?"

My blood froze. What was this about? Had he seen the Immaculatize spell? Did he know it was Chaotic magic?

Jax and Nico lowered me to the ground. Heart pounding, I stepped over the magic rope. "Sir?"

"That was quite sloppy," he said, greeting me next to the HMQ. "Fortunately for you, Mr. Garrington was worn out from the previous games."

"Are you blind?" Leandra gave him a scornful look. "Randy crushed him."

Boltstar trained his gaze upon her. "Do you have something to add to this conversation, Ms. Chen?"

"Uh, no, Sir." Her face was red as a beet as she melted into the crowd of staffers.

"Even so, you won," Boltstar said, turning his attention back to me. "And that's no small achievement, especially for one with your, uh, limited academic success. I hope I'll be seeing more of this from you in the future."

My fear melted away and I beamed with pride. Yeah, I knew I shouldn't care about his opinion. But hey, it wasn't every day I got complimented by the world's most famous magician. "Thank you, Sir."

With a nod, he took his leave. By that time, the students and staffers were filtering out of the arena. I lingered a few moments, waiting for them to leave.

When I was finally alone, I reentered the HMQ. Blood raced through my veins and my heart was filled with excitement. Winning the game had felt utterly amazing. The only way to top it would be if I were to keep winning.

The thought dazzled me. What if I were to win more HMQ games? What if I continued to impress Boltstar? What if he came to see me as being equal to, say, a Porter or a Kell? What then?

An odd possibility, weird but intriguing, began to take shape in my head. What if Boltstar plucked me out of the staffer ranks? What if he let me return to class? What if I, in turn, actually studied for a change?

A door cracked open. Nico poked his head into the arena. "Hey, Randy!"

"What?"

"You're coming right?" He grinned. "We're going to throw you a little party."

I nodded. "Yeah, I'm coming."

"Excellent, man. See you back at the dorm."

As the door banged shut, I found myself grinning from ear to ear. My mind returned to the dream of going back to school and I knew it was silly. Not only silly, but downright wrong. After all, I was trying to figure out a way to bring down Boltstar, not impress him.

Still, it was fun to consider. The benefits were endless. A bright future. An end to my self-loathing as well as Porter's insults. No more lectures from Mom and Dad. The list went on and on. It was all so enticing, so exciting. And yet, completely unrealistic. Oh, well.

A guy could always dream, right?

CHAPTER 37

Tad, memory mirror in hand, munched on an apple as we climbed into the celestarium a few days later. He shot us a sideways glance, his eyes glistening in the moonlight.

"Oh, good," he said. "I was starting to get worried."

"Boltstar kept us late." Scowling under her breath, Leandra hoisted herself through the aperture. Gaining her feet, she gave him the once-over. "What are you so happy about?"

With a wide grin, he lifted his shirt. "I'm cured," he exclaimed. "That healing potion did the trick."

We all crowded around him, gawking at his shoulder. The Gratlan had been healing for weeks now, gradually shrinking and fading in color. Now, it was gone.

"Awesome." I gave him a curious look. "So, how's the itching?"

"Gone, thank goodness." He chuckled. "Another day of that and I'd have scratched a hole right through my skin."

I knew what he meant. If my busted ribs hadn't healed by now, I'd be going crazy.

"It looks great." Piper poked his shoulder a few times, then smiled. "We should celebrate."

"Definitely." He cocked his head. "But first, how was class?"

"Ask him." Leandra jabbed a thumb at me. "He's the big winner."

He swung my way. "Yeah?"

My cheeks started to burn. Since that first victory four days earlier, I'd won multiple HMQ games, thanks to the timely use of Chaotic spells. Nobody, not even Porter, was laughing at me now. But I was also beginning to feel the pressure of added eyeballs. People were watching me closely, trying to figure out the secret to my sudden success. It was becoming harder and harder to use Chaotic magic without arousing suspicion.

"I got lucky," I said.

"Luck had nothing to do with it." Piper attempted to smooth out her frizzy hair. "You earned those wins."

For the next few minutes, we filled him in on the class as well as the HMQ games. Afterward, he sat back in his chair, looking thoughtful.

"How'd you do with letting go?" he asked.

"Letting go?"

"I mean, did you try letting your emotions guide the process? Did you forget the spells we've practiced up here and just go with the flow?"

Oh, no. Not this again. Tad had been bugging me about this very issue on a nightly basis. Curiously enough, my first Chaotic spell—Vanista—had been driven by real emotions. But since then, I'd focused on ginning up fake ones, casting spells, and recording the results. I just felt more comfortable working that way. Anyway, my process was producing results, so why change it?

"No," I replied. "Not yet."

He shrugged. "I always let my emotions guide my magic."

"Good for you. But I'm trying to learn as many spells as possible. And the fastest way to do that is to keep trying different emotional combinations."

"Fair enough." He tossed his apple core into a magic trash can and it instantly vanished. Wiping his lips, he walked to the window. The moon was gigantic that evening, shining so brightly that it all but blotted out the evening stars. "Not to change the subject, but we need to talk. All of us."

I knew what he was going to say before he even said it. "Yes," I said.

He frowned. "Yes?"

"Yes, we'll still help you with Womigia."

"Are you sure you want to go up against Boltstar? And his inner circle, too?"

I thought about Boltstar's underhanded attack on the Chaotics. I thought about the lives he'd ended, the people he'd drodiated. But most of all, I thought about Tad. I thought about him living each and every day in utter agony, hating himself for something that had never happened.

I checked with Leandra and Piper. They offered me small nods in return.

"We're sure," I said.

"Thank you," he said gratefully.

"If we're doing this, we need to do it right," Leandra said. "So, what's the plan?"

"I've got an idea. More of a strategy, really." He paused. "Divide and conquer."

We stared at him expectantly.

"Divide and conquer?" She arched an eyebrow. "That's it? That's all you've got?"

"What I mean is that we confront them one at a time. Then, bam, bam, bam, bam! We take them down."

"Bam?" Leandra looked skeptical. "It's going to take a little more than 'bam' to defeat the greatest witches and wizards of all time."

"You're right," I said thoughtfully. "Even if we fought them one at a time, we might not outduel them. We need a distraction, something to keep them occupied while we take them down."

Her skepticism melted away. "I know how to distract them."

"How?" Tad wondered.

"My simulator mirror."

"Forget it," I said.

"But—"

"But nothing. This isn't the time to fool around with unproven inventions. We need something we can count on."

She glared at me.

"How about you?" I looked at Piper. "Got any ideas?"

"No," she replied. "But I know how we can divide them, so to speak."

"How?"

"Simple. We follow them. Get their schedules down cold. We figure out when and where they're most vulnerable." She brushed some strands of frizzy hair out of her eyes. "We use Shadow Madkey to get the drop on them. Then we strike."

I gave her a thoughtful look. "Can you take point on that?"

She bobbed her head in response.

"What about me?" Tad asked.

"We still need a distraction," I replied. "If you think of anything, let us know. In the meantime, I need your help with Chaotic magic. I need to practice Vanista. Plus, I need more spells, better spells."

For the next couple of hours, we worked in relative silence. Leandra sat at a table, stewing silently, fiddling with her simulator mirror. Piper sat across from her, drawing maps of Shadow Madkey from memory. Meanwhile, Tad and I worked in our usual way. I'd cast spells using fabricated emotions and he'd record the results in a notebook.

"Hang on." Hunched over his notebook, Tad scribbled down a few notes. "What was that wording again?"

I scratched my head, befuddled and more than a bit amused. On the far side of the room, the bust had undergone a rather amazing transformation. Its mouth had popped open. Now, the mouth was moving in-time with my own mouth. If I curled my lip, its lip curled as well. It was freaky, to say the least.

"Copy-talk," I said.

"Copy-talk?"

"Yup." I sighed. "I can't imagine it'll be all that helpful."

"We'll put it in the 'Maybe' pile," he replied with a wink.

I felt annoyed and frustrated. Pouncing on those emotions, I began to move my wand.

"Herd Crash," I said.

Multiple bolts of auburn light raced across the room. The first one slammed into the bust, the others struck the table and the chairs. The table jolted across the floor. The chairs went airborne, tumbling a few times before smashing back to the ground. The bust, meanwhile, sailed into the glass windows. Clearly well-enchanted, they held firm, but the bust exploded into a billion tiny pieces.

Startled, Leandra and Piper looked up.

Tad cocked his head. "What was that?"

I blinked, awed by the unexpected display of power. "Herd Crash."

"Try it again." He scribbled down a few notes, then stood up. "On me."

I stared at him. "Uh, did you see what I just did to that bust?"

"That old thing?" He snorted. "You could've blown on it and it would've cracked right down the middle."

Before I could lodge another protest, he ventured out into the line of fire. "Are you sure about this?" I asked.

He answered me with a confident nod.

I took a second to recall the process. Then I vacated my emotions. I filled my innards with frustration and annoyance. This sent my wand into motion. My lips opened wide. "Herd Crash," I said.

Tad grunted as a bolt of auburn light smashed into his belly. Other bolts hit him in the chest and limbs. Combined, they sent him crashing to the floor, winded and red in the face.

I went to check on him. "Are you okay?"

"Herd Crash is right," he managed as he sat up. "That spell's like getting run over by a bunch of wild animals."

"What kind of animals?" Leandra wanted to know.

"Does it matter?"

"Of course," she replied, a teasing smile upon her lips. "A herd of teakettlers is very different than a herd of glawackuses."

"Actually, teakettlers don't have herds," Piper said. "The word you mean is—"

"Sasquatches," Tad muttered as he stood up again. "Definitely sasquatches."

CHAPTER 38

Boltstar whistled loudly, then removed his derby. Gently, he wiped droplets of sweat from his forehead. "Mr. Wolf is the victor."

Beaming from ear to ear, I loped across the HMQ. Extending my hand, I offered it to a fallen Kell. "Nice match."

Ignoring me, he rose to his full height. One hand clenched his belly, which was clearly still aching from the Herd Crash. His other hand stayed firmly at his side.

Just a few minutes ago, we'd been the last two contenders in a Havoc Royal. The clear favorite, he'd been bearing down hard on me. Eager to turn the tables, I'd decided to try out the latest spell in my arsenal. Churning up the right emotions, I'd sent waves of light hurtling his way. At the same time, I'd kept my wand moving, doing my best to make it look like I was firing off multiple Elertfa spells at top speed. He'd dodged a few bolts of light, but the rest had knocked him for a loop.

The staffers roared their approval. Meanwhile, the students were silent.

"How'd you get so fast, Wolf?" he demanded.

I shrugged.

He grunted. "Next chance I get, I'm wiping that smirk right off your face."

Boltstar left the bleachers. With long strides, he hiked to the HMQ. The staffer applause died off. The students perked up. Something, it appeared, was about to happen.

He stopped just short of the magic rope. Replacing his derby, he looked me over. "Congratulations, Mr. Wolf. What's your secret?"

"Practice." I offered him a nervous grin. "Loads and loads of practice."

"I see." He checked the clock. Then he turned a bit, angling toward the crowd. "I know it's quitting time. But how would you feel about one last game?"

A dull murmur rose up from the assembled audience. There was agreement, but not much in the way of enthusiasm. I figured it was because everyone was tired, but too scared to defy the likes of Boltstar.

"I'm not talking about a Havoc Royal," he continued. "Instead, I thought we'd mix things up a bit with a Havoc Duel. On one side, Mr. Randy Wolf, tonight's champion. That is, if he's up for it."

Truthfully, I was pretty tired, too. Plus, I was eager to get back to the celestarium, to work on my Chaotic magic. But how could I say no to Boltstar?

"I guess so," I said. "Who's the opponent?"

His bottom lip curled the tiniest amount. "Me."

The students erupted into raucous chatter. It grew louder and louder until I could barely hear myself think. But a single look from Boltstar, fierce and unrelenting, quelled the noise.

He pulled his wand out of his vest. Never breaking his gaze, he twirled it in his hand.

"Well?" he asked. "What do you say?"

I could feel the audience staring at me, drilling holes into my head. "No, thank you, Sir."

"Come on." His lips shifted and he gave me a full-blown smile. It caught me off-guard. I'd rarely seen him smile, at least not at me. "Let's give them a good show."

Truth be told, I was a little curious. I'd been performing quite well in the HMQ as of late. So, how good was I? Was I skilled enough to take on the legendary Boltstar? I knew I'd never beat him, but could I hold my own for a few minutes?

I sighed. "Okay."

The crowd exploded.

"There's just one rule," he said, his eyes never leaving my face. "The first person to be driven off his feet by a direct hit, or knocked unconscious, loses. Nothing is illegal, nothing is frowned upon. We duel until one magician bests the other one."

I licked my lips as my nerves began to frazzle. Then I nodded.

To enormous cheers, he crossed the magic rope and entered the HMQ. He walked to one end of the quadrant, then turned toward the bleachers.

"Since I'll be competing, I need someone to act as referee. Someone beyond reproach, someone who wouldn't possibly favor either one of us." He scanned the crowd. "Ms. Shaw, would you please do the honors?"

Hesitantly, Piper rose to her feet. "I've never refereed a match before, Headmaster," she said in a wavering tone.

"I'm sure you'll do fine. You need only deliver two whistles. One to begin the match and the other to end it."

Shooting me a helpless look, she left the bleachers and walked onto the field. I exhaled. Piper was a good choice and I knew she'd be utterly fair. But I couldn't help thinking that this was part of Boltstar's game. Not only would he defeat me, he'd force one of my best friends to make it official.

Feeling increasingly uneasy, I walked to the opposite end of the HMQ. Taking no chances, I ducked behind one of the enchanted barriers.

My breaths came short and fast. I clutched my wand so hard, my fingers started to hurt. The crowd died down and I could hear people shuffling lightly in the stands.

Twisting my neck, I eyed the bleachers. Leandra, Jax, Nico, and Fyla had moved to the front row. They leaned forward, worried looks upon their visages. I caught Leandra's gaze and cast her a small smile.

She didn't return it.

Piper's whistle, soft and musical, rang out. A hint of cyan light caught my eye and something crashed into the barrier. Now, that particular barrier had survived thousands of spells over the last few weeks without so much as a scratch. But Boltstar's spell caused it to utterly explode. The impact blew me backward and I rolled a couple of times. Bits and pieces of rubble proceeded to rain down on me.

Whoa, I thought.

Scrambling to my feet, I dove behind another enchanted barrier. A bolt of magic arrived at the same time. There was another explosion, another rain of rubble.

Any faint possibility I'd harbored of winning the duel was long gone. All I could think about was survival. Rising up, I retreated to the very back of the quadrant. My feet slammed into the turf. My arms pumped hard and fast.

Bolts of magic struck the ground. The impact drove clumps of dirt into the air and into my lungs. I coughed, then tripped on an old crate. Arms spinning like windmills, I fought a losing battle to keep my balance.

Seconds later, I crashed to the ground. Grabbing a quick breath, I glanced at Boltstar. He hadn't moved an inch. His wand was steady and he wore a look of pure concentration.

I winced, steeling myself for the finishing blow. But there was no sudden blaze of light, no crashing jolt to my gut.

He's not even trying, I realized. *He's toying with me!*

That just about crushed any confidence I had left. And yet, it also gave me the tiniest window of opportunity. Obviously, he wasn't going to take me seriously. Maybe I could use that against him.

The soles of my shoes scraped the ground. Then I was up again and running for cover. I charged past a battered boat, stacks of empty Bizzlum crates, and piles of scorched and broken furniture. Then I ducked behind a pile of cylindrical stones. Now, there were a few layers of obstacles between us.

A flurry of cyan light filled the HMQ. Ear-splitting cracking noises caused me to cringe. Peeking out, I saw one half of the boat skid and twist across the field and smash up against the magic rope. The side closest to me had a big hole in it. Gray smoke poured out of the gap.

I leaned my back against the stones. I could see part of the crowd from my vantage point. They were silent, still. They looked as shell-shocked as I felt.

More crashes rang out. Lockers, dented and scorched, went airborne. A wall of tires exploded into flames. Crates shattered into tiny slivers of wood.

His spells were coming way too fast to block. And any Structuralist spell I cast would surely be turned to smoke. If I wanted to win this thing, I'd have to use Herd Crash. If I could pull it off, I'd send a whole bunch of magic straight at Boltstar. There was no way he could block it all.

Wood cracked and metal groaned as he directed his attention to the piles of broken furniture. Chairs shot in all directions.

I closed my eyes. Digging deep, I got in touch with my inner core. Unfortunately, my emotions were little more than a frazzled bundle of nerves.

My brow furrowed. A frown creased my face. My emotions dulled, then came under my control. I thought about the Herd Crash spell, about what it would take to pull it off.

A thunderous blow deafened me. The stones quivered, then collapsed in a heap. I spilled onto the rubble. How long would Boltstar keep this up? Probably not long, I figured. Sooner or later, he'd tire of the game.

I steered my emotions to the correct mixture. My wand danced. My lips opened, the spell on the tip of my tongue. Suddenly, the warmth and comfort of Instinctia flooded my senses. I fought back and my wand began to shake. My tongue flicked as I kept myself from saying the wrong spell.

The lure of Instinctia faded away. Looking ahead, I saw Boltstar. He had yet to move even an inch. His face was calm and his brow remained unfurrowed. Twirling his wand in one hand, he appraised me for a long moment.

"Herd Crash," I whispered.

Auburn bolts burst forth, one after the other. I shifted my hand quickly, so as to mimic the casting of multiple Elertfa spells. Meanwhile, the bolts blazed a fiery trail across the HMQ.

A collective gasp rose up from the crowd. Boltstar's face tightened just a smidgeon. Dropping his casual manner, his wand flew into action. It sliced through the air, this way and that. A string of words tumbled out of his mouth.

Orbs of cyan light appeared. My auburn bolts smashed into the orbs and vanished into a cloud of colorful smoke. I barely had time to register what had happened when a heavy, weird blow struck my left shoulder. My eyes popped wide and I felt my feet leave the ground.

My back slammed into the soil. The impact drove the air out of my lungs. Unable to move, unable to breathe, I lay there, staring at the ceiling through hazy eyes.

Distant cheers, loud and raucous, reached my ears. I managed to choke out a breath. My lungs seized up and I began coughing and hacking. The sudden movements sent fierce aches up and down my torso.

My shoulder felt, well, wrong. Like it didn't even belong to my body. Blinking through the pain, I saw Piper. She looked at me with concerned eyes, then blew a loud whistle. Twisting my head, I saw Boltstar, still situated on the far end of the HMQ. He stood in the same place, twirling his wand in his hand. He wasn't bragging or playing to the crowd. He didn't have to. They'd seen what he could do.

They'd seen him crush me.

CHAPTER 39

Something jarred my shoulder, driving me out of a deep slumber. Opening my eyes, I saw Professor Tuckerson's face, jaw jutted outward, mere inches from my own. I recoiled in surprise and fear. That was when I noticed that I felt no pain, no agony. Instead, there was just a light itching sensation around my left shoulder.

"Rise and shine, dropout." He yanked his jaw back, then appraised me with a cold, stern eye. "I want you gone within the hour."

"How long have I been out?"

"How should I know?" He heaved out a sigh. "Do you even know what that stupid havoc magic class of yours has done to me? This used to be a nice, quiet job. Now, I'm inundated with all of you little twerps."

I frowned.

He sighed, as if it took him every ounce of energy he possessed to even talk to me. "Two hours sounds about right," he said.

"That's it?"

He clucked his tongue. "If you want to play Rip Van Winkle, you'd best do it on somebody else's time."

After the duel, Jax and Nico had helped me to the clinic. Ignoring Tuckerson's protests, they'd hauled me to an empty room. They'd slathered my shoulder with healing potion, fed me a glass of Canfee—Afternoon Nap-flavored—and put me to bed.

Ignoring the itching, I rose to a sitting position. Then I shifted to the side and prepared to step down.

"And just where do you think you're going?"

"I thought you wanted me to leave."

"I do. But not yet." He smiled, baring his teeth. "You've got company."

"I do?"

"Your folks. They sent a bubbler this way." He snarled. "I'd prefer to pop it, but the headmaster tends to frown on that kind of thing."

"I can't imagine why."

Grumbling, he opened the door. A whizzing noise started up and the bubbler slid into the room. He gave it a nasty look, then shoved it aside.

The door slammed shut. Slowly, the bubbler approached the bed. The temperature dropped a few degrees. A bit of mist sprayed over me.

Peering at the watery image, I saw my parents sitting at the kitchen table. They were in their usual places, digging into giant platefuls of doughcream. Just the sight of it made my stomach rumble. And that was *before* the ever-changing aromas reached my nose.

"Oh, Randy." Mom dropped her fork and it clattered against the wooden table. "Are you okay?"

"Yeah." I rubbed the back of my head. "I'm fine. Listen, I'm hungry and—"

"And nothing, buster." Dad's eyes met mine. "We need to talk."

I froze in place. This could only be about one thing …

YuckYuck.

Plenty of time had passed since that particular conversation. As such, I'd nearly forgotten about their desire to pull me out of Madkey. But now, the mere thought sent me into a panic. I couldn't leave, not yet. Not after all I'd learned and all of our plans. Not when we were so close to making our move on Boltstar.

"We got a message from Lanctin," he continued. "He told us everything."

That caught me by surprise. What had he told them? Forgetting YuckYuck for a moment, my mind began to reel through possibilities. Had he told them about how he'd crushed me in a duel? Or worse, that he suspected I was using Chaotic magic?

Dad's serious face suddenly broke and I found myself staring at a huge smile. I blinked, caught off guard. Needless to say, he wasn't the smiley type. "He says you show a real penchant for havoc magic." His voice took on a note of distinct pride. "He says if you keep it up, he just might be inclined to give you another shot."

I blinked again. "Another shot?"

"Yes, at Madkey," he exclaimed. "He's thinking about taking you back. You could be a student again!"

I sat up, unsure of whether I'd heard him correctly or not. "Are you serious?"

"Oh, Randy," Mom gushed. "We're so proud of you. I always knew you'd be a star."

That wasn't exactly true. In fact, she'd said the exact opposite ever since I'd dropped out of school. But I was way too dumbfounded to point that out to her.

"Can you believe it?" Dad looked so proud, I thought he'd burst. "Lanctin Boltstar, the father of modern magic, thinks you've got a bright future."

"But I lost," I replied. "I fought him and I lost."

"We know," Mom said.

"You might've lost," Dad added. "But it was to the greatest magician of all time. Heck, you're just a freshman."

"I'm a staffer," I reminded him.

He snorted. "Not for long. The way he spoke about you, it's just a matter of time before you're out of that lousy assembly-line job."

"Isn't this wonderful, Randy?" Mom gushed. "Your dreams are finally coming true."

My parents were in a rush to go brag to their friends, so the conversation ended quickly. After popping the bubbler, I sat in bed for a long while.

Rematriculation? Until that very moment, it had been little more than a pipedream. A lark, a nice little fantasy. But now, I found myself taking it seriously. On one hand, the idea made my heart thump. I could still earn a Madkey degree and get a good job. I could still have a normal life.

Or could I? After all, I knew the truth about Boltstar now, about Structuralism. And Tad had opened my eyes to a much deeper world of magic. A world of wonder, a world that didn't depend on the Capsudra.

Still, the thought of going back to school stuck with me. And as I climbed out of the bed, I found myself thinking about how it would feel to earn a Madkey degree. To stand on stage, accepting a diploma. To prove myself as one of the world's elite magicians. It made for a nice fantasy and I continued to think about it as I got dressed in my soiled, scorched clothing. I thought about it as I quietly exited the clinic. And I thought about it as I made my way back to the staffer dorm. It was still on my mind as I climbed into bed. Ahh, if only there was a way to have it all.

If only.

CHAPTER 40

"It's Randy, right?" Hannah asked.

She stood a couple of feet away, waiting to ride a chair into Madkey Station Grille. A couple of girls, all freshmen, were with her. Kell Masters was farther back, his face dark and ugly.

"Uh ..." I glanced over both shoulders and saw no one. Yup, she was talking to me alright. I couldn't remember the last time a student talked to me like I was an actual person. And Hannah, no less!

"Yeah," I replied. "What's up?"

Her friends giggled. What was so funny? Feeling self-conscious, I ran a hand through my hair.

"You looked good last night," she said.

Her smile could've lit a thousand cool-lights. Kell's expression, on the other hand, could've darkened them and then some. It occurred to me to tread carefully.

"Thanks. Listen, I need to, uh, find my friends." I scanned the dinner crowd. A bunch of staffers sat in Mid-Torso, not far from the windows. Jax, Nico, and Jenny occupied one table. Piper and Leandra sat at another one.

Hannah and the other girls followed my gaze. One of Hannah's friends, a freshman named Nella Shorp, sniffed. "But those are staffers."

I gave her an odd look. "And?"

Hannah glared at the girl. Immediately, Nella clamped her mouth shut.

"I think what she's trying to say is that you've got options. You don't have to hang out with them if you don't want to." She stepped up to me, so close you couldn't fit a sheet of paper between us. "You could hang out with us instead."

"My man!" An unfamiliar arm slipped around my shoulder. Peering to my right, I saw Calvin Hayes, flanked by sophomores. "It's Randy, right? Randy Wolf?"

I stood still, utterly confused. I wasn't used to attention. Well, except for the negative kind, as dished out by Porter and company.

"Nice job last night," he said with a chuckle. "I thought Kell had you beat for sure. Shows what I know, huh?"

"Yeah," I said uncertainly.

"Hey, Ronny." Dean Rinzler, a cocky sophomore with a penchant for being annoying, gave me a fake jab to the ribs. "You're looking pretty tough these days."

"Well, I—" I started to say.

"It's Randy, dummy." Calvin released my shoulder and edged between us. "His name is Randy."

Dean rolled his eyes. "Yeah, yeah, that's what I said. Listen, Randy, you've got to show me your secret sometime. Woo boy, I've never seen anyone get off so many spells at once."

Right about that time, my ears began to detect whispers from around the Grille.

"He's cute," someone said. "What's his name again?"

"No, no, you're way off-base," a guy told his friend. "He's better than Porter. Heck, he might be as good as Kell."

"A staffer?" A snort rang out. "That's just stupid. Someone needs to get that kid into a classroom."

That last comment came courtesy of Iliana Diaz, a popular senior with a bright future ahead of her. Word had it that Garrington Magic had offered her a sweet deal to join their ranks. So, her compliment felt especially good.

"Come on, Hannah." Kell turned our way as he reached the front of the chair line. His gaze passed over my face and it felt as if the temperature had dropped to freezing. "Let's go."

Reluctantly, she tore herself from my side. "Just think about it," she said with a cute wink. Then she and her friends slid through the small crowd and boarded chairs. Lifting off, they quickly found a table in Lower-Torso.

Calvin, Dean, and the other sophomores continued to chat my ear off, so much in fact that I didn't get a chance to respond. Soon, we reached the front of the line. I hopped onto a chair, said my goodbyes, then kicked myself into the air.

As I gained altitude, I became aware of people watching me. My cheeks burned with embarrassment. But it was the good kind of embarrassment and I found myself sitting a bit taller than usual.

I rose to Mid-Torso, then kicked my way across the Grille. As I slid into the open spot between Leandra and Piper, the ghostly face of Yordlo appeared.

"Ahoy, mateys," he said, barely fighting off a yawn. "And welcome to—" He blinked, then did a double-take as if seeing me for the first time. "Aye, it's ye! Indeed, this is a pleasure, lad. It seems ye are quite famous these days."

My cheeks burned even hotter. I realized that Leandra was watching me closely. Piper, meanwhile, gave me an amused look.

"I'm not famous," I protested.

"Ye most certainly are, at least within these walls." He lowered his voice to a conspiratorial whisper. "Ye may not know this, but I can hear the words of everyone here."

I looked around, seeing a bunch of furtive looks and admiring glances. This was my first brush with fame and to be honest, I kind of liked it.

"Now, what'll it be?" Yordlo asked. "It's on the house."

"It's always on the house," Leandra pointed out.

Yordlo scowled at her. "If I want ye opinion, lass, I'll ask ye for it."

I checked the glowing menu on the table, then used my finger to flip a few pages. "I'll take the Abyss Gobbler," I said. "With cheesy french fries on the side."

"Would ye like a second one to go?"

Leandra and Piper gave me knowing looks. I always ordered an extra meal for Tad.

"Actually, could you have a fresh one ready for me after class?" I asked. "I'll take it back to the dorm."

"Surely, lad."

"Hey, Randy. Hey … you guys." Before I knew what was happening, Calvin slid smoothly between Leandra and I. Folding his hands on the table, he gave Yordlo a big grin. "Say, buddy, can you bring my food here instead? I could use a change of scenery."

Yordlo gave him a withering look. Without a word or even a nod, his ghostly presence vanished.

"Scoot over." Dean slid into the spot on my other side, nicking Piper's chair in the process. She nearly fell off, but Dean didn't notice. Instead, he swiveled toward me. "So, whatcha getting, Randy? Wait, wait … don't tell me. You're a steak guy, right?"

Just then, Hannah appeared. Girlfriends in tow, she directed her chair into the space between Piper and Leandra. "Hey, Pepper." She offered her a brilliant smile, which quickly faded. Reaching out, she touched a strand of Piper's tresses. "Oh, no. Bad hair day, huh?"

Piper's lips clamped together. She stewed in silence for a couple of seconds. Then Hannah's girlfriends elbowed their way to the table and she looked about ready to explode.

"I've got some special Garrington Magic shampoo that'll really help you with those split-ends," Hannah said earnestly. "Of course, that's only a small part of the problem. What you really need is—"

Piper was primed to boil over. She was normally mild-tempered, so I was kind of curious to see it. But instead, she pushed herself away from the table. Slipping through the crowd, she rode her chair to Upper-Torso. She parked it on one of the bridges, then headed straight for Left Arm.

My first instinct was to follow her. But by that time, the crowd was four chairs deep. It was so tight, I could barely breathe. Which was unfortunate since everyone seemed interested in talking to me.

I turned my head, cramped yet marveling at my sudden popularity. Yesterday, these people refused to acknowledge my existence. Now, they treated me like a best friend. In fact, the only students who didn't seem interested in talking to me were Porter and his goons. They sat by themselves in Upper-Torso, casting an occasional nasty look in my direction.

"How rude." Nella slid into Piper's old space. "Well, that's what you get for trying to help a staffer."

Leandra arched an eyebrow. "What's wrong with staffers?"

She stammered for a moment. "Uhh, nothing. I mean, well, what I was trying to say is—"

"She was trying to say that you guys are great at helping other people," Hannah said, smoothly and with a nice smile. "But you're not always good at receiving help."

Leandra wasn't buying it. "You think insulting her hair was help?"

"It wasn't an insult. It was the truth." She flipped her hair over one shoulder. "But I see what you mean. The truth can be hard to take sometimes."

"Riiiiighhhhtttt." Leandra gave me an apologetic look. "I need to get going. See you later."

My eyes bulged and I lunged for her arm. But she dodged me and kicked backward. The crowd parted for her. Another chair, with Jayce Azul perched on its edge, filled the gap.

"Hi, Randy," she said with a bright smile. "Remember me? We sat next to each other in Conveyance 9."

Glancing past her, I saw Leandra reach the Upper-Torso bridge. Hopping onto solid ground, she shot me a look. Seeing my crestfallen face, she laughed lightly.

"Good luck," she mouthed, as she made her way toward Left Arm.

I decided I wasn't hungry after all. Kicking my legs, I tried to follow her.

"Hey, don't leave yet." Calvin grabbed my chair, arresting its movement. "We've got to talk magic. Man, you're almost as fast as Boltstar. How do you do it?"

The others leaned closer, waiting for me to spill my guts. I shifted my gaze one last time, searching for my friends. But they were already gone. For a moment, I thought about wrenching my way out of Calvin's grip. But ultimately, I decided I could hang around for a bit. Hey, I was famous, right? How often was that going to happen in my lifetime?

I might as well enjoy it.

CHAPTER 41

"Thus far, our focus has been on the individual magician," Boltstar said solemnly as he strode back and forth across the wall. "But in real life, teamwork is absolutely essential to waging a successful havoc magic campaign. If Chaotic magicians return to this institution—and rest assured they're trying to do exactly *that* at this very moment—you'll need to depend on each other. If you choose to do otherwise, your arrogance may very well cost you your life."

I shifted uneasily in my seat. Why did these chairs have to be so darn uncomfortable? And where was Boltstar going with this? Why couldn't he just finish his lecture already?

Truth be told, I didn't want to be there. No, I wanted to be back in the celestarium with my friends, working on new Chaotic spells. But like it or not, class was mandatory. And so, I'd sat through the daily lecture like always, eyes trained on the ground, praying Boltstar didn't call on me.

He smiled broadly. "With that said, we're going to switch things up today in the HMQ."

Nico elbowed my ribs. "In other words, he doesn't want you to win again."

Boltstar looked at him. "Do you have something you'd like to share with the class, Mr. Stotem?"

His face turned beet red. "Uh, yes, Headmaster. I just wanted to say that I think it's a fine idea."

He gave Nico a long look, then began pacing again. "Tonight, we're going to play a game called Havoc Flag.

When you enter the field of play, you'll do so as part of a team. Specifically, students will divide themselves up by grade. Staffers will constitute the fifth team.

"The rules of Havoc Royal largely apply to this game with two exceptions. First, play will not be limited to the HMQ. Instead, all of Madkey Arena—save the locker room area—will be open to you. Second, instead of eliminating individuals, you will instead be eliminating entire teams. This can only be done by stealing their flags."

Boltstar let his words linger for a moment. "Each team will be issued a flag along with a base somewhere within the confines of the arena. You must protect your flag while attempting to steal the flags of other teams. You may use any spell you like. If a player is knocked to the ground by a direct spell, he or she is eliminated and must go to the locker room area. We'll continue playing until one team is left standing."

"Oh, this is real fair," Piper muttered. "The game's all about numbers and we're the smallest team here."

In total, the various classes numbered close to two hundred people apiece. Us staffers, on the other hand, numbered less than a hundred. So, yeah. We were at a pretty serious disadvantage.

"If you obtain an opponent's flag, take it back to your base," he continued. "If you get eliminated along the way, you must drop it and leave the field. At that point, anyone can grab it. If, however, you manage to secure it to your own flag first, the other team will be eliminated and must leave the playing field."

"Headmaster?" Felicia raised her hand. "What happens if we eliminate every member of another team prior to capturing their flag?"

Boltstar arched an eyebrow as if he found the question, well, kind of dumb. "If you eliminate an entire team, it shouldn't be too hard to grab their flag, should it?"

Her face turned pink with embarrassment. "No, Headmaster."

"I didn't think so. Now, you cannot win the game until all other flags are affixed to your own flag. Are there any questions?"

"Yeah, I've got a question," Leandra mumbled under her breath. "Why are you such a jerk?"

He looked straight at her.

She stiffened up, but still held his gaze.

"Freshmen." Boltstar held up a pennant with an image of the Sasquatch mascot on it. "This is your flag. Your base is the Wilshire Luxury Box, directly across from the locker room tunnel."

Porter hiked down the steps and retrieved the flag. Then he led the Freshmen toward their base.

Boltstar proceeded to hand out flags and assign bases for the other grades. They were all given luxury boxes to defend so I expected the same for us. But the headmaster, as it turned out, had other ideas.

"Staffers." He held up a ragged old Madkey pennant, dated 1954 and displaying a cartoon hidebehind. "This will serve as your flag. Your base is the field. The HMQ, to be specific."

Piper frowned. "We don't get a luxury box?"

"Is that a problem, Ms. Shaw?"

"Yeah, it's a problem," Leandra said. "A big one. We'll be sitting ducks out there."

"Not if you work together, Ms. Chen." He gave us an appraising look. "Now, come get your flag."

Jax led us down the bleachers. Nico took the flag and we hiked toward the HMQ.

Cupping his hands around his mouth, Boltstar turned in a slow circle. "Your flag must be in plain sight," he hollered.

"Hiding it is grounds for elimination. You have ten minutes to prepare. The game starts on my whistle."

Jax grunted as we stepped over the magic rope. "Well, we're screwed."

Jenny scowled. "What's Boltstar's problem anyway? I swear he's got it out for us."

"Oh, you think so?" Leandra said, sarcastically. "What was your first clue?"

Dorph bit his lip. "So, uh, does anyone have a plan?"

Gazes were shared. Slowly, everyone turned toward Piper.

Her eyes widened. "Hey, wait a second ..."

None of us were havoc magic experts. So, we needed the next best thing ... a history buff. Someone who'd studied old battles, who knew a thing or two about strategy. Tad would've been my first choice, given his obsession with magic history. Unfortunately, he wasn't an option.

"You're the best student we've got," I said.

"Not that that's saying much," Leandra added.

I gave her a dirty look before shifting back to Piper. "Think hard," I said. "Have you ever read about a battle that resembles this one?"

"Yeah," Jeff added. "Ideally, one where the underdogs came out on top."

Looking uncertain, she scanned the terrain. "I don't know," she said. "I mean, the other teams have a better sightline than us and they can use the seats for concealment. Plus, we're surrounded on all sides."

Leandra gave her a hard look. "Are you trying to tell us no havoc army has ever won a battle from the low ground?"

"Well, no," she conceded. "The Battle of Tafarge Hill comes to mind. Back in 1754—"

"We don't have time for a history lesson," Jax growled. "Just tell us what to do."

"Well, okay," she said, turning back to face us. "Listen, this isn't a great idea. It's not even good. But, well ..."

Huddling up tight, we listened to her idea. She was right. It wasn't great or even good. But it was something.

We broke the huddle. Nico led a group of staffers into the HMQ. They picked up sizable pieces of debris, then snuck off to their assigned posts.

Meanwhile, I headed for the middle of the quadrant. Turning a table upward, I set our flag on its scorched surface. Then I scouted the region, taking sight of the other teams and evaluating cover options. Nearby, I spotted a bunch of lockers. They stood tall and proud, having withstood the brunt of countless spells.

Holstering my wand, I grabbed a locker and rocked it over to two other ones. Then I moved a few more lockers into position, forming a small L-shaped cave. The cave would be my refuge, a place to hide when things got hairy. And things were about to get very hairy, indeed.

Time was running short. So, I stepped away from the lockers, making sure I was within eyesight of the other teams. Then I cupped my hands around my mouth and tilted my chin toward the bleachers. "I've beaten all of you," I shouted, turning in a slow circle. "Over and over again. How's that feel? How's it feel to lose to a dropout?"

The other teams, drawn together in large conferences, glanced my way. Their faces registered collective surprise. And why not? Staffers weren't supposed to be braggarts.

"Well, get used to it," I continued. "Because you're about to lose yet again."

Chez glared at me. Porter gnashed his teeth. Even Calvin, my recent admirer, slammed a fist into his palm.

"You're going down, Wolf," Gordon yelled. A bunch of other people shouted their concurrence. And that was just fine. The more attention they paid to me, the less they worried about what my teammates were doing.

Swarmed by insults and threats, I closed my eyes. Gently, I massaged my mind into blankness, then relaxed my muscles. The first part of Piper's plan was complete. Now, I needed to wreak, well, havoc.

Boltstar whistled.

Here we go.

Opening my eyes, I spun in a circle. Several dozen colorful spells zoomed toward me.

Oh, boy.

They drew close, a feast of dangerous color. There was no way I could block them all. So, I did the next best thing.

I ran.

Dodging and zigzagging, I darted into the L-shaped locker cave and veered into the back portion.

Spells slammed into the lockers. The air smelled of smoke and hot metal. The temperature lifted a few degrees and sweat began to trickle down the back of my neck.

The spells kept right on coming, banging into the lockers with relentless fury. Every instinct I possessed told me to stay low, to keep my head down. Unfortunately, that wasn't going to work. Piper's plan, like it or not, called for us to make our presence known.

Clearing my head again, I churned up a couple of emotions. My wrist shifted and my wand started to move.

As Instinctia washed through me, I popped up and took aim at the Freshmen base. "Elertfa Lokwhan," I said.

A thin auburn light left my wand. I ducked quickly, dodging a torrent of attacks. Perking my ears, I listened hard. The telltale "oof"—courtesy of Felicia—came a moment later. A grin creased my face.

Chalk one up for the staffers.

Other staffers, hidden in deep cover, rose up. They fired off spells, then quickly ducked down again. The students attacked us with extra intensity for a few seconds. Then they slowed up to take stock of the situation.

Look at our flag, I thought. *It's right there. Right out in the open. All you have to do is grab it.*

I rose up for a quick peek. The other teams were still tightly clustered around their bases. They looked tense and more than a bit uncertain.

"There he is," Sya screamed.

Ducking, I dodged another wave of spells. As expected, the teams had banded together to crush us. But only one of them could take our flag. So, which team wanted the honors?

"We've got them pinned down," Calvin shouted. "Who wants to get the staffer flag? How about you, Porter?"

"No, thanks," he called out, his voice tight and stiff.

"What's the matter?" Calvin's tone turned mocking. "Scared?"

Porter didn't respond. A big part of me hoped that meant he'd taken the bait, that he was descending the bleachers. But I knew better. He was far too savvy to expose himself that way.

"You guys are such wimps." The voice belonged to Carl Isku, the de-facto leader of the Seniors. "I'll get it."

Pulse racing, I stood up. Carl and a dozen other seniors were hiking down the stairs. He had his wand aimed in my direction. His companions had their wands at the ready as well, prepared to fight back if one of the other teams took a potshot at them.

Lowering my gaze, I caught sight of two broken tables leaning up against the wall. I grinned. Carl thought he had us beat. He was about to find out how wrong he was.

I threw myself to the ground, evading yet another volley of magic. Impatiently, I counted to twenty, just enough time for them to finish descending the steps. Then I stood up. All eyes were on Carl. He'd reached the wall, only to find a broken table in his way. Scowling, he stooped down to push it aside.

An emerald glow appeared, seemingly from the ground itself. Carl's head jolted backward. His body sagged and he collapsed in a heap.

And then Dorph was on his feet, waving his wand and spitting out spells. Four seniors went down immediately. The others spun toward Dorph. For a moment, it looked like he was in trouble. But then Jenny shrugged off a table of her own. Rising up, she issued a pair of spells. They hit home and two more seniors crashed into the bleachers. Dorph and Jenny continued to cast spells and in a matter of moments, the rest of Carl's group had been eliminated.

Other seniors, seven of them, rushed forward. They waved their wands and a bunch of spells zoomed toward Dorph and Jenny. The staffers crouched next to the wall and the spells passed overhead without incident. Meanwhile, the Sophomores and Juniors took advantage of the situation. Swarming forward, they pinned down the Seniors. A flurry of spells followed, with the Seniors taking the brunt of them.

Piper's plan was working better than any of us could've expected. The other teams may have had the high ground, which she called the crest. But thanks to the wall, they didn't have the havoc crest. That is, they didn't have unimpeded eyesight or a clear line of fire.

With this in mind, she'd instructed Nico and a few others to grab items from the HMQ. They were to sneak to the wall and, while the other teams were plotting their strategies, cover themselves with the items. Then they would wait, wands at the ready.

The Seniors continued to wilt under heavy fire. Then Gordon made his move. During the commotion, he'd silently crawled through the bleachers, then climbed on top of the Seniors' luxury box. Now, he leapt to the ground. Blasting Kylie Davis with a Genphor spell, he ripped the flag right off of a seat. Then he hightailed it back to his base.

In less than fifteen minutes, the Seniors were eliminated. Meanwhile, the other teams were involved in close-quarter fighting, taking heavy casualties in the process. Only us staffers remained relatively unscathed.

I crept outside the locker cave. Sliding out from under a boat, Piper hustled over to join me. Pressing our backs together, we took stock of the fighting. "Looks good so far," I said. "What now?"

She grinned. "We let them destroy each other."

Kell and the Juniors began to bombard the Sophomores and Freshmen with long-distance magic. Most of the spells were wild, but enough hit pay dirt to take out the last of the Sophomores.

Meanwhile, Porter, Sya, and Royce Miller hurried down a few rows. Porter lifted his wand and aimed it at the far end of the field.

"What's he doing? It's almost as if ..." Piper stiffened up. "Jenny, get out of there!"

Jenny, still ducked down behind the wall, heard the warning. Confused, she stood up. But before she could run, a chestnut blaze struck her legs. And then she was on her back, rolling and screaming.

We'd known this was a risk. Our fellow staffers, hunkered behind the walls and hidden amongst debris, were relatively safe from frontal assaults. But they had no rear defenses.

"Staffers," she shouted. "Back to the flag."

Nico, Leandra, Fyla, and others rose up, shedding crates, tables, boxes, blankets, and other items. But Porter, Sya, and Royce were ready for them. Fyla and Leandra quickly succumbed to their spells. And just like that, our numbers began to fall.

Leaving cover, Nico and Jeff ran alongside the wall. Jeff took the offensive, lobbing spells at everyone in sight. Nico played defense, using spells to negate incoming streaks of light. Taking no chances, Porter and his friends ducked behind some seats.

With Piper and I providing cover spells, Nico and Jeff rallied the other staffers. They raced back to the HMQ. Circling our flag, they took whatever cover they could find.

Up in the bleachers, Kell and the Juniors were starting to hunker down. Casting a glimpse at the Freshmen, I saw only a few people at their base, all in defensive postures. Shifting my gaze, I noticed shadows moving through the bleachers at all levels and in all directions. The Freshmen, I realized, were staking out positions for the inevitable battle with the Juniors.

For the moment, both teams had seemingly forgotten about us. Which was just fine by me. Catching my breath, I put my brain to work. Potential tactics and strategies whirled in my head and I realized just how badly I wanted to win. Sure, it was just a game. But it was something else, too.

Us staffers suffered untold daily indignities. Not only did we serve an unappreciative student body, but we also acted as their magical punching bags. As such, we didn't get many chances to celebrate as a team, to feel like winners. A victory tonight, in Havoc Flag, would change that.

Up in the bleachers, the Juniors spotted the incoming Freshmen and laid down a thick barrage of spells. Hannah, Sya, Gordon, and many others fell under the onslaught. Porter retreated to his base and tried to organize a counter-attack. But the Juniors overran them in no time.

I inhaled a sharp breath. The Freshmen had fallen much faster than I'd expected. One moment, they were in close combat. The next, the Juniors were taking the Freshmen flag back to their base.

"The Freshmen are eliminated," Boltstar called out. "The Juniors and Staffers are our final teams." Curiously enough, he said 'Staffers' with more than a little respect.

Muscles tensed, I waited for the Juniors to cluster up and celebrate their near-victory. It had to be a sweet win for Kell, seeing as how Porter was his most formidable challenger.

But true to form, he was all-business. Ducking down, he began shouting out instructions. "Mike and London, you're with me. You three, go that way. Defenders, I want you to work your way toward the field. Make sure to keep our flag in sight though." He paused to take a breath. "Now, spread out. I want people on every level and with plenty of space between them."

I didn't like the sound of that. Frowning, I watched the Juniors break into three separate units. The units split up and spread out. They quickly surrounded the field and began to bombard us with attacks.

Piper's face turned anxious. "What do we do?"

"Head for the lockers," I called out, my heart sinking as I realized I was playing right into Kell's hands.

Dorph raced out from behind cover. A well-placed spell hit his back and he fell hard, smacking against the ground.

Piper and I slid into the makeshift locker cave. As Nico, Jax, and the remaining staffers hurried toward us, a variety of attacks went airborne. One spell wrenched Nico's leg and he collapsed to the turf. Jax took a hit to the side, stumbled, and fell on his face. Others bit the dust as well. Soon, Piper and I were the only staffers left.

I stayed at the cave entrance long enough to make sure no one was seriously hurt. Then I ducked out of sight.

"Kell's got us pinned down," I said. "My guess is that he'll go for the flag rather than take us out. So, we have to keep up our offense."

"What's the point?" Leaning against a locker, she slid to the ground.

"We can still win this thing," I said. "We just have to—"

"It's only a game," she reminded me.

Spells began to cascade against the lockers. Metal banged loudly and the acrid smell of smoke filled my nostrils.

"We made it this far," I said.

"And that's great. But there must be at least a dozen of them to just the two of us." She gave me a pointed look. "And we need to stay healthy if we want to have any hope of defeating Boltstar."

"Hey, Wolf," Kell shouted. "I've got your flag. What are you going to do about it?"

I glanced at Piper. She stared back at me.

"You're not even going to try?" I asked.

She shook her head. "It's not worth it."

Kell lifted his voice a few decibels. "Ahh, so you're a coward," he shouted. "That's what I figured."

I wasn't stupid. I knew he was goading me. If I kept my head down, he'd take our flag back to his base. If I stood up, I'd get blasted from all sides. It was a lose-lose situation. But maybe it didn't have to be that way. Maybe I could still find a way to win this thing without ending up in the clinic.

Rising to full-height, I rammed my shoulder into a locker. As it tipped over, I shifted my wand. A tall kid, dark-haired and wearing glasses, was right in front of me. Caught off-guard, he froze.

That was all I needed. My emotions and wand movements came together in an instant. Instinctia took over and I blasted the kid with Elertfa.

The locker hit earth and I leapt over it. Running fast, I zig-zagged, then ran behind a maze of debris. Spells sped my way. Tables exploded. A cabinet splintered and cracked. Stacked metal crates came tumbling down.

"You four take him out," Kell shouted as he headed for the bleachers. "Everyone else with me."

I dove behind an antique chest. Spells slammed into it, slowly reducing it to smithereens. Peeking out, I saw Piper huddled within the now-broken locker cave. Farther back, Kell raced toward the bleachers, the other juniors in tow.

I can use Herd Crash, I realized. *I can take them all down at once.*

There was just one problem.

Piper.

She was in the line of fire, her arms wrapped over her head. Given the nature of Herd Crash, as well as my inexperience with using it, there was more than a decent chance I'd wind up hitting her.

Kell paused at the wall. Looking over his shoulder, he shot me the worst kind of smile. An extra-cocky grin that made my lip curl and my heart burn with intense anger.

I forced my emotions into place. My wand flicked through a series of movements. Instinctia welled up within me. It tugged at my feelings, my wand, my lips. But I fought back, denying its warm embrace. As it faded away, my wand began to move. The words that left my mouth were entirely my own.

"Herd Crash," I whispered softly so no one else would hear it.

Multiple jets of auburn raced forward. As per usual, I kept my wand moving, making it look like I'd just gotten off a series of quick Elertfas.

Fiery light crashed into the Juniors. Some got hit on the back, others got slammed in the stomach. Regardless, they went flying and I do mean flying. Best of all was Kell. He was climbing over the wall at the time. At the last second, he turned to look at me, only to get smacked in the noggin. The impact drove him off his perch and he crashed into the seats.

Silence settled over the arena. Twisting my head, I looked at Boltstar, wondering if he'd make me go get the flags before calling the game.

"The Juniors are eliminated," he said slowly, as if still processing it. "Staffers win."

I lifted my arms in victory. Madkey students glowered at me while the staffers raced onto the field.

"Wow," Dorph said, staring at the carnage in disbelief. "How'd you do that?"

Before I could reply, Nico, Fyla, Jax, Jenny, and a bunch of others swarmed around me. I felt myself lifted off of my feet and hoisted into the air.

"Piper?" Leandra scanned the HMQ. "Where are you? Can you hear me?"

"Over … here." The tiny voice was filled with agony.

My heart froze. Turning my gaze, I saw the cave had collapsed in a heap, a victim of the Herd Crash. Piper lay underneath a locker, her face twisted to the side, her jaw clenched in pain.

Twisting violently, I climbed down from my perch. Leandra and Jax lifted the fallen locker and I pulled Piper to safety. She had a huge welt on her forehead and blood on her shoulder. Her eyes were dazed, too.

"Impressive, Mr. Wolf." Boltstar's eyes flicked from me, to Piper, then back to me again. "Very impressive."

It was a compliment, a real one. Competing emotions tugged at my heart strings. She was my friend and deserved more from me. Way more. And yet, Boltstar's words rang loudly in my ears, replaying themselves over and over again.

He was pleased with me, not just for winning but for sacrificing Piper to do it.

I felt terrible for hurting her. And I knew better than to care what he thought of me. But I couldn't help it.

Like it or not, I was bursting with pride.

CHAPTER 42

"Oh ho!" Tad lowered his memory mirror as the floating tray rose into the celestarium. "And just in time, too. I'm so hungry I was thinking about eating this remembra."

"It's probably healthier than doughcream," Leandra quipped as she followed me into the large room. She was acting normal, at least for her. Unfortunately, the same couldn't be said for Piper.

Piper was clearly mad at me. And really, who could blame her? That welt on her forehead was no accident. Part of me wanted to apologize. But the bigger part of me thought it best to wait for her to cool down.

Complicating things was the palpable frustration within our little group. Diligently, Piper had spied on Boltstar's inner circle. She'd developed ambush points, easily accessible via Shadow Madkey. We'd also created a general plan of attack. First, we'd distract the target. Then Tad would cast Hibernuction, putting the magician to sleep. I'd cast Vanista, effectively hiding the slumbering person from view. Afterward, we'd move on to the next target. It seemed manageable and we were chomping at the bit to get started. Unfortunately, we still needed a good distraction. Something to keep them occupied while Tad cast his sleeping curse. And try as we might, we had yet to come up with a workable solution.

Entering the giant room, I walked to the windows. Outside, large snowflakes fell gently from the sky. There were so many of them, they effectively blotted out the landscape.

Hungrily, Tad gazed upon his sandwich. Or rather, at the ingredients strewn about the tray. The main course consisted of a soft sesame seed roll, ample amounts of fresh roast turkey, bacon, swiss cheese, lettuce, and sweet pickles. Condiments included jars of mayonnaise, mustard, and Thousand Island dressing as well as tiny salt and pepper shakers. Uncooked french fries, a bowl of cheese sauce, and utensils completed the tray.

"Sandwich, please," he said. "And make it sloppy."

Small, heatless sparks flew outward. Then the roll flopped open. The jars emptied their condiments onto the bread and a knife went to work spreading them out. The turkey, bacon, cheese, lettuce, and pickles drifted into place. Finally, the sub closed over and pressed down, just enough to offer a good grip without squeezing out the condiments.

"French fries, too," he added. "Crispy and drippy, please."

The french fries and bowl of cheese sauce emitted heatless sparks as well. The bowl lifted a few inches off of the tray and dumped its contents onto the fries.

My stomach growled. Not because I was hungry, but because everything smelled so darn good.

Tad licked his lips. "Thanks."

The sparks pulsed for a second as if to say, *You're welcome.* Then they vanished.

As he ate his sandwich, Leandra and I took seats at the table. Piper, meanwhile, remained standing.

"How is it?" I asked.

"Awesome," he mumbled between chews.

I grinned. "I guess Structuralism has its perks."

"No doubt," he replied, stuffing a wad of cheese fries into his mouth. "But Chaotic magicians could make this quicker and with far less manpower."

"Maybe." Leandra watched him eat for a moment. "There's no way to know for sure."

"Actually, I do know. My buddy Teresa's got a gift for cooking spells. She could whip up a meal like this before you could say, 'Please.'"

The contrast between Chaotic magic and Structuralism brought up another question that had been on my mind as of late. "I've been meaning to ask you something. What does a Chaotic school look like?"

"School?" he asked.

"You guys have schools, right?"

"Actually, no."

"Really?" Leandra frowned. "Then how'd you learn your spells?"

"Trial and error."

"You mean like how you've been teaching Randy?"

"Not exactly. I learned by doing." His brow furrowed. "I remember folding laundry when I was a kid. I hated it and so one day I found myself holding my wand, awash in emotions. Next thing I knew, I cast a spell and ..."

"And it folded itself?"

"Actually, no." He grinned at the memory. "It tied one of my shirts into a knot. It was so tight I couldn't undo it."

Leandra chuckled.

"I tried again later, when I wasn't so frustrated. That time, the spell worked." He shrugged. "Chaotic magic isn't always what you expect. But it's always consistent with your emotions."

"But you used to have schools," I said. "Heck, Madkey was once a Chaotic school."

He nodded. "That's true. From what I understand, this place used to be very different. There were no classes, no bells, no schedules. It was more like a hangout, a place where magicians could work on their spells and help each other."

"What about homework?" Piper asked, speaking up at last and looking horrified in the process. "And tests?"

He shook his head. "I don't think those things existed."

"But how did people learn anything?"

"Well, the school employed a bunch of expert magicians who could offer help and guidance." He shrugged. "Overall though, I think people learned what they wanted to learn."

"So, if they didn't want to study Numerology ..."

"Then I guess they didn't learn about it."

Her jaw dropped wide open. "But ... but ..."

"I'm not saying it's right or wrong. I'm just saying that's how I think it used to be done." Putting down his sandwich, he licked his lips. "So, what's the deal? Are we ready yet?"

I shook my head. "We still need a distraction."

He nodded slowly. "I know I've brought this up before, but I feel like I should do it again ..."

"We're not backing out," I said firmly.

"Thank you for saying that." He exhaled. "But keep in mind that we're going to be casting spells on some of the most renowned witches and wizards of all time. There's a very good chance this turns out badly for us."

"Oh, don't worry." Piper sniffed. "I'm sure Randy will save us all."

"Huh?" He looked at her, then at me. "Am I missing something?"

Piper pursed her lips.

I cleared my throat. "I was trying to win the game."

"A meaningless game."

"Boltstar didn't see it that way."

"Who cares what he thinks?"

"My parents, for one." I straightened my spine. "He told them I've got a bright future, you know."

For the last few days, I'd fantasized about rematriculating at Madkey. I'd pictured myself sitting at a desk, a confident smile upon my face. I'd imagined Porter's shocked visage on my first day back. I'd wondered what it would feel like to walk around with my head held up high for a change. To feel proud of myself rather than ashamed.

Eyes flicking back and forth, Tad took another bite of his sandwich. Sitting down, Leandra turned her attention to her simulator mirror.

Piper gave me an icy look. "What do you want?" she asked. "A pat on the back?"

As I stared at her, I suddenly felt silly and kind of stupid. Most of all, I felt like a big jerk. The dreams and fantasies vanished and then it was just the two of us.

"Well?" she asked.

"No. I ..." I sighed. "You're right."

"And?"

"And I'm sorry."

Her frown wavered. A slight smile began to take its place. "Yeah, well ..." Her smile vanished. Her jaw opened wide and she went rigid.

I spun around. Horror set in as a shadowy figure climbed through the hatch. He stepped onto the carpet, then rose to his full height. No, this couldn't be happening. It was impossible. It was ...

"Boltstar." Snapping to attention, Tad drew his wand.

"Hello," the headmaster said, with nods at each of us.

Piper swallowed. "This isn't what it looks like."

"Isn't it?"

She gaped at him.

"There's no sense in denying it," he said. "I know what you did. I know everything."

Carefully, I pulled my wand from its holster. A quick peek at Piper confirmed she'd drawn her wand as well.

"What'd you expect?" Tad said angrily. "A hearty handshake? You destroyed us. You destroyed *me*."

"The time for conversation has passed." With a dangerous glitter in his eyes, he aimed his wand at Piper. "Now, it's time to die."

My emotions slid into place and Instinctia took control. "Elertfa Lokwhan," I called out.

Auburn light zoomed toward Boltstar's heart. He didn't duck or try to dodge it. Instead, he whispered a few words and flicked his wand.

A cyan glow, brimming with energy, collided with my light. Both spells vaporized in a puff of smoke.

Boltstar looked my way. More than anything, I wanted to enchant his smile right off of his face. But the sheer magnitude of everything had thrown my brain into a tizzy. Try as I might, I couldn't recall the Herd Crash or any other Chaotic spell.

He aimed his wand at me. A cyan bolt sizzled through the air. I tried to run, but my feet were glued to the ground.

Air left my lungs as Tad crashed into me. We tumbled to the carpet, narrowly eluding the spell.

Piper sprang into action. Scurrying across the celestarium, she fired spells at the headmaster. He blocked them without breaking a sweat.

Tad and I scrambled to our feet. Wands in hand, we fired spells of our own.

Boltstar blocked our magic with ease. He stared at us for a moment, his eyes glittering with a strange kind of darkness. Then he spun on his heels. With casual flicks, he sent cyan streaks flying in all directions.

I took cover behind the enchanted fireplace. "You take one side," I whispered to Tad. "I'll take the other one."

I waited for his response. When it didn't come, I glanced over my shoulder. Tad lay face down on the carpet. His skin looked pale and he wasn't moving. At all.

Throwing caution to the wind, I sprinted to his side. My fingers touched his neck and I discovered his skin was cold and clammy. Breathlessly, I maneuvered my hand into position and waited.

There was no pulse.

I stared at his lifeless body for a few seconds, shocked to the core. Memories flooded my brain and I realized how empty my life would be without him. No more meals, no more late-night spell sessions. I'd never hear his weird laugh again or squirm restlessly as he rambled on about some historical event I didn't care about.

At that moment, I realized what a fool I'd been. All along, I'd bought into the idea that the underdog always came out on top, that evil always got its comeuppance. That people like Tad and me ultimately won the day.

But that wasn't the way the world worked. I could see that now. Furthermore, I realized how ill-prepared we were for this situation. All of those HMQ games had been a complete waste of time. Squaring off against a bunch of students, trying to one-up each other, was nothing like this. This was no game where the losers ended up with a couple of bumps and bruises. This was real. This was gritty, to-the-death magic.

Shouts and screams penetrated my ears. I smelled smoke and felt the heat of active spells. Tad was dead and that would haunt me for the rest of my life. There was nothing I could do about that. But Piper was still out there, still fighting.

Turning toward Boltstar, I tried to think. But my head was a jumbled mess of emotions. Gritting my teeth, I considered my options. Herd Crash was my best bet. Yes, he'd blocked it during our duel. But if I could catch him by surprise …

With tremendous force, he heaved spells at Piper. She was running like mad to get away from him but the cyan streaks were getting closer and closer.

I forced my emotions into the correct arrangement. My wand underwent the necessary sequence. "Herd Crash."

A series of auburn lights raced toward Boltstar. But at the last second, he saw them coming. Like before, his wand went to work. Whispered words left his mouth and orbs of cyan light materialized. My lights crashed into his orbs and colorful smoke appeared.

This wasn't working. We needed help. Speaking of which, where was Leandra?

In an instant, he fired another spell. Piper froze, her body contorted. Then she slumped to the carpet.

No. Please, no.

Fury and sorrow consumed me. Tears welled up in my eyes and I could barely see. Clutching my wand, I swiveled toward Boltstar.

Cyan light slammed into my stomach.

And then all was black.

CHAPTER 43

"Wake up, Randy."

That voice … it belonged to Leandra. A bit of happiness streaked through me, but it was quickly crushed by overwhelming sadness. Tad was dead. Piper, too, I figured.

"Welcome back to the land of the living," she said. "Oh, and by the way … congratulations."

I felt complete befuddlement. What was this? What was going on? With a soft groan, I shifted one arm, then the other one. I kicked my legs a bit.

Slowly, my eyes peeled open. Moonlight poured through the glass windows. I shied away for a moment, giving myself time to adjust. When I looked again, I saw Leandra standing at my feet, hands on hips, a smirk plastered across her face.

Confusion filtered through me. "What happened?"

"Leandra happened," Tad said sourly. "That's what we get for trusting a jerk."

I followed his voice to a nearby table. Tad and Piper sat on either side of it, their hands wrapped around steaming mugs of canfee. To say they looked furious was an understatement.

"You should've told us," Piper complained.

Leandra grinned. "And spoil all of the fun?"

Now, I was really confused.

I pulled my back off the carpet. I felt sore, but it was nothing serious.

"So, what'd you think?" Leandra nodded at the table. A blanket-covered object rested between Tad and Piper. "Pretty amazing, huh?"

"Uh, what?"

Standing up, Piper pushed a warm mug of canfee into my hands. I took a quick whiff. Mhmm ... End of Exams, one of my favorites.

"Leandra chose the flavor," Tad told me. "Probably so we wouldn't kill her."

I sipped the canfee. Instantly, I felt a surge of happiness as well as a sense of a job well-done. Even better, I felt relaxed and free, like I didn't have a care in the world.

But while the canfee gave me an overall good feeling, it certainly didn't erase my memories. Now that we were no longer fighting to the death, I had questions.

Lots of questions.

"What did you do to us?" I asked.

"Me? Nothing." Leandra smiled. "All credit goes to the simulator mirror."

"Your invention?"

She nodded. "Like I told you guys, it's similar to a memory mirror, only you can actually participate in it."

I thought back to the battle with Boltstar. "So, it was all a fake."

"Yes. A simulation, if you will."

"But it felt so real."

"That's the idea."

"Are there other simulations?" Tad asked.

"A few," she said. "But the one you just experienced is the most complete. Plus, it has a defined ending."

Piper's eyes widened as the truth dawned on her. "We were destined to die?"

"Not just you. Anyone who experiences that particular simulation will die."

"Is that when we lost consciousness?" Tad wondered. "The moment Boltstar killed us?"

She nodded.

"Do me a favor." I glared at her. "Next time, leave me out of your pranks, okay?"

"Oh, this was no prank." She glared at each of us in turn. "I told you we could use my simulator mirror as a distraction. But none of you wanted to give me a chance."

"You killed us just to prove a point?" Tad asked.

She crossed her arms.

He gawked at her for a moment. "Well, consider your point made."

"What kind of simulation do you plan to use on Boltstar and the others?" Piper wondered.

"The one you just experienced," Leandra replied.

"Are you sure they'll buy it?"

"Oh, without a doubt. Essentially, the simulator mirror inserts a fake Boltstar into one's present reality. And the fake Boltstar is pretty generic. You'll notice he didn't call us by our names. Nor did he actually accuse us of anything."

"You're right," Piper said slowly. "All he said was that he knew what we'd done. I took that to mean he knew about our plan."

"Exactly," Leandra replied. "When Galison sees the mirror, he'll find himself face-to-face with fake Boltstar. Boltstar will level his general accusation and start casting spells. Galison will have no choice but to run or fight back."

Piper frowned. "Does that mean he'll do those things in real life?"

She shook her head. "It's all in the mind. Even though it felt like you were running and throwing spells, you didn't actually move at all."

"What about the real Boltstar?" I asked. "Will he fall for the simulation?"

"He should," she replied. "You see, I developed an alternative to the fake Boltstar. Namely, a fake Galison character. He uses the same body language and the same spells. But his voice and appearance are obviously different. When we go after Boltstar, I'll make the switch."

"Amazing." Tad shook his head. "Simply amazing."

"Thanks," she replied proudly. "Creating the fake Boltstar character took a long time. I gave him every spell I could think of. I even gave him a few fake ones to keep people on their toes."

A small part of me still wanted to throttle her for scaring us. But admiration slowly took hold and I saw her in a whole new light. She'd invented something new in a world that was sorely lacking in freshness.

"Well?" Leandra asked, hands on hips. "What do you think? Can we use it as our distraction?"

I shared glimpses with Tad and Piper. "Yes," I replied. "I think it'll do just fine."

CHAPTER 44

"Okay." Crouching down, I peered through the thin crack in the door. Galison's legs swished past me. "I see him."

Two days had passed since our 'deaths' at the hands of Leandra's fake Boltstar. Two long days of planning, practice, and rehearsal. Now, at long last, we were ready to make our move.

Piper gave me a little nod. It was all going down just as she'd said it would. Galison worked late nights, often staying in his office until close to midnight. Then he took a short, no-

nonsense walk back to his room. He moved quickly and with no detours. He passed numerous alumni, all on nightly guard-duty, along the way. It was the same thing every day, with no exceptions.

That left little room or time for an ambush. After some deliberation, Piper decided to focus our efforts on the hallway just outside his office. It was always empty when he retired for the evening. Even better, it curved in a complete circle, following the contours of Right Leg. So, a sizable portion of it was invisible from the nearest hoist.

"How does he look?" Tad whispered, licking his lips nervously.

Cracking the door open a little farther, I peered into the semi-darkness. To my left, Galison strode through the hallway, wand in one hand and a steaming mug of canfee in the other one. His gait was fast and clipped.

"Alert," I replied. "Very alert."

Our plan was simple. Simulator mirror in hand, Leandra would race around the opposite end of the circular hallway. She'd confront Galison before he could reach the hoist. With the distraction in place, Tad would cast Hibernuction, sending the professor to dreamland. We'd stash him in an isolated part of Shadow Madkey and I'd use Vanista to shield the man from view.

Afterward, we'd move on, taking out the rest of Boltstar's inner circle one at a time. We'd leave the headmaster for last. Once he was subdued, we'd sneak back into the archive. Then, at long last, we could fix Womigia.

I wasn't sure what would happen after the collective memory had been restored. Would the students see the light? How about the rest of the faculty? Would the alumni put down their wands? And what would we do once the deed was done? Would we attempt to bring the Chaotics back into Madkey, peacefully this time? Would we send out a mass bubbler, explaining everything that had transpired? What kind of long-term implications would arise from our actions?

All of these unknowns quickly smothered me. Shaking my head, I returned my thoughts to the matter at hand. We'd gone over our plan dozens of times. We'd worked out the kinks and considered every possible contingency. In my head, it seemed rather easy. But I knew this was an illusion. If even one little thing went wrong, we'd be finished. Goodbye Madkey, hello Gutlore.

Leandra slipped past me, simulator mirror held tightly in her hands. Turning away from Galison, she hustled around the opposite end of the circular hallway.

Galison's footsteps, now faint, filtered into my eardrums. My fingers began to tremble. I curled them into fists, but they still quivered. Leandra should've reached him by now. What was taking so long?

Finally, his footsteps halted. My fists slowly relaxed. Tad, Piper, and I shared a knowing look, then hurried into the hallway. Just ahead, I saw Galison. His back faced us. His feet were rooted to the floor, his eyes were fixed on Leandra's simulator mirror.

Taking care not to look at the glass, Tad snuck up behind the professor. Whispering a few words, he flicked his wand.

Tawny light flooded into Galison and the man went limp. Stretching out, I caught him by the shoulders. He released his mug, but Piper snagged it before it could hit the ground.

Lowering the simulator mirror, Leandra peered over both shoulders. Her neck muscles relaxed. "We're good," she said. "Nobody saw us."

"Let's keep it that way," Tad replied.

Galison was in a deep sleep, with a very light snore upon his lips. With Piper's help, I carried him into Shadow

Madkey. We took him to a hidden alcove, then laid him on the floor.

My muscles felt sore and my back ached. So, I took a moment to stretch. At the same time, I recalled the exact emotions that had allowed me to pull off the vanishing spell back in the archive. Harnessing them, I lifted my wand. "Vanista," I whispered.

The auburn light came fast and fierce. It swept over Galison, enveloping him completely. Then it vanished, taking him with it.

Piper nudged his cloaked body with the tip of her shoe. His light snoring ceased and we found ourselves in silence.

A triumphant spirit crested through me.

One down.

Three to go.

CHAPTER 45

"I don't like this." Tad cast an anxious look in either direction as we crept out of the shadows. "We shouldn't be out in the open."

"I know," I replied. "But we don't have a choice."

Speedily, we made our way onto the Upper-Torso bridge. Norch faced us, her steely gaze riveted at Leandra's simulator mirror.

Equal amounts of fear and excitement churned within me. Thirty minutes ago, we'd teamed up to take down Wadflow. Like Galison, it had gone without a hitch. Professor Norch was our current target. After that, we'd go after

Boltstar. So, yeah, there was plenty of reason to feel enthused. But that didn't mean we were out of the woods yet.

The problem was one of location. Norch was an early-riser, so Piper had planned the ambush for the area just outside her bedroom. But that plan became untenable when Norch exited her room earlier than expected. Panicking, we'd followed her to the Upper-Torso bridge. It quickly became apparent that she'd agreed to stand guard so that some of the alumni might get a brief break.

Leandra had raced ahead. With great stealth, she crept behind the professor, then touched the woman's shoulder. Spinning around, Norch stared at the simulator mirror and immediately went rigid. So, that was good. But we still had a lot to do and we had to do it fast before the normal guards returned to Torso.

Tad's Hibernuction spell engulfed Norch and she started to sag. Grabbing hold of her armpits, I lowered her to the ground. Then I grabbed my own wand, figuring I'd use Vanista before we hid her in Shadow Madkey.

But my excitement quickly turned to apprehension when I heard something strike the floor. Peering down, I saw a small stick of wood, knobby and slightly crooked, roll softly across the bridge.

Her wand!

It must have slipped out of her holster by accident. Now, it was rolling toward the edge. If we didn't grab it in time, it would clatter against the Mid-Torso bridge, right outside of Boltstar's quarters.

Piper leapt into action. Her fingers stretched at the wand, but it squirted out of her grasp. Horrified, I watched it disappear over the edge. Moments later, it banged against the Mid-Torso bridge. Breathlessly, I waited. Waited and hoped. But my prayers were for naught. For a few seconds later, a door opened. Footsteps struck stone. Clothing rustled as Boltstar stooped down to retrieve the wand.

Biting her lip, Piper pulled back from the edge. Leandra and I grabbed Norch's limbs and pulled her to the back wall. Unfortunately, not everyone got clear in time.

"You must be Mr. Crucible." Boltstar's voice thundered through all of Torso. "I recognize you from your picture. I must say, it's good to finally meet you in person."

"I wish I could say the same," Tad replied icily.

"I'm surprised to see you here. I figured you were gone for good."

"What can I say?" He gave us a quick glance. *Go*, he mouthed. "I guess Madkey's in my blood."

A blaze of cyan soared into view. It flew just over Tad's head and struck the back wall. Sizable chunks of concrete crumbled onto the bridge.

Piper gave me a helpless look. I knew how she felt. The falling wand was a freak accident. But it was about to ruin all of our lives.

"Well, what's it going to be?" Leandra asked, gritting her teeth. "Fight or run?"

I'd felt Boltstar's power, I'd seen his skills. Even with the element of surprise, taking him down would've been no easy task. Without it, our chances were exactly zero.

Hand shaking, I aimed my wand at Leandra and Piper. "Vanista," I whispered.

Breathless, I waited for a moment. But there was no auburn streak.

My brow furrowed. Clenching my teeth, I tried again. Again, the spell failed. Why wasn't it working? My wand movements had been flawless. And I'd gotten the emotions right, hadn't I?

Frustrated, I tore my eyes off of my wand. "Head to the dorm," I said. "Don't tell anyone you were here."

"What about you?" Piper asked.

"I'm going to help Tad."

"Are you crazy?" Tad hissed. "Go with them."

"I'm not leaving."

"Me either," Piper added.

"Yeah," Leandra said. "If he captures you, he'll get your anchor. Your people will—"

"You can't help them now. But you can help yourselves." Wand held high, he began muttering spells. Tawny rays soared toward the Mid-Torso bridge. "Now, go."

Leandra shared a steely look with Piper. Something unspoken passed between them. "Will do."

Keeping low, they hustled toward Left Arm. Reaching the entranceway, they turned to look for me.

Piper saw me first, huddled on the ground near Tad. Her face morphed into one of helpless fury. *What are you doing?* she mouthed.

I'll catch up, I mouthed in response.

I was lying. And I felt pretty certain she knew that. I just hoped she understood.

Be careful, she mouthed, her expression softening a bit. Then she followed Leandra into Left Arm.

"Are you crazy?" Lowering his wand, Tad glared at me. "I told you to leave."

"I'm a dropout, remember? I'm not so good at following directions."

He sighed, then peered down either end of the lower bridge. "I don't see him. He must be coming up here."

"Then we'd better go."

"Where to?"

"Shadow Madkey," I decided.

Tad ran to a door marked, *Faculty and Students Are Your Priority. Serve Them Always and Without Question.* He threw it open and with long, loping steps, sprinted down a flight of stairs. I raced after him.

"Mr. Wolf." Boltstar's voice, brimming with anger and self-assuredness, sounded out from behind me. "Stop."

My spirits hit rock-bottom. I couldn't hide the truth any longer. It was all out in the open now.

Cyan spells crashed into the stairwell as I turned a corner. Holding the banisters, I vaulted to the landing. Twisting around again, I vaulted down another flight of stairs.

We ran like that for a bit, with Boltstar in hot pursuit. Finally, Tad reeled to a stop.

"It's no use." He grabbed my wand. Aiming it at his gut, he steeled himself. "Herd Crash me."

"Are you nuts?" I yanked away from him. Above, I heard footsteps striking stairs. In a couple of seconds, Boltstar would be on top of us.

"I got you into this. So, let me get you out of it." He aimed his wand at his belly. His eyes closed over and words left his lips. A quick glimpse of tawny light filled my eyes. Then he folded in half and slumped to the ground.

Shoes slapped against steps as Boltstar descended to the landing. He aimed his wand at me, then at Tad. "Please drop your wand, Mr. Wolf."

I clutched it for another second or two before I finally let my fingers loosen. The staffer wand tumbled to the landing. I stared at it, my chest heaving in and out in perfect rhythm.

"I …" I knew what I had say. I mean, what else could I do? Tad had sacrificed himself to save me and I couldn't let that be in vain. Still, it felt like the words had to be dragged out of me by a team of sasquatches. "I got him."

His brow furrowed. "What happened?"

"I woke up early. You know, to get some practice in at the arena before my first shift." My voice gained strength as I gazed down at Tad's unconscious form. "When I walked into Torso, I saw him shooting spells at you. He ran and I followed him."

"You weren't helping him?"

My cheeks burned and I wondered if I was blushing. "No, Sir. Of course not."

"He's your friend."

"He *was* my friend."

"I see." Stooping down, he retrieved my wand. Frowning, he gave it a close look. "What foul manner of wand is this?"

"That's a staffer wand, Sir."

"You're telling me you won all of those HMQ games with this ... this abomination?"

I nodded.

Boltstar stared at me a few seconds longer, as if hoping to read my mind. Then he relaxed. "Excellent work, Mr. Wolf." Handing me the wand, he clapped me on the back. "Excellent work, indeed."

CHAPTER 46

The murmurs started the moment I set foot upon the field. Ignoring them, I joined the other staffers in the bleachers. Leandra stood up to give me a little hug. Piper, edgy and nervous, did the same.

"Thank goodness you got out of there. We were worried sick." Her cheeks were flushed and she looked about as tired as I felt. "Where have you been?"

"The celestarium."

"All day?"

I nodded. Racked with guilt and fear, I'd spent the entire day holed up in our secret meeting spot. I'd skipped my shifts, meals, everything. I spent most of that time pacing the floor, considering my options. Unfortunately, they weren't great.

Eventually, day turned into night. With Havoc Magic on the docket, I dragged myself out of Shadow Madkey and made my way to the arena. Truthfully, I would've preferred to skip class, too. But that didn't seem like a good idea, given my recent altercation with Boltstar.

"Where is you-know-who?" Leandra asked.

"Boltstar caught him," I whispered.

She winced. "Oh, no."

"How'd you get away?" Piper wondered.

"I didn't. Boltstar let me go."

She gaped at me.

"He thinks I stopped Tad." Speaking in a bare whisper, I recounted what Tad had done after they'd left, how he'd blasted himself to make it look like I'd taken him out. When I was finished, they shared a thin-lipped look.

"Where is he?" Leandra wanted to know.

My gaze turned to the locker room area. I recalled the time I'd gone there looking for Boltstar, only to hear him talking to Galison about Ivan Gully's escape. "Locked up, I guess." I nodded at the locker rooms. "Probably in there."

"They're going to skin him," Piper said in a low voice. "Maybe not right away, but eventually."

I didn't disagree. It was just a matter of time before Boltstar skinned Tad of his magic. In the process, the headmaster would seize control of Tad's anchor. He'd follow it with an army of witches and wizards at his command. Tad's friends wouldn't stand a chance.

I checked the enchanted clock. Eleven minutes remained until the start of class. Feeling restless, I trained my gaze on the locker rooms. I had to rescue Tad. But how?

"Hey guys," Jax climbed down from an upper aisle and flopped into the seat next to Piper. "Did you hear anything weird?"

Piper shook her head. "Why?"

"There's a rumor going around that Boltstar captured another Chaotic this morning."

"Where?" I asked, acting dumb.

"Nobody knows. It's all real hush-hush."

Jenny and a few other staffers joined us. Theories were floated and Piper and Leandra played along, feigning ignorance. As for me, well, I did my best to participate. But really, I barely paid attention. Instead, I considered various rescue plans, each more outlandish than the previous one.

The whispers ceased at six o'clock. Dozens of kids, sporting stupefied expressions, turned toward the locker room area.

Following their gaze, I saw Boltstar walking up the ramp. The rest of the faculty—sans MacPherson, Galison, Norch, and Wadflow—followed him, traveling in pairs. They wore their finest attire and carried their wands with formality.

We'd left Norch on the Upper-Torso bridge, fast asleep but still visible. Presumably, she was now in the clinic, sleeping next to MacPherson. As for Galison and Wadflow, I assumed they were right where we'd stashed them, still asleep and still invisible. How long would my Vanista spells last? And what about Tad's sleeping curses? Would they become undone once Boltstar skinned him?

Boltstar waved his wand. White sparks blazed upward. As they arced over his head in a perfect curve, he marched onto the field. The faculty members, two by two, followed him out. Coming to a halt, they split up and faced each other, forming two long lines, separated by a wide aisle.

Tad Crucible, slack-jawed and pale-skinned, hiked up the ramp. Well-scrubbed, he was dressed in a green dress shirt, slacks, and neatly-polished dress shoes.

Prodded by Professors Stewart and Whitlock, he strode down the aisle, passing the faculty on the way. He ignored them, choosing instead to scan the crowd. They returned the favor, their faces hard and lined.

"Boltstar's going to skin him." Piper bit her lip. "Right here, right now."

Tucking his wand under his armpit, the headmaster walked toward us. Tad, still flanked by Stewart and Whitlock, followed him at a short distance. Meanwhile, the faculty paired up again and joined the procession.

A dozen faculty members broke away from the main group. Joining together, they waved their wands in all sorts of crazy, sweeping patterns. A beautiful tune, soft and mournful, filled the arena. Despite everything, it brought a small smile to my face. It was truly wondrous, a magnificent testament to the good things magic could do.

Boltstar led the procession to the HMQ, then turned in a slow circle. He waved his wand for a second time, emitting another curving shower of white sparks. The music stopped. Shuffling rang out as kids gained their feet.

Filled with dread, I stood up. Meanwhile, down on the field, Stewart jabbed Tad with his wand. Tad took a few halting steps forward. Although his outfit looked nice, I noticed clear signs of his ordeal. His eyes looked hazy and unfocused. His jaw drooped and he appeared to be having trouble keeping his head up.

"Good evening, ladies and gentlemen," Boltstar proclaimed, facing the bleachers. "For certain reasons that will soon become clear, tonight's class will start a little later than expected."

He looked freshly shaved and nicely rested. His shirt was pressed and his derby cap hung at a jaunty angle.

"This, as some of you already know, is Mr. Tad Crucible." He waved a hand at Tad. "Many weeks ago, on Victory Day, Mr. Crucible conspired with the Chaotics to invade our beloved school."

Everyone stood still, staring at him with bated breath.

"Early this morning, Mr. Crucible surfaced yet again, brazenly attacking at least one member of the faculty."

I winced.

"As headmaster of the Roderick J. Madkey School of Magical Administration, it's my responsibility to enforce the laws that govern this institution. It's also my responsibility to decide on a punishment, should one prove necessary."

He paused to take a breath. Students edged forward in their seats, their eyes glittering with darkness and anger.

"I find Mr. Crucible guilty of treason, sedition, the usage of non-sanctioned magic, and injurious actions to magicians as well as school property."

My heart seized up. I could barely breathe.

"Mr. Crucible, while committing grave crimes against this institution, is still quite young. In addition, he cannot bear responsibility for his shameful upbringing. With that said, justice demands we punish him for his crimes." He turned to face Tad. "I do not believe your actions warrant the death penalty. However, your sentence will be far from merciful. First, you will undergo an immediate skinning of any and all magic. Second, you will spend the rest of your life locked away at Gutlore Penitentiary."

I cringed. Boltstar wasn't lying. That punishment was anything but merciful.

"Before we commence with the skinning ceremony, I'd like to recognize a certain individual." Boltstar scanned the bleachers. "Where are you, Mr. Wolf?"

I froze in horror as a bunch of heads turned my way. I wanted to hide, to vanish. But the kids in front of me moved aside and then I was right out there in the open for all to see.

"Please join me on the HMQ, Mr. Wolf," he said in a calm, authoritative manner.

I glanced at Piper and Leandra. They returned my gaze with dark, hooded eyes.

I left my aisle and hiked down the steps, aware that every single person in the arena was staring at me. Hopping the wall, I headed out onto the field. Boltstar's hands were intertwined and hung loosely in front of him. A bit hesitant, I stepped over the magic rope. My gaze shifted quickly to Tad. In turn, he stared dully in my direction, as if not even seeing me.

"Students, staffers, and faculty members." Boltstar grabbed hold of my shoulder and twisted me around so I stood by his side. "This is Mr. Randy Wolf. Like Mr. Crucible, he's a former student of this school. But unlike the aforementioned criminal, Mr. Wolf is a bona fide hero."

People recoiled in shock. Eyelids fluttered all over the arena. Even Porter looked vaguely impressed. Personally, I felt like a fraud. No, I felt like a traitor. Not to Madkey or Boltstar, but to Tad and worse, to myself.

"Mr. Wolf chased Mr. Crucible down and ultimately, apprehended him." Boltstar smiled at me. My heart, influenced by the collective memory, lit up. Quickly, I scolded it back to coldness.

"Thank you, Mr. Wolf," he said with genuine kindness. "I and the rest of the school owe you a debt of gratitude that can never be repaid."

Awkwardness and guilt flooded my veins. "It was, uh, nothing."

"There's no need for modesty." His smile widened as he turned back to the crowd. "Mr. Wolf dropped out of Madkey last semester. Undoubtedly, that was the right decision at the time. But things have changed. He has, as all of you have seen for yourselves, excelled in the field of Havoc Magic. I believe he's earned a second chance."

Murmurs turned to whispers and whispers turned to full-blown chatter. My face grew redder and redder as guilt spread to every part of my body. I knew what was about to happen. And in a way, it was worse than a permanent stint at Gutlore or even getting skinned.

"Mr. Wolf," Boltstar said. "It's my proud honor to restore you to this year's Freshmen class. Your tuition, room, and board will, at my suggestion, be completely covered by the school's sizable endowment fund."

And there it was.

Rematriculation.

I'd wanted a Madkey degree for so long, I'd nearly forgotten why it had been so important to me. And at that moment, it all came flooding back into my mind. The approval of my parents, the respect of my peers, and once I graduated, a good job at one of the Big Three. Once again, it was all there for the taking. All I had to do was grasp it.

"No need to thank me right now, Mr. Wolf. You may return to your seat." Twisting on his heels, he faced Tad. His face twisted into one of grave concern. "As for you, Mr. Crucible, it's time to commence with the skinning ceremony. May your name be forgotten from this day forward and all through the annals of time so that those you love, and those who love you in turn, may avoid your everlasting shame."

Tad stared straight ahead, his visage betraying nothing.

Boltstar's brow furrowed. His wand moved with effortless grace and he spoke a series of quiet enchantments.

Blazing cyan light zoomed out of his wand. Tad grunted as it struck his belly. At first, he merely cringed. Then he started to recoil in shock and pain. His head lifted to the ceiling. His mouth opened wide and he screamed.

A tawny glow oozed out of Tad's nose, ears, and mouth. It came very slowly, as if it were fighting the entire way. Meanwhile, he shrieked and yelled at the top of his lungs.

I saw it all. The determined glint in Boltstar's eyes. The magic slipping away from Tad. And then, I could take it no longer.

My emotions shifted into place and I grabbed my wand. Whirling around, I waved it at the air.

"Herd Crash," I shouted.

Multiple auburn bolts slammed into Boltstar's waist. Grunting loudly, he stumbled to the side. His spell vanished and the tawny glow flooded back into Tad's body.

The headmaster recovered quickly and started to turn toward me. But I fired off another Herd Crash and more auburn bolts slammed into him. They struck his torso, his legs, his shoulders. He fell down and the jarring impact sent his wand skidding along the grass.

"Headmaster Boltstar is a liar and a murderer," I shouted, my voice trembling. "He doctored the collective memory to make us think otherwise. And I can prove it."

A moment of sheer panic passed through me. There was no going back now. In a single moment, I'd thrown away everything that had ever mattered to me. My chance at a Madkey degree, my job prospects, my very reputation. And yet, I felt better than I'd ever felt in my entire life. It was as if my chains had melted away. For the first time in forever, I felt truly free.

"Help me make this right." My voice swelled to a crescendo. "Help me stop Boltstar."

CHAPTER 47

The bleachers erupted into a pure frenzy. It took me a minute to realize what was happening. But when I heard multiple cries of "traitor" and saw Kell fire an unannounced spell at Jeff's chin, it became clear. The students weren't helping me. No, they were doing the exact opposite, taking out anyone they thought might be on my side.

Confusion and terror set in amongst the staffers. Some fought to get down to the field. Others vaulted over their seats, hoping to reach higher ground.

Helplessly, I watched Calvin deck Jax with a spell. Liza Raico tripped Jenny, then began firing spells at her once she was on the ground. Chez Skalant and Charlie Ridges, meanwhile, blasted Dorph with spells from either end, causing him to bounce around like a pinball.

Piper and Leandra fought valiantly, trying to escape the growing insanity. But the crowd quickly gobbled them up. Within seconds, I couldn't see them. I couldn't see anyone, in fact. All I saw was a big blob of flesh, punctuated by a dizzying array of colorful spells.

The brawl distracted Stewart and Whitlock. Taking advantage, Tad sprinted at the former. He slammed his shoulder into the wizard's gut and at the same time, relieved the man of his wand. Twirling the wand in his fingers, Tad fired off a quick spell, catching Stewart in the forehead. Eyes rolling backward, the professor slumped to the ground.

Tad spun toward Whitlock and snapped off another spell. She, however, was ready. With a twist of the wrist, she defused his spell. Then she stalked forward, wand at the ready, preparing to dish out blows of her own.

I pinned down my emotions. My wand went into action. "Herd Crash," I called out.

Auburn streaks flooded the air. Clenching her jaw, Whitlock dropped to a crouch. Methodically, she waved her wand, forming a bunch of colorful orbs. One by one, my streaks collided with her orbs, reducing them to airy vapor. But a single streak managed to slip through her defenses. With a satisfying crunch, it struck her hip. Emitting a soft scream, she dropped the wand and sank to her knees.

Lips trembling, she stared daggers at me. "Traitor," she spat. "Chaotic scum. Skinning is too good for you. I hope you rot—"

A tawny bolt struck her cheek. Eyes bulging, she wrenched violently to the side before collapsing on the ground.

Tad lowered his wand. "I never liked her," he explained with a shrug.

I chanced another look at the bleachers. Gordon, his eyes pinched and tight, held Nico's arms behind his back. Forgoing his wand, Porter pounded the staffer with vicious belly shots. Elsewhere, Leandra extracted herself from the scuffle. Bleeding from cuts on her arms, she fled to a higher row. Sya surged after her, wand in hand. But before she could do additional damage, Piper stepped in.

She waved her wand and raspberry streaks filled the air. They hit their mark and Sya fell hard, crashing into the bleachers. Furious students, their eyes hard and unyielding, turned on Piper. Staffers rushed over to help her.

I was tempted to do the same. But at that very moment, I became aware of people closing in on Tad and I. Twisting in either direction, I saw the rest of the faculty. They held their wands at the ready, but didn't fire any spells our way. It took me a few seconds to realize they were holding back, so as to avoid hitting Boltstar by accident.

"It wasn't the ramballs that set off the alarm. It was you. You broke into the archive." Boltstar was back on his feet. Looking stiff, yet majestic, he waved off the other professors. Offering him nods, they hurried toward the bleachers. "How'd you manage to stay hidden from me?"

My heart began to thump against my chest. With more bluster than bravery, I stared him down. "Chaotic magic."

"I see. So, you're with *them* now."

"It's better than being with you." My lip curled into a snarl. "I know what happened on Victory Day. I mean, what really happened, not the fake history you concocted."

"You saw a few memories and now you think you know best?" He shook his head. "You weren't there, Mr. Wolf. You didn't have to live in a world run by Chaotic magic."

I said nothing.

"The Chaotics weren't innocent, Mr. Wolf," he continued. "Far from it. They supported a system of free, unregulated magic. Magic that could maim or even kill. Just think about that for a moment. Would you want to live in a world where anyone could cast any spell at any moment?"

My brow furrowed. It was difficult to imagine such a reality. But I could see his point. Structuralist magic was safe, if a bit boring. Chaotic magic running rampant sounded, well, kind of scary.

"We put an end to that, Mr. Wolf. We put an end to the fear, the terror. The Chaotics purge was unfortunate. I won't deny that. But it was the only way to move forward." He sighed. "Sometimes, difficult things must be done in order to serve a greater cause."

"You're full of it," Tad spat. "The Chaotics period wasn't dangerous. Sure, there were injuries, even a few deaths. But it was never as bad as you're claiming."

"No," he conceded. "It wasn't. But it was just a matter of time. All it would've taken was one rogue magician. And then, pointless tragedy."

"Isn't that why Madkey was founded?" Tad retorted. "To help people learn magic in a safe place? To help them become responsible witches and wizards?"

"Yes, and I commend the Chaotics for that. They went to great lengths to make their magic as safe as possible. And that served us quite well for many years. But even then, we were on borrowed time. Eventually, something would've gone wrong. Maybe it would've been a witch who couldn't control her magic. Or a wizard with incredible powers and a particularly dark heart. Regardless, it was bound to happen." He spoke with strength, with conviction. Regardless of his argument's merits, he believed them to his core. "But the Capsudra changed everything. It gave us a chance to evolve, to move past a time when one wizard could destroy everything we'd worked so hard to build. Unfortunately, the Chaotics didn't see it that way."

"You could've debated them," I said. "You could've tried to convince them."

"We tried. Oh, how we tried. We debated them for years. But they were too stuck in their ways."

I recalled one of the memories I'd seen in the archive. The one with Boris Hynor lecturing at the Magical Structuralism Society. His speech had been given two years prior to Victory Day. And that was just one memory. Undoubtedly, there were others from that period. Memories of speeches, debates, lectures, arguments, all sorts of stuff.

"You couldn't win the debate, so you killed or drodiated everyone." I frowned. "Is that about it?"

Boltstar's gaze lifted and I could see he was scanning the bleachers, watching as the faculty tried to reign in the violence. "An unfortunate outcome, to be sure. But still, far better than the alternative."

"You're a monster," Tad said, shaking with fury.

"Sometimes one must be a monster, Mr. Crucible, if only to correct the inherent wrongs of a cruel world."

"Chaotic magic might be dangerous," I said slowly. "But that doesn't make it wrong."

His gaze, attentive and keen, turned toward me.

"Under Structuralism, magic doesn't change. There's no evolution, no improvement. It's just ... dormant."

"That's not true at all, Mr. Wolf. The Big Three—"

"The Big Three have been making the same stuff my entire life," I said. "It changes a little every year, but never by much."

"I'm afraid I don't see your point, Mr. Wolf. Are you upset that you don't have more products to buy?"

"No, I'm upset that we've reached our pinnacle. Sure, the world is a little safer. But it's a little less alive, too. You've capped us off, ended our growth."

"And you've made everyone the same," Tad added. "You've crushed the very thing that made people unique. The thing that made us special."

"A small price to pay for stability, Mr. Crucible," Boltstar replied with a dismissive wave. "Now, I bade you both to lower your wands. Place them gently on the soil and back away."

I swallowed hard. However, I didn't budge an inch. Neither did Tad.

"This is your last chance," he warned. "Surrender your wands or I'll take them by force."

I'd fought Boltstar, I'd felt his power. It dwarfed mine and I knew there was no way we could beat him.

But we had to try.

Squaring off, he lifted his wand.

Tad slid one foot forward. He held his wand in a loose grip at his side.

With almost effortless ease, the headmaster flicked his wrist. "Drodiate," he said.

Sparks flew as cyan light zipped through the air.

Tad managed to dodge the spell, but just barely. Darting to his right, he began throwing off spells of his own. The ground rumbled softly. Acrid smoke filled my nostrils.

Boltstar flicked his wand, throwing up a whole heap of cyan orbs. Tad's spells struck them, turning the orbs into colorful vapor. Undeterred, Tad kept running, kept fighting. But the headmaster vaporized each and every attack.

Changing tactics, Boltstar gave his wand a little flourish. A jagged bolt of cyan light zoomed forth.

Tad's eyes widened and he attempted to reverse course. But the spell struck his side before he could get clear. Going limp, he collapsed to the turf.

Seeing him like that, still and unconscious, made my pulse quicken. I tried to move, to react. But my wand felt too heavy to lift and my feet remained rooted to the ground.

Boltstar twisted toward me. "I have to know something, Mr. Wolf," he said. "Did you use Chaotic magic to win all of those HMQ games?"

I nodded.

"That must've taken a herculean effort on your part. It's too bad you never put that kind of effort into your classes. Imagine what kind of student you might've been." With a sigh, he waved his wand and whispered something too soft to hear.

I raced to line up my emotions. But my mind blanked and I couldn't get off a spell in time.

Cyan light struck my stomach with the force of a sucker punch. It seized my breath and knocked me for a loop. Dropping my wand, I sank to my knees.

"A decent effort, Mr. Wolf." Stooping down, Boltstar retrieved my wand. "But you lose."

CHAPTER 48

"Nearly a century ago, we defeated the Chaotics. We converted many and chased down the stragglers, following them to the ends of the Earth. We thought we'd finished them. Unfortunately, we were wrong." Staring straight ahead, Boltstar addressed the attentive crowd. "That was my mistake, one for which I must take full responsibility. Because of my oversight, they were able to infiltrate us, invade us. They've attacked us three separate times this quarter. They even turned one of our own against us. And that won't be the end of it."

Loud boos and angry shouts rang out.

"Screw the Chaotics!"

"Destroy them!"

"Skin them all!"

A familiar chant started up. It drowned out the individual shouts and soon, every single person in attendance spoke in one voice.

"Struc-tur-al-ize," all of Madkey chanted. "Struc-tur-al-ize. Struc-tur-al-ize. Struc-tur-al-ize."

Tad and I stood in the HMQ. Numerous faculty members hovered around us, their wands ready to start blasting away if we tried anything.

I had a pretty good view of the stands, so I caught occasional glimpses of my friends. With the fighting now over, they sat in the bleachers, straight-backed and with their hands in their laps. Their faces were red, their cheeks were bruised. They'd clearly taken a beating, victims of guilt-by-association. Unfortunately, I had a feeling the beatings were just getting started.

"They'll keep coming," Boltstar continued. "And they won't stop until they've finished us off for good. Our only recourse is to get tougher, stronger, and more proficient with our spells. And so, that's what we'll do. Starting next quarter, this little introductory class of ours is going to develop into a full-fledged affair, complete with rigorous testing and grading. We also plan to cancel summer vacation, replacing it with an intensive, three-month havoc magic seminar. By this time next year, Madkey will be known as the world's premiere destination for havoc magic."

The last few minutes had passed in a blur. After defeating us, Boltstar had turned his wand toward the ceiling. A giant flurry of sparking streaks flew upward, casting a bright glow over the arena. The brawling came to a halt. People swiveled toward the headmaster. At his command, they took their seats. Professor Tuckerson and Assistant Professor Kinder began circulating in the stands, using magical first aid on the injured, leaving the staffers for last.

"But first things first." Boltstar tilted his head toward us. His eyes were cold and fierce. "Mr. Crucible has already been found guilty. His sentencing will proceed shortly with one minor change. Namely, he won't be going to Gutlore. Instead, he'll serve out his sentence at a location of my choosing."

My brow furrowed. If Tad wasn't being sent to Gutlore, then where was he going to go?

"I think it's only fair that his co-conspirator, Mr. Randy Wolf, receive the same sentence."

My blood turned icy as agreeable shouts rang out from the crowd.

"Mr. Wolf, may your name be forgotten from this day forward and all through the annals of time so that those you love, and those who love you in turn, may avoid your everlasting shame."

His words washed over me like an icy shower. What would my parents think? And what about my friends? I knew Piper and Leandra would never turn on me. But what about my more casual buddies? People like Jax, Jenny, and Nico? Would they curse my name? Would I ever get a chance to explain myself to them?

The answer, I realized, was no. I wouldn't get that chance. In short order, I'd lose my magic. I'd spend the rest of my life locked up in some kind of cell.

Still, I had no regrets. Well, that wasn't entirely true. I certainly regretted not getting to Norch's wand before it had a chance to fall and alert Boltstar. But besides that, I felt pleased with my actions. Maybe things hadn't worked out the way I'd hoped. But at least I'd tried to do the right thing.

Leandra's face reddened just a bit and she fidgeted in her chair. Meanwhile, Piper stared hard at me, as if hoping to memorize every inch of a face she'd never see again.

"Skin the Wolf." Porter cupped his hands around his mouth. "Skin the Wolf."

Cheers rang out, along with some scattered applause. Others joined in and the chant reached an ear-shattering crescendo. Even the staffers, sans my closest friends, were chanting in time.

"Skin the Wolf! Skin the Wolf! Skin the Wolf!"

The headmaster turned to face me. His wand flowed through a complex series of movements. His lips shifted softly, speaking words I couldn't quite hear.

Cyan light engulfed me. I felt a slight jostle. For a moment, I was confused. Everyone else had screamed when skinned of magic. So, why wasn't I—?

A fierce jolt of pain struck my abdomen. I couldn't do anything. I couldn't even scream. And then I started shrieking like crazy.

My agony intensified and I froze up. It felt like Boltstar was tearing open my stomach. Then the pain shifted just a bit. It felt different, but no less horrible. Kind of like Boltstar was ripping out my intestines.

My mind wanted to slip into unconsciousness. But the pain kept me awake. Horrified, I watched as auburn light— my auburn light—flowed out of my ears, mouth, and nose.

With a soft pop, the auburn light broke free from me, leaving a horrid emptiness in its wake. Engulfed by cyan light, my magic flowed into Boltstar's wand.

A shocked silence came over the crowd.

My frozen muscles thawed. Gasping and wheezing, I flopped onto the field.

Something hit the grass, a few inches from my left hand. Blinking a few times, I saw it was my wand.

"Yes, Mr. Wolf," Boltstar said. "You may retrieve it."

I tried to meet his gaze. But my head felt too tired, too heavy.

"Come, come. We don't have all evening."

My body ached and I could barely think. Still, I managed to wrap my fingers around the wand.

"Very good. Now, please rise."

I got my feet under me. Standing up, I took a few wobbly steps. I could feel hundreds of pairs of eyes upon me. But I could only see one of them.

"Please cast a spell." The headmaster smiled. "Any spell you like."

I knew I'd been skinned. Heck, I'd watched the magic flow right out of me. But this might very well be the last time I ever got my hands on a wand. If there was even a chance I still had magic, I had to make use of it.

My emotions felt dull, diminished. But I still managed to get them into the right mixture. My wand didn't move on instinct and so I directed it through the proper motions. "Herd Crash," I said.

I'd hoped and prayed for a little bit of magic, just enough to catch the mighty Boltstar by surprise. But of course, nothing happened.

Laughter, harsh and loud, rang out.

I felt empty inside, the emotional equivalent of a statue. It was utterly terrifying, even as my ability to feel terrified was rapidly diminishing.

I fell to my knees. The crowd roared and a raucous chant flooded my ears.

"The Wolf is skinned! The Wolf is skinned! The Wolf is skinned!"

CHAPTER 49

A blast of magic struck my back. It bowled me over and I tumbled into a shadowy room. I heard another blast of magic, followed by creaking metal. Light faded, then largely vanished with a loud slam.

"Tad?" I whispered. "Are you okay?"

He groaned in response.

I rolled onto my back and sat up. A bit of light snaked in under the door. It took a few minutes for my eyes to adjust.

But eventually, I saw we were in a large room with stone walls, outfitted with a couple of dusty mattresses.

The room was located at the back end of the locker room area. I was pretty sure it was the same one that had once held Ivan Gully. That seemed so long ago.

I touched my palms to the floor, then winced. A quick look showed my hands were all scraped up from where I'd caught myself. Gently, I rubbed them on my jeans, cleaning away the dirt.

Tad shifted, then unfolded. Moments later, he stood up, then stumbled to a wall. His skin looked haggard and gray. His hair was drenched with sweat. Like me, he'd been skinned of magic and was clearly suffering from the fallout.

"See a way out?" he asked without even a shred of hope.

I scanned the room. "Nope."

"Is this where they kept Ivan?"

"I think so."

"He escaped, right? How do you think he did it?"

"He got hold of a wand," I recalled. "That was, well … it was before he'd been skinned."

"Oh." His shoulders, already slumped, slumped a bit farther. "Boltstar's got my magic now," he said quietly. "He's got my anchor."

"Maybe it won't work for him."

"Wishful thinking." He sighed, then stared at the ceiling. "Do you feel … weird?"

"Weird how?"

"It's like I can't feel much." He exhaled. "I should be furious and scared. But I'm just kind of tired."

"Yeah, I know what you mean."

"Well, it could be worse, I guess. At least we're not going to Gutlore."

"What do you think Boltstar's got planned for us?"

"Who knows?" He grunted. "Regardless, I'll bet we're in for some questioning first. Maybe some torture, too."

"He's already got our spells and your anchor. What else does he need from us?"

"Information. He's going to want to know if anyone else helped us. Plus, he'll want to know what we did with Galison and Wadflow."

Falling into silence, we scoured the room, looking for a way out. The door was sturdy. The walls and floor were solid. I couldn't reach the ceiling, but it was made of stone and free of cracks.

Eventually, we gave up. Tad caught a catnap on one of the mattresses. I tried to do the same. Unfortunately, sleep eluded me.

Hours later, a soft whizzing noise caught my ear. The door clanked a few times, then swung open. Light flooded my eyes. Then MacPherson, wand in hand, marched into the room.

"Hello, Mr. Wolf." He glared at Tad. "And to you, as well, Mr. Crucible."

He looked well-rested. His hair was perfect. His clothes were perfect. Everything about him was perfect. Seriously, the mere sight of his relaxed face made me want to give that sleeping curse a try.

"What do you want? An apology?" Rubbing his eyes, Tad sat up. "Well, you can forget it."

"How are you awake?" I wondered.

"Boltstar possesses his magic now," he said with a nod at Tad. "And since he had an intimate acquaintance with Mr. Crucible's relative, Mr. Boris Hynor, he's quite familiar with the mechanics of the Hibernuction spell."

"Intimate acquaintance?" Tad shook his head. "He Drodiated poor Boris."

MacPherson clucked his tongue, impatiently. "Look, I've lost enough time already so I'm going to get right to the point." He gave us a pointed look. "We need to be face-to-face with our colleagues before we can free them from the Hibernuction Curse. So, we'd like to know where you stashed them."

"I'll bet you would," Tad replied.

MacPherson looked my way. "How about you, Mr. Wolf? Would you like the chance to redeem yourself?"

"What's it worth to you?" I asked.

"Worth?"

"Will you let us go?"

He arched an eyebrow. "What do you think?"

"Then forget it."

"I can make things very difficult for you, Mr. Wolf."

"How?" I wondered. "By skinning us? Oh, wait. Boltstar already did that."

"True." He gave me a strange smile. "But things can always get worse."

I heard the whizzing noise again. A cool mist splashed against my skin. The temperature dropped a few degrees and I began to shiver.

A bubbler entered the room. Looking at it, I saw my parents sitting at the kitchen table. Two witches, dressed in elegant pantsuits and carrying fancy wands, stood behind them. My parents looked afraid. Actually, afraid didn't begin to cover it. No, they looked downright petrified.

MacPherson wasn't joking. Things could get worse alright.

Much worse.

CHAPTER 50

"I'm going to make this simple for you," MacPherson said. "Tell me where you hid my colleagues or your parents will suffer the consequences."

"Why are you doing this?" Mom asked in a small, wavering tone.

One of the witches waved her wand and whispered a spell. A blast of magic struck the table, just inches from Mom's hand. The fine wood exploded into smithereens.

Startled, Mom reared up. Then she whimpered and made herself small again. Meanwhile, Dad remained perfectly still. His expression was serene and I suspected he was in a state of shock.

"This is no idle threat, Mr. Wolf," MacPherson said. "Now, where are they?"

I had zero leverage. And besides, what did I really gain by remaining quiet? Sooner or later, someone would stumble upon the sleeping professors.

"Promise you won't harm them," I said, my gaze locked on my parents.

"You have my word."

I exchanged looks with Tad. Then I told MacPherson exactly what we'd done to Galison and Wadflow.

He listened carefully, then headed for the door. He slammed it shut behind him and then I was alone with Tad and my parents.

And the witches, too.

I shifted my gaze to them. They hovered behind my parents, looking callous and bored. One had a pixie-like face, framed with shoulder-length black hair. The other sported wide cheeks, thin lips, and way too much make-up. At first glance, I wouldn't have pegged them as havoc magicians. But a closer look revealed they carried a myriad of scars, blemishes, and other battle wounds.

Dad stared down at a bowl of chattering cereal. The enchanted sugary flakes saw him looking and got all excited. Immediately, they started chirping at him in their squeaky, soft voices, begging to be eaten.

"It isn't so, is it Randy?" Mom blurted out. "Please tell us it isn't so."

They were dressed for work. Their eyes were hooded and baggy. They wore the expression of people who'd mistakenly tried Casafortro's Sourest of Them All candies.

"Were you skinned?" Dad asked.

"Yes," I replied.

"And the Chaotics? Did you help them?"

Clearly, he knew the score. And besides, there was no point in lying about it. "Not with the initial invasion. But afterword."

"Oh, Randy." Mom's eyes flooded with tears. She cast a fearful look at the two witches, then slowly lowered a mug to the table. "Do you realize what you've done?"

Her accusatory tone set off a tiny spark deep inside of me. "I helped a friend. I tried to right a wrong."

"And in the process, you ruined us," Dad said quietly. "Even if we get out of this in one piece, our lives are over. There's no way anyone will employ us once word gets out."

"I …" I frowned.

Part of me wanted to be furious with him, not that I was capable of such emotion. After all, what right did he have to make this about them? On the other hand, I saw his point. I hadn't really thought through all of the implications of getting caught. But now, they were impossible to ignore.

My parents would almost certainly lose their jobs. Their neighbors would ostracize them. Their friends would drift away. Other family members would turn their backs on them, desperate to avoid the stench of disgrace.

"Sorry," I said. "I … just … I'm sorry."

They were quiet for a minute. Then Mom gave me a small nod. "We know," she said softly. "And it's okay. We'll get through this."

"Just tell me one thing," Dad demanded. "Why would you help *those people*?

I decided to be honest about it because, well, why not? It wasn't like the truth could hurt anyone.

"Because they didn't do anything wrong," I replied. "They didn't attack Boltstar on Victory Day. He attacked them, then lied about it. Afterward, he tampered with the collective memory to make us—"

"Falsehoods and fabrications," spat one of the witches. The other witch, the one with the heavy make-up, jabbed Dad's jugular with her wand.

Mom winced. "Let's, uh, change the subject."

Dad remained frozen until the witch retracted her wand. Then he shoved his bowl away and the little flakes squealed in protest. "You can still fix this, Randy. Talk to Lanctin. Beg him for another chance. Do whatever it takes."

"Yes." Mom's head bobbed up and down. "Tell him you'll help. Tell him you'll be there when he rounds up the Chaotics."

I glanced at Tad. He sat on the mattress, staring off into space. "I can't do that," I replied.

"Why not?"

"I just can't."

They looked at each other. Then Dad sighed. "Look, we know what it's like to be passionate about something. But you can't let it ruin your life."

"I'm doing what I have to do," I replied. "And you should do the same."

Mom frowned. "What's that supposed to mean?"

"It means you need to disavow me. Publicly and as often as possible."

"But—"

"You have to. Promise me you'll do it."

Dad was unable to meet my gaze. "No."

"You must."

Mom burst into tears. Staring at the table, Dad wiped his eyes. They were defiant, so I didn't push the issue.

The conversation shifted and we talked about other things. Mostly, old memories. Vacations and Christmas mornings, birthdays and family walks. I recalled some of it. Other recollections were new to me.

I did my best to memorize every detail, sealing the stories deep into my memory banks. Whatever happened next, I couldn't forget them.

No matter what.

CHAPTER 51

Furrowing my brow, I tried to recall Piper's face. Oh, I remembered it in a general sense. I knew the shape of her eyes, the curl of her mouth, the frizziness of her hair. If pressed, I could glean up a pretty good image of her. And yet, it wasn't perfect. I was missing something. Maybe even a few things.

The same held true for Leandra. I recalled her general appearance, her essence. But when I tried to dig deeper, to remember the smallest details, I came up short. The realization sent a wave of panic through me. If I couldn't remember my friends now, how would my memories fare in the days to come?

I shifted uneasily on the floor. Tad was still on the mattress, his knees clutched tight to his body.

The conversation with my parents had eventually dwindled away into awkward silence. One of the witches had popped the bubbler, sending our little cell back into near-darkness.

Clanking noises flooded my ears. Nerves frazzling, I twisted toward the door.

MacPherson strode into the room a moment later, brandishing his wand like it was a sword. "On your feet, gentlemen," he said. "The headmaster wishes to address you."

I was too tired to stand, too tired to even think properly. "Not now," I replied. "Tell him to come back later."

"And tell him that we could use some doughcream," Tad added. "Lots of doughcream."

A hand steered MacPherson to one side. Then Galison appeared. His clothes were ruffled and his suspenders were in place, useless as always. Behind him, I saw Norch and Wadflow. Dust covered Wadflow from head to toe, a consequence of the forgotten corner in which we'd stashed her. Meanwhile, Norch's makeup was smeared and her hair was a tangled mess.

They were obviously furious. And that probably should've scared me. But it was hard to take them seriously.

Despite their steely expressions, they looked like a trio of chimney cleaners.

"Hey, guys," I said. "How are you feeling? Rested, I hope?"

Galison sneered. "I should wring your neck."

"No, no." Wadflow, hands on hips, glared down at Tad. "I say we turn them into squonks."

"Using what spell?" I wondered. "The Professor Wadflow Duplicator?"

Her face turned purple. She took a few menacing steps in our direction.

"That's quite alright, Professor," Boltstar said in a soothing tone. "I'll take it from here."

The professors stared at us for a long moment, their eyes full of animosity. Then MacPherson led them out of the room.

"I see you found your colleagues." Tad forced a smile. "You're welcome, by the way."

Boltstar stepped forward. He wore black trousers along with matching suspenders. A thin gold vest rested on top of his white dress shirt. His wand was tucked into his vest and he wore his derby pulled low over his eyes. "Mr. Crucible, I'd appreciate your help with something."

Tad regarded him for a long moment. "No."

"I'm afraid your participation is mandatory."

"You can't make me do something I don't want to do."

"Very true. That's why I intend to fraptize you."

I inhaled a sharp breath. Fraptize was a forbidden spell. Nearly as barbaric as the Gratlan or Drodiation Curses, it involved turning a person into, well, a puppet. I'd never seen it before, but I'd heard nightmarish stories about it. If done correctly, it could make a person do anything.

"You wouldn't dare," Tad sputtered.

"I'll take no joy in it, Mr. Crucible. But it must be done."

He fell silent.

"I take no joy in this either." He exhaled. "But you have the right to know the terms of your punishment. After careful consideration, I've decided to lock the two of you into a state of drodiation."

I experienced a tiny twinge of fear amongst my near-emptiness. Spending the rest of my life as a statue? Unable to move, to talk, even to close my eyes? Left alone with nothing but my thoughts for company? Coupled with the skinning ceremony, I couldn't imagine a worse fate. "No," I muttered. "You can't …"

"It's either that or I kill you. And I've got enough blood on my hands for one lifetime."

"Send us to Gutlore," Tad implored. "Please."

"I'm afraid I can't risk the two of you infecting others with your ideas. However, you should know that Gutlore will be getting two other prisoners today." He gave me a meaningful look. "I'm sorry, Mr. Wolf."

My eyes widened. "My parents?"

He nodded.

"But MacPherson promised—"

"Professor MacPherson promised no harm would come to them. And it won't. They'll be perfectly safe at Gutlore."

"They're innocent," Tad said. "They didn't do anything wrong."

"I know. Unfortunately, it's not what they've done that concerns me. It's what they might do." He sighed. "People will go to great lengths to help a loved one. Just like you, Mr. Crucible. You risked everything to get your people into Madkey."

"Can you blame me?" He gave Boltstar a close look. "Do you even know what you did to us?"

The headmaster gave him a curious look.

"The changes you made to Womigia made everyone hate the Chaotics." Tad exhaled. "And I do mean everyone."

"You mean …?"

"Yeah. We hate ourselves. We can't help it."

"I see. Well, I sympathize with your plight, Mr. Crucible. I do. Unfortunately, I had no other choice. It wasn't enough to defeat the Chaotic leaders. I needed to kill their philosophy. And to do that, I had to turn everyone against it."

"And for all your trouble, it didn't work," I pointed out. "Chaotics is still alive."

"Indeed. But not for long."

"Don't you get it?" Tad said. "You can't kill an idea."

"Oh, but I can, Mr. Crucible." Boltstar wiped sweat off of the back of his neck. "Your people are the only true advocates left. Once they're gone, the Chaotic philosophy will wither away once and for all."

Tad shook his head. Meanwhile, I glanced at the open door. Galison and the others stood just outside it, wands drawn and ready for action.

"Professor Galison." Boltstar glanced over his shoulder. "Please take Mr. Crucible to Torso. The Upper-Torso bridge, specifically. Prepare him to be fraptized."

Galison hiked into the room. Gripping Tad by the shoulder, he directed him toward the doorway. "Don't worry," he said with a sneer. "You won't feel a thing."

Tad tried to shrug him off, but the man's grip was strong as steel. "Why are you doing this?"

"You'll find out soon enough." The headmaster turned to leave. "Remember this moment, gentlemen. For the next time you see each other, you'll both be drodiated."

CHAPTER 52

As soon as they were gone, I tried the door. Finding it locked, I pounded on it with all of my might. But no one came to my aide.

The reality of the situation sank in and I slumped to the ground. This was it. There would be no escape, no way out.

A couple of soft blasts rang out, followed by agonized grunts. Puzzled, I crawled to the door. Placing my ear against the cool metal, I listened hard.

Seconds later, the bolt clanked open. The knob started to turn. Balling up my fists, I hid behind the door.

It swung ajar and footsteps clattered into the semi-dark room. I waited three seconds, then leapt out. A silhouetted figure stood in front of me. Grabbing its shoulders, I shoved the figure up against a wall.

"Ease up there." A hand touched my arm. "It's just us."

"Leandra?" Squinting, I peered at the figure in front of me. "Piper?"

She peeled my hands off her shoulders and gave me an appraising look. "Who else?"

Surprised, I spun toward the open doorway. Norch and Wadflow lay sprawled on the floor, unmoving.

I blinked. "You knocked them out?"

Leandra released my arm. She clutched Norch's and Wadflow's wands in her other hand. "Of course."

"But how?"

"It was easy." She shrugged. "I think they're still recovering from Tad's sleeping curses."

They'd taken an enormous risk. Part of me wanted to scold them and part of me wanted to thank them profusely. But instead, I hurried to the door. Turning my head in either direction, I scanned the exterior hallway. It was empty. Turning my gaze toward the ramp, I checked the field and the bleachers. Again, I saw no one. "Boltstar's got Tad. He's going to fraptize him."

"Why?" Leandra asked.

"He didn't say."

Piper furrowed her brow. "It must have something to do with the curfew."

"Curfew?"

She nodded. "Boltstar ordered students and staffers back to their dorms over an hour ago."

"What about the faculty?"

"They're gathered in Torso with the alumni." Leandra exhaled. "We think they're preparing to go after the Chaotics."

"Then why fraptize Tad?" I wondered. "Boltstar already has his anchor."

"Maybe they're going to use him as a distraction," Piper suggested.

"Why bother? They've already got the element of surprise."

We stood there for a few moments, puzzled. Finally, she shrugged. "It doesn't matter. What matters is stopping that attack."

"How are we going to do that?" I wondered.

"This should help." Leandra tossed me Norch's wand. As soon as it left her fingers, she winced. "Sorry. I forgot."

I fumbled for the wand, then grabbed hold of it. Lifting it to my eyes, I gave it a long look.

"Give it a shot," Piper urged. "Who knows? Maybe Boltstar didn't get all of your magic."

My eyes closed over. I searched my soul for magic, but came up empty. Grunting softly, I focused on my emotions. They remained quite dull, but with some effort I was able to churn them into a reasonable facsimile of the right combination. My wand didn't move on instinct, so I maneuvered it myself.

"Herd Crash," I said.

I waited for a few seconds, hoping against hope that I'd see auburn light. But nothing happened.

Piper's jaw twisted with disappointment. Leandra emitted a soft sigh.

With a deep exhalation, I pocketed the wand. "Well, at least we know."

"We should get going," Piper said.

"First, we need a plan," Leandra replied. "We can't very well run into Torso, casting spells left and right. The faculty and alumni will crush us."

"They can't crush us if we don't fight," Piper replied, a mischievous gleam in her eyes.

Leandra gave her a questioning look.

"Boltstar's army will have to travel through the Floating Abyss, right? So, we'll go with them. When we get to wherever we're going, we'll sneak ahead and warn the Chaotics. That'll give them time to evacuate."

She looked thoughtful. "You know, that just might work. But what if they see us?"

"They probably will." She gave us a pointed look. "Once we do this, there's a good chance we'll spend the rest of our lives on the run."

"Send bubblers to your parents," I told them. "Tell them to go someplace safe."

They looked at me.

"Trust me."

They exchanged glances. "We'll do it before we leave," Piper said.

"Three dropouts on one side. The greatest magicians in the world on the other one." Leandra chuckled darkly. "We must be crazy."

"Indeed." I gave them a meaningful look. "Now, let's get to work."

CHAPTER 53

Sweat dripped down my cheeks as we slipped into Lower Torso. It was late now and quite dark. In fact, it was far darker than normal. Looking around, I saw every single cool-light in the area had been extinguished.

Steering clear of moonlight, I eyed the cavernous space. Madkey Station Grille's tables and chairs were unoccupied. The Lower-Torso bridge was completely vacant. The Upper-Torso bridge also appeared empty. But the Mid-Torso bridge was another story.

"They're above us. Galison, MacPherson, Lellpoppy, Hunt …" I scanned the faces for Boltstar. Oddly enough, I didn't see him. "What are they waiting for?"

"Don't know." Brow furrowed, Leandra scanned the rest of Torso. "Look," she whispered. "Up there."

Following her gaze, I saw Tad. He stood at the very edge of the Upper-Torso bridge, near the entrance to Left Arm. His eyes were unfocused and he looked dazed. A few seconds passed. Then he lifted a wand.

"What's he doing?" I wondered.

Piper bit her lip. "Whatever Boltstar wants him to do."

My gaze shifted back a few feet and I caught a glimpse of Boltstar. His body was shifting this way and that, in perfect time with Tad's movements.

"Tad's been fraptized, alright," Leandra said, clenching her fingers into fists.

A tawny hue appeared, seemingly from Tad's wand. But in actuality, I could see it came from just behind him, from Boltstar's wand. Apparently, the headmaster hadn't just taken Tad's magic. He'd taken his spell color as well.

The tawny glow sped out to the Grille and began to wrap itself around the ancient conveyance station. It wrapped once, then twice. It soared around for a third time, gradually covering every inch of the mystical energy.

"They're making it look like Tad's handiwork." Piper frowned. "But why?"

"Because they're not invading the Chaotics." Leandra's tone turned breathless. "They're luring them here."

Her explanation sped through my brain and I knew it was true. Boltstar wasn't planning to attack the Chaotics on their turf. Instead, he was going to draw them to Madkey. That was why he needed Tad. The remaining Chaotics would be wary after the last battle. They'd enter Torso with great caution, ready to flee at a moment's notice. Seeing Tad would put them at ease. Heck, Boltstar could even force him to speak, to tell the Chaotics everything was fine. And everything would be fine. That is, until Boltstar decided to launch his ambush.

"They've got the high ground," Leandra said slowly.

"The havoc crest, too," Piper pointed out. "When the ambush starts, the Chaotics will be out in the open, totally exposed."

"We have to warn them," I said.

Leandra and Piper exchanged a glance. "I think we can manage that," Leandra said with surprising confidence.

"But we'll still need to get them out of harm's way," Piper added.

"So, we'll tell them to return home," I said. "Before Boltstar can close the station."

She shook her head. "He'll just use the anchor to follow them. No, they've got to fight."

Leandra's gaze drifted across the Lower-Torso bridge. "We could steer them to the library. Plenty of space, lots of places to hide.

"They could regroup in there, then launch a counter-attack." Piper looked thoughtful for a moment. Then she frowned. "It's a good idea. But that's a long way to go, considering they'll be under fire the entire time."

"So, we'll offer up a distraction."

"That could work. But someone still needs to get them into the library."

"I'll do it," I volunteered.

Piper turned my way. Her hair hung in damp, frazzled curls. Smudges of grease and dirt dotted her clothing. She looked totally helpless, yet completely unbeatable.

"Forget it," she said.

"Somebody's got to do it. And since I can't do magic, it might as well be me."

She shook her head. "You won't be able to protect yourself. And—"

"And it's our best chance," I said softly.

She exhaled. "If you get hurt …"

"I won't."

"We need to get ready." Leandra patted my shoulder. "Good luck."

"You, too."

She darted to the nearest hoist. Piper lingered for an extra moment. Suddenly, she lunged at me. Her head burrowed into my chest. Her arms folded around me and I felt a tight squeeze along with a surge of positivity.

As it washed over me, I felt stirrings of joy and gratitude. The emotions came from deep inside, from a place that I'd thought was empty. Surprised, I hugged her back.

She released me, then retreated a few feet. She didn't cry or sob or anything like that. Instead, she fixed me with a tough glare.

"Take care of yourself," she warned. "Or else."

"I will. And do me a favor." I grinned. "Make Boltstar regret he ever taught you havoc magic."

With a nod, she darted to the hoist. She slipped inside of it and it sped silently up to Upper-Torso.

The tawny glow continued to surge until it had completely enveloped the ancient conveyance station. Then it began to pulse and throb, faster and faster.

A shadowy figure materialized within the Grille. It belonged to a woman, approximately twenty years of age. She wore a purple shirt and a long green skirt. Her shoes had little buckles on them and looked freshly polished.

A chair rose up from Lower-Torso and caught the woman. Panicked, she emitted a light gasp. Then she gave her legs a little kick. The chair shifted sideways a few inches. She kicked again and the chair slid in the opposite direction.

Hovering in mid-air, she set her jaw and clenched her wand in a steely grip. Then she trained her eyes on the bridges. Her gaze settled on Tad. Fraptized by Boltstar, he gave her a calming wave with his free hand. Then he lifted his finger to his mouth, shushing her. Her jaw relaxed and she lowered her wand.

More shadowy figures appeared. The early arrivals were a young bunch, ranging from the teens to the thirties. Older folks were next to arrive.

Chairs rose up to grab each and every one of them. Silently, the Chaotics conducted quick checks of the area. At first, they were tense and uneasy. But as they caught sight of Tad, they relaxed a bit.

The flow of new arrivals started to slow. I did a quick count of the Chaotics. There were roughly forty of them. How many more were coming? Another dozen or so? It couldn't be much more than that.

Ducking down, I hurried across the Lower-Torso bridge. Time, I knew, was short. If I didn't get them to safety in the next few minutes, they'd be finished.

CHAPTER 54

As I hustled across the stone bridge, Norch's wand rode up in my pocket. Annoyed, I pushed it back down.

The air sizzled just as I reached the library. Looking over my shoulder, I caught a glimpse of aureolin light. A grunt rang out. Slowly, the tawny glow began to unravel from the ancient conveyance station.

Going after Boltstar himself, huh? I couldn't help but grin. *Gutsy move, Leandra.*

Almost immediately, the Chaotics knew something was wrong. Gathering in a tight group, they scanned the bridges.

"They must be on to us," Galison shouted. "Attack!"

Stewart turned her attention to the Upper-Torso bridge. Spotting Leandra, she fired off a quick spell. Stone crunched and metal squealed. Leandra yelped. Then part of the bridge broke away, the debris crashing near Stewart's feet.

I raced to the railing and peered up. Through the smoke and dust, I saw Leandra hanging from the broken bridge. Her legs kicked for purchase and she was starting to make some headway. But Stewart was ready for her. Shifting her wand, the professor readied another spell.

A raspberry-colored jet came screaming down from another section of the Upper-Torso bridge. It hit Stewart's hand and she dropped her wand. Caught by surprise, she took a stumbling step backward, then crashed onto her rear.

Leaping onto a chair, I rode it out into the Grille. "Follow me," I shouted. "And hurry."

The Chaotics got the message and raced after me. Waves of magic, all the colors of the rainbow, assailed them. A young girl, no more than fourteen, slumped in her chair. A quick peek revealed she'd been hit by the Gratlan. Evidently, Boltstar and his allies were playing for keeps.

Stopping my chair just short of the bridge, I pointed at the library. "In there."

A bunch of Chaotics leapt to the bridge. Wands aimed high, they fired spells at the faculty and alumni. Farther up, I heard Leandra and Piper calling to each other. I strained my ears, but couldn't make out their words.

Other Chaotics reached the bridge and ran for the library. Throwing the doors open, they disappeared inside. Meanwhile, the faculty and alumni mounted chairs and zoomed out into the open. They began hurling spells at the library.

Keeping a low profile, I rode my chair into the middle of the Grille. Sticking close to the curving glass windows, I turned my attention to the Upper-Torso bridge.

Boltstar stood on one side of it. Looking serene, he aimed a spell at a fleeing Piper and Leandra. He missed and his magic hit the stonework in front of them. An explosion rang out as another section of the bridge collapsed.

My friends skidded to a halt. With the bridge broken on either side, their options were limited. So, they scrambled toward the railing, ready to leap into the Grille.

Looking determined now, the headmaster shifted his wand and I knew he wouldn't miss again. Maneuvering my knees, I directed my chair toward the ceiling. "Hey, Boltstar," I bellowed. "Up here."

His wand paused as he caught sight of me. Then he leapt off the bridge. A chair flew up and he landed neatly on its seat. He directed it out into the open, stopping just a few feet from me.

I shot a quick glimpse at Piper and Leandra. They were still on the bridge, looking dazed, but okay. My gaze twisted to Tad. He sat on the ground, holding his head in his hands. Clearly, he was no longer under Boltstar's control.

"Hello again, Mr. Wolf." Boltstar gave me a long look. "I see that I underestimated you."

My mind went blank. I had no idea what to do, what to say. All I could think about was how I was facing the greatest magician of all time without a lick of magic to call my own. Had I lost my mind?

I felt Norch's wand in my pocket. Even though it was useless, I held it up anyway.

He arched an amused eyebrow. "Tell me something, Mr. Wolf. Just what do you hope to accomplish here?"

"Peace." I inhaled a slow breath. "Let's lower our wands, see if we can't figure this out, wizard to wizard."

"And just how would that work?"

"We could start by telling the truth and restoring Womigia, warts and all."

"I'm afraid that's a non-starter, Mr. Wolf."

"Is it? Because you can't just expect people to go on hating themselves for something they didn't do."

"Fair point." He rubbed his jaw. "Perhaps we can make an alternative arrangement."

"Like what?"

"We skin them. Without magic, they'd no longer be subjected to the whims of Womigia."

I arched an eyebrow. "Don't you mean *your* whims?"

"Call it whatever you like."

"Absolutely not." Tad rose to unsteady footing. "No way we're giving up our magic."

As I looked his way, Leandra and Piper hopped off the bridge. Chairs sailed upward, grabbing both of them. Right away, Galison opened fire. Another section of bridge exploded, sending metal and stone to all ends of Torso. Meanwhile, my friends zipped across the Grille, dodging havoc magic the entire way.

"Be skinned or suffer the consequences." Boltstar clasped his hands behind his back. Tilting his chair upward, he rode it toward the ceiling. "It's your choice."

Tad gritted his teeth. "If I still had magic …"

"I take it you'd prefer the latter option." His eyes glittered with a strange kind of darkness. Tilting his chair, he rode it around the window side of Torso. With casual flicks, he sent a series of spells flying in all directions. "Drodiate. Drodiate. Drodiate."

I directed my chair out of the way, narrowly dodging the ensuing wave of cyan bolts.

Tad leapt out into the open. A chair caught him and he flew after Boltstar. Meanwhile, Galison continued to aim spells at Leandra and Piper.

The library door burst open and Chaotics flooded out into Torso. Now organized, they hopped onto chairs and split up into groups. Within seconds, the entire area was a web of spells.

Dodging magic on all sides, I rode my chair down to the Lower-Torso bridge. As I watched the battle rage all around me, I had a sudden realization.

We were going to lose.

Although fast-paced, the battle had a long and drawn-out feel to it. This was a war of attrition. Which was a problem, seeing as how our side was outnumbered by the faculty and alumni.

I exhaled. Unfortunately, good didn't always win nor did evil always get its comeuppance. Reality was messier than that. Sometimes, good people died. Sometimes, bad people were hailed as heroes.

Fury and helplessness churned up within me as I watched the Chaotics fall one-by-one to Boltstar's army. I couldn't just stay on the sidelines. Skinned or not, I had to help.

Riding my chair into the fray, I tried to formulate a plan. But my head was a jumble of newfound emotions.

"Drodiate, Drodiate, Drodiate."

Boltstar heaved spells at Piper. She flew like mad to get away from him but the cyan bolts were getting closer and closer. Finally, one of them struck her back. She froze and her chair paused in mid-air.

My heart slowed to a near-stop. My veins iced over.

No.

Boltstar didn't waste any time. Turning his wand toward a zigzagging Leandra, he took careful aim.

Emotions surged within me. They bubbled up, filling that horrible emptiness I'd felt since the skinning ceremony. The emotions brought something else with them. A familiar, longing sensation. I found myself reaching toward it, straining for even a touch.

Without thinking, I lifted Norch's wand. I didn't know what was happening. All I knew that was that for a single moment in time, I felt utterly and completely whole.

"Dissolate," I said. The word just came out of my mouth. I hadn't planned it or anything.

Brilliant auburn light exploded out of the wand. The force was so powerful, it sent me and my chair soaring backward a couple of feet.

Twirling and shimmering, the light raced across Torso. At the exact same instant, Boltstar cast his spell.

"Drodiate," he said.

A blaze of cyan left his wand and raced toward Leandra.

The auburn light gained speed. Faster and faster it flew, crackling like lightning. It caught up with Boltstar's spell in the blink of an eye. Auburn swept over cyan, swallowing it up before blinking out of existence.

I'd seen it with my own eyes. But it barely registered in my brain. Boltstar had skinned me. I'd felt it happen. I'd seen the magic leave my body. And yet, I'd managed to perform a spell anyway. Right out in the open, for all to see. Somehow, despite his best efforts, I still had magic.

And now, it was time to use it.

CHAPTER 55

Boltstar twisted at the waist. His bulging eyes met mine. For the first time, I noticed a trace of uncertainty within them. Adjusting his derby, he stared at me again. And just like that, the uncertainty was gone.

His wand moved in a very precise fashion. "Drodiate."

A burst of cyan raced toward me. There was no time to think, to plan. And so, my instincts took over. My emotions solidified. My wand shifted, duplicating its previous movements. "Dissolate," I said.

I hadn't planned to do the same spell again. It had just sort of happened. But I was grateful nonetheless. For a split-second later, my wand exploded just like before. An auburn streak soared straight and true. It swallowed up Boltstar's spell, then vanished.

Cocking his head, he studied me from afar. Meanwhile, spells flew back and forth, overhead and beneath our chairs. We were smack dab in the middle of a havoc magic war. And yet, it felt like we were the only two people in existence.

Racking my brain, I tried to understand how this had happened. Either something had gone wrong with the skinning ceremony or it simply hadn't worked on me.

While I contemplated this, fury and disbelief started to swirl inside of me. Boltstar had drodiated Piper and tried to do the same to Leandra. He'd drodiated a generation of Chaotics and caused the next generation to hate itself for crimes it had never committed.

My wand shifted, flowing with my emotions. My lips opened wide and I knew just what to say.

"Pulverize."

An auburn spell raced out of my wand. Immediately, Boltstar went to work. Little orbs of cyan light appeared, darting this way and that, constantly shifting positions. It was a veritable minefield of magic and I saw no way for my spell to penetrate it.

Abruptly, the auburn light began to stretch and unfold. It grew longer and wider, forming something akin to a flying blanket. Then it careened into the minefield and the orbs detonated all at once. They shredded the blanket.

But they didn't destroy it.

Bits of auburn sailed onward. Boltstar lifted his arm and braced himself. The little bits stuck fast to his clothes for a split-second. Then they exploded.

The impact sent him hurtling off of his chair. Spinning sideways, he slammed into the back wall. Then he dropped to the Mid-Torso bridge.

For the briefest of moments, the room fell still. There were no spells, no shouts, no movement at all. Every head in Torso, save none, swiveled my way.

I blinked, utterly and completely shocked by this turn of events. I had stood toe-to-toe with the greatest magician of all time. And with a few unplanned, unknown spells, I'd driven him to his knees. How could that be possible? How was it even possible that I was doing magic in the first place?

Maybe magic can't really be skinned, I thought. *Maybe it exists in an endless, inner well.*

That actually made a lot of sense. A skinning ceremony might drain one of magic. But maybe one could generate more magic under certain circumstances.

Grunts rang out and the fighting resumed. Meanwhile, Boltstar was quick to his feet. His gaze fell on me and I saw no fear in his visage. My knees began to quake just a bit.

Climbing over the railing, he leapt toward the Grille. His chair grabbed him and he rode it straight up until he was level with me.

Magic flowed inside of me like a restless ocean. I felt strong and powerful. Like a great wizard, one capable of tearing down all of Madkey with a simple wave of the wand. But that strength was tempered by sheer terror.

I was a dropout. And Boltstar was, well, *Boltstar*. The greatest magician of all time. The memory of our first duel flooded my mind. I recalled racing around the HMQ, desperately trying to escape his power. And I recalled the exact moment he'd vanquished me. I'd used Chaotic magic back then and he'd defeated me with ease.

So, how had I gotten the upper hand this time? It must've been a fluke. Yes, that was it. I'd gotten lucky.

Unfortunately, I couldn't count on luck to bail me out again. And so, I racked my brain, trying to recall the exact emotions that had led to the Pulverize spell. I'd experienced tremendous fury for what he'd done to Piper, for what he'd tried to do to Leandra. I'd also felt disbelief over how far he'd gone in his pursuit to destroy the Chaotics. Yes, that was it … fury and disbelief, in just the right amounts.

"It appears you're fairly adept with Chaotic magic," Boltstar said, his wand at his side. "But tell me something, Mr. Wolf. Can you control it?"

My fingers twitched nervously. "Control it?"

He nodded. "For all you know, your next spell might turn someone into an amputee. Or perhaps you'll bring this entire building down upon us." He gave me a keen look. "So, can you control it, Mr. Wolf?"

His words hit me hard, even as I tried to ignore them.

"The simple answer, Mr. Wolf, is no. You can't control it. That's not your fault, by the way. It's a fundamental flaw of Chaotic magic."

Panicking, I tried to recall the Pulverize emotions all over again. I'd felt fury, right? But how much? And what was that other emotion again?

"In my youth, decent witches and wizards couldn't walk down the street without looking over their shoulders, lest they fall victim to some errant spell." He gave me an appraising look. "Is that what you want your legacy to be, Mr. Wolf? The wizard who brought the magic community back to the Dark Ages?"

As much as I tried to resist, his words were getting to me. I'd always taken my safety for granted. Oh sure, rogue witches and wizards existed. And they sometimes used the Capsudra to cast the forbidden spells. But such magicians were few and far between.

Did I really want to live in a world where anyone could cast any spell at any time? A world where witches and wizards might not even know what spell they were casting until it had already left their wands? It sounded frightening. But the more I thought about it, the more it intrigued me as well.

Structuralist magic was so dull, so boring. So … contained. Every spell, save the forbidden ones, was known by everyone. That was what made Chaotics so interesting. Yes, it could cause problems. But it also held the promise of newness, of invention.

"Chaotics might be dangerous," I replied. "But it could be good, too. Someone might come up with a spell to cure Hickets. Or to solve hunger. Or maybe to just sprout some lapsas and brighten everyone's day."

He stared at me, unmoving and unemotional. "I can see we're at a philosophical stalemate, Mr. Wolf, the same one I reached with Mr. Hynor many years ago. Since debate won't settle our differences, I'm afraid wands will have to do."

The emotions I'd used for the Pulverize spell popped into my head. I steeled my heart, letting my anxiety and everything else melt away. Disbelief and fear began to rise up inside of me. The amounts of each varied as I sought to find just the right balance.

"Drodiate," Boltstar said, his voice tinged with sadness and regret.

A flash of cyan caught my eye and I knew I was in trouble. My brain shifted into defensive mode and I recalled the spell I'd used to save Leandra from drodiation.

New emotions stirred inside of me. With quick, arcing movements, I shifted my wand. "Dissolate," I said.

To my surprise, there was no sudden explosion of auburn magic. In fact, there was no magic at all.

Panicking, I lunged to the right. The chair tilted just enough and Boltstar's spell flew past me. It struck one of the Chaotics, a bearded, heavyset man, in mid-spell. He gurgled and froze solid in his chair.

"How very interesting," Boltstar said. "It appears you haven't mastered Chaotics magic quite yet, Mr. Wolf."

Goosebumps sprang up on my arms and legs. I felt like the proverbial emperor, exposed for my nakedness. With my options dwindling, I took the only choice I had left.

I fled.

CHAPTER 56

Cyan jets, bright and sizzling, flew past me. They were so close I could feel their heat, their dangerous energy.

I directed my chair to the right, then climbed toward the ceiling. A cyan streak just missed me, crashing into a thin witch with wide hips and big eyes. As I hurtled by, I caught a brief glimpse of her going rigid.

I kept the chair moving, zigzagging across the Grille, shifting up and down. The cyan streaks kept coming, getting ever closer to my body.

All around me, the war continued without pause. Galison, perched on the Mid-Torso bridge, fired a spell at a tall guy with glasses. The spell hit home and the guy dropped his wand. Screaming, he raked his fingers across his skin, clawing away imaginary terrors. Another spell put him out of his misery and he slumped in his chair.

On Lower-Torso, an elderly woman with a stooped posture and silver hair fired a spell at Whitlock. It found its mark and the professor shrieked in pain.

It was like that all around me. Sometimes a faculty member or alumnus took out a Chaotic, sometimes it was the other way around.

I heard a soft bump, followed by a grunt. Chancing a look over my shoulder, I saw a Chaotic tackle Boltstar right off his chair. The two of them started to fall before being caught by their respective chairs. Boltstar fired off a quick spell and the Chaotic went stiff.

I looked for Leandra and Piper. While I didn't see them, I did notice Tad. He was on an undamaged section of the Upper-Torso bridge, the part connected to Left Arm. MacPherson was there as well. There wasn't a wand to be seen and instead, the two of them were fighting the old-fashioned way.

Riding my chair to the bridge, I dove over the railing. My shoulder smacked into MacPherson's back. The impact drove him forward and he hit his head on the wall. Eyes glazed over, he slumped to the ground.

"You okay?" I asked.

"Fine, now that my strings are cut." He gave me a curious look. "Were you doing magic out there?"

I nodded.

"But you were skinned."

"Yeah, well, I—" A cyan blast struck the railing. Swiveling around, I saw Boltstar on his chair, racing toward us. "We need to go."

"Where?"

"Anywhere but here."

Keeping low, we dove into the nearest hoist.

"Don't leave, Mr. Wolf." Boltstar's voice thundered through Torso. "I'm not finished with you yet."

As the gate slid up, the headmaster vaulted off of his chair. Landing squarely on the bridge, he stalked toward us.

"Where are we going?" Tad asked frantically.

"Lower-Torso," I whispered to the hoist. "And hurry."

Spells flew our way and I ducked down. They struck the gate and the hoist emitted an angry squeak.

It descended abruptly, leaving my stomach behind. Wind whistled in my ears. Then, just as abruptly, it slid to a screaming halt.

"Lower-Torso," it snarled. "Everyone out. And hey, who hit me with that spell up there?"

"Boltstar," I said as I followed Tad off of the hoist.

"Really?" The hoist's tune changed instantly. "Well, sheesh. What'd you two idiots do to piss him off?"

We didn't answer. Grumbling loudly, the hoist closed its gate and took off again, presumably to pick up the headmaster.

Tad gave me a look. "What now?"

I scanned Torso. The Chaotics were still putting up a good fight, but their numbers were definitely dwindling. "We need help."

He snapped his fingers. "How about the archive? All of the old Chaotic magicians are in there."

I considered that for a moment. "Didn't you already try to free them?"

"Yeah," he admitted.

"Even if it works, who says they'll help us?" I added. "I mean, they've been frozen for decades. They could be insane for all we know."

"True." He eyed me. "Do you have a better plan?"

I racked my brain. "We could try to fix Womigia."

"What good will that do?"

"It'll stop your people from hating themselves, for one thing. That might empower them to fight harder. And it'll strip away the faculty's and alumni's blind loyalty toward Boltstar. That could weaken their resolve."

He thought about it, then shook his head. "Even if we did fix it, Boltstar would just mess it all up again."

"Then we'll have to find a way to stop him."

We broke out into a sprint. Using another hoist, we descended to Right Foot. Then we darted toward the archive's secret entrance, passing trash and broken furniture along the way.

We halted just shy of the old plaque. Without a word, we shifted it to one side, exposing the conveyance portal.

Tad cocked his ear. "I don't hear him," he said between light gasps.

"Me neither."

"Do you think he knows what we're doing?"

"Undoubtedly." My brow furrowed into a ridge. "There's something I don't understand."

"What's that?" he asked.

"Boltstar wanted to keep Womigia a secret, right? So, why didn't he destroy this portal?"

"I don't think he could." He shrugged. "Boltstar's a great magician, but much of Chaotic magic is beyond even his grasp."

We touched the portal at roughly the same time. The bundled magic buzzed softly and then I found myself in complete darkness, twisting and turning and sliding at a million miles per hour.

Wind rushed against my face. Air vacated my lungs and I could no longer breathe. I started to panic. And that's when I spilled out onto a concrete platform.

There was no garden this time. Instead, we found ourselves in a vast room, dimly lit with cool-lights. Mirrors were positioned across the floor. Not memory mirrors. Not even regular mirrors. No, these mirrors were something else.

When I stared into them, I saw different versions of myself. In one mirror, I was sobbing on a dingy floor, a cold body lying next to me. Another mirror showed me dumping a bowl of soup over a humiliated Porter's head. Still another mirror depicted me sitting in class, taking a test with a confident expression etched upon my face.

Tad made a face at one of the mirrors, then winced. "Holy smokes, that's freaky."

"What's freaky?"

"Believe me, you don't want to know."

He'd visited the archive in the past and hence, had some experience with its rotating traps. "Please tell me you've seen this one before," I said.

"No such luck." He exhaled. "What do you make of it?"

"It looks like a hall of mirrors."

"A hall of what?"

"A hall of mirrors. You know, a fun house attraction."

He studied another mirror up close, then recoiled from it. "Doesn't seem very fun to me," he said, inhaling a sharp breath.

I strode deeper into the room, searching for traps. After a short walk, I stopped in front of a tall, skinny mirror. It stood on a short stand. Its edging was made from gold, which looked like it hadn't been cleaned in years. I gave the glass a quick glance. The surface swirled and I saw myself ten or fifteen years into the future. I stood in front of my workstation in Madkey's kitchen. A ball of sticky doughcream rested before me. As I watched, the older me maneuvered a wand and issued a spell. The doughcream began to knead itself. Then it vanished and another ball of doughcream appeared.

Frowning, I lowered my gaze to the floor. What had I just seen? It definitely wasn't my future. Heck, I'd be surprised if I survived that long. And even if I did, there was no way I'd work at Madkey again.

"Hey," Tad called out. "Over here."

Hiking over to him, I noticed a small sign posted on stilts. The text, written in living ink, chilled my bones.

"Welcome to the Hall of Souls," I read aloud. "Know thyself … or die."

CHAPTER 57

"Know thyself or die?" I exhaled. "Whoever built these traps was as twisted as they come."

"What do you think it means?"

"Know thyself, know thyself, know thyself …" Deep in thought, I stood up. My gaze traced the room. There must have been over one thousand mirrors, all of them unique in terms of size, shape, and ornamentation. "What did you see when you looked in the mirrors?"

"A whole bunch of stuff." He pointed at three mirrors in turn. "In that one, I was back home, lying in bed. My mom kept checking on me and I'm pretty sure I was faking a stomachache. Over there, I was playing ramball in Madkey Arena. The stands were filled with all kinds of magicians, Structuralists and Chaotics alike. From what I could tell, everyone got along just fine. And I was a little kid in that one over there, dancing in the middle of a crowded street."

"Weird."

"Tell me about it."

"I saw strange stuff, too. Different than yours. But still strange." I thought about what Tad had described and what

I'd seen as well. And I thought about the sign on stilts and its cryptic message. "According to the sign, we're supposed to know ourselves. So, what if the mirrors show different versions of us?"

"You mean different parts of our personality?"

"Not exactly." I paused, considering the possibilities. "This is the Hall of Souls, right? So, maybe they depict our potential souls. But only one of them shows the truth."

"Oh, I see. So, if I'm a big faker who likes hanging out in bed all day, I'd choose that first mirror?"

"Pretty much."

"And if I chose the wrong one?"

I glanced at the sign again. *Welcome to the Hall of Souls*, it read. *Know thyself … or die.*

"Don't," I replied

"Got it."

Splitting up, we began searching the massive room. Tad stopped in front of a short, skinny mirror with plain metal edging and gave it a quick look. Two seconds later, he broke off eye-contact and moved to another mirror.

Meanwhile, I checked out an oval-shaped mirror, propped up by a cherry wooden stand. The glass appeared old and dusty at first glance. But when I peered into it, the dust melted away and a clear image appeared.

I saw myself standing on a chair in the middle of Madkey Station Grille, trading spells with Boltstar. It felt so familiar, so recent that I thought I'd found the right one. My fingers reached out, stretching toward the glass.

Then I saw something a bit off. This Randy's posture was firm, unyielding, completely lacking in fear. His expression was one of cruel confidence. With reckless abandon, he threw spell after spell at an equally reckless Boltstar.

Halting my fingers, I watched as one of the spells slipped past the headmaster. It flew another few feet before striking

Piper. Eyes rolling into the back of her head, she collapsed on the Upper-Torso bridge.

Horrified, I looked away. Only then did I realize I was breathing rapidly, my heart thumping against my chest.

That wasn't her, I reminded myself. *It wasn't real.*

My heart kept thumping as I contemplated what I'd just seen. Apparently, that version of me relished the opportunity to fight Boltstar. To turn the tables on him for all that he'd done, to kill him instead of the other way around. So, was that the real me? Possibly. After all, I'd sacrificed Piper to win that HMQ game.

But the longer I thought about it, the more I came to doubt the mirror. Yes, I'd sacrificed Piper. I'd hurt her to win a meaningless competition. But I'd learned from that experience. I'd grown, evolved. Now, I couldn't imagine myself doing something like that ever again.

It made me wonder about Boltstar. What had twisted him into a monster? How had he come to physically attack those who held dissenting opinions from his own? He'd told me he'd done it to protect the magic community. And I believed that to a certain extent. But surely, he hadn't always wanted to drodiate his enemies. Something must've happened to make him that way.

I walked to another mirror. This one was framed by long lengths of curling ivy. The ivy stretched all the way to the floor, forming an elaborate, beautiful stand.

I stared into the glass. It swirled into a liquid-like texture and then I saw myself, sitting on a field of grass, my back up against the wheel of a rickety wagon. A sign posted on the wooden siding read, *Randy Wolf's Magical & Amazing Wonders! Admission: Dirt Cheap at just Ten Quadrods!*

There was a faraway look in this Randy's eyes. A red apple, big and juicy, filled his hand. In-between bites, he casually fired spells at a tall oak tree. The spells came at a fast clip, altering the roots, bark, branches, and leaves in various ways.

One of his spells struck the tree and vanished. Immediately, the green leaves began to change color, morphing into a vibrant purple.

That seemed to excite this version of me. Climbing to his feet, he trotted out to the tree. He pulled down a branch and removed a couple of leaves. As they broke free, their color reverted to green. A big grin creased his face and he chortled with happiness.

My eyes left the mirror and the surface swirled back into a glass-like substance. The very idea of a traveling showman was ludicrous, especially in an era of memory mirrors capable of providing endless, cheap entertainment. And even if such a job existed, I'd never want it.

I traveled around to other mirrors, seeing many strange versions of myself. Some were curious, others made me think. Some were even frightening. Regardless, none of them seemed quite right.

"I've got it," Tad shouted. "Over here."

I continued to stare at a pocket-sized mirror for an extra second or two. The glass showed me stripped entirely of skin. My insides were out there for anyone to see, which made for a unique, if unsettling, picture.

Tearing my eyes away, I trotted across the room. Tad stood in front of an eight-foot tall mirror. It featured steel edging, one side of which was welded to the floor.

"What do you see?" I asked.

"An older version of me," he said, his eyes locked on the glass. "I'm sitting in Boltstar's quarters, only they're not his anymore. They're mine … I'm Madkey's new headmaster! There's a bunch of students with me and we're just chatting. There's no homework, no tests, no grades. No stress or animosity. We're all on the same side. Everyone's learning what they want to learn."

"And ...?"

"And what?" he said. "Don't you see? Taking back Madkey, running it the right away ... that's my life's purpose. That's what I'm meant to do."

Intrigued, I looked at the mirror head-on. The glass swirled into liquid and I saw myself. This version of Randy Wolf sat in a large auditorium, back straight and fully at attention.

"Welcome to Magicology 9, ladies and gentlemen." Professor Norch gazed out at a sea of freshmen students. "Before we get started, did anyone forget to bring a mug?"

This Randy, along with his classmates, remained quiet. If they'd forgotten to bring their mugs, they sure weren't about to admit it.

"Very good," she said approvingly. "Today, we'll take our first look at one of history's most esteemed spellcasters ... Isaac Donaldson. Can any of you tell me something substantial about this esteemed wizard?"

Magicology was the study of magic as the primary language of the magician. Its purpose was to teach students how to read and write Structuralist spells as well as how to talk about and listen to them. Typical coursework involved taking a magician from the Structuralist era and analyzing his or her use of spells in the context of the period.

A couple of students slunk down in their chairs. Not that it helped much, given the auditorium's stadium-seating. Only one person seemed eager to answer the question.

I blinked in surprise as I saw my hand—well, Randy's hand—shoot into the air.

"Yes, Mr. Wolf?" she said.

"Isaac Donaldson lived in England during the early part of the 1900s," this Randy replied in a soft, confident voice.

"He's best known for helping to fully develop the Structuralist philosophy."

She beamed. "Very good, Mr. Wolf."

Slowly, I twisted my head away from the mirror. The imagery stopped and the liquid glass hardened up again. The mirror was a strong candidate. After all, I'd harbored a lifelong fascination with studying at Madkey. But was that really my true self?

"I'm not sure," I said at last. "I think we should … wait, what are you …? Tad, stop!"

Tad, totally transfixed by the mirror, reached for its surface. His fingers touched the glass and it vibrated ever so slightly. Then, with a soft sizzle, it began to melt.

"Ouch." With a soft yelp, he jumped back a few feet. He wrung his hand, then clutched it close to his chest. I saw his fingers were bright red and raw, the outer layer of skin having been stripped away from them.

The liquid glass dripped to the ground, then ate through the bottom portion of the steel frame. The entire mirror toppled into the sizzling liquid and quickly melted as well.

"But that was the right mirror." Still clutching his hand, Tad backpedaled across the room. "It showed my destiny."

"It showed you what you think you want," I said, realizing the truth. "But not what you need."

"What are you talking about?"

"Do you really want to take over as headmaster? Or do you just think it's the right thing to do?"

He bit his cheeks and said nothing.

The liquid glass oozed toward a towering, magnificent mirror. This one was at least fourteen-feet tall and held up by a diamond-encrusted frame. Holding my breath, I watched as the liquid glass dissolved the frame like it was nothing. The large mirror fell into the liquid glass and turned into liquid as well. Just like that, the ooze doubled in size.

"When I looked into it, I saw myself at Madkey." My head twisted from side to side, searching for refuge. "Sitting in a normal class, being a good student. That's all I ever wanted. But it's not what I need."

The liquid glass swallowed up three more mirrors. Again, it doubled in size.

We retreated to the other side of the room. Licking his lips, Tad eyed the molten glass. "You know what I need? A way out of here."

"What about the other mirrors? Did you see anything promising?"

He shook his head. "You?"

"I'm ... not sure." As I backed away from the searing glass, my thoughts turned inward. I thought about myself, about what really mattered to me.

You're a daydreamer, I thought. *You'd never do well at school. You didn't even like it.*

Tad looked at me like I'd gone crazy. "Earth to Randy. We need a plan and fast."

You'd never fit into a Big Three job, I told myself. *You'd hate it. No, you were meant to do something new, something different. That's why Chaotics appealed to you. You liked the idea of discovering new spells. Deep down, you're a daydreamer, an inventor ...*

"Randy," Tad yelled in my ear. "Wake up, will you? We need to get out of here."

I came crashing back into reality. What was once a puddle had turned enormous, covering half of the room with over a foot of molten glass. Steam floated up to the ceiling, filling the rest of the room with insufferably hot air. It was difficult to breathe and buckets of sweat began to pour down my body.

"Follow me," I yelled, breaking out into a sprint.

The liquid glass grew deeper and began to slosh upon itself, akin to the waves of a churning sea. Crashing across the room, it consumed everything in its path.

"Go faster," Tad yelled.

Peering backward, I saw a sizable wave take shape within the molten glass. The wave grew taller and taller, until it stood some twelve-feet in height. Stretching outward, it curled over us.

The steam thickened until I could barely see. Hanging a slight right, I galloped toward a hazy object. It was the mirror I'd looked at earlier, the one covered in ivy. The one that had depicted me sitting in a field with a rickety cart, chomping on an apple while trying out new spells. Chaotic spells.

You're a dreamer, I told myself. *An inventor.*

So, maybe I'd never sit in an open field, shooting random spells at trees. And I was pretty sure I'd never work out of a rickety old cart. But the spirit of that scene, well, it seemed kind of perfect.

The wave crested. Drops of sizzling glass burnt my skin. Taking one final stride, I leapt forward. Arms extended, I reached for the ivy-encased mirror. It buzzed softly.

And then I was gone.

CHAPTER 58

Conveyance portal journeys are like snowflakes … no two are ever alike. This time, the route was extremely twisty. I shot around tight bends and loose ones headfirst and on my stomach. I plunged down short hills, twisted around, then plunged down much longer ones. Occasionally, I got tossed about so that I was going feet first. During those periods, I had to deal with Tad kicking my head. Not exactly fun. But hey, it was better than taking a bath in molten glass.

Space unfolded upon itself with an ear-splitting crack and Tad and I hurtled out into the archive. We slid across the curved floor, scraping our bellies against the smooth stones.

Feeling queasy, I rose to an unsteady footing. A few deep breaths calmed my stomach. Swiveling on my toes, I studied the giant spherical room.

My gaze passed over the shelving racks that lined the curving walls. From my vantage point, I could just make out the massive *Enter Here for Womigia* sign.

Boltstar was nowhere in sight. But I had no doubt he'd show up sooner or later.

Wasting no time, we began to scale the shelves. The first few steps were easy, like walking up a gently sloping metal staircase. But as we gained altitude, they grew increasingly vertical. Even worse, they began to wobble under our feet.

My teeth gritted as metal dug into my palms. My shoulders and thighs started to ache. As the shelves grew steeper, we switched tactics. Tad would boost me up to the next shelf. I, in turn, would help him up after me. Then we'd switch.

We passed the halfway point. The shelving racks began to slope backward. We still helped each other, but our progress slowed considerably. More than once, I nearly lost my grip. If it weren't for Tad's steady hands, I would've splatted against the floor for sure.

"Almost …" Chest heaving, he pulled me up to another shelf. "… there."

Grabbing hold of a strut, I took a few deep breaths, catching my wind. Shifting my gaze, I focused my attention on the next shelf. It hovered above my head, with the edge jutting out over open space.

"Want me to go first?" Tad asked between breaths.

I shook my head. "It's my turn."

Releasing the strut, I moved to the very edge of the shelf. Craning my neck backward, I took a good look at my target. Then I gathered my strength and pushed off.

Flying up and backward, I stretched out my hands. My fingers latched onto the metal. But they were slippery with sweat and I found myself clawing for purchase.

Terror welled up inside of me. And with it, I felt the distinct presence of magic. I couldn't harness it, not without a wand. But I could feel it inside of me nonetheless.

Steeling my fingertips, I managed to get a decent grip on the edge. Then I performed a pull-up, propelling myself onto the next shelf. My muscles were near exhaustion and my breaths came in short gasps. But my mind moved at the speed of a spell. Skinned or not, I was still able to feel magic, to access it. And yet, it had failed me during the fight with Boltstar. Why was that?

Rising to my knees, I braced myself behind a strut. "Your turn," I mumbled.

"Lucky me," Tad quipped.

He propelled himself into the air. His fingertips struck the metallic edge and he began scraping every which way for a grip. Leaning forward, I grabbed his wrists. He kicked his legs and a few seconds later, I dragged him onto the shelf with me.

While he caught his breath, I strode to the back wall. The sign, etched out of tarnished silver, was still there. *Danger: Restricted Area,* it read. *Authorized Wizards Only.*

I opened the door and found myself facing what seemed like a million cool-lights. Shielding my eyes, I strode into the cavernous room. Everything was the same as before. The walls, the ceiling, the carpeting.

The statues.

My stomach churned as I glimpsed the drodiated witches and wizards from days gone by. They stood still and tall, frozen in time and space, monuments to an era that was all but forgotten. Could they see us? Were they hoping we'd free them? Or had their minds been turned to mush by decades of mental isolation?

I turned toward Womigia. It was still the size of a cottage, still emitting strange energy. Jets of sparking magic crossed through it, sometimes dimming or dying out, sometimes gaining intensity, sometimes igniting still other sparks.

Memories—big, important ones—played out before me. I saw Ayla Fodge, the fearless adventurer, hiking through lava-filled caverns on her infamous journey to the Earth's core. I also saw sasquatches gathered on a mystical, hazy mountain. They carried torches and were engaged in some kind of solemn, silent ceremony. It was, I realized, the precursor to the famous Craggin Oodlai. Which was kind of weird, given that I'd never actually seen it. In fact, no person, magician or humdrum, had ever witnessed it. And yet, it was still a part of the collective memory. How did that work?

I mulled that question for a moment before reaching a possible explanation. Maybe what I was looking at wasn't the actual ritual. Maybe it was how we perceived it, shaped by centuries of fiction as well as our general knowledge of the sasquatches and their habitat.

"Hello, gentlemen." Boltstar stepped out from behind Womigia. His voice was low and steady. His visage lacked any trace of concern. "It's good to see you again."

My lip curled even as my heart fell. I knew he had a separate way into the archive. I'd just hoped it would take him a lot longer to access it.

"I wish I could say the same," I replied.

He took a step forward, his wand already moving. His posture was relaxed and his attire looked unruffled, as if he'd gotten a chance to clean up a bit since our previous encounter.

Panic surged inside of me. Grabbing my wand, I tried to recall the exact steps required to cast Herd Crash.

"Drodiate," he whispered.

Cyan light burst out of his wand. I panicked again, the Herd Crash spell on the tip of my tongue. Unable to finish it, I dove out of the way, narrowly dodging disaster.

Putting on a burst of speed, Tad and I raced around to the other side of Womigia. Cyan jets zoomed through the air, missing us by mere inches. Meanwhile, memories continued to surge within Womigia, utterly ignorant of what was transpiring all around them.

Sliding to a halt, I perked my ears. One second later, I heard soft footsteps. Boltstar was following us, albeit at a slow, restrained pace.

I glanced at Womigia, focusing my gaze on the many mirrors jutting out of its sides. We'd never beat Boltstar by ourselves. No, our only hope was to shake things up. To strengthen the Chaotics' resolve while weakening that of the faculty members and alumni. And to do that, we needed to restore the collective memory.

Tad and I backed up slowly, in time with the headmaster's footsteps. "Get rid of the mirrors," I whispered. "I'll keep Boltstar busy."

As he turned his attention to Womigia, I continued to back up, wand at the ready. My brain reeled through various spells before halting at Dissolate. It had stopped Boltstar's spells back in Torso. Maybe it would work here, too.

"This has gone on long enough, Mr. Wolf," Boltstar called out, his voice disturbingly calm.

"Agreed," I replied, continuing to match his footsteps with my own. "So, why don't you surrender already?"

Selecting a mirror, Tad gripped it with both hands. Pulling hard, he struggled to move it. But it didn't budge.

"Break it," I whispered.

He slammed his elbow into the glass. It clunked loudly, but didn't shatter. Uttering a silent scream, he clutched his sore limb.

"Try magic," I urged quietly.

"What magic? I was skinned, remember?"

"Yeah. But so was I."

His face twisted in thought. "I need a wand."

Looking around the room, I spotted the drodiated magicians. Many of them held wands in their stony grips. "How about one of those?"

He gave his elbow a good shake. Then he raced to a statue. Grabbing hold of its wand, he tried to wrench it free. But it refused to move.

Boltstar came into view. He held his wand loosely, almost casually. His derby hat was propped up just a bit, allowing me to see his swirling eyes.

He sent a blast of magic our way. Ducking down, we beat a path around Womigia.

Air rushed softly. Whispered voices reached my ears. Peeking toward the doorway, I saw a hoist descend to the outer shelf. Faculty members, armed with wands, stepped off it and entered the room.

My heart fell as I caught sight of Galison and MacPherson. Wadflow and Norch, too, armed with brand new wands. To a magician, they stared at us with cold, sullen eyes.

"It's over, Lanctin," Galison reported. "The Chaotics are finished."

"Not yet. But they will be." Boltstar slid around the edge of Womigia. His wand moved and he uttered that one horrible word. "Drodiate."

A cyan bolt raced toward me. I dropped to my knees and it hurtled overhead. Something shattered and shimmering shards of glass rained down upon me.

Eyes wide, I glanced up. A formerly-pristine mirror, one of the many embedded into Womigia, was now broken. Abruptly, the collective memory began to pulse and throb. Then the broken mirror slid out of its side and crashed to the carpet. Other mirrors, untouched by the spell, began to slide out as well. One by one, they hit the floor.

"The mirrors." Tad's jaw opened wide. "Womigia's rejecting them."

It occurred to me that the mirrors were akin to a precarious spider web. A single broken strand could cause the entire structure to unravel.

The faculty members gripped their skulls, horrible looks upon their faces. Suddenly, my brain started to ache, as if a bubble was growing within it. Gritting my teeth, I fell to a knee. My hands pressed against my ears.

My head roiled as a series of ideas fought their way into my mind. The pain lasted maybe fifteen seconds. When it finally vanished, long-held certainties came into doubt. On a very deep level, I began to wonder if the Chaotics were really all that bad after all. At the same time, complexity entered my feelings toward Boltstar and his allies. The heroes of Victory Day no longer seemed quite so pure, quite so perfect.

Excitement surged within me. I wasn't questioning conventional truth because of something I'd seen in a memory mirror. No, I was questioning it in my soul, in the place that knew the grass was green and the sky was blue. And that meant one thing.

Womigia had been restored.

CHAPTER 59

It was amazing, really. All my life, I'd *known* the evils of the Chaotics. I'd known about the terrors they were capable of inflicting upon our world. I'd known how they'd attacked the Structuralists in cowardly fashion. And I'd known that Boltstar had heroically pushed them back and in the process, saved magic from itself. I'd known all of these things at a very deep level. So deep, in fact, that just being in the presence of a Chaotic magician like Tad had made me uneasy.

And then, in a single moment, all of that changed.

It was as if someone had flipped a switch deep inside of me, shedding light on long-forgotten memories. Of course, I'd known the truth ever since my first trip to the archive. But back then, I'd only known it at an academic level. Now, I knew it for real and the knowledge made me feel powerful, emboldened.

Knees wobbling, I gained my feet. My head felt heavy, burdened by the weight of all of this new knowledge. Twisting my face from side to side, I took stock of the situation.

Tad knelt next to me. His face was cherubic and youthful. His eyes shone brightly. Clearly, a great emotional load had been lifted off his shoulders.

Boltstar, meanwhile, stood still. He held his wand aloft in a steady grip. His eyes had a faraway look to them. His face was unreadable.

His allies—Galison, Wadflow, MacPherson, and Norch— continued to hold their heads. Their brows were scrunched up tight. Then something happened that surprised me. Slowly at first, then much more quickly, guilt began to etch its way across their features.

Tad and I weren't the only ones having deep revelations. The faculty was realizing stuff as well. For the first time in nearly a century, they weren't seeing themselves as pure heroes. Instead, they were forced to confront the horrifying reality of what they'd done to win the Philosophical War.

I wondered what was happening in the rest of Madkey. Students, staffers, alumni, the other faculty members ... they all knew the truth now. Heck, everyone knew the truth. My folks, my friends back home, everyone.

"What ...?" MacPherson's eyes and tight-knit brows reflected confusion and anxiety. "What is this?"

"The truth," Tad said without a trace of pity.

I could only imagine how wonderful he felt. After a lifetime of self-loathing, he now knew the truth at the deepest level.

"Good God." MacPherson began to quiver and shake. "What did we do?"

"We destroyed the Chaotic philosophy," Boltstar replied, snapping out of his temporary daze.

MacPherson sank to his knees. "Think of the lives we ruined. Think of—"

Boltstar shifted his wand. "Drodiate."

A cyan streak raced past me. MacPherson, head down, never saw it coming.

"Have you lost your mind?" Wadflow looked back and forth between Boltstar and the now-frozen MacPherson. Lifting her wand, she aimed it at the headmaster. "Undo it. Now."

"I will," he promised. "Just as soon as Womigia is fixed."

"No, no." Norch shook her head. "We have to think about this. We have to—"

"Drodiate," he said, waving his wand in a well-practiced manner. "Drodiate."

Wadflow's lips curled in disbelief as the spell careened into her chest. Then she went rigid.

Norch managed to dodge the spell meant for her. But her hesitation to return fire cost her big-time when Boltstar hit her with a follow-up spell.

Like Wadflow, she hardened into a human statue. And then she just stood there, a passive observer to whatever came next.

Boltstar eyed Galison with distinct suspicion. "George?"

"I'm with you," he replied a moment later.

Sighing, Boltstar lowered his wand. His gaze focused on MacPherson, Wadflow, and Norch. "I'm sorry. I truly am. But you're not in your right minds right now. Once Womigia is returned to its proper state, I promise to make this right. We can go back to the way things were."

I wondered about that. While Boltstar could influence the collective memory, he couldn't erase actual memories. Like it or not, MacPherson, Wadflow, and Norch would always remember these last few minutes. They'd remember how he'd turned on them, how he'd drodiated them without warning or hesitation.

Boltstar's normally serene face took on a dark hue. "Well?" he asked, turning our way. "Are you pleased with yourselves?"

"Are *we* pleased?" Tad's eyes practically popped out of his head. "What about you? You ruined my people. You doomed us to a lifetime of guilt and self-hatred."

"A small price to pay, Mr. Crucible." He tugged his derby down over his head. The effort cast a shadow over much of his visage. "In any event, enjoy this while it lasts. Soon, it will be nothing but a distant memory."

"You've got to get past us first," I said.

"Very well, Mr. Wolf." He twirled his wand in his hand. "Let's finish this."

CHAPTER 60

I saw his wand shift before I heard him utter the actual spell. My brain shifted back to panic mode and I darted around Womigia.

"Drodiate," Boltstar said.

I saw a flash of cyan light. Desperately, I dove to the floor. I landed on my belly and the spell careened harmlessly against the wall.

Scrambling to my feet, I pressed my back against Womigia. Despite its magical origin, it felt hard to the touch.

"Show yourself, Mr. Wolf." Boltstar's voice was soft and sickeningly smooth.

"And become one of your statues?" I retorted. "I don't think so."

He passed into view again. "Drodiate."

A soft cyan glow cast a deadly pall over the room. Tad sidestepped the spell but got his legs twisted up in the process. One second later, he fell to the ground.

As I stooped down to help him, I heard Galison's footsteps coming up on our other side. We were trapped.

Helplessness and fury boiled up within me. The emotions felt powerful, yet fluid. Like they could morph into something else at a moment's notice.

Before I could help Tad to his feet, Boltstar arrived. He stopped a few feet away, his wand aimed at Tad's heart. Tad froze just as surely as if he'd already been drodiated.

Boltstar didn't smile. He didn't even look all that happy. But his determination was evident.

"Drodiate," he uttered, waving his wand in precise, defined ways. His wand opened fire, sending a cyan spell straight at Tad.

There was no time to recall a spell or even prepare my emotions. "Dissolate," I responded, my wand moving in time with a symphony only I could hear.

A spell, auburn in color, raced forth. It expanded quickly, like a hungry lion stretching for its prey. Then it swallowed up his streak.

Dumbfounded, I stared at my wand. The spell had worked this time. But why? I hadn't prepared my emotions or anything. In fact, I wasn't even sure what emotions I'd been feeling.

I realized I was breathing fast and hard. Forcing myself to calm down, I shot a glance at Boltstar.

He arched his eyebrow. "More luck, Mr. Wolf?"

That, of course, was precisely the problem. It was all luck. My mind swept over the last few seconds. What had I felt right before the spell? Helplessness? Fury? A bit of both?

Yes, a bit of both. That was how I'd done it. But I'd done the same thing earlier, back in Torso, and the spell had failed to materialize. What was different about this time?

Boltstar tucked his derby down low, shrouding his eyes in even more darkness. "And so, we find ourselves in a havoc magic duel, Mr. Wolf," he said. "Too bad nobody outside this room will ever know about it."

I could feel Galison behind me, but I didn't dare look at him. "Oh, they will," I replied, hoping my tone exuded more confidence than I actually felt. "After I beat you, I'll make sure the whole world knows about it."

His wand moved in very precise ways. "Drodiate."

Another spell raced toward me. Again, my emotions shifted ever so slightly. I felt tons of fury, tempered by the helplessness of the situation. My wand moved in arcing fashion, driven by the deep harmony of my emotions.

"Dissolate," I said.

A fiery auburn streak soared straight and true. Once again, it swallowed up Boltstar's magic, then vanished.

His jaw hardened.

Meanwhile, I stood still, enjoying the wondrous feeling of unplanned magic. It was quite amazing, really. His spell had roiled my emotions. My emotions, in turn, caused my wand to shift. I'd uttered the spell not because I was thinking about it. It had just felt right, almost as if some part of me was programmed to say it.

His wand moved quickly and he threw another Drodiate spell at me. My emotions mixed themselves. My wand moved via instinct. And then I issued a spell of my own, dissolving his cyan jet into a cloud of harmless smoke.

Something occurred to me. Against Tad's advice, I'd been trying to perform Chaotic magic as if it were Structuralist magic. I'd treated it as something foreign to me, something that needed to be memorized and practiced. But was that really the best approach?

Magic required exacting emotions. And exacting emotions were difficult to fake. That was why Instinctia existed. It helped people duplicate the emotions, wand movements, and words once used by the Capsudra's inventor, Xavier Capsudra.

But such a process didn't exist for Chaotic magic. In other words, if I couldn't pin down the exact emotions, the spell simply wouldn't work. So, maybe I'd been going about this the wrong way. Maybe the Madkey method—memorization and repetition—didn't work for Chaotic magic. Maybe the real trick was, as Tad had insisted, to *just let go.* To let my instincts and emotions run wild.

Boltstar's face twisted into one of complete concentration. He swept his wand through a familiar series of movements. "Drodiate," he said.

I took a deep breath.

And let go.

Emotions swirled inside of me, all on their own. The sudden freedom roiled me to the core. I'd spent my entire life trying to feel someone else's emotions. Feeling my own was, to put it mildly, a revelation.

My wand shifted, flowing with my emotions like a dancer to the sound of music. "Dissolate," I said.

A fiery auburn bolt swallowed his cyan streak, snuffing it out of existence.

My emotions shifted again. I still felt a strong desire for self-preservation. But I also felt a need for justice. A deep longing to make Boltstar pay for his crimes.

My wand twirled. My lips opened wide and I knew just what to say.

"Pulverize," I called out.

Sweeping his wand, Boltstar threw up a bunch of spells. Orbs of light appeared before him, darting this way and that, constantly shifting positions.

My spell spread out in mid-air. It stretched in every direction until it resembled a flying blanket.

Moving faster and faster, Boltstar threw up even more orbs. There must've been hundreds of them, all lined up, all waiting to intercept my attack.

The blanket careened into the minefield and the orbs detonated. They did a lot of damage.

But they didn't get the entire spell.

His eyes widened as the tattered, enchanted blanket swept over him. It stuck fast to his body for a split-second, then exploded. The impact sent him reeling toward Womigia. He slammed into it, then dropped to the floor.

I spun around, my wand aimed at a stunned Galison. "What's it going to be?"

He hesitated, his eyes reflecting pure disbelief. Then he placed his wand on the floor and backed away.

Tad picked up Galison's wand. Then he approached Boltstar. Confirming the man was unconscious, Tad grabbed his wand as well. "So, you finally figured it out?" he asked.

I nodded.

"How?"

"I forgot everything I learned." I grinned. "And just followed my instincts."

CHAPTER 61

"I, Randy Wolf, was a magic school dropout." I paused, my gaze passing over thousands of faces. For the first time in known memory, every single seat within Madkey Arena was filled. "And that surprised the heck out of me. You see, I spent my entire life dreaming of this place. Of being a student here, of earning a diploma. And then it all just fell apart. My dreams died. Or so I thought."

The audience stayed quiet, hanging on to my every word.

"Today, I'm pleased to say that my dreams are coming true. Not the dreams I expected, mind you. My real dreams, my true dreams." I grinned. "That's the way it is with dreams. You don't always get what you want. Sometimes, if you're lucky, you get what you actually need."

Thunderous applause ripped through the audience. My cheeks burned with pleasure and more than a bit of embarrassment. I'd gone from disgraced dropout to full-blown celebrity in record time. In a lot of ways, it was pretty awesome. But it also felt really weird.

I studied the audience. From my elevated platform above the old HMQ, I had a pretty good view of everyone. But it was so packed that I found it hard to focus on any one person in particular.

I took a second to hone in on a few faces. Porter Garrington sat in the very top row. Sya, Felicia, and Gordon were with him, along with some other freshmen. They looked bored and annoyed. Much had changed at Madkey over the last two weeks. But Porter's hatred of me, as well as his immense popularity, were still the same.

I looked at other people. Calvin. Jenny. Nico. Jax. Ivan Gully, back from Gutlore. Some of the Chaotic magicians, fresh out of drodiation. Plus, thousands of alumni I'd never met, hooting and hollering at the top of their lungs.

My gaze shifted to the front row. Tad stared hard at a memory mirror, probably reliving some newly-released moment from his people's history. Leandra, in turn, stared hard at him. She had a devilish look about her and I knew she was already plotting her next prank. Piper, meanwhile, shot me a thumbs-up along with the brightest smile I'd ever seen.

I turned in a slow circle. I probably looked like some stuck-up jerk, basking in the glow of an adoring crowd. But really, I was just looking for two people. And after an excruciatingly long time, I finally saw them. My parents stood in the lower half of the bleachers, well off to my left side. They clapped loudly and with great enthusiasm.

Our relationship had improved tenfold since Boltstar's fall from power. Don't get me wrong. It still had its fair share of problems. But the restoring of Womigia, along with my role in it, had caused them to lay off of me as of late.

I shot them a slight nod, then took in the rest of the crowd. "Thank you," I said.

I let Professor Whitlock take my place, then descended to the field. Tad, looking highly uncomfortable in a sport coat and tie, left the bleachers to come meet me.

"Well?" he asked, pumping my hand. "How's it feel to be famous?"

"I should be asking you that question."

After I'd defeated Boltstar, Tad had reconnected with his own magic. Swiftly, he'd cast the Hibernuction Curse upon the headmaster. We'd carried him back to Torso and explained everything to a waiting crowd of confused witches and wizards. Within hours, bubblers flew in all directions and we were household names.

That wasn't all that had changed. Boltstar, still fast asleep, was now at Gutlore awaiting trial, along with Galison, Norch, Wadflow, and MacPherson. The Chaotics, the ones who'd survived the battle, had been allotted space at Madkey. They were standing a little straighter these days. A little taller, too.

With Boltstar gone, a power vacuum had appeared at Madkey. As of this moment, nobody had stepped forward to fill it. There were rumors, though. Piper said that Whitlock was thinking about throwing her hat into the ring. The Chaotics were pushing for one of their own to take the slot. I wasn't really sure how it would all shake out. But the next headmaster would have a lot to do. For one thing, he or she would need to figure out a new curriculum, something to satisfy Structuralists as well as Chaotics. What would that look like? Would school continue to consist of a rigorous course schedule, bells, reading assignments, homework, tests, and grades? Or would it become something else?

For another thing, the new headmaster would need to make some decisions regarding Boris Hynor and his allies. After skinning Boltstar of magic, Whitlock had reversed all of the headmaster's Drodiation Curses. She'd started with the most recent victims, including Piper. Then she'd moved to Madkey Archive, freeing Boris as well as the other old Chaotics from their horrible fate.

Acting quickly, Tad had cast sleeping curses upon the old Chaotics and we'd moved them to the clinic. But they couldn't stay there forever. Sooner or later, we would have to wake them. But that carried an element of risk to it. After all, they'd spent decades as human statues, a fate which had undoubtedly taken a toll on their sanity. Could they be trusted to run free anytime soon? What kind of precautions would need to be taken?

I glanced up at the stands again. My gaze drifted to where I'd seen Piper and Leandra. Their seats were now empty and I had a pretty good idea where they'd gone.

As Whitlock began to speak, Tad and I snuck away. Entering Torso, we took a hoist up to Left Arm. Along, the way, I considered my future. For the moment, I was still working my assembly-line job. However, there was talk of me joining the faculty once things settled down. I found that a little hard to swallow. Sure, I could probably help a few Structuralists learn the ins and outs of Chaotics. But a full-blown professor? I was just a kid, for cripes sake.

We walked into Shadow Madkey, then made our way to the celestarium. It looked great, thanks to a whole bunch of my Immaculatize spells. The bronze and silver contraptions, now free of dust, gleamed softly. The fine tables and chairs looked like new and the carpet had undergone a thorough cleaning. The busts and statues had been polished and repaired.

"Nice speech, Randy." Leandra, situated in front of the enchanted fireplace, spun around to face us. "It was just what I needed."

I twirled my wand absent-mindedly. "Yeah?"

She nodded. "I haven't slept that good in years."

I tossed my wand at her. She dodged it and it clattered against the glass wall.

"You did fine." Piper stopped scribbling in her notebook just long enough to shoot me an encouraging look. "No, you did great."

I smiled at her. "Thanks."

I retrieved my wand. The sun shone brightly in the sky, filling the celestarium with incredible light. Twisting my head to either side, I saw mountains, icy blue lakes, and snow-covered valleys.

All this time, I'd thought there was something wrong with me, that I was a failure. But the real problem was that I'd never followed my instincts. I'd been so busy trying to be another Xavier Capsudra that I'd forgotten to be myself.

Piper placed her notebook on the floor. Shoving her pencil behind her ear, she joined me at the window. "I talked to my parents this morning," she said.

I caught an edgy tone to her voice. "Yeah?"

"They told me to be careful. They said Chaotics is a real threat to the Big Three. Not just to the owners, but to the workers, too."

I frowned. "How so?"

"I bet I know," Tad said. "Structuralism limited the types of spells that could be done, which meant there was a need for binding spells and thus, assembly-line magicians. But now, the spell book has been thrown wide open, so to speak."

"Right." Piper nodded. "There've got to be people out there who have a natural gift for making, say, furniture. They'll be able to do it in a single spell. The Big Three can't compete with that. They'll go out of business. Assembly-line magicians will lose their jobs."

"But they can tap into their Chaotic magic," I argued. "They can learn new trades."

"Maybe. But it'll take time. And some witches and wizards might never make the change." Leandra sighed. "Things are going to get worse before they get better."

"But they will get better," Piper added quickly. "It's just going to take time."

I continued to stare outside. Meanwhile, Piper returned to her reading. Tad picked up his memory mirror again. As for Leandra, she stared at the ceiling in deep concentration, perhaps mulling over her next invention.

As I watched the outside world, I found myself thinking about the future, about how rapidly things were changing. If truth be told, it scared me. A lot. But my heart still sung and my chest was filled with nervous excitement. For the first time in my life, I wasn't following the path laid out for me. Rather, I was following my own path.

And that felt pretty darn terrific.

AUTHOR'S NOTE

Even now, I remember the day I stopped laughing at Grandpa's jokes.

My grandfather was a real trickster with a deep love of puns and wordplay. He could always get a laugh out of me, even when telling the same joke for the billionth time. But during my early twenties, something changed.

His gentle jokes began to fall on deaf ears. My laughter dried up, then turned fake. I had to force myself not to roll my eyes in front of him. At the time, I figured it was just a sign of growing up. Now, I know differently.

It wasn't just my sense of humor that changed, by the way. Around that same time, I developed brain fog, which manifested itself as a weird, floaty feeling in my head. I found it harder to think, to concentrate. Doctors were stumped. X-rays and MRIs found nothing unusual. I tried balance training and other forms of therapy, but nothing corrected the problem.

Slowly, but surely, my emotions began to dull. I stopped crying. My smiles thinned, then turned fake. Little annoyances became big ones. I turned into a crank, an introvert, and a homebody. Not because I liked staying at home all that much, but because of inertia. I felt fatigued and old. My "get up and go" faded away and I started having trouble getting out of bed each morning.

Happy moments were few and far between. Soon, I lost interest in entertainment. I stopped reading. I only half-watched television shows and movies. I became listless and mechanical in everything I did. My constant negativity and general emptiness made me wonder if I suffered from depression. Later, I concluded that I probably was depressed, albeit at what I considered to be a sustainable level.

And yet, life went on. I got an MBA and a CFA charter. Moving to New York City, I worked as an equity research analyst. It left me miserable and unfulfilled. So, I took a risk. Quitting my job, I tried my hand as a storyteller. Years ago, it would've been my dream profession. But to my surprise, I found it a real struggle. Negativity and crippling self-doubt plagued me at every turn. Still, all storytellers face those things, so I thought little of it.

But writing became increasingly difficult with time. Worse, my well of creativity, which had been shallow for years, all but dried up. I experienced no real joy in telling stories and had to depend on a strict schedule to get anything accomplished.

Physically, it became increasingly difficult to move. My head ached constantly. I developed bone pain and began to experience lingering injuries. Knee problems cut into my running time. Shoulder and wrist injuries made it nearly impossible to lift my son.

Now, this didn't happen all at once. Rather, my decline took place rather slowly over the course of some fifteen years. Even so, I still noticed it. More than once, I wondered if I was going crazy. Now, I know the answer to that question.

In 2011, I was diagnosed with a disease known as hyperparathyroidism. Parathyroid glands regulate the calcium in your blood and bones. When one turns tumorous, it begins making excess PTH hormones. Those hormones circulate in the body, leaching calcium from your bones. The excess calcium then circulates in your bloodstream. Given enough time, this can cause a gigantic and weird list of symptoms known as, "moans, groans, stones, and bones, with psychic overtones."

Since I was young, male, and appeared asymptomatic on the surface, a surgeon suggested I wait to have the tumor removed. This is rather common, and unfortunately, outdated advice. In any event, I put off the surgery for five years. In mid-2017, the surgeon suggested I wait another five years. But by that time, the true cost of the disease was becoming impossible to ignore.

Mid-2017, of course, was also when I started work on this novel. DESTROYING MAGIC began as an experimental journey into the creative process, which I'd planned to follow via a public journal on my website. Here's how I described it in my very first entry, dated May 16, 2017:

"Right now, I've got nothing. No ideas, no characters, no settings. I'm going to start from scratch with nothing more than a fake title. So, this series will depict my entire creative process from beginning to end, laughs and tears alike. You'll see how I create and develop characters and settings. You'll watch as I work without an outline, driving the story forward and backward, dreaming up new ideas and dropping old ones."

The journal, I thought, would make an interesting accompaniment to the book. But it soon fell by the wayside. I made it just twenty-four days before quietly calling it quits, as depression and a general lack of interest in pretty much everything stopped me cold.

Fortunately, I didn't stop writing altogether. As the months unfolded, I continued to build this book, word by word, line by line, and scene by scene. And all the while, I slowly awakened to the true, destructive nature of my tumor.

I began to research it in depth, reading everything I could find on the condition. And as I worked my way to this book's conclusion, I finally scheduled a surgery with the Norman Parathyroid Center, the world's leading parathyroid surgery center. A short while later, I went public with my disease, first to family and close friends, and then more generally, via Facebook. Here's that particular post, dated December 1, 2017:

"I don't know how else to say this, so I'm just going to say it. I have a disease. It's called hyperparathyroidism. Essentially, a tumor in one of my parathyroid glands is leaching calcium from my bones and into my bloodstream. This has caused me lots of problems, some physical and some mental. Worst of all, it's robbed me of my joy, my energy, and even my personality. I have very little enthusiasm for anything, including writing or creating art (which is part of the reason why it takes me so long to finish books). In general, I feel very old and listless at all times.

"Hyperparathyroidism is one of those diseases that takes 25 years to kill you and I've had it for at least 8 years now (I suspect I've had it closer to 15 years). Fortunately, there is an excellent, low-risk surgical cure. In a few short weeks, I'll be flying to Florida to get the tumor removed at a parathyroid surgery center. Hopefully, this will get my body and my life back on track.

"I'll have more to say about this later. But for now, I'd just like to note that I was first diagnosed with hyperparathyroidism six years ago. Since I was young, male, and appeared asymptomatic, I was advised to delay surgery. Unfortunately, that advice turned out to be outdated. Hyperparathyroidism is quite rare and thus, not well understood, even by endocrinological experts. Plus, I was never asymptomatic. Even then, the symptoms were creeping up on me slowly, day by day. I didn't realize how much I'd changed until it became impossible to ignore. So, please pay attention to your body, do your own research, and don't always take medical advice at face value.

"Thanks for reading. Much love to all of you."

A few weeks later, on December 22, I went under the knife, so to speak. Here's how my wife recorded it, also via Facebook, at the time:

"David did great!!!! David's tumor was hiding buried INSIDE his thyroid gland. They opened it up carefully, took out the tumor, then closed up his thyroid. His main surgeon said most other places would have taken over an hour just to think of looking inside the thyroid and may have even removed his thyroid, causing more issues for him down the line. We are so happy with our experience here - his whole team included me and Ryden as much as possible and we knew David was in the best hands in the world. Here is a life size pic of his tumor - because it was constricted inside the thyroid, its overall growth was constrained. But the amount of hormone output indicates David has had this for 10+ years. Notice that the tumor was making 765 units of hormone versus the normal level of 30 to 80!! The black dot below on the green label is the size that a normal gland should be. Thankfully his other three glands are perfect not just in size but in hormone levels! We're all together again resting, thanks for all your kind words, concern, prayers and love! We can't stress this enough - go to the best expert you can!!"

So, now, the tumor is gone. And you know what? I feel pretty darn good. Within hours of the surgery, my negativity vanished. I experienced my first real smile in years the very next day. I say "years" because I can't remember the last time I didn't have to fake it. My bones feel better. My headaches are gone. I've got tons of energy. I'm not kidding when I say it's like I'm back in my 20's again.

I'd all but given up on emotions. Now, I'm feeling stuff again. The brain fog is at least diminished, if not gone for good. For the first time in forever, I want to be around people. I want to do things, to live life. To show the world what I've got and in turn, to let it show me what it's got.

That brings me back to *DESTROYING MAGIC*. This story is curious for me in retrospect, seeing as how it was crafted both before and after the surgery. I'd rather not try to tell you what it's about on a deep level because, well, I don't really know what it's about. I'm still trying to figure that out.

But as I read through it today, months removed from the surgery, I find myself surprised by the many odd parallels to my personal journey. Life is art and art is life, I suppose.

With that said, let's bring this to a close. And to do that, we'll circle back to Grandpa. Even now, years after his death, I find myself thinking of him, of his jokes. I'll laugh, then cry my eyes out. I'll never get those years back. I'll never laugh with him again and that just makes me want to cry all over again. And that's okay, I think. Until the surgery, I'd become pretty much incapable of real grief. So, this is a blessing.

Hyperparathyroidism stole countless laughs and tears from me. Well, no more. I've got a second shot at life now. A second shot at creating great stories.

And I plan on making the most of it.

Thank you for reading *DESTROYING MAGIC*. I hope you enjoyed it. If you want to be the first to know about my upcoming stories, make sure to sign up for my newsletter.

Keep Adventuring!
David Meyer
December 2018

ABOUT THE AUTHOR

David Meyer is an adventurer and international bestselling author. He's been creating for as long as he can remember. As a kid, he made his own toys, invented games, and built elaborate cities with blocks and Legos. Before long, he was planning out murder mysteries and trap-filled treasure quests for his family and friends.

These days, his lifelong interests—lost treasure, mysteries of history, monsters, conspiracies, forgotten lands, exploration, and archaeology—fuel his personal adventures. Whether hunting for pirate treasure or exploring ancient ruins, he loves seeking out answers to the unknown. Over the years, Meyer has consulted on a variety of television shows. Most recently, he made an appearance on H2's #1 hit original series, *America Unearthed*.

Meyer lives in New Hampshire with his wife and son. For more information about him, his adventures, and his stories, please see the links below.

Connect with David!
Website: www.DavidMeyerCreations.com
Amazon Page: viewauthor.at/davidmeyer
Mailing List: eepurl.com/CVjj5
Facebook: www.facebook.com/GuerrillaExplorer
Twitter: www.twitter.com/DavidMeyer_

BOOKS BY DAVID MEYER

Cy Reed Adventures
CHAOS
ICE STORM
TORRENT
VAPOR
FURY

Apex Predator Series
BEHEMOTH
SAVAGE

Randy Wolf and the Dropout Magicians
DESTROYING MAGIC

Made in the USA
San Bernardino, CA
19 May 2019